WARRIORS WITHIN

Book One of the Fianna Cycle

First Edition

Written by
Janine De Tillio Cammarata

Highland Mountain Publishing
Rexford, New York
2006

Laura,
Believe in your
Dreams!
Janine De Tillio Cammarat
3/27/2006

Published by
Highland Mountain Publishing
PO Box 217, Rexford, NY 12148
http://www.highlandpub.com

Library of Congress Control Number: 2005911258

ISBN 0-9776912-0-9

Printed in the United States of America

Cover Design by James Russo, Channel One Design, Inc.

Interior Illustrations by Samantha Nichole De Tillio

Dedication

Lucas
My Champion

Nick and Stephen
My Warriors

Mater
For opening the world of books to me

Pater
Your spirit released my words
They are for you.

Acknowledgments

There are so many family and friends to thank for helping make this book a reality. I would like to thank Debra Young, my medieval literature teacher at The College of Saint Rose, who encouraged me to write novels instead of research papers. So much thanks and praise goes to my wonderful friends, who did a fantastic job editing my book—Kathleen Lange-Madden (thank you for introducing me to Celtic literature), Karen Patchell (you are always there to encourage me), and Karen Knowles (I couldn't have done it without your guidance and keen eye). Thank you to Arline Chase for editing my book and helping me through the writing process. To the Clifton Park-Halfmoon Public Library for your endless resources and assistance. To Scott Braman whose sword fighting lessons helped the action scenes come alive. Thanks to my martial arts instructors—Grandmaster Alex Marsal and Senior Instructor Lucas Cammarata—for your patient guidance and realism. I would like to thank The International Women's Writing Guild for their years of support and wonderful writing seminars. To my niece, Samantha Nichole De Tillio, for her fantastic illustrations. For my sister, Michele Thomas, who listened to my endless monologues, while I tried to put my dreams into words. To my husband, Lucas, for telling me to 'suck it up' and get the book done. Your unwavering support strengthens me daily.

Part One

1

New York City—2000

Tipped off about a drug exchange, Senior Narcotics Officers Jack Sommers and Frank Goodale raced to a local dry cleaner in New York City.

"Where are they?" Jack yelled as he stormed in.

"I...I don't know what you are talking about," the young clerk squealed.

Grabbing the clerk by his shirt collar, Jack lifted him off the ground and pounded him against the store wall. "Don't mess with me, punk!"

The clerk looked from Jack to Frank and pointed to a curtain at the back of the room. Jack slapped the clerk on the cheek. "Good decision, kid," he said and dropped him to the ground.

Motioning for his partner to follow, Jack yanked the curtain aside and ran up the stairs. "What about backup?" Frank asked.

"Frank, we don't have time. I can finally get him. Back me up, OK?" Jack's blue eyes burned with intensity.

"You always were a stubborn Irishman."

Frank followed him up the stairs.

Jack kicked the door in. The door opened easily, too easily.

"Freeze!" Jack counted three men and Natalie, his young informant. Tears streamed down her face as she crawled across the floor. Jack knew something was wrong. The bullets ripped through his vest.

"It wasn't me, Jack!" Natalie cried and raced from the room.

Frank yelled, "Jack!"

A fourth man, hiding behind the door, smashed Frank on the head. He slumped to the floor.

Ricky Cartillo, the leader of New York City's biggest drug enterprise, turned Jack Sommers over. Jack gasped for breath. He opened his eyes and croaked, "Why, Ricky? Why the children?"

"I am sorry, my brother, that it has to come down to this, but you leave me no choice. You may think that what I do is wrong, but in my own way, I am helping these children while they assist me with my business. I keep them off the street, feed them, and clothe them. We both want to help these poor creatures, only…our philosophies are different," Ricky explained.

Jack rasped, "You are not my brother. You'll pay for this."

"Ha, ha, Jack, my boy. I do not think you will be doing anything on this side of the ground," Ricky Cartillo said, as he stepped on Jack's chest. Jack passed out.

"What should we do with the other guy, Boss?" one of his men asked.

"Just leave him here and go find that bitch daughter of mine. I want her back by nightfall. And if I have to take care of this dirty work again, I will tear one of your heads off first!" he barked.

Frank Goodale woke up and saw his partner of 30 years lying in a congealing pool of blood. He called for help and cried while he held his friend's head in his arms.

"Hurry up, get him in there. He has to get to the hospital

now!" Frank screamed at the EMT.

"Officer, we really should get a look at your head. That cut looks deep and is still bleeding," the paramedic coaxed.

"I don't care about my head, dammit! He's dying. Just take care of him. Please," Frank said.

They rushed Jack Sommers into the hospital. Frank had asked an officer to contact Jack's daughters, Michaela and Shannon, but he hoped they weren't there yet. He didn't know how he could face them. He hadn't even fired his gun. He knew who should have been in that room, but he hadn't seen who shot his partner. He had only seen the bullets tear through Jack.

Jack was wheeled into a room where doctors attempted to save his life. A paramedic turned to Frank. "Listen, you can't do anything for him now."

After one last look, Frank Goodale turned and walked away from his lifelong friend.

Michaela Sommers waited at her dad's apartment. Used to jeans, she twisted in her black cocktail dress. Her long auburn hair hung in a tendril of curls that made her gray eyes stand out. She and her sister planned to go to dinner and celebrate their dad's 30th anniversary on the police force. Michaela admired the New York City skyline, when she heard an emergency call over the scanner. "Officers down. I repeat, officers down. Backup needed! Patrol car 47 needs assistance!" the dispatcher said.

Patrol car 47? "That's Dad!" Michaela said aloud. She ran out the door and straight into her sister, Shannon. Two years older, Shannon had reddish blond, curly hair, and blue eyes. Her freckled face made her look younger than her thirty years.

"What's the big rush?" Shannon asked.

Tears ran down Michaela's cheeks. "It's Dad. He's been hurt. I just heard it on the scanner. We have to get to the hospi-

3

tal." Without another word, they both took off to New York Hospital Center.

Michaela chewed the inside of her lip. She didn't give Shannon time to park before she jumped out of the car and ran into the emergency room. She was swallowed by chaos. Police officers were everywhere. She recognized a few, but she didn't want to talk to them. She hoped to see her dad standing against a wall saying, "It was nothing. A minor skirmish. We handled it fine." But she didn't see him or his partner.

Michaela hurried to the receptionist's desk. She said, "Excuse me. But have they brought in the injured officers?"

The nurses didn't answer her. Her shawl fell off her shoulders as she leaned over the counter and grabbed the nurse's arm. She yelled, "I need to know if Jack Sommers, a police officer, was brought in here!"

"Michaela!"

She pushed the nurse's arm away and turned to see her sister with their Uncle Frank. Being so close to the family, that was what Michaela and Shannon called him. Michaela's throat constricted, when she saw Shannon's pale face.

"Uncle Frank," she said and hugged him. "You're hurt. Are you supposed to be walking around?" Frank touched the bandaged wound around his balding blond head.

"I'm OK. I wanted to find you two first. Come on. Let's sit down over here," he said as he led them away from the crowd.

"What happened, Uncle Frank?" Shannon asked.

"Your father was shot during a drug raid that we tried to handle ourselves. He's in serious condition and they are trying their best to save him. I'm really sorry. I'm even sorrier that it wasn't me," he looked down at his hands and cried.

"I'm sure you did all you could," Shannon said, placing her arm around him.

Shannon looked at Michaela, but she paced back and forth in front of them.

4

Shannon spoke in a calm voice and said, "Michaela, why don't you sit down?"

"How could he do this to us? He knows better than to go into a dangerous situation without proper backup. What if he dies, Shannon?"

Shannon grabbed Michaela's hand and said, "All we can do right now is wait and hope that he pulls through."

Jack Sommers died that night. Fellow officers had to carry Frank out of the hospital to take him home. Shannon and Michaela just sat on either side of their father's bed, not knowing what to do. Shannon cried and held her father's cold hand, while Michaela watched her, not wanting to see their father's face. She had just spoken to him that morning, when he was so full of energy and life. And now he was gone. His soul had moved along to wherever souls go when the body can no longer sustain them. Michaela wanted to remember his cheerful face and robust laugh. His once bright red hair was lifeless. His blue eyes would never sparkle as they shared a joke together. Michaela couldn't look at this dead man who was supposed to be her father. She watched Shannon spill out her grief and wondered what they would do next.

2

Run, keep running. Swirls of black clouds enveloping the field, people screaming, horses falling all around, bloodshed, death, darkness. Sword covered with blood coming closer, too close. Screaming, a hand comes through the darkness. Safe for now.

"Oh my head! When will these crazy dreams and headaches end?" Michaela thought aloud as she tried to pry her head off the pillow. "It's been two months since Dad died and still these dreams plague my mind. I felt like I was in Celtic Ireland, with screaming warriors running toward their enemy. There is so much blood."

Shannon banged on her sister's bedroom door and yelled, "Are you up yet, Michaela? If you want to get a run in, you had better move it!"

"I'm coming!" Michaela yelled back to her. "Hey Max, wake up you big, black, hairy hunk of mine!" Michaela called to her Rottweiler. "OK, OK, stop all the licking; you need some exercise."

Running with her dog was Michaela's favorite way to clear her head of dream cobwebs. They would run through Central Park, chase each other, and just exhaust themselves.

After they ran two miles, Michaela and Shannon stopped.

"How are you feeling, Michaela?" Shannon asked, while she stretched her calves.

"OK, I guess. Why do you ask?" Michaela replied, not wanting to go into her crazy dreams again.

"You just seem distant lately, that's all. I can always tell when something is brewing in that dreamy head of yours," Shannon said.

It was true. Shannon always knew what was going on in Michaela's head and vice versa. They were inseparable, since their mother had died of breast cancer when they were just children. Most couldn't see the family resemblance. Michaela was the picture of her mother. Genevieve was an Italian born beauty with deep olive skin, long dark hair, and a petite nose and chin. Michaela's hair was redder, but she had that Mediterranean look that caused men to stare often.

Shannon, on the other hand, was Irish down to the freckles on her nose. Both sisters were tall at 5' 7" and athletic. Shannon was a dancer and Michaela a martial artist. Their lives often ran parallel to each other. Shannon became a doctor of psychology when Michaela became a doctor of Celtic and medieval literature. Shannon opened a flourishing private practice, while Michaela was the first woman in Manhattan to open her own karate school. Not much to do with literature, but Michaela dreamed about being the Irish woman warrior, Scathach, and karate was the closest she was going to get.

"I just wake up sometimes thinking about Dad and I can't get back to sleep," Michaela said.

"I know you can't sleep. I hear you punching that bag in the living room!" she said. "Did you have another one of those dreams?"

Michaela rolled her eyes. "Yes, I had another one of my dreams about swords and bloodshed. It has something to do with Dad. I don't know how to stop them, and I really don't want to talk about it."

"Your dreams could be telling you that you are not dealing with Dad's death very well. You need to let the past go and move forward just a little bit," Shannon coaxed.

"How can I let the past rest? Dad is in that past. I have so many questions that haven't been answered. I want to know what happened on that drug raid. I can't go on until I know the truth," Michaela said shaking.

"And how will you do that? Are you going to start your own investigation?" Shannon joked.

"Maybe I am. They have stopped the investigation, calling it a 'drug raid gone bad.' A man spends thirty years of his life protecting the law and they just sit back and say 'oh well.' Is it me or is everybody screwed up a little?" she retorted.

Breathing out in exasperation, Shannon said, "Michaela, they haven't stopped the investigation. They just took Frank off the case and it's probably a good idea. He is too close, too filled with guilt. You have to trust the system and let the professionals do their job. Dad's death hit you hard and I don't think you've dealt with it. Plus, you have been avoiding the karate studio, because it brings back memories of him. Dad influenced your love for karate. All I can remember is the two of you watching endless Bruce Lee movies and Dad attacking you like Cato in the *Pink Panther* to see how you would react."

"Yeah, most of the time, I would react with a doubled over 'Augh'," Michaela laughed. "We had so many great times and maybe my grief is coming out in my dreams. I don't know. What I do know is that there is something strange about how he died. Being a police officer is a dangerous job, but he knew better than to go into a crack house alone and stop a raid. It just feels wrong and no one has given us a specific explanation. I just want some answers. That's all."

"I understand your frustrations, because I feel the same way. But Frank was there and he said Dad just ran in, wanting to save the world. I'm sure he was tired of seeing all these children dealing drugs. Maybe he temporarily flipped out," Shannon said.

Michaela looked at her sister. "Do you really believe that our father could just lose it?"

"No, I don't. But at this point, I don't know what else to think," she said. Grabbing Michaela's hand, Shannon smiled, and suggested, "Listen, let's go away to some remote place where we can relax and heal. There's a peaceful bed and breakfast in upstate New York. We can hike and get back to nature."

All Michaela thought about was running in the fields with her Celtic warrior. "I have been thinking about going away, but I really can't until I finish the self-defense seminar with the police force. It'll be in two weeks and then I'll be able to go. Plus you're right. I have been ignoring the studio, so I need to get back to business."

Next to her family, Michaela's greatest love was her karate school. It wasn't a big school, but her students were hardworking and loyal, and they shared the same enthusiasm for the martial arts that she did. She seemed to attract students who couldn't get enough of the physical and mental challenges that any martial arts required. She also used her school as a diversion for the kids that her dad had worked so hard to get off the streets. For some it was either karate or jail. Michaela believed that a child who was trained in the martial arts would have the confidence to say 'no' and walk away.

Michaela entered the dojo. Vince commanded the students to move to their ready position.

"Standing, set, move," Vince called.

The students snapped to their set position.

"Bow to show respect to Instructor Sommers," yelled Instructor Vince Cardosa.

Bowing, Michaela motioned for them to carry on. With a

stiff smile to her boyfriend, Vince, she entered her office and shut the door. Vince and Michaela had been close friends since grade school and had been together since high school. He knew her moods before she could even identify them and they were always there for one another. Next to her sister, Michaela considered Vince to be her best friend.

However, since her dad had died, they hadn't been as close. Vince did not believe in the dream world like Michaela did and, since it had been such a major part of her life, she had a tough time talking to him. Michaela watched Vince through her one-way office window as he tumbled with the little tykes. Much like a kid himself, Vince was demonstrating the tumble, which ended up in a big wrestling match. All the kids jumped on his 5'10" frame and tried to hold his muscular body down. In addition to extensive karate workouts, Vince liked to lift weights, so he was built like a bulldozer and could take all the punishment the kids were prepared to offer.

Michaela's office was often a haven for thought. Unless a dire emergency, everyone knew to leave her alone. This was where she could sort out studio concerns, think about which students should be promoted, and prepare her day. What she loved best about her office was that she could watch her students without them knowing. They would often be surprised at the end of their class with a new belt rank. She believed that you never knew when a situation to defend yourself would occur, so every class must be your best.

After the wrestling match ended, Vince stood up and smiled at the window. He knew that Michaela watched. Despite herself, she smiled back and watched as he smoothed back his wavy, dark brown hair. She wanted to be out there, but she couldn't right now.

At the end of the day, Michaela and Vince discussed the format for their self-defense seminar and promotions, while they sparred.

"It looks like the kids are doing well," she said and threw a fast kick.

"Yeah, I think they're ready for their promotions," he responded as he hit her leg with a downward block and reciprocated with a backhand to the head.

"Did you review the self-defense outline for the police rookies?" Michaela spoke as she swept Vince's leg and jabbed him in the ribs.

"Sure did," Vince answered. He stepped to the side and hit Michaela with a rear roundhouse.

Michaela saw it and deflected the kick with her hand and spun around nailing Vince with a side kick.

Without pause, she continued, "I figured we would keep it hands-on and utilize their tonfa sticks for most of the techniques."

With a smile, Vince bowed, "The program looks good. You lead and I'll follow."

Michaela answered with a backhand, reverse punch, and leg sweep, which dropped Vince to the floor.

"Are you really that mad at me?"

Michaela sat on Vince's stomach.

"I just don't like you teasing about my dreams," Michaela replied.

"I'm sorry I tease you, but that's what I do when I don't get something—and I don't get these dreams of yours. Plus, it scares me that you take them so seriously, like you think they are going to come true."

Michaela rolled off Vince and lay on the mat.

"They are real, Vince, and my dreams lead me in my everyday life. You need to realize that they are a part of who I am. I can't stop them."

Vince leaned up on his elbow and turned Michaela to face

him. "Listen. I may not understand them, but if they come with the package, then I'll accept them. I know it was hard losing your dad. I miss him, too. He was an incredible man. I am here to support you in any way I can. I love you, Michaela and I'll take all the beatings you can muster."

"Really?"

"Really," Vince said as he leaned over to kiss her. "What are you doing tonight?" Vince asked in his best husky voice.

"Sorry, but I'm meeting Shannon for dinner," Michaela replied.

Even though they lived together, Shannon and Michaela had kept the traditional weekly dinner outing that they had started with their dad years ago. It was a great way to unwind after their hectic week and there were always some crazy stories to be told.

"Damn, I'm stuck with the boys again. Well, I'll walk you over to the restaurant to say hello to that lovely sister of yours," Vince said.

"Hi, sorry I'm late. Vince and I had some extra work at the studio," Michaela said, slipping into her chair.

"Hi Shannon."

"Hi Vince. Do you want to join us?"

"No. I know how you girls like your weekly rap session. I'm going to meet the guys to shoot some pool. I'll see you later," Vince said. He kissed Michaela and left.

"I need a man like that," Shannon said.

Michaela turned and watched Vince leave. She admired his broad frame and noticed that several other women did, too.

"Yeah, he is incredible."

"Rub it in, why don't you!"

"Your day will come, Shannon."

Michaela knew that Shannon was still thinking about the

dream she had last night and Michaela figured she would indulge her sister and see what analysis she would get. "All right. Do you want to hear about my dream?"

"Well, it's up to you. I don't want to pressure you, but my sleep keeps getting interrupted by the sound of that heavy bag!" Shannon said looking around at the other customers. Analyzing people was her life and it was often hard to stop.

Michaela began, "I'm at some type of stone fortress by an open field. I walk toward the field and a huge man steps in my way. He is our father dressed as a Celtic king. He is afraid to let me fight and says that there is danger bigger than both of us. He bids me to go back to our fortress. I refuse. His shoulders slump forward as he turns to leave. Then a tall Celtic warrior appears. His hair is black and it trails down his back in a thick braid entwined with deep brown leather thongs. His shoulders are broad and his muscular body flows through the steps of something called *cada'me,* which he does using a sword. His strength is like an aura around him and no one can stand against him. He turns and his deep green eyes look right into mine. He knows me. Not as the daughter of the king in some Celtic land, but as me, Michaela, here in Manhattan. He beckons me to join him. He has been waiting for a warrior with my skills and we don't have much time. I tell him I am coming and I walk toward him. I step forward and my sword lays secure against my leg. I am dressed like him and my hair is pulled back in the same way. We are one and then I wake up." Michaela looked around to make sure no one had heard. These dreams were embarrassing.

Shannon thought for a while and then asked, "What is *cada'me?*"

"I don't know. I think *cada'me* must be some type of sword fighting, but I recognized some of our self-defenses," Michaela said.

"Well, my guess is that either you have relived a past life experience or you are spending too much time at the studio getting your head knocked in," Shannon joked.

13

"Really, Shannon, this is serious. Why do I keep dreaming of Dad, a form of fighting called *cada'me*, crazy bloodthirsty warriors, and a beautiful man with a ponytail? I know I tend to be eccentric with my dreams, but this was real. Plus, this man knew me and I'll be damned, but I felt I knew him, too."

"Michaela, I can't imagine how Dad and these dreams are related, even with him in the dream. Are you still keeping a dream journal?" she asked.

"I am, but these dreams are like novels and it's hard to get it all down," Michaela said.

"Try to be more diligent about it. The answers may be right there. And please remember that you can always talk to me. We need to stick together and protect each other. It's OK to let others help you, Michaela," Shannon said.

"I know. But I feel like this is something I'm going to have to work through myself," Michaela said.

After dinner, the two sisters headed home. Upon entering their place, Michaela whistled for Max. Max nosed open her bedroom door and jumped happily onto his owner. Shannon walked in and placed her purse on the table. Their apartment was small, but comfortable. It was one big room with two bedrooms and a bath off one end. To the right of the room was an open kitchen with a small table. The living room, which had a fireplace along the wall, was also used as Michaela's workout area. An 80-pound bag hung toward the left wall and various targets and equipment took up the corner by the window. A bay window looked out the back of their apartment with a view of their small back yard.

She had seen everything—the drugs, the kidnappings, the files, and that poor man getting killed. He was going to help her and the other kids start a new life, but their drug lord, Ricky Cartillo, stopped him. Natalie Fischer had been a 'daughter' of Ricky Cartillo for four years now. Her mother died one night while she was with Ricky. At the time he had told Natalie some story about her health, but now she knew it was drugs and Ricky had provided them for her. Natalie was told that he was her father and she would be taken care of as long as she helped with the family business. The business was a document destruction company, but it was a front for the real business of drugs: cocaine, heroin, and ecstasy. Natalie managed to stay away from it all, even with Ricky always pushing it on her. The other kids weren't so lucky. They would be found on the streets, runaways needing shelter and they figured this life was better than the lives they were running from. Of course, they found out too late that they were wrong.

On the run since her friend had been killed, Natalie had no place to go. She felt guilty about his death, since it was probably because of her that he was in the room that night. Daddy Cartillo had always trusted Natalie and he had been giving her more and more responsibility with his document business. Natalie knew more than a 10-year old would ever want to know or see. Her 'dad' owned a bunch of warehouses where companies' files were supposed to be shredded or stored. These files were highly confidential and Cartillo's supposedly 'good' reputation had earned him the best clients in Manhattan.

Of course what the executives didn't know was that Cartillo would copy incriminating files and use them to blackmail the companies. He also focused on smaller companies where he could run his drug business in the background. He kept the drugs moving to different businesses so they would be harder to trace. He moved the drugs in the file boxes, which were supposed to have confidential material in them.

Even at 10 years old, Natalie proved to be a useful and hard worker. She would spend 12-hour days copying files. One day, while shredding some original documents, Natalie came across some photos. They were pictures of a man who had been horribly beaten. Natalie looked at the name on the documents and saw that it was a local restaurant where Cartillo ate. She

15

remembered the owner's wife, a kind and very quiet woman. Even though she couldn't begin to recognize this man from the pictures, she knew it must be her husband. This restaurant was a front for Cartillo's drug exchange and Natalie believed that this was a persuasive action to keep the man's mouth shut. She swallowed the bile that lurched up from her guts. She feared her father and understood that everyone else did, too.

Finding those pictures was the whole reason Natalie was running for her life. She remembered it clearly.

"What are you looking at?" Boris, Cartillo's head bodyguard, had growled from the copier room door.

Natalie was scared of Boris. Not only because he was the meanest person, next to Cartillo, but also because he was grotesquely disfigured from a warehouse fire. But having lots of experience in deception and lying, Natalie said, "Nothing."

"What's in your hand?" he asked.

Natalie had slipped the photos inside her pants and backed away from Boris as he towered over her. He grabbed her by the shoulders and shook her.

Luckily, another one of Cartillo's thugs interrupted, "Hey Boris, the boss wants you upstairs."

Boris had pushed Natalie into a carton of boxes and said, "I'm not finished with you yet, kid."

Natalie went into the basement of the warehouse where all of Cartillo's kids were kept. There were cots lined up and no windows. It was damp and dark with only a couple lamps to light the entire area. They had enough food to keep them going and were kept high until they were needed to move drugs around.

Natalie was always able to keep straight. She would hide the tiny pills in her pocket and act as though she was high. Her mind would often go elsewhere and remove her from all the drug-induced chaos that surrounded her. She had visions that the other kids thought were brought on by the drugs, but she would often see events that appeared to be from some future time and knew that she would somehow play a part in Cartillo's downfall.

That night Natalie sat in her corner of the warehouse and took out some needle and thread that she had collected to repair her clothing. She might have been Ricky Cartillo's daughter, but he didn't lavish her with gifts to keep her here. He used fear. She had a pink sash that was the only reminder of her mother. She was wearing it when she died and for some reason, Ricky had given it to Natalie. Natalie kept it in her small box of possessions. She took out the pink sash and carefully made an opening, folded the pictures and placed them inside. She sewed the hole and tied the sash around her neck.

Minutes later, Ricky showed up and asked her if she was hiding anything. His gaze was ice and, mirroring his image, she denied everything. Cartillo noticed her sash and asked why she wore that crappy thing. Natalie had said it reminded her of her mother. "Be a good girl and you won't end up like her," was all Cartillo said.

Natalie had known that it was time to get away from that monster. She thought she was saved when Jack had found her. He promised he would take care of her. Now, he was gone.

"Wha..?" Michaela woke up. She searched the darkness and cried, "Oh Dad, what did you get into?" She checked out the time. 2:00 A.M. "Max, come here, boy. Why didn't you wake me up? Something's happening that I don't have any control over. But I'm going to try. I'd better write this one down."

Dream Journal—September 27, 2000, 2AM

On a side street waiting for Shannon, watching the cars go by. Hear muffled sounds and look down an alley to see four men pulling a girl from a car. She is just a child with ratty orange-red hair and a pink sash around her neck. She is strug-

17

gling and I know that they are going to kill her. I look around and see that everyone is making a deliberate attempt to avoid my eyes and the alley. I yell for someone to call for the police and I walk down the alley. I yell, "Hey!" All five of them stop and look at me. I see her eyes, know her pain, and am urged to continue. Two of the men are mean bastards who are probably doing this for some big bucks. They are dressed in suits, with mid-length black leather jackets on. It looks like a scene from *The Godfather*. They tell me to mind my own business and I say this is my business. They lunge for me. I move to a fighting stance, and throw heel kicks and spinning back kicks. I hit their weak spots, but they don't even flinch. Glancing beyond the car, I catch sight of my father. He is upset. I stop and turn to see what has caused him such pain. It's the girl. He knows her. I turn back to him and understand that this has something to do with his death and he wants it stopped. I'm frightened with the knowledge that Dad was set up. I continue to fight, but begin to doubt my abilities as a martial artist. I look at my father again, but he is gone. In his place is a woman on a horse. She is clad in leather armor, with a shield covering most of her face, and her hand on the hilt of a sword. I hear her call to me. She says, "Invoke me and I will come." I know she is Macha, Goddess of War, but I don't call to her. I am afraid. The men come upon me.

Michaela closed her journal. Now awake, she decided that this was the perfect time to work out. This was what her life had come down to. Have dreams that unraveled a story she may not want to hear and fight reality with a heavy bag. Donning her gloves, she went into the living room. Thinking about her frame of my mind, she turned on the *Rocky* theme and visualized each target as the men in her nightmare. After countless backhands, reverse punches, and soul-ripping kicks, she tore off her gloves and fell on her bed.

Later that morning, Michaela ran over to her father's old precinct to find his partner. Frank and Jack had been partners the entire time they were on the force, so they were like brothers. You had to be to work as a police officer in New York City. There were so few people you could trust with your life.

She hadn't been there since her dad died, and walking in caused a flow of memories that overwhelmed her. Michaela rushed into the restroom to calm down and breathe again. Part of her died with her father and it was hard not to just leave and run away from the hurt. But she had been doing that for two months now and her dream last night revealed that her dad wanted her help.

Calm, she walked out into the hall, right into her father's partner. "Hey there, pretty lady, you want a ticket for reckless walking?" Frank Goodale said, taking her into a big bear hug. He was big and cuddly like her dad and she gripped him.

Looking up at him, Michaela could see the pain and sorrow etched around his eyes and felt bad that she had ignored him since the funeral. "How are you, Uncle Frank?"

He put his arm around her and led her to his office.

Frank said, "OK, Michaela. I try not to blame myself too much. Hey, where's that mutt of yours?"

"He's outside. Captain Newman always yelled at me when I brought him in. Of course, I ignored him, but without Dad here …I thought I'd better listen."

She sat down and looked around his office. There were commendations and countless awards for his years of service and outstanding dedication to children. He and Jack were of the same mold and they both had enthusiastically joined the D.A.R.E. (Drug Abuse Resistance Education) team. They counseled children on how to steer clear of drugs, what to do if approached, and they had recently begun this string of raids on local businesses that were reportedly hiring children to cart their drugs around town. Of course, these kids were first hooked on the crap, so selling drugs for drugs was their only way to survive. Frank and Jack committed their lives to make a difference. Her dad sacrificed his and she hoped it was worth it.

Remembering her father's conviction, Michaela looked up at his partner and started, "Uncle Frank, can you tell me what happened?" Looking down at her hands, she blurted out, "I just feel that something went wrong and it's being covered up…or ignored."

Alarmed, Frank walked around his desk and leaned back on it, so that he was standing over Michaela like a parent getting ready to preach some sermon to his kid. He bent forward and whispered, "Now hold on, Michaela. I'm sure that there are lots of questions about what went on that day, but don't go around telling people that you think something went askew. Your father and I always followed procedures and so does this department."

Michaela didn't move.

He added, "We were responding to a call about a drug exchange at a crack house. It was fronted by a local dry cleaning business and run by a big time mobster."

"Who?" Michaela demanded.

"You know I can't tell you that, Michaela. And it's for your own good. The less you know the better. All I can say is that your father was mad. We had been on constant raids looking to find the person or group responsible and this seemed to be a real breakthrough. We arrived on the scene and the dispatcher told us that help was on the way. A guy working there tried to shut the door on us. Jack and I rushed in." He stopped and averted his gaze to look at anything else but Michaela.

"That's it? That's all you can tell me?"

Taking a deep breath, he looked her in the eyes. He continued, "Your father felt that we had stumbled onto something big that day. He always had these strong feelings about situations, and people for that matter. And that day, he knew he had found a link and he wasn't going to let this guy stop him. I tried to make him wait, but you know how he would get when he wanted something bad. Anyway, he grabbed the shopkeeper, demanding an entrance to the upstairs. The man pointed to the back of his store and Jack ran in that direction. I followed. We pulled back a curtain and there was a stairway leading upward. It was like we were in a battle frenzy and fate pushed us forward. We heard screaming and Jack ran up the stairs. He busted the door down and rushed in. I swear, Michaela, I ran in right behind him. But as soon as I entered the doorway, I was hit on the back of the head, and I don't remember anything."

Ashamed, he walked away from Michaela and stared out the window. His broad shoulders were hunched in despair. "I loved your father and I would have given my life for him. And I would do just about anything to bring him back for you and Shannon, but I can't. It was a bad move and I have to live with the pain of not being able to help my partner." He turned and, as tears streamed down his face, he beseeched Michaela, "Let it go and move on with your life. Spend time with your sister to heal from this tragedy."

Michaela thought about everything he said and asked, "Uncle Frank, you didn't see anything?"

He said, "You are stubborn like your father. I saw men with guns pointed at Jack. My gun was in my hand, but I still wasn't fast enough to stop any of them."

She stood up and put an arm around him. "I know it must be so hard for you, Uncle Frank, and I know that Dad would never blame you for anything that happened. I just need closure to this, that's all."

"I understand, little one, who's not so little anymore." He closed his eyes, breathed deep, and thought. Slowly he started, "The room was kind of dark and tables were overturned like a fight had been going on. I tried to scope the room to see how many were there. As I turned to my left, I saw a pink sash and that's when I got hit." He stopped and opened his eyes. He continued, "That's funny, because I didn't remember the sash before now. Was there a girl there? I think I remember a girl. Yes, I do! I remember her in the corner to my left and she was trying to reach for the pink sash. Sort of crazy with all the chaos going on that she would want that sash. Anyway, she must have been one of the kids these guys were using to move their drugs. I know that your father was in contact with one of the kids, but I never knew who it was."

Michaela felt chills through her body when he mentioned the pink sash. She now knew that her dreams were true and her father sent them. "Maybe the sash is all she had from her past. Maybe she was waiting for her champion to save her and she was hoping it would be you or Dad," she said. "What happened to this little girl, Uncle Frank?"

Frank looked unsure and he led her to the door. "That's really all I know, Michaela."

"Are you going to look into this further?" she asked. "I mean about the little girl? Maybe she can tell you what happened. Dad could have been set up!"

Averting his eyes, he stumbled, "Michaela, I am off the case. This was a bad raid and I wouldn't even know where to start with this girl. Hell, she may have been a figment of my imagination, my mind playing tricks on me. The police captain put a detective on the case and I'm sure he will find out some answers soon. I don't know what else to tell you. I just hope that what I've told you helps you to move on." He watched Michaela and saw her father's conviction filling her soul and he looked scared.

"Uh, like I said, I hope this helps you. Don't ask questions around the precinct and it is way too dangerous out on the streets. Please take care of yourself and tell Shannon I said hello. You both know that if ever, and I mean ever, you need me, I'll be there for you just like your father would." Disguising her anger and disappointment, Michaela said goodbye and walked out onto the street.

"Come on, Max, we have some work to do," Michaela said as she led him down the street. They jogged to Central Park where she ran with her thoughts. *Who is this little girl, Dad? Is she still alive and does she know something?* Michaela was almost positive her dad and Frank were set up, although why Frank wasn't killed was a mystery. Maybe they thought they killed him or maybe he wasn't the threat they had to eliminate. Michaela knew her father wouldn't let the threat of a mobster deter him from saving children from a life of despair. Her guess was that someone would lose a lot of money and a comfortable business arrangement if Jack Sommers lived. She didn't know what she could do about it, but having her father appear in her dream meant that he wanted her to do something and she wasn't about to let him down. What she couldn't understand was why a Celtic warrior had appeared with her father, but somehow they were connected.

Michaela decided that, despite Frank's warning, she was going to pursue her own investigation. Michaela ran along the west part of Central Park and, before she knew it, she was standing in front of the dry cleaners where her dad had been shot. She tied Max up outside and walked in. It looked like a regular place and she had arrived at a busy time. There was an older man behind the counter bustling around and barking orders toward the back room. Michaela could see the curtain that led to the staircase.

She saw that no one was watching and slipped behind the curtain. She ran up the stairs to the first doorway. Yellow tape still blocked the door, but she walked under it. It was strange standing in the room where her dad was last seen alive. She knelt down and could still see where his blood had stained the wood floor. The room was small and she couldn't imagine how Frank wouldn't have been able to recognize anyone.

Michaela closed her eyes to envision what it must have been like. She never knew how police officers could deal with the uncertainty of entering a dangerous area, where anything could happen. Just like martial arts, they were trained to react with speed and efficiency. A few seconds could make a difference in whether or not they lived.

Michaela's vision wavered. She saw her father on a battle-field. Another warrior fought with him. Then the warrior turned and stabbed her father with a sword. Her father fell. Michaela opened her eyes and gasped. Jack Sommers didn't have a chance. She knew he would never hesitate. So someone, who also knew him well, was ready and waiting.

Michaela heard footsteps. "What are you doing here?!" The shop owner yelled. "No one is allowed up here. Get out before I call the police!" He pushed Michaela out of the room. His face was beaded with sweat and he looked ready to have a heart attack.

"OK, I'm going. No harm done," Michaela said and she raced out the door, grabbed Max, and ran to the studio.

"We couldn't find her, Boss," Boris Nielson said with his hat tilted low over his face, looking at his gloved hands. He hoped that Cartillo wouldn't take his anger out on him.

Ricky Cartillo looked out his window that loomed forty stories high. He could see so much of Manhattan. He owned much of Manhattan and yet a little girl had managed to evade him. He turned to look at the three men he had sent to find her.

"All right. So what do we know?" he asked, staring at each man. They all kept quiet. "Her contact, Jack Sommers, is dead. Frank Goodale may be righteous, but he does not have the courage to go against his captain's orders and go after his partner's killer. So who does that leave us?" he asked.

"Jack's daughters?" said a thin, pale guy, named Tommy.

Cartillo grabbed him and pushed him against the wall. "What do you know about his daughters and why would she go to them?"

"Ah, because the dry cleaner owner left a message that a young woman was snooping in the room where Jack was killed," he stammered.

Cartillo shook his head and pushed Tommy away. "And why was I not told this?"

Boris interjected. "We were going to tell you when you were done."

Ricky Cartillo rubbed his smooth chin and thought. "Very well. This is what we shall do. Keep an eye on the two daughters, but make sure they do not see you. I do not think they could be involved, but you never know with Jack Sommers' family. See if Natalie tries to contact them and if either one is trying to find out what happened to their beloved daddy. It has been a long time, but I will have to reunite with the Sommers' family. Leave me," he said.

Just thinking about the Sommers' girls caused Ricky pain—especially Michaela. He had seen her at her father's funeral and her beauty blazed over everyone and cut his heart open. She looked so much like Genevieve that for a moment he thought she was still alive. He had loved her, even though she never returned that love and married Jack instead.

Jack. That righteous bastard was the cause of all his misery. Even dead he managed to foil his plans. He wasn't sure how much Natalie knew, but it was enough to get Jack too close. So he did what he always had to do—protect his family and what was his—no matter what. When he found Natalie, she would pay and so would anyone who helped her.

As Michaela walked into her karate school, she knew that Shannon had been right. She had been avoiding this place. It felt good to work out with Vince the other day. The school resonated with memories of her dad, and he would be disappointed, if she just let it all go. Plus, this was her way of keeping the children off the street and teaching them how to love and respect themselves, as well as others. Luckily, Vince had kept the place in order, but it was time to get back to her business.

After bowing to her students and observing them for a few minutes, Michaela immersed herself in paperwork. Classes had been done for about an hour and her shoulders ached. It was nice to be able to totally concentrate on something for a change. Her dad's death consumed her and her dreams were exhausting.

With her head pounding and her neck in a tight knot, she tried to massage the source of pain. She heard the door open and knew it was Vince, since he was the only one she didn't scold for entering unannounced. He rubbed her shoulders and asked, "What are you still doing here, Michaela?"

"How are the students doing?" she asked, not wanting to concern him. Although after her visit with Frank Goodale, he would probably be very concerned. Michaela placed her hand on his and he kissed the top of her head.

"The students are doing great, but they miss you. I've been trying to fill your shoes, but it's tough with the younger groups," he said sitting down next to her.

"I know, Vince. It felt good to spar the other night and I do miss the kids. I'll take the pee wee classes back," Michaela said.

"Are you sure?"

"Yes, I'm sure," she said.

"Great! Is there anything else you need to tell me?" Vince coaxed.

"Why would you ask?"

"You always chew your bottom lip when you need to tell me something," Vince laughed.

Michaela decided to test her theory to see what his reaction would be. "I went to see Uncle Frank today and I ended up with more questions than answers. I think something was covered up concerning my dad's death and I don't know what to do about it." She looked up at him to see his reaction. His face was serious and his concern was genuine. That made her even more upset.

"What do you think you can do about it?" he asked.

"Well," she began and stood up. "I thought I'd go to the mob and ask if they killed my father and where the girl with the pink sash is."

"The girl with the pink sash?" Vince looked confused, as he should be.

"She's part of the story. I just don't know what to do, Vince, but I need answers. I know my father would want me to find out."

"This is a serious situation, 'Aela', and you can't become a detective. You don't know who may be involved."

'Aela' was a nickname Vince had bestowed on Michaela at a very young age and he always used it when he was serious.

"Wouldn't you want to know? I'm not going to become a detective, but I need answers. I need to know who killed my father," Michaela pleaded.

Vince knew that when Michaela had something in her head, she would stop at nothing to do it. "Ok, ok. I understand. I'll help you where I can, but this is dangerous business. Don't do anything crazy. Think before you act for once. The kids need you in one piece," he said and pulled her his arms.

Michaela looked up at him and laughed. "Just the kids?"

"Well you know I need you and it sure isn't for a paycheck! You need me. I'm here. Got it?" Michaela nodded. "Good. Now

27

come on, I'll walk you home."

They walked the ten blocks to Michaela's apartment and caught up on the students and life in general. Vince was talking about the kids. "Little Joe Verducci is doing great on his self-defenses and finally started punching Susan VerPlanck when they spar. He has a crush on her and is afraid that if he hits her, she won't like him," he said laughing. Michaela was half listening to him and half tuning into her swirling thoughts, when she saw two men sitting in a Cadillac watching her. She just stared at them, because they set her sixth sense reeling. She couldn't see them too well in the dark, but when they realized that Michaela had seen them, they started their car and took off. "Michaela? Hey. Are you listening to me?" Vince asked.

"Huh, oh yeah, Vince. There were two men in that Cadillac watching us," she said.

Vince ran into the street to get the license plate. The car turned a corner and Vince ran back to the safety of the sidewalk as cars honked and blasted by him.

"I couldn't see the license plate. Probably just some drug dealers," he offered.

"What did you ask?" Michaela changed the subject, because she felt strongly that they were watching her.

"I wanted to know if you would be at the promotion this Thursday for the pee wees," he said.

"Of course I'll be there, Vince," Michaela said stepping up to her apartment building. "Do you want to come up?"

"Absolutely," Vince said following her.

Michaela opened the door and Max sat in front of it whimpering.

"Max, you poor thing. Vince can you take him out?" Michaela asked.

"Max, you are cutting into my girl time," Vince said while he scratched both of Max's ears.

"I'll make us something to eat," Michaela called as they

went out the door.

The light on the answering machine was blinking and Michaela checked the messages before starting dinner.

"Hello, Michaela and Shannon. It is Ricky Cartillo. I wanted to see how you ladies were faring since the funeral. I would love to take you both out to dinner sometime. Please give me a call."

Michaela stared at the answering machine, not knowing what to make of the message. Mr. Cartillo was their father's foster brother. Michaela's grandfather was a missionary in Colombia and had brought Ricky back with him to live, so he could get an education. Ricky decided to stay in the United States, but provided for his family still in Colombia. Michaela hadn't heard from him since their mother died. Michaela remembered asking her father about Uncle Ricky and her father had snapped, "He's not your uncle and he's not my brother. I don't ever want to hear his name in this house again! Do you understand?"

Michaela had been upset and confused and she had never even thought of him again until she had seen him at her dad's funeral.

"Who was that on the answering machine?" Vince asked.

"Just someone from my father's past. A man named Ricky Cartillo. He's a wealthy businessman here in Manhattan. He runs some kind of document destruction company. He wants to take Shannon and me out to dinner, but I don't want to go," Michaela said.

"Well then don't, but I'm going to pass out if you don't feed me soon," Vince said as he wrapped his arms around her waist and kissed her neck.

Mall. Pink sash. Turn and see girl run. Two men chase her. One has cropped red hair, short and stocky. Other is tall, big with brown hair. Call mall security, but don't help. Men grab girl. Natalie. Clutches her sash. She sees me and yells my name. I run toward her. The tall one draws his gun and BANG! My arm! I keep running and grab the other guy and try to release Natalie. He hits me, kicks me. I fall. Natalie screams as they take her away. Blackness.

Michaela woke up stiff and agitated. Her body felt like it had been whipped and beaten and her head throbbed. As she stood and stretched, her dream drifted back to her. She remembered Natalie screaming and calling her name. Michaela showered and came out to the kitchen just as Shannon finished breakfast. One look at Michaela and Shannon knew she had had another rough night.

Sitting down, Shannon asked, "What happened this time?"

Michaela told her the dream.

"It was like this Natalie girl knew me and was trying to find me, Shannon. It felt so real. How can that be? Is it my mind playing out some drama or does this girl know about me? Dad would never have told her his daughters' names or where they could be found. So what's the deal? Is this girl dreaming about me as I'm dreaming about her!?" Michaela asked.

Shannon thought and said, "I don't think we can ignore what your dream is telling you. If this girl saw Dad get shot, then she is a witness to a crime. Whoever killed Dad must want to find her and keep her quiet. I think she's probably still out there Michaela, but I don't know how you are going to convince anyone about that."

"What about Uncle Frank?"

"I think Uncle Frank is feeling the pressure from his superiors and, as much as he would like to find Dad's killers, they have cut him off from the whole investigation," Shannon offered.

"Cut him off! I think they have stopped the whole inves-

30

tigation. I don't understand how they can get away with this. Captain Newman loved Dad. He was the best policeman on that force. I need to get some information from someone." Michaela thought. "Hey, my self-defense seminar for the police force is next week. Maybe I can hint around about it and see who is working on it," Michaela said.

"Just be careful, Michaela. I know you don't want to hear it, but this isn't your area of expertise, even though it affects you," Shannon pleaded.

"I know. I know. But casually asking is very different from being a big time sleuth," she said. "By the way, guess who called last night."

"Who?"

"Ricky Cartillo. He wants to take us out to dinner. It sounds weird to me," Michaela said.

"Well, he is coming to the annual D.A.R.E. fundraiser, so maybe that reminded him of us," Shannon offered. "We'll just see him there. Don't worry about him. I'll see you tonight," Shannon said and left for work.

Michaela sat and stared at her cereal for a long time, thinking about her dream. As Shannon had said Natalie was the key player in her dreams, so it would make sense to try and find her. Whether or not anyone on the police force was looking for her didn't matter. Michaela needed to find Natalie before her dad's killers did.

Although Michaela had never actually seen this girl, she had a clear picture of her from her dreams. She guessed that Natalie was about 10 years old. She was a small girl with curly red hair and pale blue eyes. Michaela remembered her eyes very clearly, because each time she had seen them, they had a far away look. It was like she was looking at something beyond this life.

Vince and Michaela were planning to meet for lunch to go over promotion possibilities and the seminar, so she took Max for a walk. As she passed an ice cream and candy store a boy and girl raced out of the door. The owner of the store came out and yelled, "Stop those two! They just robbed my store!"

Michaela let Max go. "Go get 'em, Max!"

Max took off barking after the kids and Michaela followed. Max ran around a corner into an alley and Michaela caught up. The kids stood against the brick wall while Max sat in front of them and growled.

Their clothes were dirty and too small. Michaela could see the fear in their eyes, but also a look of defiance. She knew they wanted to get out of there before the police came.

"What did you take from the candy store?" Michaela asked.

"Just some candy," the boy snapped. "Are you gonna let us go?"

"And where will you go to?" Michaela wanted to know.

"Wherever we want. We take care of ourselves," the boy retorted.

"Yeah, and Natalie will help us," the girl yapped.

"Shut up, Amanda," the boy yelled.

Amanda's eyes filled with tears.

Natalie, Michaela looked surprised, but thought quickly. "Does this Natalie wear a pink sash?"

The boy looked at her with suspicion and yapped, "That question will cost ya', lady."

"That's fine with me. I'll pay for good information," Michaela responded.

The two kids looked at each other and once again the boy spoke, "Maybe." Michaela pulled out a twenty-dollar bill. His eyes bulged in excitement and he tried to grab the bill.

"Ah, answer the question first," she said.

The girl answered, "We had seen her around the streets now and then. She used to work for her father. But now she's not with her father anymore and she lives on her own like us. She's really good at finding food and work for us, so we help her out when we can."

Michaela's head reeled. She tried to process all they told her.

"Who's her father?" Michaela asked.

"Ricky Cartillo," the boy said looking like she should have known.

"Ricky Cartillo? Are you sure?" Michaela asked.

The boy, excited that he had shocked her, retorted, "Of course I'm sure. We've seen them together and everyone knows he took her in when her mother died." Michaela was sure that there had to be some sort of mistake. Ricky Cartillo ran a respectful business and was well-known around the community. Plus, he had just called her and Shannon. Then she thought about her father's words. *Maybe....*

Pulling herself together, she asked, "Do you both work for him?"

"Not really," said the boy. "Sometimes we are his lookouts, but we make sure we stay out of the warehouse."

"Yeah," said the girl. "We heard that once you go in there, you never get away."

"Why not?"

Getting tough again, the boy said, "I think we answered enough questions and the cops are going to be here any minute. Where's our money?"

"Wait. Do you know where this warehouse is?" she further questioned.

"No," he said.

Michaela held out the money and he grabbed it and turned to take off. "Hey, where are your parents?" Michaela asked.

"Dead," they both said.

"Listen, you tell Natalie that Michaela is looking for her. Tell her I want to help. You both come with her and I'll help you, too," Michaela said.

"We're fine," the boy said and pulled the girl, as the sound of police cars raced toward them. Michaela stepped out of the alley and saw Uncle Frank questioning the shop owner. The shop

33

owner pointed to Michaela. She just smiled at Frank when his mouth gaped open.

"What are you doing here?" he asked.

"Hi, Uncle Frank. I was walking with Max, when this man yelled to stop the kids. We chased them, but they got away," Michaela said. She felt bad about lying to her uncle, but these kids were a clue to help her find Natalie.

Michaela looked at the police officer next to Frank.

"Hi, I'm Michaela Sommers," she said.

"I'm Frank's new partner, Benjamin Walker. It's a pleasure meeting you. I admired your father very much," Ben said.

"So now that you have a partner, they'll let you back on my father's case?" Michaela asked Frank.

"Michaela, not here," Frank warned.

"I take that as a no?"

Frank didn't answer.

"Interesting. Can I go now? I'm late meeting Vince," Michaela coolly asked.

"Yes, I'll call you later," Frank replied.

She nodded to Ben and walked away.

Michaela was overwhelmed. She was so excited about meeting those kids, but she was upset about the information they had given her. And what was up with Frank and that damn department. How could they give him a new partner when her father's death was unsolved?

Michaela focused on what the kids told her about Natalie and Ricky Cartillo. Even if Ricky was involved in all of this, why would he want to kill his own daughter or use her in such a horrible way? Did he kill her father? And what was this warehouse that sounded more like a dungeon? She remembered her dad saying that he and Frank would pick up kids who had been dealing drugs and would be high. Maybe Cartillo kept them corralled in some abandoned warehouse and that was where he ran his main operation.

Still distracted, Michaela met Vince at a little Italian deli. She had barely sat down before she was telling him all about her adventure. She was excited and mad at the same time.

"Is this the same man who just called to ask you and Shannon out to dinner?" Vince asked.

"Yes, and he is also coming to the D.A.R.E. fundraiser," Michaela answered.

"Don't you think it odd that out of the blue he is taking an interest in you? What else have you done besides visit Frank?" Vince asked.

Michaela stammered, "I...uh...went to the dry cleaner where Dad was shot, but just looked around. I didn't talk to anyone!"

Vince leaned back in his chair, struggling to remain calm. "Did anyone see you?"

"The store owner," Michaela mumbled.

"Who?" Vince asked, leaning close to her.

"The store owner saw me," Michaela answered stronger. "And so what if he did? What does that have to do with Ricky Cartillo?"

"Maybe if he is involved in the drug dealing, then the dry cleaner could be working for him," Vince responded, letting the consequences of her actions sink in.

Michaela's face sank, "Vince, I didn't think...."

Vince grabbed her hands. "I know this is important to you, so I'm going to see you through this, but you have to be careful! I can't stress it enough. You need to keep your uncle abreast of everything that you are doing, and if he doesn't want you to do it, then you had better stop. Now how do you know about this Natalie girl that the kids were talking about?"

Michaela explained, "I told you that I've been having dreams about this girl with a pink sash. Dad is urging me to find her. She has seen everything, and if by some horrible chance Ricky Cartillo is involved, Natalie can lead the police right to him."

Vince waited not knowing what to say.

"You don't believe me, do you?" Michaela said.

"I want to, but it is so hard to believe that you are dreaming of the same girl these kids were talking about. Like I said, I think you need to tell Frank and let him deal with it. I have a bad feeling about all of this."

Michaela slumped back in her chair and sighed, "Maybe you're right."

After lunch Michaela and Vince walked to the precinct to find Frank, but he was still out of the building. She left Frank a message to call her.

3

Lying on bags of garbage, Natalie relived the brutal murders at the hand of Ricky Cartillo. She had never seen him so mad. He had dragged her to some shop and shoved her in the corner, while he dealt with one of his men.

"My friend, Roger, was in charge of the restaurant operation and he informed me that he took pictures of Mr. Randall to show his wife what would happen to her if she did not help with the business. That was stupid. He also told me he placed the pictures with the documents so they could be destroyed. That was not intelligent. Now I do not like brainless people and I do not like to fix their mistakes. So I make sure that they never make mistakes again."

He aimed a gun at Roger's head and pulled the trigger. Natalie backed away, shocked by all the blood. Ricky grabbed her by her pink sash and threw her into the wall.

Natalie cried.

"Now I am only going to ask you one more time," he said. "Did you find these pictures and did you show them to anyone?"

"No," Natalie sobbed.

Cartillo pulled her up by her shirt and held her there, forcing her to look at him. "Unfortunately, I do not believe you. You see, Boris had a bad feeling when he saw you in the copy room and followed you. He saw you with a narcotics officer named Jack Sommers."

Natalie looked scared. "I…I don't know what you're talking about. I always do what you tell me, Dad…dy."

"Enough of this daddy crap. And take this goddamn sash off," he yelled as he ripped it off her neck and threw it on the ground. "Your mother was such a whore, who the hell knows who your daddy was. All I know is that you must pay for your own stupidity—after I take care of your friend."

"No…please," Natalie began, but the door opened and Ricky shoved her to the ground.

"They're downstairs, Boss," Boris said and Natalie knew what they were going to do to Jack. Her dreams of a new life were wiped away by her violent reality.

Minutes later, Natalie watched Jack Sommers walk into a trap. She yelled to warn him, but it was too late. She screamed as she saw the bullets rip through his body. As he fell to the floor, Natalie grabbed her sash and raced out the door. She knew that if Ricky Cartillo found her, he would kill her.

Natalie stared at her putrid surroundings. She touched the pink sash around her neck. It held what she needed to pay back Ricky Cartillo for killing everyone who cared for her.

"You look gorgeous, Michaela," Vince said as they walked into the hotel for the D.A.R.E. fundraiser. Michaela wore an elegant silk charmeuse halter top gown. The gown was high-waisted and the collar halter top cut low in the back. The dark brown material shimmered in the evening light.

The fund raiser was an annual event to help raise money to fund school programs about drug prevention. It was a special night, since they were also honoring Jack Sommers' dedication to D.A.R.E.

"Thank you, Vince," Michaela said and kissed him on the cheek.

They held hands and walked into the ballroom. "I'm going to get us a drink. Why don't you find your sister and I'll meet you at our table," Vince said.

There were so many faces Michaela hadn't seen in a long time. It was difficult not seeing her dad with them. "Brings back memories, doesn't it?" Michaela said to Shannon at their table.

Shannon wiped the tears that threatened to spill over onto her eyelashes. "Yes it does. I remember growing up we would always come to the police galas. It was so much fun dancing with Dad," she said.

Michaela wrapped her arm around Shannon and nodded. She didn't trust herself to speak. The emotional turmoil was too close to the surface.

Vince sat down and made a toast. "To Jack Sommers. May his work not be done in vain," Vince said.

"Hello, Shannon," Michaela heard a voice behind her. Shannon smiled stiffly and Michaela turned to see who had made her so uncomfortable. Ricky Cartillo hovered behind Michaela like a hawk circling its prey. "Well, Michaela, you are certainly looking ravishing compared to the last time I saw you," he said while placing himself in the seat next to her. Since the last time was at her father's funeral, she didn't consider it a compliment.

Michaela shifted away from him. "Hello, Mr. Cartillo. This is my boyfriend, Vince Cardosa," she said.

Michaela couldn't believe this man was right next to her. She didn't have any proof against him, except for those children, but she still felt sick. He made her skin crawl for fear of his touch. The music was loud, so she didn't have to search for small talk.

Standing, Ricky Cartillo held out his hand and asked, "A lady as lovely as you should not be sitting down hiding at the table. Would you like to dance with me, Michaela?"

Michaela had been looking at Vince and she was sure her

eyes had gone back into her head at that question.

"No, she would not," Vince spoke as he stood up and offered his hand to Michaela. They walked onto the dance floor.

"Your sister reminds me so much of your mother," Ricky said moving next to Shannon. "Such a waste to die so young."

Shannon forced herself to speak, "You seem to miss her very much. Have you ever married?"

"No, I have never found someone who could match your mother's beauty or vivacious love for life," Ricky admitted.

Shannon's laugh was bitter. "You sound as if it was you who lost a wife and not my father."

Ricky's eyes were cold. "She should have been mine," and he left to search for Michaela on the dance floor.

He grasped Vince's shoulder.

"May I cut in?"

Vince's temper flared. "No."

"Such beauty cannot be contained. It must be shared for all to enjoy," Ricky implored.

"Michaela is not an object to be shared," Vince raised his voice and stepped toward Ricky.

Two bodyguards showed up behind Vince.

Vince saw them and looked at Ricky. "Now why would a businessman need bodyguards?"

Michaela stepped in and whispered to Vince, "Please don't make a scene. I'll dance once and then he'll leave us alone."

Vince turned to her, "A man like him gets what he wants."

He noted Michaela's stubborn gaze and stepped back. Ricky bowed.

He held her hand and placed his other on the small of her back and pulled her close enough so that his suit jacket rubbed against her chest. He leaned in closer and whispered, "Why do you fear me, Michaela?"

Michaela tensed and pretended not to hear him. He pulled back and looked her in the eyes. "Please tell me. I wish to know this."

Blinking, Michaela averted her gaze and responded, "What makes you think that I am afraid of you, Mr...?"

"Please, call me Ricky. I insist," he said while he moved her gracefully along the floor. "Perhaps it is the way you turn your eyes from me when I look at you or the nervous laugh that comes through when I speak to you. One knows that it is either fear or attraction, perhaps?"

Michaela began to laugh and reproached herself. She replied, "Why would I have to fear you, Mr. Cartillo? You and my father grew up together. You were practically brothers. I am trying to adjust to life without my father. I'm sorry if I appear afraid...or anything else."

Tightening his grasp on her hand, he continued, "I hope that this evening will start you on your way to healing, Michaela. I know what it is like to lose a loved one to an obsession or a drug. It consumes a person until life no longer can stand in the way of obtaining it."

Michaela was enraged. She pulled back. "I would not compare my father to an addict. He lived to free children from the confines of drug addiction and drug lords who used the children's dependency to fulfill their own greed. My father died in a battle, not in a prison."

The song ended and Michaela tried to move away. Cartillo held her and she looked into his eyes with defiance and anger.

"Ha, now that is what I like to see in a woman," he said as he led her off the dance floor. His hand touched the small of Michaela's back and it burned her skin like a snake bite, the sting lingering long after the first painful puncture. Moving his hand along her arm, he took her hand and brought it to his lips. He softly kissed the back of Michaela's hand and said, "Remember, sometimes fear is a good thing and it tells you when to run or when to lay dead. Of course now that I know you do not fear me, I will see you again."

41

As Michaela watched Cartillo walk away, her vision shifted. She saw warriors dying. A man walked away from her, horns protruded from his helmet; blood dripped from his sword. Her father lay on the ground wounded.

"Michaela? Michaela?!" Shannon yelled, shaking her sister.

"Huh?" Michaela asked, finally focusing her eyes on Shannon.

"Are you all right? You look like you're going to pass out. What did he say to you?" Shannon asked.

"Well, he didn't say too much. I just thought I saw…," she stopped when Vince touched her arm.

"Saw what?" Vince asked, his face twisted with anger and concern.

"Nothing," she said. "It was nothing," and she walked back to their table.

Shannon stared after her sister and, as her gaze found Ricky Cartillo, she saw that he also watched Michaela, with a hungry look in his eyes.

"Can you believe that loser had the nerve to ask me to dance?" Michaela said when she and Shannon arrived home. The two sisters sat in front of the fireplace and drank tea.

"He bothers me. He spoke about Mom as if they were lovers. Do you think they could have been?" Shannon asked.

Michaela looked at Shannon like she was mad, but Shannon was quite serious.

"What did he say to you?"

"He said that he used to teach Mom how to speak Spanish and when Dad had to work after school, Ricky and Mom would sit and talk on the front steps until Dad came home. He seemed to spend a lot of time with her when Dad wasn't around."

"Ricky was part of the family," Michaela said.

"I guess. But why the sudden interest in us?"

"I'm sorry, Shannon. I haven't been completely honest with you about what I have been doing."

Michaela told Shannon about her discussion with Frank, his new partner, and the kids she had met. She also told Shannon about the dry cleaner and her vision. She always told Shannon her dreams, so all their information was out in the open.

"If Frank knew Ricky was the suspect, why didn't they question him? How did he get away without even a subpoena to search his house for a gun? Someone else has to be protecting him, but who?" Shannon thought out loud.

"Sounds like we need to see more of Ricky to find out," Michaela asked.

"From what you told me, it would seem that Ricky likes you. You remind him of Mom, which makes it even creepier. If it wasn't so creepy, I would say to be friendly with him just to find out more about his contacts," Shannon said flippantly.

"That's it," Michaela agreed. "I could reunite with Ricky and find out where he keeps his warehouses."

"Besides the fact that Vince would kill him, that is too dangerous. You told me that Vince wants you to talk to Uncle Frank. I think that's a good idea."

"I left Frank a message and he still hasn't called me. I feel that someone on the inside is protecting Ricky. When Ricky left me on the dance floor I had another vision. I saw a warrior stab Dad. It was someone who should have been on his side. Maybe Uncle Frank isn't all he says he is."

Shannon crossed her legs and laughed. "I don't know what is more unreal—you having a dream vision while awake or Uncle Frank being a crooked cop. Tonight has upset you, so let's slow down and think things through before we do anything we may regret."

"All right," Michaela said and got up to go to bed. "Where are we going to eat tomorrow? Pepe's is closed for remodeling."

"There's another Italian restaurant called Pasta Belle. It's near the park. Why don't we try there?" Shannon said.

"I'll stop by and make a reservation. Goodnight, Shannon," Michaela said jumping into bed with Max right behind her.

Michaela didn't have a chance to exercise in the morning, so at lunchtime she took Max for a run. They made their way around Central Park and stopped at the restaurant Shannon had recommended. It looked authentic enough with the red and white canopy on the outside, the bottles of wine hanging from the ceiling, and vine paper lining the walls. She was walking toward the front when she heard a familiar voice that once again made her skin crawl. She turned and saw Ricky Cartillo sitting with a detective that she had recognized from her dad's precinct. Suspicious and scared, Michaela attempted to walk out, but Cartillo saw her. He was just as surprised as she was, but managed to recover much quicker.

"Michaela! How nice it is to see you again. I was going to call you," he said with a big, bright smile. "Do you know Detective Malowski from the precinct?"

Scott Malowski stood up and shook Michaela's hand. "I thought you looked familiar, Detective. Are you out solving any crimes today?" Michaela said taking her hand back.

"Nothing that should worry a pretty thing like you, Ms. Sommers," he said.

Cartillo's eyes never left Michaela's face and he continued, "What brings you to the Pasta Belle?"

"I was going to make a reservation. I heard the food was good. Do you come here often?" she asked.

"I do and the food is delicious. The owners are dear friends of mine. We do business together," he said waving down the hostess. "Maria. My friend here would like to make a reservation. Can you help her and make sure that she has the best service possible."

"Yes, Mr. Cartillo. Please follow me," she said.

Michaela followed the hostess. As she came up to the reservation desk, a young boy with straggly hair and baggy jeans ran out of the back door with a box in his arms. He crashed right into Michaela and dropped the box. Flustered, he bent down to pick up the box.

"Here, let me help you," Michaela said bending down. The boy looked up and Michaela saw his huge, haunted blue eyes. "This is kind of heavy for a young guy like you."

He looked at her and then darted a look toward the table where Cartillo and Malowski were having lunch. Cartillo watched and the boy stammered, "I can handle it." He grabbed the box and scurried out the door.

Michaela turned to the hostess. "You sure do hire them young here." When the hostess didn't respond, Michaela made her reservation and turned to leave.

Malowski stood up and took his leave of Cartillo. "I will see you soon, Michaela," Ricky said smiling.

Nodding Michaela left the restaurant with Malowski behind her. Her head was swirling with questions.

"Can I give you a ride somewhere, Ms. Sommers? The city can be a dangerous place for someone as beautiful as you," Malowski said.

Michaela unhooked Max and he let out a low growl toward the detective. Malowski backed away. "As you can see, I'm well protected. But tell me, Detective, do you know who is in charge of my father's case?" Michaela asked.

Malowski's smile was evil, but he managed to sound sympathetic. "I am."

"So can you tell me if you have found the men who killed my father?"

"We have some leads, but nothing that would interest you," Malowski said to close the conversation.

"Oh, but it all interests me. Two months have gone by without any results. I would like to be updated on any progress."

"Well, most of it is confidential, but I'll let you know if I find anything. Maybe we could get together and talk about it," Malowski said as he stepped closer.

Max's growl held him back.

"I'll call you," Michaela said and she turned and walked away.

Scott Malowski relaxed his clenched fists and knew that Jack Sommers' daughter was going to be a problem.

That evening was the students' test for their next karate belt. Joe Verducci had come a long way. He and Susan VerPlanck had sparred and Susan didn't yell at him for punching her. Actually, she seemed to like him more. The students were tested for their self-defense, kata, and sparring. Michaela and Vince walked around evaluating the students while black belt students ran the drills. Michaela stopped to help a student with a side kick. Something outside caught her eye. She turned her back to the window and observed through her large mirror on the back wall. A tall figure loomed just outside the streetlight and all she saw were shadows. Vince came and stood next to her.

"Who is that?" he asked.

"I don't know. Probably just someone interested in joining the studio," Michaela answered.

"I'll go see what he wants," Vince fumed.

"No, let it go, Vince. We are here for the kids," Michaela said in exasperation.

"Detective Malowski. What a surprise to see you. Do you always attend seminars for rookies or do you have information about my father?" Michaela said.

Michaela noticed how big Scott Malowski was when he stood next to her. "Even a detective needs to protect himself. And no, I don't have any new information for you, but I am working on some leads. Besides I didn't want to miss all the karate action. Hwaaaa!" he screamed pretending to be Bruce Lee.

Annoyed, Michaela had a feeling this detective wasn't here for the seminar.

"Good morning, ladies and gentlemen. I am Instructor Michaela Sommers and this is Instructor Vince Cardosa. Today we will be working on techniques that will allow you to utilize your tonfa stick in a defensive mode and take a criminal down with efficiency and speed. The tonfa is basically an extension of your hand and protects your arm as well as other areas of the body when used properly.

"When using the tonfa, the key to successfully maneuvering it is in the grip. The grip is very similar to a karate fist, but you must keep the grip loose enough to move the stick, but not drop it. At the moment of a strike or blow, squeeze or tighten your grip on the handle and thrust your hips forward to add power," Michaela explained.

"Hey, I like that thrusting part!" Malowski shouted from the back. Some rookies laughed, while Vince walked over to stand behind Malowski.

Michaela continued, seeing that Vince would keep an eye on the detective. "Let's look at a basic technique. You are in a situation where a drugged up lowlife attacks you. Release your tonfa and thrust the front head into his midsection and he'll double over," Michaela spoke as she demonstrated the technique. "Plus if the attacker has a weapon, you can use the tonfa to block, just as you would block with your arm. There's an upper-block, where the bottom edge of the tonfa deflects the blow. Then you have the inward and outward block. The tonfa is held vertically, the back head pointed down. You can use this to deflect a weapon aimed toward the chest." Everyone tried these techniques.

"Of course, the tonfa can be used to strike your attacker and cause enough damage to stop him with a single strike," Michaela began.

"One strike?! Man, you're taking all the fun out of it!" Detective Malowski yelled out.

The rest of the class felt the tension between Malowski and the instructors. They fell silent and waited for Michaela to continue.

Michaela could see from Vince's strained face that he wanted to hit the obnoxious man. "Detective Malowski! Could you come forward, please?" she asked.

With his chest pushed out, he strutted forward like the barnyard's favorite cock. "You need my assistance?" he asked.

"No, I just need you to dummy for me," Michaela replied. "OK, so once again, we know that the tonfa is an extension of your fist. So, instead of punching a certain area, use the front head like this," she said as she planted the tip of the tonfa under Malowski's chin and pushed back hard enough to make his teeth rattle. Keeping him there, she continued, "You temporarily cut off his breathing and his whole body is open to you now. There are numerous pressure points available. For instance, Detective Malowski's throat is wide open to me, so I can press in like so and cause him to gag." Gurgling sounds came from the detective's throat. "Behind the ear is another effective point or under the nose. Or perhaps the hooligan is trying to be tough and doesn't respond. After you've cut off his breathing, ram the tonfa into his solarplex, avoiding the stomach please, unless you would like to get puked on. It doesn't take much," she explained as she tapped Malowski in his solarplex and he reeled forward. Michaela then twisted his hand behind his back and forced him to his knees and cuffed him. "Thank you, Detective," she said uncuffing him.

Nursing his jaw, Malowski was quiet for the first time that day.

Michaela walked around the studio taking in everyone's facial expressions. She noted several satisfied grins, especially from the women. She figured Malowski was probably harsh to most of them.

"Let's try another technique. You are attacked by a violent criminal, who may or may not be high. You swing your tonfa up and loosening your grip let the back end swing up and around to nail him in the bridge of the nose. Besides causing intense pain, this would cause his eyes to water. However, he ducks out of the way. Keeping the motion of the tonfa moving forward over his head, swing it back around and drop your body down onto your opposite knee and quickly flip the side edge of the tonfa into the criminal's shin. This will drop him without further strikes." Michaela had them practice on one another.

Unfortunately, a female rookie had Malowski for a partner. He kept moving behind her or pushing her over when she was trying to hit him in the shin. Vince walked over to help. "Let's stick to the drill so she can get the technique down," he commanded.

Malowski laughed. "She isn't going to be able to get any power with this thing. I can take this stick right away from her," he said grabbing it.

"And that is why she is here, Detective, so she can get the skills needed to protect her from morons like you. If you cannot help her with this, then we need to change partners," Vince warned.

Malowski stepped closer and barked, "Who are you calling a moron, kung fu man?"

Vince lost it. Taking his tonfa, he hit Malowski in the chest, doubling him over. Pushing him upright, Vince grabbed Malowski's hand and twisted it so that the hand locked at Malowski's side. Vince proceeded to lead Malowski to a corner and all he could do was comply. On his toes, Malowski winced from the pain.

"Now, I'm only going to say this once," Vince whispered through gritted teeth. "We are here to help the rookies defend themselves in life or death situations. I don't know what you are doing here, but it is obvious that it's not to learn anything. If I have to talk to you again, then your hand might get broken. Are we clear?"

Malowski nodded.

"Good." Vince released him and walked back to join the class.

Malowski rubbed his hand, pissed.

Michaela addressed the group. "We are not here to fight each other. Instructor Cardosa is a professional martial artist and he deserves respect for his level of expertise. Let's take a break and change partners when we continue," she said.

"How's everyone doing?" Michaela asked as they resumed their instruction. "While it's important to know how to hit, it is also helpful to know what it feels like to get hit, so we will give you the opportunity to be the target. Now, chances are a simple technique is going to work to bring someone down. But sometimes, there are other circumstances involved where you may have to use some force to gain control. The assailant could have a weapon, be high on drugs, and most likely desperate not to get caught," she said. She turned to Vince and motioned for him to join her.

"Let's say you are trying to apprehend someone and he pulls out a knife. The most important point to remember is to not be there when the assailant attacks. Step out of the way to the side of your assailant. Release your tonfa, spin it out, and hit the hand holding the knife. Then grab your assailant's hand and quickly twist the arm down and away from you. This does a few things. His arm is now useless, and you have him on his knees and in your control, and his knife cannot hurt you. If he fails to go all the way down to the ground, twist his arm more and push down with the tonfa. His arm will break. Just hold on to it until he is submissive and cuffed. Let's try it."

Michaela and Vince walked around helping everyone with the different techniques. Malowski had been paired up with another officer who was about his size and they easily took one another down.

Once again Malowski had something to say. "This technique is fine for a 200-pound cop, but no woman is going to able to make it work. Look at Kampton! She can't even twist the guy's arm!"

Michaela saw that this was true and had Vince help the officer to be more effective. "All techniques are not for everyone. What works for a larger person may not work for someone smaller. In such a case, it is necessary to modify the movement so that you are comfortable with it. I was able to take Instructor Cardosa down and with practice and modications, so could Officer Kampton," Michaela replied.

"I bet you can't take me down," Malowski challenged.

In an instant, Michaela was behind Detective Malowski. She swung her tonfa at his feet and swept them clean out from under him. He hit the ground hard, losing his breath. Michaela placed the handle on his neck and pressed hard.

"I would use a different technique with you, Malowski," she said, not smiling. She stood up and surveyed her students. Some snickered and some were very solemn. Officer Kampton looked avenged.

Michaela continued in her loudest voice. "You are not here to see who is better or to mock one another's weaknesses. You are here to find out your strengths, work on your weaknesses, and to protect yourself and your partner beyond all extreme measures. This is not a joke. This is not an afternoon away from

51

serious training. This training will save your life and the citizens that you have sworn to protect!"

Malowski stood up rubbing his behind. "You just surprised me," he challenged.

Michaela was done with this moron of a man. "Of course I surprised you. The element of surprise and even deception comes in very handy when there is a huge difference in size. You can't let your opponent know what you are going to do. Sometimes surprise is all you have!" She paused and scanned his body. "How much do you weigh, Detective?" she asked.

"About 220 on a light day," he replied, knowing he was going to get his chance.

"Please step forward," Michaela said motioning to him with her hand. "This is a good lesson in case the lowlife happens to be much bigger than you, which can happen with a man or a woman. In this case, he is coming at me with a knife." She motioned for Malowski to stab her. "Hit the arm down with the tonfa. He's not going to use that arm anymore. While your attacker is stunned, ram the tonfa into his jaw. Sweep him onto his back, retrieve the knife, and cuff him." Michaela finished and turned to Malowski.

"Detective, you are a scumbag. Pretend you are going to stab me," she said. Happy to oblige, Malowski lunged toward Michaela. Michaela stepped to the side maintaining her balance. Malowski lunged again, and Michaela whipped her tonfa into his forearm and touched the front end of the tonfa off his jaw. She twisted his hand and flipped him down to the ground with his face planted on the floor. He tried to get up, but she only twisted more. "Now apply pressure until the assailant stops. For the sake of training, when you feel that you have given your all, you should tap out and submit. Do you submit, Detective?" Michaela asked.

He tried to move again, but she only twisted more and everyone could hear the ligaments pop in his arm. As he grumbled in pain, he mumbled, "I submit," and Michaela let him up.

"Getting the bastard under control as fast as you can is the key to survival on the streets. Never underestimate anyone—man or woman. It could cost you more than your pride. You have partners. Use them well and stick together. We have ended our time together. Thank you and good luck out on the streets," Michaela finished. Malowski slipped, not unnoticed, out of the studio and left Michaela wondering what he would be up to next.

Detective Malowski made a quick call once he left the studio. "Yeah, it's me. The seminar was fine, but Jack's daughter keeps asking me about her dad's case." Malowski listened. "She's seems pretty confident with all her karate crap. Do you want me to teach her a little lesson?" Malowski waited and then smiled.

"Whatever you say. Just don't start getting soft on me. This girl is trouble and I'd rather get all the loose ends tied up," he said and hung up.

"What did you find out?" Vince asked Michaela after the seminar.

Michaela hit the heavy bag. *Punch, punch, kick.* "Scott—*punch*—Malowski is working on my dad's case," she said. *Kick.*

"So why was he here harassing rookies when he should be conducting an investigation? Maybe this was part of his investigation," Vince wondered.

Spin kick, backhand, punch. "I don't know, but I ran into him with—*jab*—Ricky Cartillo the other day and he was just as arrogant. *Kick.* I don't like him and his association with Cartillo makes it worse!" Michaela slammed the bag once more and dropped down to the mats.

Vince sat next to her. "Let's try to see Frank again tomorrow, Michaela. We don't know what we are doing and I feel like you are being watched. Something serious must be going on if they have their eye on you already and you haven't done anything."

"All right, we'll go see him tomorrow. Now enough of this, what are you doing tonight?" Michaela asked tired of all the worries.

"I'm supposed to go over Josh's house to watch the fight tonight. But I don't have to. We could go see a movie or go to my place?" Vince offered.

"No, you go have some fun. I'm actually going to finish some balance sheets for the month. Then I'll head home and see what Shannon's doing."

"I'm not comfortable leaving you here alone."

Michaela laughed. "I'll call Shannon."

"All right, but call me when you get home."

"Yes, Vince."

"I'll see you tomorrow, 'Aela'," Vince kissed her goodbye.

"Have fun," she said and settled into her office to work.

Michaela couldn't get in touch with Shannon, so she left the studio to go home. As she walked the few blocks to her apartment, she had the feeling again that someone was watching her. She turned and saw a limousine following her. The streets were busy and there were people walking around eating and shopping, so she wasn't too worried. However, once she turned the corner and the car was still there, she began to look for a shop to go into.

"Michaela!" she heard someone call. She turned thinking it was Vince, and was surprised to see Ricky Cartillo step out of his limousine.

Michaela stopped and confronted him. "Why are you fol-

54

lowing me?"

"I apologize. I was speaking on the phone and I did not want to lose you. May I offer you a ride home?" Ricky offered.

"No, I can take care of myself," Michaela said not wanting to be around the man. Her thoughts of finding out more about her father were overcome by her revulsion of what this man could be.

"Please. I would like to talk to you about your father," he spoke softly, but his eyes were insistent.

"Well, just to my apartment. Shannon is waiting for me and will want to know where I am," she lied.

"Wonderful," Ricky said smiling. "Would you like some wine?"

"I don't think so," Michaela said, settling into the leather seats.

He poured her a glass anyway and gave it to her.

"You certainly like to get your way, don't you?" Michaela asked not taking the wine.

"I just like to make sure that my guests are comfortable. Please, just a toast to you and your sister," Ricky said.

Not seeing the harm, Michaela drank the wine.

"So, how was your day at your studio?" Cartillo asked.

Loosening up a little, Michaela said, "Well, it started out great. I had my self-defense seminar for the police force. Your friend, Detective Malowski, showed up."

"Really? Well, he is always one for learning new things," he said.

"How do you know Detective Malowski?" Michaela asked.

"I am involved in some projects with the police department and he keeps me apprised of progress," Ricky replied.

"You certainly are involved in what is happening around you," Michaela noted.

"Yes, I like to be aware of what affects me. As a martial artist, I would think you would be very good at that." Ricky had refilled her glass and already her head was beginning to feel light. Normally wine wouldn't affect her so quickly, since she often had it with dinner. She wondered if something was in the wine.

"What is in this wine? I don't feel right," Michaela asked.

"It is my own special recipe. Do not worry. I will take good care of you. I just need to talk to you for a while."

Michaela felt giddy and very thirsty. "I need some water."

BEEP, BEEP. Michaela searched in her pocket to grab her cell phone. She dropped it on the floor and when she bent over to get it, her heart began to race. She sat up and felt the blood pounding in her head. "Woah," was all she could manage while blinking her eyes to try and clear her head.

"Here, let me get that for you," Cartillo said. He picked it up and turned it off. "It seems as though they gave up." He placed it on the seat across from them.

Michaela leaned her head back against the seat. Her throat and mouth were dry and her senses reeled. Cartillo's cologne smelled so strong to her now and her skin tingled. She felt good and her body wanted to be active.

She looked out the window. The limo had pulled around a circular driveway and Michaela saw a mansion looming high above the grounds.

"Where are we?" she asked amazed.

"This is my home," he replied.

"You said you would take me home," Michaela said.

"Not until we have a little talk," Cartillo said.

The limo driver opened the door for Michaela. She hesitated. She was sure that Cartillo put something in her wine, but she couldn't prove it. Cartillo stepped in front of the door and held out his hand. She took it. She knew she shouldn't, but her body didn't feel like it was her own and even his touch made her feel good.

The house was open and bright. Two banisters encircled the foyer and led to the upper levels of the house. On the left was a cozy room with a fire burning. Candles were lit and the room glowed.

"Please sit down. Can I get you anything?" he asked sitting across from her.

"Just some water, please," she said picking up a piece of candy from a dish on the table. "I feel very warm."

Cartillo left the room and came back with a tray of sweets and drinks. Michaela was standing by a mantel looking at some photos.

"Is this your family in Colombia?" she asked.

"Yes, this is my mother, father, and my sister. And this is my sister with her husband and two children," he said.

"They are beautiful. Why don't they come here to live closer to you?" she asked.

Cartillo looked at Michaela. "My father is set in his ways and so is my sister's husband. They have come to visit, but prefer their life in Colombia. I have shared my wealth with them and so they are comfortable and can come here any time they like. My door is always open to my family," he finished.

"It must be hard not having your family close to you. I don't know what I would do without my sister," Michaela said. Thinking of Shannon made Michaela stop talking. She needed to leave this place soon.

"You learn to do whatever you must in order to survive and help those you love," he said.

"And have you done whatever you must to help them?" Michaela asked.

"Whatever I have done, I have done for myself and my family. I help others who cannot help themselves. I would like to help you to get on with your life," he said moving closer.

"What do you mean?" she asked trying to keep her head from spinning.

"I mean about your father. You miss him?" Cartillo asked taking Michaela's hand.

Michaela stepped back. "Of course I miss him, don't you? After all, the two of you grew up together. Besides, what happened between the two of you? After my mother died, my father told me to never speak of you again and you never came around."

Cartillo led Michaela into another room. It was a small ballroom. Before Michaela could object, Ricky Cartillo pulled her into his arms and swayed her around the floor. Michaela thought about the dinner when she first danced with him and how repulsed she felt. She still felt repulsed, but she couldn't move her body away. Her mind felt intoxicated and his touch sent chills throughout her body. He led and she followed, falling into the magic of the music that had begun to play.

"Your father and I were teenagers when we met. We always had a tumultuous friendship. He was my foster-brother, but beyond that we never did become close. His philosophy and mine were always at odds. He came from a different world. He never had to work as hard as I did. Your grandfather always provided for him and things came easier for your father," he explained as he twirled Michaela around the floor.

"But didn't my grandfather provide for you?" she asked.

"He did, but I was taught to earn what I had, so that I would never have to owe others. As it was I felt that I would always owe your grandfather more than I could ever repay. He helped me at a time when I was desperate and I will always appreciate that, but people change and must move on. Just as you must move on and stop trying to find out the answers to your father's death," he said.

Michaela stopped. "I just want to know how a seasoned officer could get caught off guard."

Cartillo held her closer and Michaela's body tensed. "There are many enemies within, Michaela. You must always know who they are before they reveal themselves…and it is too late. Perhaps your father's enemy was his friend."

"You were his friend," she whispered.

"That was a long time ago. But know this. I will never hurt you," he said as his lips came closer.

Michaela shoved Ricky away from her. "I don't know what game you are playing, but I will not have any of it."

Ricky could have been enraged by her actions, but he found her too attractive. "And what game are you playing, Michaela? I see how you look at me. Do you deny that you are attracted to me?"

"What? You told me that you wanted to talk to me about my father. I want to find out who killed him. That's why I came here. I'm young enough to be your daughter!"

Ricky grabbed Michaela's arm and swung her around hard against him. Her equilibrium was gone and the room started spinning. He held her tight and whispered in her ear.

"For your own safety, you need to let this go. I cannot control what may happen to you if you are too persistent."

"The wine. What did you put in the wine?"

"Remember what I said. Stop finding answers concerning your father," Ricky implored her.

Michaela could see from his face that he was sincere. "I will never hurt you, Michaela. You are safe here with me," Ricky promised.

Michaela's head pounded and she could no longer focus on the man her father said to never speak about again. She felt danger, but her body was beyond her control. She slumped in Cartillo's arms.

Cartillo easily picked up Michaela and laid her down on the couch.

"Boris!"

"Yeah, Boss?"

"Please prepare the guest room for Ms. Sommers," he requested.

Boris moved to touch Michaela. "I'll prepare my room for her," he said.

With a fast and hard backhand, Cartillo sent Boris flying across the room. He walked to him, grabbed his collar, and twisted.

"If you lay a hand on her, I will personally remove them and stuff them down your throat! Do you understand me?" he yelled.

"Yeah, yeah. Why are you so defensive about her? You know she's trying to find her father's killer. Shouldn't we just get rid of her?" he asked, wiping the blood from his mouth.

Cartillo looked at Michaela Sommers and spoke almost to himself. "I made a promise a long time ago. Michaela will never be harmed by my hand. Now go and do what I asked."

Shannon called Michaela's cell phone from work, but the phone was turned off. She called the studio, but no one answered. She went home thinking that maybe Michaela was sick or asleep. The apartment was quiet and Max whined for his owner. He rubbed his head on her leg. "Max, I don't have time for this. I don't know where Michaela is."

She dialed Vince's cell phone. "Vince? It's Shannon. Is Michaela with you?"

"No. I haven't seen her since the seminar. She was going to catch up on paperwork and call you for a ride home," he said.

"Her cell phone is turned off, she's not at the studio, and she's not home," she said.

"I'll be right over," Vince said.

Michaela still had not shown up at 11:30 pm. She had been missing for two and a half hours.

"We need to call Frank," Vince said.

Sick to her stomach, Shannon agreed, but before she picked up the phone, it rang. Shannon didn't recognize the number, but Vince motioned for her to answer.

"Hello?"

"Shannon! This is Ricky Cartillo. You must be wondering where Michaela is, yes?" he asked lightly.

"How did you know that?" Shannon replied.

"I met up with Michaela earlier this evening and she came over to my house. I'm afraid she had too much wine. I did not want you to worry. She can stay here for the evening and I will bring her home in the morning," Ricky offered.

"No! Uh, I mean, can you hold on?" Shannon blurted.

"What's wrong?" Vince asked.

"It's Ricky Cartillo. He said that Michaela came over to his house and she had too much wine. He wants her to stay over."

Vince grabbed the phone. "You disgusting scum! Where are you? I'm coming to get Michaela."

"Ah, this must be Vince. Your girlfriend is in good hands. I will bring her home when she wakes up," Cartillo said and he hung up.

"What? The bastard hung up on me. How can we get his address?" Vince yelled.

"I have his address from the fundraiser. But what are you going to do?" Shannon asked.

"I'm going to get Michaela. There is no way in hell that I'm letting her stay there with that creep! Are you coming?" Vince asked.

"Shouldn't we call Frank?" Shannon wanted to know.

"We'll call him on the way," Vince said and they rushed out the door.

He walks toward her across the broken battlefield. His arms glisten with sweat and he holds his flail steady, prepared to kill anyone who should cross his path. His face is hidden behind an elaborate helmet, but his eyes hold hers and she waits for him. He shifts his eyes to above her head and as they widen in surprise, she turns and screams.

Michaela woke up and could barely lift her head off the pillow. Her tongue was stuck to the roof of her mouth. Moving her head, she realized she wasn't home. The room was small, but elaborately decorated. Her bed was covered by a canopy over mahogany bedposts. The sheets were white silk and felt cool on her skin. Michaela forced her eyes to stay open and sat up.

There was a connecting bathroom and she washed her face and mouth with cold water trying to remember what happened. Michaela remembered dancing with Ricky and he told her not to do something, but beyond that was blank. She remembered that all she drank was wine. It had never affected her in that way and she had had more than three glasses before. Ricky had to have put something in her wine.

She cursed herself for getting in his limo and opened the bedroom door to leave. She heard yelling in the foyer.

"Where is she?" Vince yelled in another man's face.

"Vince!" Michaela called and swooned.

Vince shoved the man out of his way, but the young man, Tommy, attempted to stop him. Vince kneed him in the groin and ran up the stairs. He grabbed Michaela and held her tight.

"Are you all right?" he asked.

Cartillo sauntered from his room smoking a cigar.

Vince lunged at Cartillo and jammed his elbow into Cartillo's throat.

"Don't you ever, ever come near Michaela again!" Vince yelled.

Another of Ricky's bodyguards grabbed Vince and pulled

him off Cartillo. Vince fell to the ground, but was up in an instant, eager to smash someone's face in.

The bodyguard moved to attack Vince, but Ricky stopped him. He massaged his throat and spoke, "Leave him, he is upset."

"Damn right I'm upset. You just remember what I said, Cartillo. Let's go, Michaela," Vince said and he took her hand. They walked down the stairs and out the door and no one stopped them.

"Now him, I could do without," Ricky said.

"You want me to take him out, Boss?" the burly bodyguard asked.

"No, but see to Tommy. All will end well in time," Ricky said.

Michaela slept well into the morning. When she woke up, her body felt like it had been battered. She dragged her feet into the living room, where Vince and Shannon were talking. Vince jumped up when he saw her.

"Hey, baby. How are you feeling?" Vince asked, helping her to the couch.

"Like I've been run over. What happened last night?"

Shannon filled her in on all the events.

"I remember being on the balcony and Vince arguing with someone, but it was like I was in a dream. Then of course I was dreaming about my warriors on the battlefield. Do you think Cartillo drugged me?" Michaela asked worried.

"I don't know, Michaela, but we called Uncle Frank and he is on his way over. It's time that you spoke to him and told him what has been going on. Plus, you need to try and remember what you and Cartillo spoke about last night," Shannon said.

About a half hour later, Frank showed up with his partner, Ben Walker.

"How are you, Michaela?" Frank asked as he bent down to kiss her on the forehead.

"I've been better, Uncle Frank. Hello, Ben. Feel free to introduce yourself," Michaela said, holding her head.

"Hi, I'm Ben Walker, Frank's new partner," he said as he shook Vince's hand.

Vince noted his strong handshake.

"Hello, Ben, it's nice to meet you," Shannon said smiling. Ben smiled back.

Michaela explained how Ricky had followed her in his limo and offered to drive her home. "He was so insistent about drinking the wine. After one glass I felt funny and was unable to control my actions. My heart was pounding out of my chest and I was very warm and thirsty," Michaela recalled. "Then instead of bringing me home, he took me to his mansion. I felt like I didn't even own my own body. He kept talking to me about his family and about Dad."

"The effects you describe sound like Ecstasy," Frank replied.

Vince clenched his fists.

"What did he say about your father?"

"He talked about how they didn't get along when growing up and he insinuated that someone close to Dad was responsible for killing him." Michaela thought for a moment. "Then he discouraged me from inquiring about my father's case in any way. He said he could only do so much to protect me."

"Uncle Frank, is Ricky Cartillo a suspect in our father's case?" Shannon asked.

Frank shifted in his chair. He stole a glance at Ben and then the girls. "I don't know if Cartillo was involved with your father's death. All I can tell you is that he was reportedly involved in the string of drug raids that your father and I were conducting. We have never been able to pin anything on him. I want you to take a test, Michaela to see if you were drugged. If you were, then we might be able to get into Cartillo's warehouses and gather some evidence."

"Well, there's more, Frank," Vince started. He told them how Michaela had spoken with the kids from the candy store and that they said Ricky Cartillo was this girl Natalie's father.

"Are you trying to get yourself killed? I told you not to get involved and now all three of you are in this. There is only so much I can do and I can't protect you if you are running around acting stupid. Now let's go down to the hospital and get you checked out, Michaela," Frank said.

Two hours later, Michaela was cleared to leave the hospital.

"I'll call you when I get the results. I should have something for you later this afternoon. Until then, just lay low and relax, OK?" Frank asked with an anxious face.

"We promise, Uncle Frank," Shannon and Michaela said in unison.

Later that afternoon at the precinct, Scott Malowski stopped Frank and Ben in the hall.

"Hey Goodale! I got the results from the Sommers' girl and she was clear, no drugs in her system," Scott said.

"But she had classic symptoms of Ecstasy use," Frank implored.

"Maybe it's out of her system already," Malowski replied, bored.

"Ecstasy can be detected in the urine up to four days. Can I see the report?" Frank asked.

"No can do, my man. Captain Newman has it and says it's done with. Tell your girl not to drink so much next time and maybe she'll remember what she was doing," Scott cracked and left.

"That doesn't sound right, Frank. Do you want to talk to the captain about it?" Ben asked.

"No, Ben. If the captain looked at the report, then Malowski must be right. I'll let Michaela know," Frank said dejected.

Ben grabbed Frank's arm. "What are you afraid of, Frank? Someone you care about is in danger and you are just going to sit back and let it happen?"

"I'll talk to him later," Frank lied.

Ben just watched his partner slink back to his office and wondered where the heroic Frank that he heard about had gone.

4

Michaela was angry. Ricky Cartillo had taken advantage of her and she fell for it. She didn't understand what was going on, but she was involved now. Even her Uncle Frank was playing some kind of game and it wasn't leading to her father's killer. She didn't actually believe that he could be involved, but someone higher than him was and he was being coerced into playing the puppet role. Michaela's father would never have done that and it saddened her. At least Michaela knew she could always count on her sister and Vince, but she needed to start coming up with some proof.

Michaela decided that her next step would be to find one of these warehouses. Michaela went by the restaurant where she had seen Malowski and Ricky eating. She suspected that the boy who had run into her might be one of the kids involved in this drug delivery deal. She shopped in the boutique across the street from the restaurant and watched. After about an hour of snooping and pretending to want to buy something, Michaela saw the same teenager rush out of the restaurant. He haggardly looked in both directions and walked up the street.

Michaela flew out of the boutique. She tried to remember the streets he ran down. The boy stopped at an abandoned warehouse and, looking around, pushed a large steel door open and squeezed inside. Michaela looked for an open window, but could only find one boarded up. She ran around the back and climbed up the fire escape ladder. She managed to squeeze through a broken window, but cut the back of her hand. "Damn," she whispered and listened for some movement. Michaela saw the teenager with a man in a long coat and hat. She couldn't see his face, but knew that he was too bulky to be Cartillo.

"Is it all here?" the large man growled.

"Yes," said the teenager.

The large man handed him a file box on a cart. "Take this back to the restaurant and return to the warehouse when you are done," the large man said and he followed the teenager out of the building.

Michaela jumped down and ran out of the alley. She collided into the man in the long coat. He grabbed her. "What do you think you're doing?" he yelled.

Michaela shoved his elbows up to release his hands. "Back off, I was just jogging. I didn't see you," Michaela said. Her hand dripped blood on the ground and she saw that some of it was on his coat. She couldn't see his face. His hat was pulled down so far, she only saw shadows.

"Watch where you run next time," he barked at her.

"Yeah, whatever," Michaela said as she turned and jogged away without looking back at the strange man. She held her hand tight to her chest.

Boris smiled his crooked smile. He didn't know what Cartillo's plan was for this woman. Doubtless, it was probably lust, but he wasn't about to let all he had worked for be ruined by a woman—especially Jack Sommers' daughter. He touched the blood on his coat and licked it off his finger. Oh yes, he thought. He would have a piece of this woman. He figured she had heard everything and he was tired of listening to his boss go on and on about her. It was time to scare this woman.

Michaela was in her office. She heard a knock and one of her students popped his head in. "Instructor Sommers?" Joseph Geiser said.

Michaela turned to him and noted the concern in his eyes. "What is it, Joseph?"

"There's a man out here who says he needs to see you," he continued.

Michaela peered through her window and dropped her pen at the sight of Ricky Cartillo.

"Where is Instructor Cardosa?" Michaela asked.

"He's not here."

"Show him in Joseph and keep the class going," she said. Anger seethed inside Michaela. This man had some nerve coming to see her.

"Michaela!" Ricky came in and tried to hug her. Michaela slapped him across the face.

"How dare you come here all smiling like nothing happened? I want to know what you put in my wine!" Michaela yelled.

Ricky touched his cheek and smiled like he knew a big secret. "Now, now, Michaela. Calm down. The police brought me in and I explained that we had a good time."

"You were supposed to bring me home!" Michaela retorted.

"You did not mind when we were dancing," Ricky laughed.

"That was the wine," Michaela replied.

"My wine often has that effect on people. Besides, the report came back clear, so how could you blame me," Ricky answered.

"Yeah, and your friend wouldn't give the report to my Uncle Frank," Michaela accused.

Ricky turned and watched Michaela's students. Michaela allowed herself to look at this man. He was clad in a long black overcoat and his dark hair was once again meticulously pulled back into a shiny, smooth ponytail. He turned to look at her and she held his gaze. His deep black eyes squinted as they stared back at her as if he was trying to see within her mind.

"What did you do to your hand?"

Michaela hid her bandaged hand behind her back. "I broke a glass, that's all."

He raised an eyebrow and continued, "Well, I would like to apologize for the other night. I swear to you that it was never my intention to do you any harm. I care for you very much."

Ricky sat down. He crossed his legs and smoothed his coat. He watched Michaela before he continued. "As much as your father and I hated each other, your mother and I were very close friends. She helped me adjust to my new life in America and I am not ashamed to say that I loved her with all the intensity that a man could possibly have for a woman. When you and Shannon were born, I adored both of you; not because you were Jack Sommers' daughters, but because you were a part of Genevieve that I would never share. So when your mother became ill, she worried about your father's dangerous career and asked me to care for the two of you if anything ever happened to him. I promised your mother, on my love for her, that I would never...never let any harm come to either one of you." Cartillo laughed. Michaela heard the bitterness and sense of loss in that laugh. "I will confess that when I see you I feel as though I am looking at your mother again. She was so beautiful and you encompass all that she was and more. I am attracted to you, Michaela, but I will never force myself on you, that I promise. And, if you cannot return my love, then I at least want you to think that I am a fine and respectable man. I have heard that

70

there is some speculation that my warehouses might be more than just a storage area. That...," he feigned shock. "That I could be using them as a front to sell *drugs*."

Balls of sweat had broken and the cold stream trickled down Michaela's sides and chilled her body. He loved her mother, he loves her, and he is telling her about his warehouses. She was so angry that this man took advantage of her, yet he was giving her the opportunity to see the warehouse that the children may have been talking about. She played along. "I certainly don't blame you for being upset by such a scandalous rumor and I can assure you that I have not heard any such thing, nor will I condone it. And as for your feelings, I am not sure what to think about you. A part of me wants to trust you, but another part warns me to stay away. I still feel you betrayed me. Besides, I love Vince Cardosa and I want to be with him."

Cartillo grabbed Michaela's good hand and entwined her fingers with his own. "I respect your feelings and I respect you." Ricky paused. "Would you like to see one of my warehouses?"

"I would love to," she found herself saying.

Michaela motioned to Jorge Bartolomew, who was a black belt.

"Jorge, I need to go out for about an hour. Please let Instructor Cardosa know that I will be back soon. You are in charge."

"Yes, Instructor Sommers," Jorge said and bowed.

A car was waiting for them and they drove around the city with Cartillo talking about his business. It seemed as though he wanted to impress her with how many warehouses he owned, and the prestigious companies that trusted him with their most confidential files.

Again Michaela tried to remember the roads they were taking and noticed that they had turned onto a road that led away from the city. They stopped in front of a warehouse that barely looked inhabited. Run down, dilapidated buildings enclosed it on each side. The place was deserted and that made Michaela nervous.

"It is not much from the outside," Cartillo said, "but it keeps inquisitive people away."

They walked into a front reception room and Michaela was surprised to see a very well-dressed woman sitting at the desk. "Mr. Cartillo! What a pleasant surprise!" she said.

"You look marvelous, Lucy. This is my dear friend, Michaela Sommers. I was going to show her around the warehouse," he said motioning Michaela forward. They came to a huge vaulted door that appeared to have no entrance. Ricky Cartillo motioned to someone guarding the door and Michaela watched him punch some numbers into a keypad. The door slowly opened to a huge area.

"One can never have too much security in a place like this," Ricky said.

The warehouse looked like a regular storage facility. There were metal doors along the walls and shelves strategically set to make the most efficient use of all the space. Some boxes were arranged on the open shelves.

"I thought you destroyed documents, not stored them," Michaela stated.

"We do a little of both," Cartillo explained. "Some companies want us to store their documents for a certain number of years and then destroy them. Others do not have the space for files not needed very often, and so we store them and deliver them when needed."

"Does that boy I ran into at the restaurant work for you?" Michaela asked.

Cartillo's face clouded for a moment. "You have a wonderful memory. He is one of my employees who helps make deliveries."

"Well, he looked very young and frazzled," Michaela replied walking further.

Michaela looked around for any door that might lead to a basement or room where he could keep children. She saw some wooden doors and asked Cartillo what was in there.

Ricky unlocked one of the doors and let Michaela go in. It was a small room with a desk and chair. "I provide these private rooms for my clients if they need to look at some files."

Michaela turned to leave and found Ricky once again very close to her. He seemed to have this habit of being inside one's personal space. The scent of his cologne and cigars swirled around her head like a drug. His face was intense as he looked down into hers, forcing her to look up at him. He touched her chin.

Michaela moved his hand away. "Didn't we take care of this attraction deal?" Michaela asked, trying to keep the situation light.

"Ah, yes, you are right. Please excuse my indiscretion. I do hope this tour puts your mind at ease," he said still close to Michaela.

"Uh, excuse me, Boss," someone said.

Not moving Cartillo asked through clenched teeth, "What is it?"

"We found her," the man said.

Cartillo pulled away from Michaela. "Excuse me for a moment."

"Where is she?" he whispered.

"She's been spotted by the wharf," he said.

"Get the car ready. I will take care of this myself," Cartillo said and went back to Michaela.

"Everything OK?" she asked putting her hand on his arm.

Ricky looked at Michaela's hand and then at her, "All is well, but I am afraid that I will have to cut our visit short today. Lucy has called you a cab to take you back to your studio. I will call you to have lunch very soon."

The cab was outside already. Cartillo walked Michaela to the cab door. She turned around and Ricky leaned over and kissed

Michaela on her cheek. Michaela tried not to flinch.

"Take Ms. Sommers wherever she would like." Michaela watched Cartillo's limo drive away and was determined to follow.

She asked the driver. "Is it possible to let me off by the water?"

The driver nodded his head and drove.

Michaela thanked the driver and hurried to the wharf. She searched for Natalie. Michaela caught sight of Cartillo and three of his men near a boathouse. She backed up against the wall and watched them talking to someone. She couldn't hear what they were saying, but she could tell that Cartillo was mad. Michaela watched in horror as Cartillo picked up a heavy stick and jabbed the man in his gut while his thugs grabbed him to keep him up. The man screamed in agony as his knees were broken and he gasped for air as Cartillo held the stick up against his throat. Michaela was afraid he was going to kill him, but he stopped and let the crying man fall to the ground. Cartillo's men both kicked him in his side and, as Cartillo turned, Michaela saw his cold face.

Michaela turned to run away and fell over some trash cans. The men heard her and Cartillo yelled for them to see who it was. A fast runner, Michaela lost them and hoped that they didn't catch sight of her. They probably took her for Natalie and she was glad that maybe she deterred them from finding the girl. Of course now she had lost her opportunity to find Natalie, but she couldn't stop. Michaela didn't stop running until she found a taxi and reached her studio. She had thought she might be wrong about Cartillo, but she knew he was a man who would get what he wanted no matter what the cost. She just didn't know if that price was her father's life. She was afraid of him, but she was too far involved now and she knew that he would come looking for her to pursue whatever relationship his arrogant mind thought that they might have. Or maybe he just wanted to keep a close eye on her. She didn't know anymore, but what she did know was that for her safety and Shannon's she couldn't stop now.

5

With the seminar and promotions over, Michaela and Shannon prepared for their trip. Michaela started packing for her vacation and noticed her lack of warm clothing. It was the beginning of October and she knew that the Catskills would be much cooler than New York City. She called to see if Shannon wanted to join her.

"Hi Sonya, is Shannon still in her office?" Michaela asked.

"Sorry, Michaela, she is at a court hearing and will probably head home after that," she said. "Want me to leave a message for her anyway?"

"No thanks, I'll leave her a note at home," Michaela said, as she wrote a quick note to Shannon.

Max whined and pushed his head against her leg. "You know I can't take you into the store. I won't be long." She patted his head and tried to go past him. He continued to whine, so Michaela knelt down and rubbed his cheeks. Michaela thought Max looked worried and tried to soothe him, "It's OK, boy. Why are you so anxious? I'll see you in a couple hours."

The subway terminal was about two blocks from Michaela's apartment. The air was cool, so Michaela put on her sweatshirt and took off down the stairs to wait for a car. Michaela stepped in and took note of the people around her. She was wary of her surroundings now that Max had seemed nervous. She remembered the men she had seen a couple weeks ago while walking home, the children she questioned, and the burly man outside the warehouse.

There was a couple necking in the far end, unaware of anyone's presence and of where they were going. An elderly woman kept her eyes to the ground. Michaela smiled at her when she glanced her way, and she squinted as her way of saying hello. The car made another stop and two men strolled in. One looked like a bodyguard and towered over his buddy. He had long dark greasy hair pulled back into a semblance of a ponytail and a goatee outlined his chin and traveled down toward his chest. He surveyed the car and glanced toward Michaela with a cold hard stare. Michaela stared right back at him and straightened her back. His buddy was half his size. He looked familiar with his dirty blond hair and thin face. He had beady eyes that seemed way too small and his nose hooked like an eagle. He reminded her of a bird of prey circling in on its next meal.

He looked at Michaela and gave her a broad, untrustworthy grin. That smile made the hairs on her arms and neck stand up and her body was chilled to the bone. These two were here for a reason and it wasn't shopping. Only a couple more minutes and she'd be gone.

The big guy sat next to the old woman. She shifted and he took advantage of her fear. "Hi there, Grandma. I'm sorry I haven't called, but I've been busy at the butcher." He sat so he faced Michaela and sneered as he took a knife out and toyed with the edge. She didn't know if these two were just thugs looking for money or if they were here on account of her.

Then the eagle man looked over at Michaela. "Mind if I join you, young lady? It seems as though my pal here has found his long lost grandma." As he sat down, Michaela stood up and walked across the aisle ignoring him. He just sat there looking down at a blade he produced from the sleeve of his jean jacket. He looked over at his friend and, while he tested the blade's sharpness on the hairs of his arm, he said, "You always give me the unfriendly ones, Hank!"

Laughing, his buddy Hank stood up and said, "Boris told us she was the inquisitive type who would want to know more about you. She seems to like to ask questions. Don't you, pretty girl?" The car stopped and they moved toward her. Michaela backed into the corner of the car. The little old lady scurried out and even the two lovers came apart enough to know that they should take off. Michaela also moved to leave, but they blocked her way. The car began to move again.

"Ah, ah. I don't think you are going anywhere. Michaela, is it? You seem to be doing a lot of snooping around that has annoyed our friend, so he thought you might want to know who you're dealing with. Maybe it will answer some of your questions," eagle man said as he came closer.

Trying to be nonchalant, Michaela asked, "I'm not quite sure what you guys are talking about, but maybe you can tell me who I'm dealing with?"

Hank the bodyguard looked at his friend, shrugged his shoulders, and attacked. The blade flashed as he lunged toward her, confident in the outcome of their little discussion. Michaela slid out of the way. She grasped his arm and, using his momentum, slammed him face first into the window. Michaela noted the look of shock on his face reflected in the window. They didn't think she would be a problem. Stunned, he sank to the floor. Eagle man jumped over him, slicing his knife through the air. Panic was setting in; this was not part of the plan. He was all over the place with his weapon, the plan forgotten, hoping to get a piece of Michaela. She watched the blade, allowing him to move forward.

"Why don't you just calm down and we can talk about this," Michaela said.

Eagle man paused and spat, "It's too late for talking, you see. We are going to tear you to pieces. Teach you a lesson!"

Michaela's foot came up in a short roundhouse motion, catching him just below the wrist and the knife flew to the side of the car. Michaela grabbed his wrist and slammed her fist into the back of his elbow. The sound of bone giving way was only drowned out by the scream that escaped eagle man's twisted mouth. She stepped in and hammered his shoulder joint, dislocating the limb that again caused a hair-raising scream.

Hank had recovered. Still holding eagle man's twisted arm, Michaela side-kicked Hank, but he caught her foot and swung up hard. Falling over backwards, Michaela hit her head on the pole. He was on her fast, so she flipped up behind the pole. He didn't have his knife, but his hands were like tree stumps and he hit hard. She blocked his blows and tried to get to the emergency line to stop the car. He pounded her like a tough piece of meat and any kicks she delivered bounced off. He punched her in the sternum, and she flew into the rear door. As she bounced back like a rubber ball, he grabbed her in a bear hug and squeezed hard. Michaela couldn't breathe. The hit, impact, and squeeze had taken her senses away.

The car stopped and someone yelled. Michaela shook off her impending blackness and hit him on both ears with a clap that sent a roar through his head and made thunder sound like a pin drop. And drop he did. She kicked him in the face and his head snapped back as his body followed sprawled across the floor.

Michaela turned thinking that eagle man was behind her, but he leaned against a pole holding his broken wing. She stared at him and heard someone yell, "Freeze!" She saw two police officers with guns drawn.

"Stay where you are! Let's see those hands!" Michaela heard his voice echo in her head. Her ribs crushed her lungs. She uttered a thank you and fell.

"Let's move it! Get her in the ambulance."

Pulling. Pulling me down. The dead have come for me. Decomposing flesh reek of urine and decay. They moan as they pull wanting my soul. Run hard, harder, look for a place to hide. Reach battlefield and feel safer in the throng of warriors slicing one another. The dead stop hungrily waiting for their chance to suck the dying souls into their empty hearts.

"Hold her down, dammit! Give her something to calm her down. She's starting to go into shock."

Father! Try to find him. The battle frenzy fills my head and I push and run slicing back and forth through anything that stops my advance. Screaming. I hear him scream. Father! I stop. He's away from the fighting and I wonder why he yells and then I see his champion on a chariot being held by two men without faces. A third holds his neck tight and is howling up at the sky. He looks down at me and laughs. As he laughs I run, but am too late. He yanks his head back and his blade slices the champion's neck slow and ruthless. The skin separates and the blood trickles down his neck. As the gash extends the blood flows faster and I run slower. He slices again and as his head falls forward, blood sprays, covering me, congealing on me like glue, so I can't move.

"We've lost her pulse! What the hell is going on here? She just bruised her ribs. There's only a minor scrape on her head. Shock her! Go!"

He comes.

"Daddy, you've come for me," I whisper, moving toward him.

A bright path glows behind him and he looks healthy and happy.

"Michaela," he begins. "I am so sorry for getting you involved in this. I was trying to do the right thing and so many people have gotten hurt."

"It's OK, Dad. We are together now. Will you take me with you? I want to go. The light looks so…peaceful," my voice falters. I feel myself fading away. "What's happening?"

"You cannot stay, my dear, dear daughter. One day I will come for you, but it is not today. You have much to do, but I will guide and protect you as much as I can. Listen to your dreams," he says as the light begins to enclose his body.

Trying to go toward him, I yell, "I don't want to go back! I want to be with you. PLEASE!"

"Natalie Fischer lives, Michaela. Find her and the Celtic warrior and they both will lead you to the truth. I love you and Shannon. Goodbye." The light takes him in and I am spiraled back to my world.

"OK, she's stable. Let's get her into the hospital," says the EMT.

Michaela woke up. She remembered the warrior who was killed in her dream and she felt guilty like she should have been able to save him. She felt guilty about her father's death; even though she knew that she could not have prevented it. She tried to remember all her father had told her.

Michaela scared and confused the hospital staff. When she woke up the next day, Vince and Shannon hung over her. Shannon told her about going into shock in the ambulance and, despite her minor injuries, they had lost her for a couple minutes.

"Lost me."

"Yeah," Shannon had said, "like no pulse, nothing."

80

Michaela knew they blamed it on the trauma of the attack. She knew better, but wasn't going to offer any information, just yet. It's hard to stay on this side of life, when someone you love is right there showing you Heaven. Michaela could have stayed with her father and never looked back. He had touched her hand, pulled her to him, and comforted her like he had done so many times when she was little. She felt safe and she *felt* him. His body, the scent of his skin, and even the texture of his face were all real. She thought it was hard for him to hold her and then let go, but he knew that she had to continue. She was determined to find Natalie and this warrior her dad had mentioned. While she slept, she dreamt of the girl with the pink sash and knew she was special. She had to be saved and would be a key player in this whole drug related fiasco. But even more important, she knew she wasn't the only one looking for Natalie. She was furious that Ricky Cartillo would just strike out at her with such violence. Didn't he say he would never harm her? He was a liar. She thought that everything was out in the open. It was all so wrong, but with her dad pushing her along, she had no choice but to go on.

Vince and Shannon brought her home with Uncle Frank trailing close behind. Frank had felt responsible, although Michaela told him she didn't know who the thugs were and tried to convince him that they wanted to rob her. Frank hadn't looked convinced, and to make matters worse, he wasn't allowed to question Michaela's attackers. Detective Malowski was called in and Frank was sent away to finish some paperwork. The captain said something about him being too close to the victim, but that didn't feel right to Michaela. She knew Frank was capable of doing his job.

Vince helped her out of the car and Frank rushed over.

"I'm OK, Uncle Frank. I'm just going to go up and crash," Michaela reassured him. She wanted to be left alone to think everything over.

"Are you sure, Michaela? Let me come up and look over your place to make sure there aren't any surprises," he asked. Michaela gave in, so he could stop feeling guilty about divulging information to her.

When Michaela opened the door, she saw Max laying in the living room with her pillow under his head. He whimpered at her and turned his head as if asleep. Vince helped her sit on the couch.

"Max, I am so sorry that I didn't listen to you," she said to him.

Max grunted in agreement, but looked up at Michaela in forgiveness.

"Come here, Boy," she said and he climbed up on the couch and licked her face.

"Let me take him out," Vince offered, while Frank checked all the rooms.

"Everything looks fine," Frank said as he kissed Michaela goodbye. He met Shannon at the door and whispered.

Shannon turned and smiled at her. She knew Michaela would ask, so she volunteered, "He wanted Vince and I to make sure you're fine and to discourage any more detective work."

Michaela gave her a disgusted look, because everyone was treating her like a fragile child.

She decided to let it ride for now, especially since both Vince and Shannon looked like they were the ones in the scuffle.

"Fine. Now I would like to get some rest, so can you help me get into my room?" she asked. It was difficult to get off the couch, since any contraction of her abdomen pushed her ribs out and caused a great deal of pain.

She grabbed some pajamas and attempted to get her shirt and pants off.

82

Outside the door, Vince knocked. "Are you OK in there, 'Aela'?"

She opened the door with her arm stuck. "Do I look OK?" she hissed.

"I could leave," Vince looked exhausted, so she softened up a bit.

"I'm sorry. You know how I get when I can't do something and I'm tired. Please help me so we can get some sleep."

Somehow he managed to get her top off and her pajama top on. She couldn't bend down, so he had to help with her pants, too. He fumbled and looked nervous.

"Vince, what's the problem?" She teased. "It's not like you've never done this before. Just pull my pants off, please!"

Vince stopped, his hands on her knees, and put his head down. Michaela stroked his hair.

"Are you OK?"

He looked up at her with tears in his eyes. She could see his fear and realized how much she must have scared him *and* her sister.

"Michaela...," Vince began. "You really sent me for a whirl at the hospital. When I got that call at the studio, I couldn't breathe. The thought of you being attacked just made me crazy. I would be lost without you."

He broke down and she didn't know what to do. He always comforted her and she wasn't used to this show of emotion. He moved back and finished dressing her. When he started to get up, Michaela put her hands on his face and pulled him to her. She kissed him ever so lightly on the lips and they held each other for a long time.

The trip to the Catskills was delayed, so Michaela's ribs could heal. She still wanted to go, but gave in to Shannon and

Vince's nagging about her condition. She immersed herself in the studio and life slowed down to a normal pace.

Two weeks after her attack, Michaela was at the studio as usual.

"Vince, I need to go to the bank. Do you want me to pick up something for you for lunch?"

"Yeah, sure. I'll take an Italian sub with the works. Thanks," he said.

"Great. I won't be long," Michaela said. Michaela walked the short distance to Sam's Deli. She felt at ease and was so involved with her school that she hadn't had time to think about her father and his death. On her way back to the studio, Michaela looked across the street and something red caught her eye. She stopped and stared. A bus was in her way, but when it passed, a small girl with curly red hair stood there staring back at Michaela. She looked hopeless and ragged. As ragged as she was, Michaela easily spotted the pink sash around her neck.

"Natalie," she said as she dropped her subs and ran across the street. Natalie turned and ran away. It was hard for Michaela to keep up. Her ribs were holding her back and she hadn't gotten far before she was bent over in pain, gasping for breath. She saw a man sitting on the ground playing a harmonica.

"Did you see a red-haired girl with a pink sash run by here?" she asked. The man just shook his head and kept playing. "Dammit," Michaela said as she looked around. She had seen Natalie and let her get away. Michaela wondered why Natalie had run. She had looked at Michaela like she knew her, but maybe she got spooked. Michaela walked for a while, hoping to spot Natalie. Unsuccessful, she went back to buy more subs.

6

Natalie had watched Michaela for a while. She wanted to stop her from getting involved with Cartillo, but couldn't risk being seen. She hoped that Michaela would be smarter than her mother and not get caught up in his wining and dining escapades. She had seen it happen all too often and Natalie needed Michaela if either one of them was going to survive. She knew that Michaela had been hurt, and feared that Ricky Cartillo was behind that also.

Natalie had been living on the streets trying to stay away from Cartillo's spies and all the evil that lurked among the alleys. She had cut her hair short and wore it up in a baseball cap. She had removed the hat when she saw Michaela walking down the street. She wanted Michaela to recognize her and help. But Natalie didn't realize she would be spotted so soon. Cartillo's men were everywhere and she was running out of time.

That night Natalie cried. When she fell asleep, she saw Michaela drifting into blackness and riding a large stallion. Michaela swung a shining sword and beheaded people in robes. Their blood gushed from their ravaged bodies and fell on an unconscious girl who was lying on a long stone in between the robed people. Michaela picked up the small girl, with flaming red hair, and called her Niachra.

Days had gone by since Michaela saw Natalie. She feared the worst, which made her moods unstable. Shannon was concerned, because ever since she hit her head, Michaela was having blackouts more often. Michaela didn't consider them to be blackouts, since she usually saw something happening that she knew couldn't be possible. Her dreams about warriors from another time and place invaded her daytime hours.

Just that morning, Shannon had found her in the backyard staring at the building wall. Max barked next to her, but Michaela didn't respond.

Shannon asked, "Michaela. What do you see?"

Michaela had spoken in a faraway voice. "I am fighting warriors. They are very big and carry large battleaxes. I'm in a castle when they attack. I've lost my sword, so I pick up an axe and try to swing it. It's too heavy and I can't get the momentum to swing it," she stopped and cried.

"It's all right, Michaela," Shannon said and Michaela continued.

"A black-haired man laughs. His teeth are rotten. I manage to swing the axe at him and it nicks his neck. He stops laughing and lunges at me. He is going to kill me. I run and hide up some stairs. I see another girl beg for her life. It doesn't help. They kill her. I see someone else. I have to help save them. Something has to be done."

Michaela sobbed and then looked at Shannon in recognition. Michaela remembered all that she had seen. Shannon held her sister, not knowing where the visions were leading them.

Ricky Cartillo couldn't get Michaela off his mind. She reminded him so much of her mother, Genevieve. He thought of Genevieve every day, and what could have been. Seeing Michaela just brought all the memories back.

He remembered the first day he saw Genevieve. It was outside the small house he lived in with Jack and his parents in Howard Beach. It was the summer of 1973. Ricky had been with the Sommers since June and would be starting his junior year in high school. Genevieve leaned against the railing on the front steps. Her black hair flowed with the breeze as she tilted her head back and laughed. Then Genevieve had looked at Ricky and smiled with a radiance that stunned him.

"Hey, Rick!" Jack had called.

Ricky didn't move. So Jack brought him to the steps and whispered, "She's a beauty, eh?"

Ricky scoffed at Jack thinking he didn't even come close to appreciating the beauty that Ricky saw.

"Genevieve, this is my foster-brother, Ricky Cartillo. He's from Colombia. Ricky, this is my girlfriend, Genevieve," Jack introduced.

"How do you do," Ricky said in his thick, low accent. 'Girlfriend' stuck in his head.

He watched Genevieve step down, admiring her long graceful legs.

"It's so nice to meet you, Ricky. Jack has told me so much about you," she had responded.

"Time for lunch!" Jack's mom had called.

Ricky hadn't moved, so Genevieve wrapped her arm through his and then through Jack's and the trio had walked together into the house. Since that day, Ricky loved Genevieve Marcino.

"Michaela, Vince is on the phone," Shannon's voice drifted through Michaela's dreams.

"What?"

"Vince, your boyfriend, is on the phone. Can you talk?"

"Yeah." Shannon handed her the phone. "Hi. I'm coming in. I'll meet you on the way to the deli for breakfast. Bye."

Michaela felt good. For the first time since her dad died, she felt like she could really enjoy her day and let the past take care of itself. She still had her visions, but doctors attributed it to post traumatic stress. Michaela let the visions pass through her, trying not to let them shake her world anymore. After showering and taking care of Max, Michaela headed toward Sam's Deli to meet Vince. She took a shortcut through Gutless Alley, as everyone liked to call it.

"Well, well, well, if it isn't the famous champion, Michaela Sommers," the tallest one sneered as he jumped out in front of her. Michaela stopped, startled. She had been thinking about Vince.

"Do I know you or care to?" She asked while preparing herself for another attack. She needed to protect her ribs and get out of there fast. Hearing another behind her, Michaela stepped back to get them both in front of her. Next to the first guy was a rather large bald man, who held a baseball bat.

Growling like a tiger, they walked closer and the first guy said, "You should have let your old man die peacefully instead of asking so many questions and sticking your nose where it doesn't belong."

"Tell Cartillo to back off!" she yelled.

Coming closer she could smell his breath as he sneered, "Cartillo is a speck on the wall compared to the man you have pissed off. No one can protect you now."

Michaela stepped back and said, "Like I told your other buddies, I don't know what you are talking about!"

"We work alone," he said.

The bald one interrupted and said, "Let's get this done and stopped the socializing, man!" The tall one glared at his partner. "Relax. She won't be talking after we're done with her."

"Well boys, I'd really love to chat with you, but I don't have time," Michaela said. Displaying a blade with jagged, menacing teeth, the tall one lunged toward her with lethal precision. Knowing that baldy was coming right behind, she turned to the side and, grabbing the tall one by his wrist, twisted it over her shoulder, so that the knife plummeted into his partner's gut with the accuracy of a surgeon.

Instead of falling, the bald thug was thrown back. Michaela saw Vince throw him into a pile of trash. The tall one lost his courage and tried to escape, but Vince was furious and he took all his frustrations out on him. Seeing that he had to put up a fight, he pulled out another knife to try and defend himself. Vince deflected the knife while he broke his hand in a few places. Vince jumped up and kicked the thug square in the face, which sent him reeling right into the garbage bags next to his partner. Filled with rage, Vince didn't stop. He pummeled his fist into the guy's face.

"Vince!" Michaela screamed. "That's enough!" The sound of her voice brought him back to his senses and Vince stepped back to assess the damage he had caused.

Turning to Michaela, he asked, "Are you OK?"

"Yeah, I think so. Let's get out of here," she said pulling him along with her.

"Shouldn't we call the police?" Vince asked. "They could be related to the first guys and maybe now that detective, who let the other two go, will do something."

Michaela thought about the man more powerful than Ricky Cartillo. He said no one would protect her now. Ricky had told her he would always look out for her. So who were these men working for? Detective Malowski's face came to Michaela and she shivered, "Somehow I don't think it's going to matter.

Let's get to the studio."

They went into the karate school and straight to Michaela's office. Vince's knuckles were bleeding, so Michaela cleaned them up.

"Those guys weren't messing around, 'Aela'." Vince looked at her. "Usually they ask for the money first before they beat the crap out of you. If Uncle Frank isn't going to be able to help you with this, then I think it is a good idea for you to get away. Maybe if you're not here, things will settle down."

7

On a crisp October morning, Shannon and Michaela left New York City to head up north to the mountainous Catskill region. Vince had stayed over the night before and helped the two sisters pack their bags into Shannon's SUV. Max hopped in the back seat and stuck his head out the open window.

Vince rubbed Max's head. "Take care of my girl, Max."

Max licked Vince's face and barked.

Vince hugged Michaela once again.

"Are you sure you don't want to come?" Michaela asked.

"No, no," Vince said stepping away and stuffing his hands in his jean pockets. "I'll miss you, but you two need to spend some time together and I need to keep the school going."

"Well, all right. I'll see you soon. I love you," Michaela said as she kissed him again and stepped into the vehicle.

"I love you, too," Vince said.

"Take care, Vince!" Shannon called.

As they retreated further away from Manhattan, Michaela breathed in the country air and admired the foliage and beautiful changes that were still occurring so late in October. They arrived at a bed and breakfast, called The Little Lake Inn. It stood on endless acres of woods and had a lake behind it that separated it from another vast wood. There was a dock at the lake with paddleboats and canoes. It reminded her of when she and Shannon were little and their parents would take them to Pennsylvania by the Delaware River. Michaela and her dad would rent canoes and take off on the river like great explorers. Her mom and Shannon would walk through the woods trying to keep them in view, but they were fast, or at least her dad was, and determined to leave the world behind. Then they would find a spot where rocks, protruding from the earth, rose up toward the sky and they would climb to the top to be the champions of the world.

As she settled into her Victorian hideaway, Michaela stepped out onto a balcony and reveled in the cold scent of pine, and the sound of birds chirping away in endless song. She gazed toward the trees and the distant mountains feeling like a part of her belonged there. Max sniffed the air and wagged his tail. Just beyond the tree line, she noticed the top of an old house.

Michaela stood entranced. The sound of swords clashed together. Michaela turned around frightened. She looked toward the house again and the sound reverberated in her head, so that she had to cover her ears. She saw her father in the battlefield. A larger warrior protected him. It was the man with the ponytail. An equally large man tried to kill her father. The sounds of swords striking and the screams of men dying overwhelmed her. The enemy warrior was next to her father. Without hesitation, he struck Michaela's father down.

"NO!" Michaela yelled and fell to the floor. Max barked.

Shannon ran into the room. Michaela lay unconscious on the floor. "Michaela!" she exclaimed kneeling down to help.

Michaela woke up and began to cry, "I'm coming. I'll save you!"

"Michaela, you had another vision," Shannon whispered. "It's over."

Michaela's mind cleared and she saw Shannon. She looked around and realized that she was on the floor and tried to stand up.

"It's not over."

"Why don't you lie down on the bed? You are scaring me with these hallucinations," Shannon said. "And it is over. Dad is dead and you need to come to terms with that."

As Michaela walked toward the bed, she looked out the window toward the house. It held the answer to what she must do.

"It's not Dad. It's something else."

Michaela slept until the evening. Her mind and body were fatigued from all the stress she had been through. Michaela walked down to the small foyer where Shannon was busy speaking with the inn's owners.

"Hi, sleepy head!" Shannon called. "This is William and Emma Lansing. They were just telling me about the house and all the changes they have made."

"Nice to meet you," Michaela began. "I could see a house back in the woods. Do you own that, too?"

Emma Lansing looked at her husband, but he spoke. "No. We don't own it. And I would recommend that you don't venture by it. An old man, named Finnius Morgan, lived there. He was some type of archeologist and he was very interested in ancient Ireland. We never saw much of him and one day he just disappeared. He left everything behind. I keep telling the town to do something with all the weapons and books he has stashed up there, but no one seems to care."

"So the house is just abandoned?" Michaela asked astonished.

"Yup. Like I said no one has bothered to look into it. There's rumor that the house is...you know...haunted because of how he disappeared and all," William said.

Michaela kept on. "How did he disappear?"

Emma interrupted, "You have all week to hear William's

crazy stories, but I'm sure you're hungry. Why don't you go into the parlor and we'll get you some stew."

"Doesn't that house sound exciting, Shannon?" Michaela asked as they ate.

Shannon just shook her head at her adventurous sister. "Listen, you just passed out earlier, because of all your excitement. Don't add another adventure. We are here to relax. Besides, the owners told you that weird things have happened. Just stay away, Michaela."

"Yes, I know you would just stay away, but what if there are some antique weapons from Ireland! I can't believe historians have ignored it. I might have to explore just a little bit," Michaela continued.

"Just remember that your curiosity is part of the reason why we are here," Shannon warned.

"I know, but this has nothing to do with Manhattan," Michaela continued.

Ricky had been watching Michaela. So when he heard about the attack on the subway, he was furious. He didn't dare go near her since her damn boyfriend stayed close by. But he wanted answers.

He knew something was wrong when Malowski let the two hoodlums go on some technicality. Ricky had been allowed to see photos of the men, but he didn't recognize them. He did recognize a change though; a dangerous change.

Ricky was surprised and relieved when he found out that Michaela and Shannon were going away. He called for Boris.

"The Sommers' sisters are going on a little vacation in the Catskills. I need you to look after them from a distance and make sure they are safe. I do not know who was behind Michaela's attack, but no harm must come to her."

Boris hid his anger behind a docile grin. "Whatever you say, Boss." Boris felt good. He would get his revenge.

It was two days later before Michaela had the chance to explore the land. Shannon had decided to lounge on the front porch and read, but Michaela was sure that something waited for her beyond the lake and trees. She donned her hiking boots, jeans, and flannel shirt and walked out to a canoe that flopped against the deck. Max jumped in the canoe and sat down to wait for the adventure. She began to paddle taking in the breathtaking surroundings. The trees were in full change and they formed a tapestry of colors that echoed the nature around them. The yellows reflected the brightness of the sun and the orange leaves were a bright fire that led Michaela along the water.

"What a beautiful, peaceful place," she said to herself, feeling now that the peace was what had drawn her. The grass was still green and soft in the field and she could see the lining of trees that enfolded the house like a cocoon. Michaela came to the edge of the trees and saw an old path that had been covered by years of pine needles and leaves, but was still easy enough to follow.

The trail sloped uphill and she felt exhilarated. Her senses reached out for the scents of the place. Michaela smelled the heavy odor of the massive pine, maple and oak trees, and looked up at the towering trees reaching toward the sky. They formed a canopy over her, and the vines that wrapped around the trunks and smaller bushes guided her forward. She smelled the moss and mold of times gone by and the stench of animals that had made the forest their final resting place. The sounds of the birds flying tree to tree, singing their stories, welcomed her. She watched a pileated woodpecker bang rhythmically at a small birch tree. He flew to another location and Michaela followed his methodical beat. Max ran behind Michaela sniffing at the ground and pawing leaves to follow the scents.

Now deep into the woods, Michaela kneeled down to tie her boot. She thought she heard someone speak. She looked around figuring her mind was wandering way too much. Then she heard the words, "*Come to me, Maecha.*" Max stopped and the hair on his back rose up in alarm. As she looked up toward the sound, she saw his face through the woods. He sat high on a frothing, black warhorse, whose nostrils flared as it inhaled the smell of death. "*Maecha, wake up and come to me now!*"

Michaela didn't move. The warrior on the horse moved toward her and she didn't know if he was real. Then he looked at her and she saw his face. He was the man in her dreams. The Celtic warrior had come to her. Her head pounded from the unreality of this vision and her heart screamed, "Just take me and ride!" This man was a part of her life that she couldn't comprehend. He leaned over on his horse, with his huge battle scarred hand reaching to her like an anchor. Michaela lost herself in those eyes that revealed his concern for her and...his love? She wanted to thrust her hand into his and lose herself in the beauty of his existence, but love? Michaela thought of Vince and she tried to speak. She wanted him to understand and not be mad, but already his image floated away like the smoke of a smoldering fire.

Michaela was cold; cold from the wet leaves and mold that seeped into her jeans and cold from loss. For more than two months she had been running away from the loss of her father. Both her parents had been ripped away, but all the questions surrounding her father were destroying her. "What happened to you, Dad? Why did you leave us?" Michaela yelled. The only answer was the shriek of birds flying from their nests and Max whining next to her. Never allowing the tears to fully come, they came in torrents. They fell to the earth in a stream of heartache and pain, adding their suffering to all those who had come this way before and cried to the land.

Michaela forgot about the house and walked back to the inn. She was mentally exhausted and her ribs throbbed from the exertion. She found Shannon on the front porch swinging in a love seat. Michaela joined her and they rocked in silence.

"What happened?" Shannon asked.

"Come again?" Michaela asked coming back to reality.

Turning to her younger sister, she continued, "When you sat down you looked like you saw a ghost. Did you have another hallucination?"

"You would never believe me if I told you, Shannon," Michaela said putting an arm around her.

"Try me," she said.

Michaela had been open with Shannon with her dreams and her investigating. Plus, she had been witness to more than one of Michaela's 'hallucinations' as they were calling them. Shannon knew that the attacks were related to their father and that was one of the reasons she wanted to get Michaela away from Manhattan. She wanted her father's murderer to forget about Michaela. Life was too dangerous and soon they would all be involved.

"I saw my Celtic warrior in the woods," she began. "Or at least I think I did. He was on a horse and they were both dressed for battle. He called me, 'Maecha'. Even Max felt something."

"Tell me Michaela, do you think that a man from Ireland could be here in the woods? Hallucinations are false or distorted experiences that you may think are real. The fact that you could smell and see him just proves my point. These sensory impressions are generated by the mind and make you believe that it really happened," Shannon said.

Michaela thought and replied, "But he seemed so...real." Talking about it made it all seem so foolish and Michaela laughed. Shannon joined in.

"Anyway, what would Vince think if you were dreaming

about some sexy Celtic warrior? You should be thinking more about him," Shannon teased.

Michaela smiled. "Of course I have been thinking about him. I want to live a normal life and continue Dad's work. I only hope that all these attacks are over and we don't have any more problems."

"I don't think you'll have a problem with that. The biggest problem is finding a room for me when you two decide to become permanent!" Shannon said acting lost.

"Don't worry," Michaela teased. "We'll save a room for you in the basement."

"Thanks for nothing!" Shannon said and they both laughed again, while they linked arms and swung.

The sun set over the Catskill Mountains. Shafts of purple and pink rays shot threw the clouds to cast a mystical glow across the sky. The mountains retained their fake blue color and, as the wind gently blew the clean country air by them, the sisters felt positive.

8

Feeling the need to envision her Celtic warrior again, Michaela decided to walk into the woods on the last day of their stay. Shannon and Michaela had spent a lot of quiet time together, remembering and healing. A part of her was still edgy and Michaela felt like something or someone waited for her out in the woods. Plus, she hadn't made it to that house and it kept calling to her in her dreams. She wrote an entry into her journal, before leaving her room.

Dream Journal—October 28, 2000, 4:00 AM

In my dream I meet the man who built the house—Finnius Morgan. He beckons me to come in. His time is short and he has so much to teach me. He is dressed as a Druid in a white robe. His hair and beard are white and long. He shows me his weapons: battle-axes, iron-tipped maces with highly decorated hilts, swords and daggers; all displayed on his walls. He walks along another wall displaying armor, a helmet, and a beautifully designed sword. He points to the sword and I touch it. I feel its power and the pain it has inflicted on its enemies. He pushes me closer and when my hand enfolds the handle, I see the blood of the wounded, the gaping holes of the dead, the chaos of battle and the victory of the sword bearer—a woman. The images swirl around my mind enveloping me in their turmoil and I let go, not able to handle its power. I turn toward the man to tell him what I have seen, but he silences me with his finger and motions for me to follow.

We walk through the house. I notice old furniture and when I touch the walls to admire the fancy wallpaper, they disintegrate and another room opens to me. The first room is a parlor. I walk to the wall and as I touch it, it disappears and turns into a doorway. The man is there and he walks up a ladder. I follow. It is a loft, with every wall filled with books. The books are old and I know they hold the knowledge of my past. I pick up one named <u>The Annals of Ancient Ireland</u>. I hungrily skim some of the other countless titles: <u>The Brehon Laws</u>, <u>Fianaigecht</u>, <u>Book of Aicill</u>.

I want to sit down and read about my history, but he has more to show me. He leads me down the ladder and toward the back of the house. It is so dark I cannot make out what is around me. We are in a hallway and he stops at a door. He opens it and, pointing to the wall, says, "This will save you and bring you home." He turns. I follow his gaze and see a shadow. I sense danger, but when I turn back to the man, he is gone. I wake up.

Shannon enjoyed Emma's company, so Michaela found her in the parlor talking while Emma finished some paperwork. "Hey, I'm going to head back for a walk in the woods today to see if I can check out that house," she said.

Emma glanced at Shannon who walked Michaela out the door. "I think you should stay here. I have a bad feeling about it," Shannon insisted.

Michaela rolled her eyes, impatient to leave. "Shannon, I said I was starting over. I will put Dad's death behind me. This is my background and yours. I can't leave without at least seeing the front of the house!" Michaela said in a half truth.

Shannon sighed, "OK, Michaela. Do you want me to come along?"

"No, I'll take Max. I won't be long," she said. As Michaela walked down the steps she turned to her sister. Shannon looked at peace, although she was concerned. Michaela needed to see this house before she could have peace and move on.

"I love you, Sis. I'll see you...soon."

"I love you too, 'Aela'. Hurry up," Shannon said.

Michaela walked into the woods once more, admiring the beauty of her surroundings, so it would stay embedded in her mind. It would be hard to go back to the studio and begin again, but she looked forward to it and, besides that, she missed Vince. She walked quicker to get to the house.

When it came into view, Michaela stopped. It was huge. The outside was weather beaten. It looked like it used to be a light green with white trim. She saw that the front door had swung opened, but wasn't ready to go in. The porch surrounded the whole front and, as she walked around to the back, she could see a circular room that was enclosed, except for a window up high. An escape ladder and doorway also led to that room. Michaela gazed up toward the roof and, closing her eyes, took a deep breath of clean air. As she exhaled, she heard some branches crack, and then some more. Max growled. She told herself it was just animals, but then she heard the familiar sound of human feet trying to keep quiet. Shannon wouldn't have been quiet, so she walked back around the front to see if she could make it back to the inn. She saw men walking toward the house looking down and cursing.

"Dammit, Boris! Why are we wasting our time out here? We scared her off good enough! Cartillo will be mad if he finds out what we have done. We're only supposed to keep an eye on her," a tall, stringy man complained.

Michaela ran up the front steps and squatted behind the railings. She saw a younger man dragging his feet behind the other two. He was young and uncertain.

Boris, however, was different. He wore a black cowboy hat pulled down low so his face was hidden. She recognized him from the warehouse. She remembered how enormous he was. He towered over the younger man by at least a foot and his body was broad and built. He wore a long black overcoat that reminded her of the man in her dream from the alley. One arm was in his coat and he pulled out a semi-automatic. Did Cartillo send him? She was a fool to think that he would never hurt her.

Her only refuge was inside the house, so she started to crawl to avoid being seen. The porch creaked like an old man's back and all of them heard it.

Boris saw her. As she stood up and turned toward him, he took off his hat. Michaela gasped in horror. His face and hands were badly burned. One eye was enclosed by his deformed skin and the other was red and burning mad. He looked like a clay statue that had been set too close to the fire before it hardened. Michaela found him revolting and that made him madder. He smiled a lipless smile and placing his hat back on his head, she saw that his hands were red and looked painful.

"Remember me? I knew you were trouble when I saw you at the warehouse. You are lucky that my boss has taking a liking to you. I would have finished you off as you slept like a baby in his house," Boris said as he took a step forward.

"Ricky isn't going to be happy about this," Michaela said.

"I don't care about *Ricky*. Just like your father, you have caused a lot of trouble, bitch," he said as he turned and nodded to his men. They walked along the back as Michaela backed up toward the open door.

"Look, you guys scared me good. I plan to go back to my own life and forget about everything, so you can leave knowing that you accomplished your goal."

He laughed. "My goal is not to scare you, but to kill you in a very painful way," he sneered and Michaela grimaced.

"I disgust you. Well, it's because of your father that I look the way I do. He destroyed one of our biggest warehouses and trapped me in it leaving me for dead. 90% of my body looks like this! The worst part is that I wasn't able to take my revenge on your pitiful daddy. I didn't get the chance to make him suffer and scream from the pain of burning skin searing off his limbs." He stepped closer and snickered. "So guess who I'm going to take my revenge out on? You," he whispered and leapt forward.

Michaela was inside the house before he reached the stairs. She heard Max growl and one of the men yell in pain. They shot at the house, so she dropped to the ground to wait for the endless rounds to cease. It was dark, but she recognized the front room and crawled toward the back. She heard yelling, but didn't listen. Remembering the old man's words, 'this will save you and bring you home,' Michaela headed toward the back of the house. She saw the loft filled with books on her left, and standing up turned right down the hall. She tried to find the circular room, but the house was a hallway of mazes, with little rooms zigzagging off it. She began to open all the doors hoping to recognize the wall. Her dream had been dark and she didn't remember all these rooms. Michaela turned to go back up the hall, when she saw the younger man. He blocked her way. He looked like a child holding his hat in his hand, while attempting to hold his gun in the other. She knew he must be one of the teens enslaved by his addiction. He was scared and mighty upset that he was the one who found her.

Stepping closer she whispered, "You don't have to do this. Please let me go and I'll disappear forever."

He glanced over his shoulder. Michaela had placed her hand on a doorknob and it felt warm. She felt the old man's presence and knew that this was the circular room. "Please," she said, turning the knob.

He stepped closer and whispered, "Don't disappear. Help us."

Michaela nodded and whipped into the room. The sun streaming through the high window shed an eerie glow around the room. She noticed the spiral stairway and the books shelved along the walls. Michaela looked up toward the window and saw Boris' outline. She didn't have time to think about how he got up there. He sped down those stairs like a super villain and came at her before she had the chance to back away. Boris slammed into her with his entire body. Michaela flew back into a book ladder and flipped around it. Trying to run up the stairs, he grabbed her legs and pulled her to the ground. She turned and kicked up at him, but he was on top of her pinning her legs down. His weight overwhelmed her. He pulled out a lighter and flicked it on. His face was like the dead and Michaela was sure he was going to make her one of them. She screamed and he laughed one last time. "Scream all you want, but no one is going to help you." She tried bucking him off but he pushed his hips down and she could feel his manhood harden against her.

He turned off his light and tried to undo her jeans. He put his mouth close to her ear and drooled, "You're going to scream in ecstasy once I get in you and then I'm going to burn every last bit of you."

Michaela heard Max bark down the hall and smashed her head into Boris' nose. It bled and he pulled away in pain, which gave her just enough room to free her hands. She boxed his ears, hit his nose again, and slid out from under him. Michaela tried to get up, but he shoved her down again. Michaela hit her head and almost passed out. She heard Boris scream and knew that Max bit him. It didn't matter, because she saw the wall. It pulsed with an otherworldly light and she felt it pull her. With renewed vigor, she kicked his face and he reeled back onto the floor, with Max on top of him. She heard Max yelp, but Michaela Sommers crawled into the wall, and disappeared.

One...two...three shots were heard. Shannon lost count. She was in the back of the inn waiting for Michaela's return. Shannon had been preoccupied talking to Emma when Michaela had left, so her words hadn't registered until she had been gone for over two hours.

Shannon believed she had convinced Michaela that chasing after their dad's killers was futile and much too dangerous for all of them. But, after hearing the gunshots, she was afraid it was too late. The shots had come from the woods where Michaela had gone. William Lansing had called Sheriff Tom Macenroy. The sheriff and his men went into the woods to look around. Shannon had told them that Michaela had been interested in the old house and they all frowned.

"Weird things have been known to happen at the Morgan house. Old Finnius Morgan just disappeared one day and we never saw him again," said the sheriff frowning even more. Seeing her frantic look, the sheriff squeezed Shannon's shoulder and said, "Now don't you worry, young lady; if your sister's out there, we'll find her. My boys know every inch of these woods."

They left in the early afternoon and didn't come back until after dark. William glanced at Emma and sat down next to Shannon. Taking her hand, William began, "Uh, Shannon dear, we couldn't find her. We looked all through the house and about a two mile radius as well. Now that doesn't mean she's not out there, but we'll just have to wait and see what happens tomorrow. I'm sorry." He stood up and hugged Emma.

Shannon watched the sheriff chomp his tobacco and shift his hat. "Did you find any signs of her?" she asked.

Reaching into his coat pocket, he pulled out a silver chain. Attached to it was a silver Celtic cross etched with elaborate scrollwork and a red ruby in the middle. "That's Michaela's. I gave it to her as a graduation present," Shannon said holding out her hand. The sheriff gave it to her and turning it over, she could still read Michaela's initials and 'love your SOS'. Her full name was Shannon Olivia Sommers. When they were younger, Michaela would call out SOS when she was in trouble and needed Shannon to save her. She was often Michaela's beacon home and she hoped that the same would happen now.

Shannon started to cry, but before she could break down, the sheriff continued. "There's more, Ms. Sommers. We found evidence of a struggle. Furniture was turned over and a whole crap load of bullets was found in the front wall. Whoever was looking for your sister, wanted to kill her pretty bad. We'll need to know if your sister was in some kind of trouble."

Trouble didn't even begin to describe what Michaela was in, Shannon thought. "Whatever you need, Sheriff," Shannon replied.

"That's good, real good. We'll send some samples to the crime lab and see what we can come up with. But that's it. There's no sign of any vehicles, so they must have ventured in from the highway on foot. If your sister is out there, we'll do our best to find her," the sheriff said, then stopped and added, "Did your sister have a dog?"

"Yes, did you find him?" she asked.

"Yeah, we found him inside the house, whining by a wall. He's been hurt, stabbed by a knife, but I think he'll be OK. He wouldn't leave that wall and kept trying to paw through it. It may be a clue, so we'll look into it more. He's been taken to the local animal hospital," the sheriff explained.

9

Cartillo waited, impatient for news from his men. He needed to make sure Michaela was safe. He wished he could be open with her about his life. But he knew that the daughter of Jack and Genevieve Sommers would never go against her beliefs. It was unfortunate, because he had feelings for Michaela.

It was true. She reminded him so much of her mother. It was also true that Ricky had been in love with Genevieve for as long as he could remember. The day Jack brought her home Ricky loved her, and it broke his heart knowing that she loved Jack and not him. Nonetheless, they had been close. She had always tried to heal the rift that had grown between him and Jack, wanting them to find peace. She accepted Ricky and listened to him. That was why when she lay dying and asked Ricky to protect her girls if something happened to Jack, he had promised. He swore on his soul that he would protect them. He swore on his love for her that he would always be there for them.

Now look at him. Yeah, he was there for them and he wanted more from Michaela than he had a right to. But he would send her and Shannon away, so that they would be protected...from him and what his life had become. The door to his office opened.

Boris had to face his boss with a broken nose. His face

looked like a bruised tomato. Cartillo looked at his top man with open disgust. "What happened?"

Boris' partners looked anywhere else, except their boss's face. "Well, you see, Boss. She disappeared," Boris said knowing how stupid that sounded.

Ricky paused. He puffed on his cigar then looked at Boris through a thick cloud of smoke. "What do you mean she disappeared? Where did she go?" Cartillo asked.

"That's the weird part. We were in this old abandoned house and I was fighting with her and she got away and disappeared into a...wall," Boris explained.

Cartillo paced. His men hated when he paced. "Let me get this straight. I send out three of my top guys to protect a woman that I care about, and you tell me that you were fighting with her and now she has disappeared! Am I missing something?!" he yelled.

The young man who had let Michaela leave, blurted, "He wanted to hurt her!"

Boris slammed his fist into the man's face. He dropped to the ground. Cartillo grabbed his gun and rammed it into Boris' cheek. Boris fell back against the wall.

"What's with you and this girl, Boss? She's trouble and you know it," Boris said, pissed. He had seen Ricky Cartillo blow his ex-lovers' heads off for looking at another man and so he couldn't understand what this Sommers' girl had over him. Plus it was true—he did want a piece of her so bad, his insides boiled.

Realization dawned on Ricky's face and Boris' eyes showed fear. The two other men backed away.

"Were you responsible for the attack on the subway?" Ricky asked in a controlled voice.

Boris tried to explain, "Boss, I was just trying to protect you! She saw me at the warehouse getting a delivery. This girl will bring you and all of us down!"

Ricky stepped back to think. He walked back and forth by

Boris who knelt on the floor.

Ricky ranted, "Oh Genevieve, Genevieve. I am sorry to have failed you—to not have done what I promised."

He raised his hand over his head and with all his strength struck Boris' head with the gun.

"You will never hurt her. I will kill you if I find out that she has been hurt by you again. Find Natalie."

"Yes, Boss," Boris mumbled as he tried to stop the blood flowing through his hands.

"Bandage his head!" Cartillo barked to the other men. He walked into the bathroom and washed his hands. Ricky looked at himself in the mirror. Boris was right. He protected Michaela to the endangerment of his business and his family. He needed to settle this fast and still protect Michaela and Shannon.

If she was out there? Shannon thought about the sheriff's words on her long drive home...alone. Well, Max didn't count. He was lying in the back, still crying for Michaela with his stomach wrapped in gauze. The police had found some blood samples on Max's fur and hoped to match it to the attacker. Who had attacked Michaela? Where could she be? Shannon had to believe that this attack was yet another warning, maybe a final warning all connected with their father. She had contacted Uncle Frank and left a message for Vince.

Shannon arrived home late and ran up the stairs. She was nervous that these hoodlums knew she lived with Michaela and thought they would come for her, too. Uncle Frank and Vince were there.

"Thank God you're here, Vince. Max is in the car. Can you carry him up?" Shannon asked.

Vince nodded and went to get Max.

Not saying anything else she sat down on the couch.

Uncle Frank was nervous and started talking, "I've already had contact with Sheriff Macenroy and got most of the details. I put an APB out on her and will put some of our best men on it. The sheriff is more than willing to work with us." He looked at Shannon and seeing the anguish in her eyes, came over wrapped his arms around her. "It'll be OK, Shannon. Whoever has done this…well, I'll find him and I'm going to finish this business once and for all…for Michaela and for Jack."

Vince came in with Max and laid him on his bed by the window. Max lifted his head and moaned to Vince.

"I know, big fella. You tried your best," Vince said rubbing behind Max's ear. "What happened out there, Shannon?" he asked.

"Michaela insisted on seeing this abandoned house in the woods. A man lived there who was from Ireland and there were weapons left in the house that he had collected. I tried to get her to stay, but you know how stubborn she can be. Besides, she had Max with her. I don't know what happened. She was at peace about Dad. She was ready to move on. No one knew that we were going to be there; except for us," Shannon sobbed, not able to continue.

"Did she get any other information?" Frank asked in a calm voice.

Shannon thought. "Besides Ricky Cartillo being involved, which I can't even imagine, I don't really think so. Oh, she did say something about a warehouse where the kids were kept. Plus, she thought she has seen this Natalie girl one day and followed her. That was before the second attack."

"Second attack?" Frank asked. "What second attack?"

"Uncle Frank, I'm sorry for not telling you. Michaela said that she was through with it all and that was why we went away," Shannon said, knowing she had made a mistake.

Frank was angry. "How can I protect you if you don't come to me?"

Vince interrupted. "We came to see you and we have called you. Either that detective or Newman keep interfering and putting an end to any leads we have."

"Why couldn't she leave Cartillo out of this?! He's a very dangerous man." Frank paced the room, rubbing his face. He roughly pushed his hair back off his forehead. Trying to be calm, he asked, "Is there anything else?"

"No, you know everything," Shannon asked.

Frank walked to the door. "I'll leave a squad car outside for a couple days just to make sure that no one tries to find out for themselves just how much Michaela knows. That's why she's been taken. I'm going to take care of this myself. I thought if I trusted in the system, all would be well. I was wrong. Will you be all right, Shannon?" Uncle Frank asked.

"I'm going to stay for a while, Frank, so don't worry. Just find her," Vince said.

"OK, but if you remember anything...," he started.

"I know, Uncle Frank, we'll call you," Shannon said and kissed him on the cheek. He looked sad and lost. It was hard on him to lose his best friend and partner and now with this happening, he was ready to crumble. He left and Vince closed the door. Shannon wondered if he would be able to get near this case.

"Oh God, Shannon, what am I going to do if we don't find her?" Vince said.

Shannon couldn't bear Vince's pain, too. She turned away from the need to comfort and hardened her heart. She only had room for Michaela and her one thought was to find her little sister and end this disaster.

"We'll find her, Vince. I have a few ideas and I have to hope that maybe now Uncle Frank will get some answers. Now I'm fine. Really. But I'm exhausted and I'd like to get some sleep. I promise I'll call you before I do anything, OK?" she ended.

Vince walked to the door and hugged Shannon. "You tell me what needs to be done to get Michaela home and I'll do it. I need her back."

"I also need her, Vince," she said and closed the door after him.

Shannon was alone and could think about all that happened in the last couple months. She really didn't know much more than what she told Frank, except for Michaela's dreams. That reminded her of Michaela's dream journal. Maybe she had recorded enough of her dreams to give Shannon some sort of clue.

Michaela's door was closed. When she placed her hand on the knob, it felt warm and Shannon's arm tingled. Spooked, Shannon jumped back. She couldn't take anything else so she went to bed.

It was the day before Halloween and Shannon's legs were chilled by the fall winds. She hurried Max through his walk.

Shannon walked into her office and a week's worth of backlogged work. Her day was packed with patients and she found it hard to concentrate on any of their problems. It was early evening by the time Shannon had a break. The door to her office opened and Sonya popped her head in. "Come in, Sonya. What is it?" Shannon asked.

"Uh, there's someone here who is insistent upon seeing you, Ms. Sommers," Sonya said.

Shaking her head, Shannon asked, "Well, who is it?"

"A Mr. Cartillo?" Sonya replied.

The hairs on Shannon's arms perked up like porcupine quills. Should she let him in? He was a link to Michaela, so she said, "Let him in."

Smoothing her skirt, Shannon walked around her desk to shake Ricky Cartillo's hand. He looked handsome dressed in a dark olive suit and his shoes were so well polished, you could see your reflection in them. As usual, his hair was greased back displaying his smooth high forehead and his ponytail was hidden inside his jacket.

Not releasing Shannon's hand, Ricky spoke in deep, soft voice, "Shannon, I am so sorry to hear about Michaela. This is terrible. I tried to reach Frank Goodale, but he has not returned my call. I wanted to come to you and see how I could be of assistance."

Caught off guard, Shannon pulled her hand away and replied, "Uh, I don't know what you can do, Mr. Cartillo, but I appreciate your concern."

Cartillo looked around Shannon's office and walked to her window peering down at the street. "She could be anywhere by now. The longer anyone waits, the less chance there will be of finding her," he said turning back to her. Tears welled up in Shannon's eyes despite her desire to control them. Ricky Cartillo walked over to Shannon and placed an arm around her. "Now, now, I am here to help you. I care about you and Michaela very much. Is there anything you can tell me that might help me find her? I know she is still so distressed over your father's death. Has she spoken to anyone about this since she was attacked?"

With that question, Shannon's emotions dissolved. She reminded herself that Ricky Cartillo was a snake and, whether or not she could believe he was involved in her father's death, she knew better than to trust him. "I really don't know what you are talking about, Mr. Cartillo. Michaela is dealing with her grief much better now and has been busy with her studio. She was going to move on with her life. A person can get attacked only so many times. First it's on the subway and then in an alley and now on vacation!"

Ricky's look told Shannon that she had said more than she should have.

"Tell me about the alley," he said.

"You should know."

Ricky walked the room like a caged animal then came

close to Shannon. He held her shoulders so that she had to look at him.

"I did not send anyone to attack Michaela. On this, you must believe me. I do not want anything to happen to either one of you. I will…take care of the person who has done this. I promise you, but I need to know what happened," he whispered.

"There were two guys who followed her into an alley. Michaela asked if you were behind it." Ricky winced. "They said their boss was more powerful than you," Shannon explained.

Ricky's mouth hardened. "I will do what I can. Good day, Shannon," he said.

Shannon closed the door behind him confused. She could tell he was very angry—like he knew who was behind the attacks. She didn't know what to think anymore. One minute she was sure he was involved in Michaela's disappearance and the next she thought he may be able to help.

10

Frank Goodale walked into his precinct the next morning still shaking. He thought he had done the right thing when he decided to listen to his captain, Barry Newman, and let the whole case rest. He had tried so hard to settle the guilty feelings that kept him up for endless nights and end the nightmares where Jack called to him from the dead. That's what he thought until he received Shannon's call. He should have known that the daughter of a drug lord's worst enemy wouldn't stop until she had some answers. Now it was his turn to get some answers and to make things right.

Frank walked into his captain's office. Barry Newman looked up surprised. He sat close to Detective Scott Malowski. Barry Newman was quite young to be in the captain's seat. Some thought that he was a born leader and ran the precinct well, while others thought that he was as crooked as arthritic fingers, and bought this position with bad money. Frank believed in the loyalty and honor of the police brotherhood. He wasn't naive and knew that people were bought, but the captain was needed to keep the brotherhood together and, if he was bad, then the whole foundation was doomed. Sensing Frank's agitation, Newman began, "Uh, Frank you look like crap! What's going on?"

"Jack Sommers's daughter is missing," Frank blurted.

Newman nodded a dismissal to Malowski, who shuffled his papers and rose. He looked at Frank with a smile that never led to his eyes. He turned to the captain and said, "Just call me when you need me. OK, Cap?"

Captain Newman waved him away muttering, "Yeah, yeah," and turned his attention to Frank. "Now what's this about Jack's daughter?"

"I stopped investigating Jack's death, because you told me you were going to handle it and I was too close. Because you haven't done a damn thing, Michaela decided to take matters into her own hands and now she's gone!" Frank said getting louder.

Stepping around the desk, Barry tried to settle Frank down. "Now hold on, man. I told you that I was going to handle the whole situation and I have. Malowski just told me about some leads and I planned to inform you. This is a sticky situation, Frank, and it involves some very important people. Storming into a raid without thinking is the best way to get killed as we found out with Jack. It seems to me that his daughter is acting in the same way."

Sitting down and slumping in the chair, Frank said, "I know. I know. I told her not to go around asking questions."

"Oh, so you knew about her snooping around? You should have told me and maybe I could have done something to protect her," he said squeezing Frank's shoulder.

Guilt gripped Frank's heart. "I know, Captain. Now I'm responsible for two people who are gone. I have to do something. I have to get involved and make things right. I want to come back onto this case," he pleaded.

"Now, Frank. I know you feel responsible, but you shouldn't. Let me see what I can do to get some men up to the Catskills and check things out and maybe you can do some checking around here for me. You have to slow down though, so that a tragedy like Jack's won't happen again. I need you to play by the rules like we are supposed to do around here.

117

Understood?" he said leading Frank to the door.

Frank stopped in the doorway and grabbed his captain's hand squeezing hard. "Thanks, Captain," he said and walked away.

Frank walked out of the precinct still troubled. He thought about Newman's words and stopped when he remembered him mentioning the Catskills. He never told his captain where Michaela disappeared. Feeling lonely and disillusioned, Jack went to find his partner.

Benjamin Walker sat on a bench in the foyer of the precinct. Seeing him, Frank just shook his head. He missed Jack. Frank felt the weight of responsibility dragging him to the ground. He tried to feel excited about having a new partner, but it had been hard working with him for the last couple weeks.

"Let's go, Walker," Frank said.

"Everything all right, Frank? You look sick," Ben asked.

"I don't know anymore," Frank said walking outside. All he knew was that he had some important business to take care of.

Shannon decided it was time to see what was in Michaela's room. She touched the door handle and felt its warmth once again. However, this time she wasn't frightened. She felt comforted by the heat and turned the handle. Max limped over and pushed the door open with his nose, eager to be near his owner's belongings. He sniffed around and whimpered when he did not find Michaela.

"I know how you feel, but we'll find her. I don't think either one of us can live without her," Shannon said looking around her sister's small bedroom. She stared at all the awards Michaela earned over the years in martial arts and her school program for kids. There was a picture on her dresser of Michaela and a group of kids she had mentored. Shannon looked on Michaela's bed where her karate bag was left untouched with her uniform laying on top. Max had made himself comfortable on the floor and as Shannon walked toward him she noticed Michaela's suitcase in the corner. Vince must have put it in her room. Shannon decided to open it to wash Michaela's clothes. On top was Michaela's dream journal. Shannon picked it up and sitting on the bed opened it to the last entry.

Dream Journal—October 28, 2000, 4:00 AM

In my dream I meet the man who built the house—Finnius Morgan. He beckons me to come in. His time is short and he has so much to teach me. He is dressed as a Druid in a white robe. His hair and beard are white and long. He shows me his weapons: battle-axes, iron-tipped maces with highly decorated hilts, swords and daggers; all displayed on his walls. He walks along another wall displaying armor, a helmet, and a beautifully designed sword. He points to the sword and I touch it. I feel its power and the pain it has inflicted on its enemies. He pushes me closer and when my hand enfolds the handle, I see the blood of the wounded, the gaping holes of the dead, the chaos of battle and the victory of the sword bearer—a woman. The images swirl around my mind enveloping me in their turmoil and I let go, not able to handle its power. I turn toward the man to tell him what I have seen, but he silences me with his finger and motions for me to follow.

We walk through the house. I notice old furniture and when I touch the walls to admire the fancy wallpaper, they disintegrate and another room opens to me. The first room is a parlor. I walk to the wall and as I touch it, it disappears and turns into a doorway. The man is there and he walks up a ladder. I follow. It is a loft, with every wall filled with books. The books are old and I know they hold the knowledge of my past. I pick up one named <u>The Annals of Ancient Ireland</u>. I hungrily skim some of the other countless titles: <u>The Brehon Laws</u>, <u>Fianaigecht</u>, <u>Book of Aicill</u>.

I want to sit down and read about my history, but he has more to show me. He leads me down the ladder and toward the back of the house. It is so dark I cannot make out what is around me. We are in a hallway and he stops at a door. He opens it and, pointing to the wall, says, "This will save you and bring you home." He turns. I follow his gaze and see a shadow. I sense danger, but when I turn back to the man, he is gone. I wake up.

Response: During the day when I walked into the woods I had seen a vision or apparition of my Celtic warrior. He watched me and held out his hand urging me to come with him. I think he is somehow related to this dream and the man's house, but I don't know how. Shannon said I looked like I had seen a ghost. I had, but I knew this ghost and he seemed so very real. I feel as though a journey is about to begin and this warrior will be my guide.

We are going home this Saturday. It will be Halloween soon. Halloween is a day of reckoning, the time between times, when all doors will be open to me and perhaps this mystery will be solved.

Shannon closed the journal. Shannon was familiar with the Celtic New Year called Samhain. Michaela had often told her the story about how there was a great feast to celebrate the start of winter and, because Samhain didn't belong to the old or the new, it was a time of great magic. On that day, the doors to the Otherworld were open and spirits could walk between this world and their own.

Shannon lay down on Michaela's bed not knowing what to think anymore. Tears streamed down her face and soaked her hair as she stared at the ceiling in frustration. Max whimpered at the edge of the bed and Shannon helped him up. He cuddled next to her and, as she gently stroked his fur, she said, "Maybe Michaela will give us a clue, eh, Max?" Exhausted, Shannon fell asleep.

Floating, beams of white light flash through the starless night sky. Source of beam comes from a woman swinging a long sword, dressed in leather armor, a helmet covers her face. Swings at another woman with long auburn hair wearing a black uniform. Blocks sword with a long staff. Only see her back. They clash, scream. Sword woman falls.

That morning Shannon called Uncle Frank at the precinct again. She had tried his house, but the phone just rang. The dispatcher transferred her call, but it wasn't Frank.

"Hello, Officer Benjamin Walker of the 42nd Precinct. Can I help you?" he answered.

"Uh, hello, Officer Walker. This is Shannon Sommers. Is Frank available? I have some information for him," Shannon said.

"Officer Goodale isn't here yet, Ms. Sommers. I could take

the information for you and make sure he gets it," Ben said.

Shannon let out a frustrated sound. "No, no. He'll only understand what the information is."

"Are you in some kind of trouble? I can help," Ben said.

"I'm sure you could, but no thanks. Could you have him call me when he gets in? Please tell him that it's about Michaela and that I've been trying to get in touch with him," Shannon said.

"Okay, Ms. Sommers," Ben finished.

"Thank you and please call me Shannon. Goodbye," she said.

"Goodbye...Shannon," Ben said.

11

"Maecha Ruadh! Wake up!"

Michaela heard a familiar voice float through her head. It was the voice in her dreams. *"Kelan."*

Kelan, so that's your name. She opened her eyes and saw him. Those green hawk-like eyes pierced her own and willed her to come back to him. He held Michaela close, cradling her head in his arms. She lifted her hand to touch his chiseled chin and realized he wasn't a hallucination. His black, thick hair was pulled back tight off his forehead and strung together at the nape of his neck. His braid hung over his shoulder and, entwined with leather strappings, flowed down to touch her breast. "We must go," he stated while lifting her up into his battle built arms. Placing Michaela on his black warhorse, Octar, Kelan climbed up behind her and took off at a quick canter.

Michaela breathed in the fresh air. They rode close to a line of trees, away from the open field to their right. *So peaceful!* The sounds of distant waves caught Michaela's ears. She thought she was deep in the woods behind the old house in Catskill and so this man, dressed as a Celtic warrior with his leather tunic and battle horse, must be someone dressed for Halloween, right?

"NO!" A voice screamed in her head.

Michaela rubbed her temples. She really hit her head

123

this time.

Overhead she caught a glimpse of a huge, majestic bird. Screeching, it circled over them while lowering itself closer to Michaela. He floated with the wind tipping his tail along the current.

"His name is Aeiden."

Hearing that voice again, Michaela threw her head back into Kelan's chest.

"Easy, young warrior. We'll be back to our dwelling soon," he said in a concerned voice.

Michaela looked ahead to see what Kelan referred to as their dwelling. She saw rounded mounds of hay scattered along the fields. Rising out of the earth stood an enormous fortress. Its towers rose high into the clear blue sky. Mighty ringforts stood at each corner of the castle and a rectangular building stretched away from what looked like the main entrance. The castle walls wound around the hill and a lower wall encased it in protection. Guards could be seen along the top and Michaela heard them yell in a language she knew was not from New York.

People gathered around the lower walls and Kelan and his warriors made their way through the castle gates. The women wore colorful woolen dresses and their long hair lay braided down their backs. The men wore cloth breeches and sleeveless leather vests with swords comfortably hanging at their sides. Children with wild hair scampered along the walls, yelled that they hoped the princess wouldn't die, too.

Michaela looked down at her clothing. She wore some type of shirt *"leine"* and pants *"briogais."* She felt around her neck and touched a cold piece of metal. A torc *"torques,"* which distinguished her as…royalty? Michaela heard the voice in her head clearer now and realized it was correcting her words. She felt a heavy pressure in her head and chest.

"We are almost there, Maecha," Kelan said.

She wanted to tell him her name. She wanted her sister.

Michaela wished she was with Shannon swinging on the porch at the inn. Her head felt like it would burst and she covered her face to shut out the piercing lights that were striking her eyes like balls of fire. Feeling faint, Michaela Sommers leaned back on Kelan and was lost in this strange land.

"Shannon, Shannon? Where are you?" Scream. Blackness. Run hard from the darkness.

"Michaela! I'm over here," Shannon yells from a green ridge with hanging vines. Jump to reach the vines, but the blackness encloses me like a box. Become hysterical.

"Shannon, don't leave me here!" The blackness pulls me away from her. Shannon gasps and points. See a woman dressed in Celtic war gear carrying a glowing sword and wearing a helmet. Sense immediate danger and must confront her.

Hear Shannon calling "Michaela!" as this warrior attacks. She screams like a blood-thirsty animal and charges with her sword ready to kill. Step out of her way and grabbing her sword arm flip her over onto her back. Retreat. She jumps up and charges with her sword swinging left and right. Retreat further, keeping out of range. Jump to the side and kick her hand. Sword flies out of her hand. Attack with fast spinning kicks trying to get her off balance. The kicks penetrate her leather tunic and she seems surprised by this type of fighting. Falls to the ground. Hold the warrior down and remove her helmet.

"Michaela?" Shannon asks as she looks at the fallen warrior and begins to fade away. Her sister looks up, stretches out her hand. "Michaela," Shannon says again looking from the warrior to her sister. Their faces are the same.

12

Shannon had never dreamed like that before. She felt as though it really happened and Michaela could see her. Shannon didn't know what to think or who to talk to about her sister. She wasn't sure how Vince would be able to help her.

Shannon took Max for a walk. Shannon didn't notice the cold weather or where Max dragged her. Max stopped and, in her absentmindedness, Shannon almost ran him over.

"Why did you stop, Max?" she asked as she looked around. They were in front of Michaela's studio and Max pulled on his leash. As tears formed in Shannon's eyes, she spoke, "Your friend isn't in there and I'm not sure when she will be." Max insisted, so she went in.

She saw Vince demonstrating a kata to the upper ranks. Shannon had seen him perform in tournaments and was often impressed by Vince's strength and passion for the martial arts, but that passion was not there today. She knew that Michaela's disappearance took a heavy toll on him and she could only imagine how it affected her students.

Max barked. All the kids turned and started talking with excitement. Vince gave them permission to visit, and Shannon followed him into Michaela's office.

"How are you doing, Shannon?" asked Vince as he wiped

his face. His eyes were black and puffy and he looked pale from worry.

"I'm doing the best I can as I'm sure you are. I...," she hesitated.

"What is it, Shannon? Did they find Michaela? Is she...?" He was too scared to continue.

Shannon recovered. "No, it's not like that. We haven't found her, but frankly, I'm frustrated, Vince!"

"OK, sit down and tell me what's going on," he said.

Shannon told him about Michaela's journal and about the dream she had.

"Then," she continued, "I try to get in touch with Frank, but he doesn't return my calls, he's never home and his partner, although concerned, can't tell me anything either. He's keeping something from us. I just know it. I could never believe that he would be a part of my dad's death or Michaela's disappearance, but he just acting—suspicious, that's all."

For once, Vince didn't go off on a scientific tirade about the impossibility of dream reality. He just sat and stared out the one-way mirror watching the kids run around the studio with Max, but he was thinking. He stood up and said, "Come on, we are going to pay a visit to Frank Goodale and get to the bottom of this."

Another adult teacher took control of the class and Shannon left Max there. When they arrived at the precinct, Shannon stopped Vince. "What are you going to say?"

"I don't know. I'm going to go with my instincts," he said.

Vince's instincts made Shannon nervous. She knew that his calm façade could burst into a flaming inferno. She just hoped Uncle Frank would be cooperative.

At the front desk, Vince asked to see Officer Goodale. The receptionist picked up the phone. As she was on the phone, Captain Newman walked around the corner.

"Shannon Sommers! How are you, my dear?" he asked.

"Captain Newman. It's nice to see you. I'm doing OK, considering that my sister is missing," she spoke in a sarcastic, but friendly manner.

Ignoring the biting remark, Newman continued. "So who are you here to see?"

Vince interjected. "Hi, I'm Vince Cardosa. We are here to see Officer Goodale, who I believe is investigating her disappearance. Or did you take him off this case also?"

Captain Newman's smile disappeared. "I would watch how you talk to the people who are here to help you."

"That's what I hope you guys are doing. Excuse us," Vince said as the receptionist pointed for them to go in.

Captain Newman stared hard at Vince's back.

"Hi, Shannon. It's so nice to see you," Benjamin Walker said looking from Shannon to Vince. "Come in. Did you get in touch with Frank? I told him three times to call you."

Biting her tongue, Shannon remained pleasant. "No, I haven't spoken to him. That's why we've come down. We hoped that he was here."

"Oh, he is. He just went to get some coffee. He should be right back," Ben said.

"How is Frank doing? Has he seemed distracted from his work?" Vince asked.

Taking Vince's agitated manner in, Ben said, "He's been extremely busy, although I really couldn't tell you what he is involved in. He hasn't been including me. Do either of you want to fill me in?"

Shannon decided to give him some information. "It's about my sister's disappearance. Frank has been ignoring me and I would like to find out why."

Vince didn't think he should have to provide any more information. That was what he came for. So he asked, "You drive around with him, don't you?" Ben just nodded. "Where has he been going?"

Ben was about to answer, when they heard a voice from the door. "Hey, go easy on my partner. He doesn't know what's happening here," Frank said coming in trying to sound upbeat.

Shannon wasn't fooled. She could see the stress around his eyes as they shifted back and forth trying to figure out what to say. "Shannon, darling, I am so sorry that I haven't been in touch with you. I have been so busy, working on things and I haven't had that many leads."

"Well I have, and they might have been helpful to you. Ricky Cartillo...."

"Shhhh!!" Frank interrupted. Frank's eyes were large and round...with fear. He shut the door and explained. "Don't go yelling that name around here! I have enough guys breathing down my neck about this whole murder/disappearance thing. I can't get any information from anyone, because I'm too close and Ricky Cartillo is a heavy player in this precinct. He supports us and the local businesses, so saying that he is involved in something as bad as this could have some negative implications for him and my job!"

Vince had had it. "So you are more worried about some greasy drug lord than Michaela's safety?"

"It's not that way, Vince!" he tried to continue.

"Bull crap, man! Shannon has been trying for days to get in touch with you. You keep ignoring her, ignoring your partner, and now you give us this politically correct answer about how we can't upset the people who support your paycheck. I don't give a damn about your paycheck, your career or anyone else in this goddamn precinct! I care about Michaela and getting her back. Every day that goes by takes her further away from all of us. Do you have some detectives out in the Catskills looking for her?" he asked, wanting to give Frank a chance.

"Not yet," Frank said.

Vince was stunned. "Why not, Frank?"

"Captain Newman is supposed to send a detective out to take care of it. He is better equipped to handle this type of work and can be assigned to it full-time," he said feeling that sense of responsibility weighing all too heavily on him again.

"And why aren't you up there like you told Shannon you would be?" he asked, his temper started to ignite.

"I'd lose my job, Vinny, and then I couldn't help at all. I'm too close," he said trying to sound pitiful.

Losing it, Vince grabbed Frank and threw him into the wall of commendations. As they shattered to the floor, Vince held Frank and spat, "The girls' father would have forsaken the force, forsaken the captain to find your daughter and to find your murderer. He had a level of integrity that I thought you shared, but now I know that he was the strong one. I don't know how you are involved and maybe you're not. Maybe you're just a scared old man who is tired of fighting, but I do know that we are done with you. You have let your partner down and it sickens me."

He dropped Frank who sank to the floor.

"Ricky Cartillo came to see me and he was very shaken up about Michaela's disappearance and all her attacks. I think someone more powerful than Ricky is behind this. Find him, Frank and get my sister back," Shannon implored.

"Keep an eye on your back, Ben. You never know whom you can trust. There are enemies even within this precinct and they are closer than you think," Vince finished and left.

Ben touched her arm and whispered, "I'll call you. I want to help." Shannon just looked at him and turned away.

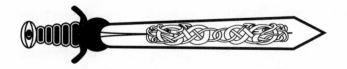

Part Two

1

Celtic Ireland—284 AD

Maecha Ruadh mac Art. I was named after the first woman to come and conquer Ireland—Macha Mong Ruadh— Macha of the Red Tresses. The story is well-known amongst our bards—how she had come to Ireland many years ago and built Emain Macha, once the largest stronghold of Ireland. The stronghold is now in Tara where my father, King Cormac mac Art, lives and rules. Ireland is a beautiful land. The green hills roll onward, until they disappear amongst the cliffs, which make their homes against the raging waters. Tara is a formidable *rath*, whose power is in its location on top of a hill. Its great hall could hold a hundred warriors with the mead and meat always plentiful. I love our land and our people as much as my father does, and I am willing to defend it with my life.

Everyone was afraid I had lost my mind after I had been hit by that cursed Pict, but I remembered who I was. Kelan mac Nessa, my trusted companion and trainer, stayed with me as much as possible I was told, but he was also needed to make sure that the enemy was gone. Brina, my nursemaid, told me that I had been possessed by some illness. I had chanted some foreign words like 'Mikala'. I dreamt of a woman who looked like me, but dressed strange and fought with her hands and feet instead of a sword.

I remembered now what happened, too. Kelan and I had been scouting our borders for any signs of invasions. Our neighbors to the north from Ulaid had recently been attacked by a foreign band of raiders called the Picts. They were a well-organized tribe from Alba. Each spring they made their way across the sea and invaded our lands, attempting to settle here or at least steal some food, women, and children to take back to their home. Their bodies, which were painted blue, brought fear even to our best warrior. They came with a vengeance and were unmerciful.

My father had left on a hunting trip with his champion, Fionn mac Cumhail, and his warrior group called the Fianna. After their trip, there was to be a great feast and all the forths would gather together in anticipation of our Samhain celebration. With twenty warriors we ventured forth hoping to be back in time for the festivities. At nineteen summers, I am training to be a warrior. Kelan is my trainer, but I long for the day when I can go to the female warrior, Scathach, to be trained like my mother, Queen Deirdre, had been. I thought I was a good warrior and I had even surprised Kelan, who was always concerned for my safety. Kelan has been my constant companion for 10 years, since his family's village was destroyed. His mother and father, the *Rig-Mor-Tuatha* of his united tuaths, were killed along with most of his relatives. Our fathers were close friends and since there wasn't much of a tuath to rule, my father took Kelan in and raised him into manhood. Kelan was only eleven summers when my father taught him to think and fight as a warrior. It was at that time that Kelan began teaching me the sword.

Moving along the southern edge of our border, near Dublin, we had been surprised by a large group of Picts. Aeiden, my peregrine falcon, dove screeching toward us and, as we turned to see what brought on his warning, a hoard of battle crazed Picts ran at us from the trees.

We were on horseback and, as long as we could stay away from their spears, we would have the advantage. We were out-numbered three to one and where our horses didn't crush the Picts down into the earth, our swords slashed through their limbs and tore our enemy apart.

I saw a rather large Pict advancing through our men while he kept his eyes on me. I could see the blood of our fallen men congealing on his blue tattooed arms. I turned my horse, Gwendor, so my sword arm could face this enemy and slice the menacing smile from his face.

He ran toward me with his battle-axe raised high above his head. While I prepared for his attack, Aeiden screeched behind me and I turned to see another Pict throwing his spear toward Gwendor. My beautiful horse bellowed out a painful howl and reared up onto her hind legs. Aeiden swooped down and tore at the killer's eyes. Kelan yelled for me to jump off my horse. I jumped away from the horse, but was hit by the big Pict. I held up my shield, but his swing was so powerful, my shield hit me in the head and that was all I remembered. Kelan later told me that the large Pict wanted to make sure that I was dead and so he and Kelan fought until the Pict's broken body lay lifeless on the ground. The others ran back into the dense forest toward the sea, with six of our remaining men chasing them, taking down any-one they could. They must have had a boat waiting to take them back to Alba. The boat had been launched, so after our men killed those left behind, they came back. Kelan had stayed with me and when the others arrived, he carried me back to Tara.

When I could remain awake long enough, Kelan told me horrible news; my father had been taken. He thought that the Picts who had attacked us were protecting their ship and thought that we might find them. The main attack had been near Tara against my father and the Fianna. The Fianna were an elite group of warriors who fought under Fionn mac Cumhail to protect the laws of our land and to protect Ireland's coastline from invaders. They were recruited from the war bands of many local chieftains and kings of Ireland, but all served under the *aegis* of the High King of Tara, Cormac mac Art. My father was responsible for setting up this strong core of warriors, but it was Fionn mac Cumhail, my father's champion, who commanded the Fianna from the forths of Mide to Laigin. Kelan described the battle.

"Who was in charge of this attack?" I asked.

Kelan answered, "We do not know who was in charge. I was told that the Picts attacked from all sides and created a thundering chaos. Goll mac Morna told me that there was a man, oddly familiar, standing up on a ridge. He appeared to be in charge, but the coward did not come forth to fight."

"And we are to trust mac Morna? Maybe he was involved. He did betray Fionn's father, did he not?" I said shuddering at the memory.

"Goll has proven his loyalty to your father and to Fionn. It was said that he fought ten men at once to reach his king, but he could not save him in time."

"We shall see how deep his loyalty runs. Did he say anything else about this man?"

"Only that he wore a helmet with tusks flaring from the top and a long tail that whipped like a fury in the wind. No one could get close enough to him and some say he disappeared like a ghost when the battle was over," Kelan finished.

Since we were children, Kelan and I dreamed of being a part of the Fianna. I had always believed that the Fianna could never lose a battle. I don't think they had in my lifetime. Kelan hoped to be put through the rigorous test soon. As a woman, I wasn't accepted as a possible member, but I wasn't going to let that stop me. I planned to prove myself a great warrior and they would have to let me in.

I thought about my father. He was gone from us, probably on that boat.

"There's more," Kelan said.

"What is it, Kelan? You can tell me. You have to tell me!" I yelled.

Kelan looked at me with sadness and pride. He began, "Maecha, Fionn, along with probably half of his men, was killed during the raid. I'm very sorry, but the king's champion is dead."

Dead? How could Fionn mac Cumhail be dead? I could see him riding his gray steed, challenging others to keep up with him on their hunt for meat. His long, orange hair held down away from his face by a leather strap, with his beard and mustache of the same color always neatly trimmed. His lime colored tunic with brown trim would be held tight to his waist by a leather belt entwined with Celtic knots. With bare feet and hands, he would ride against the largest animals. His faithful hounds, Bran and Sgeolang, were always by his side, smelling the fear of their prey. Fionn was the greatest warrior who ever lived and his warriors were the best ever to grace our land. There were countless stories about how he had braved the Otherworld, *Tir-nan-Og*, to gather the treasures that were now protected by Scathach and her warriors. He could move mountains as far as I was concerned and a hundred men couldn't take him down.

I looked at Kelan, with tears flowing and asked, "There's more isn't there?"

"Yes," Kelan began.

I wiped my face and tried to look like the warrior that I knew would make my mother proud. "What is it?"

"Your brother has declared that he will control our rath. His decision is to wait and see what ransom the Picts demand for your father," he stopped waiting for my reaction.

"Wait? Wait for a ransom or wait until they decide to kill father, so he can take over. My father is a righteous, strong, and loving king and no one will accept that snake brother of mine as his equal. Only the Sovereignty Goddess can declare the ruler of Ireland. Our land is ruled by the power of the Mother Goddess. Besides, we need to attack now. Surely, the Fianna will want to avenge their leader's death and it will be a sign of weakness if we wait."

"That is true, Maecha, but there are some leaders who believe that Cairpre should be the next ruler of Tara and so what he says will be obeyed," Kelan replied. "You must speak with your brother before he takes any further action that could threaten your father's rule. Ambitious men always look for a reason to dethrone a king and this could be the time," he said.

I stood, closing my eyes to stop my head from spinning. I was still very weak, but my father's life and throne were at stake and I would step up to this challenge. I looked at Kelan, my closest companion, and said, "Please call an assembly together, including the surrounding forths' leaders, our group of warriors, and the remaining Fianna. I will talk to my brother and then we will meet. It is close to Samhain, so most should be preparing to travel." Turning, I called, "Brina!"

My mother's servant, Brina, hurried into the room with my clothing. "What is all this, Brina?"

She smiled and said, "I am glad you are feeling better, my lady. I thought you would like some fresh clothing."

I thanked her and a younger woman struggled with a leather tunic, leggings, and a coat of chain mail that I recognized as my mother's. My mother had always dressed in this armor that she had earned through Scathach's training and today I would wear it. I hoped that I would bring honor to her and my father.

As each piece of clothing touched my skin, I felt my mother's spirit quiet my fears and still my emotions. This was the moment in my life that would make me a warrior and future queen. I did not intend to usurp the crown from my father, and I did not want to ruin the relationship with my brother, although ours was never one of great fondness. My brother tolerated me and always sought to keep me in the background. He tried to instill the idea in my father that women were not able to fight or rule. He forgot the power of the goddess and the abilities of our Celtic women. In his warped mind, Cairpre believed that our mother's death at his birth was a sign of female weakness and their inability to fight or rule.

I tamed my wild red tresses and braided them down my back. Brina spoke, "Maecha, you are truly your mother's child. I cared for her when she was younger than you and I see her in your eyes. Her spirit is with us today." She paused looking out the window. "I think that she and your father would want you to have something as a symbol of your status." Brina turned and went to my bed, where she opened a bundle of cloth. She revealed a sword and scabbard that I had only heard about.

"Brina," I began. "How did my mother get such a magical sword?"

Brina looked past me in remembrance. "When your mother was training with Scathach on the Isle of Imbas Skye, there was a band of rogues who had found their way through the mists into the island's secret entrance. Those who had been initiated into Scathach's group of warriors knew how to get to the entrance, but only the boatman could find his way through the mist that had forever kept the island safe from invaders. Most were terrified of Scathach's fury and would not take the risk to enter.

"However, one enemy of the Fianna, Conan Maol, had found his way into the mists by following a group of students."

Maecha remembered the terrible stories about how he and the sons of Morna had killed Fionn mac Cumhail's father, the first captain of the Fianna, in battle. Because of his death, Fionn's mother, Muirne, escaped with Fionn to the woods of Sleive Bladhma when he was just a babe. She feared for his life. Two women warriors, Bodhmall the Bendrui and Liath Luachra raised Fionn well.

Brina went on. "Although his followers were slain before they could reach the mists, he killed the escort and boatman and managed to find his way across. He threatened the students' lives for some of the treasures that he knew were hidden on the island. This man took the Cloak of Immortality, which would prevent him from being mortally wounded while wearing it. Conan managed to escape that day and came back two times before he was killed. He had taken the Brooch of Strength the next time and came back a third time, confident that he could not be defeated. He demanded the Sword of Souls, which carried the spirits of all those who had owned it before. Their skills, knowledge, and bravery would join the warrior who wore it and the more she used it, the stronger she and the sword would become.

"But these treasures could only be used by those deemed worthy. Thinking he was immortal with the strength of the gods, Conan invaded the island. Your mother was in her final year of training and had proved to be a cunning and powerful warrior. She was asked to bring the Sword of Souls to Conan. My dear Deirdre went into the room and when she came back with the sword it was unsheathed. Those who saw her said the golden spirits of the greatest warriors swarmed around her and blessed her as its new owner.

"Conan was furious and so challenged her. With the sword singing high over her head, your mother spun around and removed Conan's head from his body. She then removed the Cloak of Immortality and the Brooch of Strength and, sheathing the sword, presented them back to Scathach. Scathach had not told her students that those unworthy to use the sword would be killed by the spirits protecting it. So knowing that Deirdre was truly worthy of it, she presented it back to her as her gift for ridding the island of a terrible enemy."

I smiled in remembrance of my mother and only wished that I could have half her strength and confidence. Brina picked up the sword. The scabbard was plain. It was made from thick leather and was tanned to the darkest brown. Without removing the sword, Brina held the handle toward me. She respected its power and did not wish to offend any spirits. The handle was magical. The pommel was shaped like an eye and would shine as blue as the sky when the sun gleamed on it. I did not know then that the "eye" would possess its own power. The handle was made of brass and was wrapped in a thin layer of gold wire with inlayed grooves. I placed my hand around the handle and my fingers settled into the grooves. As I pulled the sword from its scabbard, I could see the polished steel of the blade begin to glow. Brina told me that it was made from Damascus steel, which no one has ever been able to find again and so was thought to be a gift from the gods.

A white light pulsed beneath the scabbard that demanded to be released. I noticed the hilt. It was a gold hand that covered and protected mine. On its finger was a red ruby ring that also glowed brighter as I pulled the sword from its sheath. It matched the ring on my left hand that my father had given me when my mother died. It was called the Ring of Mercy, which had been passed through the long line of daughters from my mother's family. Whoever wore this ring was bound to show mercy to those deserving and relentless anger to those who defied our goddess.

My ring glowed and my body sung. I felt the spirits dance around me as they praised their goddesses and laughed. Their golden bodies flitted around and hugged me with strong emotion and acceptance. I even felt my mother. My mother! Of course she would be amongst its spirits and now she was with me again. "Welcome home, Mother," I said. I turned to Brina with the power of a queen and the spirits to guide me. "Thank you, Brina. My father will be forever grateful." I hugged her and, grabbing my mother's helmet, went to meet Cairpre.

When I stepped out of my room, Kelan was there, dressed in his war gear. He looked pleased and told me that he had done what I asked. I was sure that my brother knew of the assembly, but I would show respect by telling him.

I found my brother alone in my father's weapon room. He leaned forward in my father's chair holding his sword blade to his forehead. His eyes were closed and he seemed to be struggling with some dilemma. I felt an instance of hope and sympathy, thinking that maybe what Kelan had told me was wrong. But then he looked up and the surprise and disgust at my appearance told me all I needed to know.

I walked toward him looking around at my father's weapons. He had a fondness for weaponry and had collected many different swords, battleaxes, spears, and helmets that his enemies used. I always loved coming into this room when I was a little girl. My father would sit by the fire telling me about each weapon and the man who had used it against him. The helmets, he said, told the story of the warrior. Some would be simple for the warrior who could not afford anything more than protection. But others would be decorated with plumes from birds, or wolf tails, horsehair or even animal skulls. His favorite helmet was one that he had taken from the High King of Alba's son during a raid. The helmet covered the face except for the mouth and eyes. Animal tusks protruded from the top and a tail hung from the back. I noticed it was missing. I thought of the cowardly leader on the hill and looked at my brother.

Cairpre was the first to speak. "You are looking better, Maecha." Looking at my clothing, he added, "Why are you dressed in war gear?" He had not noticed the sword I had hidden under my cloak.

"Kelan told me about Father and your plans to wait out the Picts. I am sorry that I was not here to make that decision, but I am now and I disagree. We cannot wait around like helpless fools and let the Picts attack us. We must rally the Fianna and travel to find Father. I believe we should leave Tara well protected and attack first. We must not appear weak to our people either, Cairpre. I do appreciate your concern for the kingdom, but matriarchal sovereignty still reigns in this land. As the first-born, it is my responsibility to rule our kingdom until Father arrives. I'll need your advice, but I also need you to help gather our warriors. I have arranged for an assembly and I hope that you will support me and Father," I finished happy to have done so without interruption.

Cairpre stood up and paced. His already unruly red hair stood on end like he had just rolled in the hay fields. He shifted his eyes in anxiety like a caged animal who was determined to escape, but just couldn't find the way.

"No," he said and paused. "No, my dear sister. That is not how it is going to be. These men do not want a weak woman to rule their land. The idea of the goddess and her sovereign rule over the land is old. Men are stronger and should be able to choose who will rule instead of powerless females. I should be the one to take over. You will never have the capability to lead a troop and rule a kingdom, so I must do it for you and for our father."

I shifted my cloak over my shoulder to reveal the serpent coiled around my bicep eating its tail. It had been tattooed on my arm to seal my fate as the future ruler of the kingdom. I knew that the reason my father ruled as king was because my mother was queen and had chosen him as her consort. I also knew that there were those who no longer believed in the goddess and wanted to destroy her power. The fact that the Fianna warriors were only men was dangerous to the goddess.

I looked at Cairpre with cold eyes and spoke in my strongest voice. "The serpent on my arm reflects the all-knowing and all-powerful Goddess. She gave you life and she can take it away. Father, more than anyone else, knows that I am quite able to defend myself and our kingdom and, if you need some con-

141

vincing, let's go outside and find out whose sword sings the loudest."

Cairpre didn't move. I could see the longing for power in his eyes, but he still had fear of the Goddess as he very well should.

I continued, "The assembly has been called. You can show your support or you can claim yourself a traitor. I plan to restore our father to the throne. What your plans are I am not sure at the moment, but I will watch you, Brother." I turned to leave and then stopped.

"By the way, I was told that there was a man on horseback who watched the Picts attack Father. He wore a helmet with horns that sounds very much like the one Father took from the Scots. Besides being a coward for not fighting, the man is a thief. Whoever took the helmet is a traitor to our people. When I find out who this man is, I will kill him in Father's name," I said.

I chanced a look back at Cairpre and his face was whiter than before. *He knows the person,* I thought, and my mind refused the possibility that it could have been him. I would have to wait and see. I left to find Kelan.

2

Shannon didn't know what happened to her Uncle Frank's spirit. Maybe her dad's death killed his motivation as a police officer. He no longer seemed sure of his commitments and still couldn't, or wouldn't, give her any answers.

She knew that Benjamin Walker wasn't involved in this particular investigation. That was not promising. He had followed her outside of Frank's office, and assured her that he would stay on top of the case. She wanted to believe him, but wasn't sure how much influence he would have.

As Shannon walked out of her dad's old precinct, the sky loomed dark and the clouds hung low with the threat of snow. Shannon thought of how determined her father and sister were when it came to helping children. They stood behind their beliefs 100%, no matter what it cost them. She had never put herself on the line, even in her professional career, but now it was time to make a decision. She would find her sister and end this whole drug lord escapade. She knew that Vince would help and Ben seemed to be drawn into their circle, so she would let him help her for now.

After Shannon had retrieved Max, she went home and read recent entries in Michaela's journal.

Dream Journal—September 15, 2000, 5:00 AM

A man walks up to me confused. He knows me, but he looks different. His hair is long and his mustache is thin and hangs down into his beard. His name is Cormac and he has been looking for me to take him home. He tells me the year he was born and it was a long time ago. He isn't doing well in our time, so I can't get him to talk much. He disappears and I look in books for his description and travel to cemeteries looking for his ancestors, but I must travel far to do this. I vaguely remember the man and believe that I was supposed to return to finish something. He needs me.

Response: Without his facial hair, this man looked a lot like Dad. I don't remember what he was wearing, but something around his neck looked thick and gold color? Maybe he is from Celtic Ireland. Not sure, but his presence felt warm to me and I know he needs me.

"Why have you come here?" Ricky said trying hard not to raise his voice. He was hosting a business party at his house when Frank Goodale charged in. Ricky smelled the powerful stench of alcohol steaming from Frank's pores. He needed to be careful. He led Frank into a private room and motioned for two of his men to stand guard outside the door.

Frank Goodale was scared and desperate. All those he loved had died, disappeared, or left him. No one knew the emotional turmoil that threatened to overcome him. Shannon's disappointment was more than he could handle, so he had to go to the source of the problem.

"You know damn well why I'm here, Rrricky," Frank slurred. "Where is Michaela?"

Ricky grabbed some glasses and rum.

"Settle down, Frank. Have a drink and let us talk about this," he said. "First, let me say that I am just as distraught about Michaela's disappearance as you are. I made a promise to her mother that I would take care of them if something happened to dear old Jack."

"Even if you took care of Jack yourself?" Frank blurted.

Ricky Cartillo's eyes narrowed to dangerous slits and he focused on Frank's face like it was the last time he would see him. He spoke, "If you want to live, then I suggest that you never ever think that thought again. You know who I am. I do not give a damn what you think about what I do. But I can squash you like a little bug and flick you back into the dirt where you came from."

Frank jumped up, but Ricky was too fast and pushed him back into his chair with his hand tight on his throat. "I do not know what happened to Michaela. If you are stupid enough to come to me, then I guess I was wrong thinking that you have her hidden somewhere. I will find her though, so you can just relax and go back to your lethargic life as a police officer and leave the business to those of us who have the power to get things done. This is not your league anymore, Frank. It never really was," he said releasing Frank's throat. "Jack was always the strong one and now that he is gone, you are mighty vulnerable. So watch your back." He tapped Frank on the cheek. "Boris!"

"Yeah, Boss," Boris said right at the door. A fedora covered his bandaged head.

"Make sure Mr. Goodale gets home safely tonight."

"No problem."

Without another look, Frank allowed himself to be taken from his enemy's house and brought home like a runaway teenager. Defeated and disgusted, Frank cried himself to sleep.

Captain Newman was busy at his desk sorting through the day's work. It was mid-morning and already the day seemed to drag on with all the scum filing in. He was in a bad mood, so the email that he received from Ricky Cartillo didn't cheer him up. It read:

Newman,
Meet me at my warehouse at 1pm sharp! Come alone.
RC

"What could that bastard want now?" Newman thought. They had only met together a few times in the past years and it was usually when there was a problem. He figured it had to do with the Sommers girl's disappearance.

"Barry, my boy!" Ricky called, as Newman entered the main warehouse. He put his arm around the captain's shoulder, and continued, "I hope all is well down at the precinct."

"Yes, yes all is fine, Mr. Cartillo, but I'm pretty busy. What's going on?"

"Please, sit down." Cartillo waved his hand toward a chair. At the back of the warehouse was an office that only Ricky and his most trusted men had a key to. The rich mahogany furniture and deep burgundy rug were a warm contrast to the cold steel and concrete in the rest of the warehouse. The room was windowless and the desk lamps cast shadows around the room. This was where Cartillo performed his most intimate business deals.

"As you know, I am a man of vision. You have been with my operation for a long time and you have reaped the benefits. Your children attend a prestigious private school. You own a beautiful home in Vermont to ski and a condo in Florida right on the beach. Because of my generosity, you and your family have wanted for nothing and, in return, you have allowed me to run my business the way I deem suitable. I respect your authority and trust your business integrity. But there is something that bothers me," he paused as he puffed on his fat Cuban cigar.

Newman knew better than to interrupt Cartillo's monologue so he kept quiet and waited.

Cartillo exhaled and continued. "I have a strong interest in the missing Sommers girl." Newman hid his smirk. "Her safety is of great concern to me and yet you have not found her." Ricky leaned forward, "Where is she?"

Newman shifted in his seat. "I don't know. I sent a couple guys up north to scout around and they haven't seen anything. That sheriff is a real redneck and probably couldn't find his ass in the morning, so I don't see much hope."

Cartillo slammed his hand on the desk and walked around it. "I need hope, Newman, and I want her back!"

Newman started to get up. "I'll get right on it, Mr...."

Cartillo shoved him back in his chair and kept his hands securely on Newman's shoulders. Newman winced, but remained still.

Ricky moved back and leaned on his desk. He smoked his cigar. "I heard that Michaela was attacked in an alley after she was beaten on the subway. Did you have anything to do with that?"

Newman respected and feared this man. He needed to save his ass.

"It was Malowski...augh!" Newman gasped as Ricky kicked his heel into Newman's groin. He twisted his foot.

"Malowski does what you say and so I hold you responsible. You worthless, ungrateful lout! Find Michaela," he pressed harder. "Or else I will get angry."

He stepped away and Newman fell forward.

"And get rid of that Goodale character. He is a nuisance,"

Ricky said. He turned to Newman. "Well, what are you waiting for? Get out!"

"Yes, Mr. Cartillo," Newman croaked and crawled toward the door.

Natalie woke with a start. She had forgotten where she was, but the strong stench of human excrement brought her back to reality. She fought for her life on the street and had to change her location often. The alley where she had found herself last night was especially vile with sick people coughing and vomiting all around her. She needed to stay healthy and alert, so she left her living hell.

Natalie felt very jittery this morning. She had dreamt again and knew that she would be rescued, but she would have to lead the way. There was chaos in the air and all hell was going to break loose, before this nightmare ended. She had dreamt about the woman on the horse who looked so much like Michaela and she had seen herself in a long white robe riding behind the woman and holding on for dear life. They were being chased by someone or something and whatever it was, it was after her. Even in her dreams, Natalie was on the run.

Natalie feared for Michaela. She hadn't seen her for a couple days. She knew Michaela's schedule. Natalie watched her go from her studio to her favorite restaurants, to home. She already loved her dog, Max, and wished she could pet him. But Cartillo's men knew all this and they were always one step behind Natalie. She knew that if she went to Michaela, they would both be dead. She had to figure out a way to find Michaela, but she was afraid that Cartillo had removed her like he did her father. Tears streamed down her dirty face as she thought of all the destruction Ricky Cartillo had caused.

Now Natalie was forced to take the next move and she

had to do it fast. She had to get to Michaela's sister. She had started to watch her, but wasn't sure yet if anyone else was watching Shannon. She needed to watch, listen and wait, but soon enough Shannon Sommers would meet Natalie Fischer.

3

I found Kelan by the sacred stones of Tara. These stones were used in ceremonies to anoint a new queen and her king and to celebrate our lives and ancestors during Samhain and Beltane. It was near the time of Samhain, our New Year, when all the harvest fruits are gathered and offerings are made to our ancestors. It is the time between times, when the spirits of the Otherworld come forth and mingle with us. It is a time when sovereignty is strengthened and the gods and goddesses are honored. My mother's spirit would be among them and I waited anxiously for her guidance.

I approached Kelan where he spoke with two other men. Upon my arrival they all moved away and greeted me. I recognized Caoilte mac Ronan, Fionn's nephew.

"Caoilte, I am sorry for your loss. Fionn was special to all of us and I know you were very close," I said and squeezed his arm in support.

Caoilte was fair-skinned with wispy, pale hair. He looked at me. His pale blue eyes betrayed his stoic face. He nodded and turned away with the shyness that had been with him all of his nineteen summers.

Next to him was Goll mac Morna. Goll was a very large warrior and towered over Kelan, who was not small by any means. His face had been scarred by many battles and he wore a black patch over his right eye, where he had been stabbed. Rarely seen without his battle-axe and mace in his hand, he carried his weapons like twigs; their weight nothing in his tree trunk arms. His enemies often fell to their death in fear when they saw this crazy Celt running toward them with his weapons being effortlessly swung and his red hair flying to and fro with a spiked ball tied to the end of it. Goll had been a bitter enemy of Fionn's for a long time. He had ruled parts of the Fianna long before Fionn was old enough to be its leader and it was no secret that he longed to be the leader of the entire Fianna.

However, throughout his battles, Fionn had proven his leadership and won the loyalty of Goll. When my father bestowed the captaincy of the Fianna upon Fionn, he asked Goll if he would stay and serve under Fionn mac Cumhail or suffer banishment from Ireland forever. Goll's one eye never wavered from the king. He vowed to serve under Fionn and if he failed they could strike him down where he stood. From that day on Goll's loyalty was never again questioned. But with Fionn's death, I feared that his old desire to be leader would return.

"May I ask what the three of you were discussing with such intensity?" I said.

Stepping forward, Goll surprised me by kneeling and taking my hand. He said, "My lady. First, it is very important that you know that I loved Fionn mac Cumhail and would have given my life to keep him as the true leader of the Fianna. We have been left with a gaping wound that I am not sure any leader will ever be able to fill. Second, I love the king, your father, like a brother and the injustice that has been done to him has also been done to me. I plan to travel to the end of the world to find him and bring him home alive. Finally, I will give my life for you in battle and deem you as our leader until your father returns."

Caoilte came forward and pledged his loyalty to me and Kelan did the same only with my hand touching his forehead. I felt a special bond toward him and something else that I could not recognize. When Kelan stood up, I could tell by his eyes that he had felt something, too.

After they had pledged their loyalty, they expressed their concerns about my leading the warriors and the kingdom. They were afraid that people would not support me, since I wasn't a very seasoned warrior and it appeared that Cairpre had poisoned some of their beliefs about sovereignty belonging to the Goddess.

I thought about what they had said. I asked, "What would give people confidence in my ability to rule?"

Goll began. "You can be inducted as a warrior and the acting queen at Samhain, while the other leaders are present. As for the warriors, they need to trust your leadership and there is only one way for this to happen." He hesitated, looked at the other two and continued. "We believe you and Kelan should be tested to join the Fianna."

He saw my shock and added, "And if you prove to be successful in this test, we and all of the Fianna would be honored to have you as our leader."

I walked to the sacred stone and placed my forehead against the cool rock. The coolness calmed my head and allowed me to feel the spirits that were always with the stones. They pulsed around me and gave me strength. Turning toward my three supporters, I swung my cloak over my shoulder revealing the sword that I have henceforth named Imbas Skye, after Scathach's Isle of Skye. It meant the Light of Skye and I hoped that Scathach's power and light would shine on me.

Satisfied with *their* shocked faces, I released the sword from its scabbard and swung it over my head into the Stone of Destiny that was encircled by three standing stones. The stone split into three lines pointing toward each of the outlying standing stones. The Druids believed that a true leader would pierce the stone of sovereignty. Each standing stone stood for Truth, Honor, and Justice. Upon seeing the stone yield to my sword, each man stepped within the circle and stood with his back against a stone. Goll mac Morna stood at the Stone of Justice, Caoilte mac Ronan at the Stone of Truth and Kelan mac Nessa at the Stone of Honor. I was the holder of Imbas Skye, the Sword of Souls and the Sovereign of Tara. With that I accepted the challenge of the Fianna and, along with Kelan, would take the test to join them as their leader and brethren.

"Where do you come from?" Maecha asked Michaela who had been visiting her dreams, since she hit her head.

Amazed that she could understand this warrior, Michaela replied, "I come from far away." She huddled against a tree hugging her knees, looking lost and forsaken.

Although Maecha still considered her a demon come to drive her mad, she felt pity for her. "Why are you here?" Maecha asked.

"I don't know," Michaela could only say.

Maecha sneered, "Well I have much greater concerns on my mind. Leave me be, so that I can prepare for my day." At that, Michaela watched Maecha prepare for her departure to the Otherworld and she sensed that her own fears added to the girl's lack of confidence and fear of what she would find tomorrow. With that, Michaela stood up and began to practice her katas. Seeing her, Maecha drew her sword and practiced.

Maecha knew that her skills as a swordswoman were better than most of the warriors in Kelan's band. However, she couldn't help but watch the woman named 'Mikala'. Her hands swung like swords and her feet flew like flails. She was intrigued by this type of fighting and thought that it might give her an advantage. She approached Michaela, "What do you call this type of fighting?"

"This is called Karate," Michaela said. "I am doing a kata, which is a set of movements that train the body to defend itself against an attacker."

"Cada," pronounced Maecha. "I like it. Can I use it with my sword?"

Michaela smiled, happy to be distracted from her mysterious location. "Yes. I will show you."

I felt good the next morning. I remembered my dream and the mysterious woman who seemed to have found a home in my land of dreams. I also remembered her strange way of fighting. *Cada'me* I decided to call it and looked forward to a chance to try it.

Goll mac Morna assumed leadership of the Fianna until I could pass the test. We all felt that the warriors and leaders would listen to a well-seasoned warrior rather than a young woman who had only fought in a few skirmishes before the Pict attack.

I met Kelan by the sacred stones. I was scared and uncertain of my abilities or what to expect. I only remembered the stories from my childhood about how some of our best warriors entered the Cave of the Warrior and never returned, or if they did return, their minds were gone from them forever. I didn't want to express my concerns to Kelan for fear that he would not let me go.

"I don't know what to expect Maecha and that scares me," he began. "We are fortunate to be entering together. I don't believe anyone has ever done that before, but then again, I don't think a woman has ever had the chance to join this special group."

Relieved, I smiled, "I am glad to hear you say that, Kelan. We must protect one another to come out together or not at all."

Kelan shook his head. "No. Under no circumstances should you stay behind to save me. We do not know what will confront us, but it is more important for you to remain alive."

"You don't understand, Kelan. I am not a whole warrior without you. You have always been there for me and I consider you to be part of who I am. Next to my father, there is no one that I love more. I need you. I cannot keep this group and my father's kingship together without you. So you have no choice but to return with me. I demand it," I said squeezing his arm. I hoped that the choice to come out alone wouldn't happen. Goll had arrived with the other chief warriors of the Fianna and kings who had been with King Cormac when he was taken. The other leaders would arrive in the next few days hopefully in support of what we were about to do.

Goll spoke in a deep and strong voice. "As many of you witnessed, the High King of Tara, Cormac mac Art, has been taken by the savage Picts and as far as we know is on his way back to their native land by way of sea. We do not know whether or not the king lives. I believe that if they meant to kill him, they would have done so during battle. But whether or not he is alive, he is not here to rule and guide us. In the name of sovereignty, I stand by Maecha Ruadh mac Art as acting queen until the king is returned. Maecha Ruadh agrees that we should move forward and not wait for further attacks. She has been trained by one of our best warriors, Kelan mac Nessa, and she has been schooled in the laws of our land."

Goll waited for the rumbling of the crowd to settle. Then he continued, "Also, in light of the unfortunate and tragic death of our leader and the king's champion, Fionn mac Cumhail, I have passed the leadership of the Fianna to Maecha, upon one condition. She must pass the test of the Cave of the Warrior."

First, there was silence and then the terrified and shocked looks on the warriors' faces. Next, there was the uproar about a woman joining the band of warriors. Osgar Conchobar, leader of the Fianna of Leinster, was the first to be heard. "We do not mean to be disrespectful, your ladyship, but a woman has never gone into the Cave of the Warrior. I don't think there is a woman alive who even knows where it is."

"Plus, you are too young and inexperienced to venture on such a quest," said Fercobh McDermott, King of Munster. "We cannot afford to lose you." The third leader from the county Roscommon of Connacta, Ferlaigh mac Morna, remained silent and nodded agreement with the others.

Goll was about to plead to them on my behalf, when I raised my hand for silence. "Who will lead you? I do not doubt that Goll mac Morna would make a strong and loyal leader, but he is not the chosen leader. Will you choose my brother, who has made known that he will let my father rot away in a foreign land, while he reaps the benefits? He will let this land and people fall back into the chaos that you, the Fianna, have worked so hard to end. This land is still ruled by the Sovereign Goddess. Until she has spoken, it is known that the eldest daughter shall rule in the absence of a rightful king. Cairpre was not chosen by the land and he is not blessed by the Sovereign Goddess. Let him lead and you will lose more men. So many have already fallen: Flann the eloquent hero is no more, the three sons of Criomhall, the fault-less Green Fian, Daighre the bright lad is no more, Banbh Sionna can no longer raise the shout, Fionn's offspring, Oisin of admirable warrior-skill, his children, Oisin of great beauty, and Oscar are no more! And so many more are gone from us!"

I could see the sense of loss and despair on their faces, but they still did not consider me as a possible leader. "What exactly is it that all of you are afraid of?" I asked walking up to each of them. "Is it that I will know where your special place is? Or is it that you are truly concerned for my safety as your sovereign queen? Or perhaps you are afraid that once one woman shows you that it can be done, others will want to follow in my foot-steps? And is that so bad? Doesn't the Goddess shower you with the fertility of this land? Doesn't she keep you strong and guide your kingdoms? Can you not stand to look a woman warrior equally in the eye?"

"It's not that, my lady," stammered Osgar. "It's just not right and...you don't know what horrors are out there and well...I, for one, don't think you can do it. I'm sorry," he finished.

Now everyone knew that the best way to get my father to do something was to say that he could never do it. Little did these men know that this trait ran true and strong in my soul and it made my blood boil to hear someone say I couldn't become a member of the Fianna. "Do you know who I am named after?" They all nodded. "Don't you think that Macha of the Red Tresses saw and dealt with the horrors and atrocities that all of you have dealt with in this cave? And who have all of you trained under at one time in your lives? You know—Scathach, whose name means 'the woman who strikes fear' and possibly the greatest warrior who has ever lived! Her daughter, Uatach the Terrible, could conquer any man here. And who was my mother? Queen Deirdre was the best warrior that Scathach ever trained. She was responsible for relieving the Isle of Imbas Skye of that fool Conan Maol...with this!" I said as I pulled out the Sword of Souls and raised it above my head. Once again, I saw the awesome power that the sword could display and as I marveled at its beauty and power, I saw that it had captured the men's attention as well.

Lowering the sword I planted its tip into the ground. I looked at every single man present and spoke loud and strong. "Since I was a little girl, I have dreamed of being a member of the Fianna's elite and magnificent group. I have admired all of you and I have envied the friendships that you have shared amongst yourselves and with Fionn. I cannot expect you to befriend me. But this I will tell you. I will be a faithful member and I will protect each and every one of you with my life." I paused to let my words sink in. "I will go into the Cave of the Warrior and I will come out victorious. I am fortunate enough to have my champion, Kelan mac Nessa, as another contender for this honor. But, when I emerge I will have earned the right to be called a sister of the Fianna and I hope to earn your respect," I finished and stood next to Kelan.

When no one responded, Goll stepped in between us, and grabbing our hands held them up high. "Do all present accept the contenders Maecha Ruadh mac Art and Kelan mac Nessa for entry into the Cave of the Warrior?" he asked. Caoilte was the first to accept us and then the others relented. Goll continued, "Upon their victorious return, do all here accept Maecha Ruadh mac Art as the undisputed leader of the Fianna and acting queen of Tara, and Kelan mac Nessa as her champion?"

The men looked at one another. Osgar took a deep breath and raised his hand. Caoilte did the same.

Osgar turned to the men. "We are either together or we are nothing."

The rest raised their hands.

4

I clasped arms with all the Fianna warriors. Some hugged me, while others whispered words of advice or stood aloof with resentment. I let them be, hoping that my victory would change their mind. I could bring Imbas Skye and a dagger, and Kelan carried similar weapons. Anything else we needed would be provided in the Otherworld. The three leaders who had doubted me had decided to accompany us. Ferlaigh mac Morna was eager to see his new bride, Treasa. I wanted to meet her, since she had studied weaponry under the tutelage of Scathach. I had heard that she traveled her borders with a group of female warriors and each one was more formidable than the next. I believed that Osgar Conchobar and Fercobh McDermott both accompanied us out of an obligation to my father. They each had a band of warriors with them and so just days before Samhain, we began our journey west.

I thought about all I would need to do in the few days before the festival. I thought about my mother and all that she had accomplished in her life at my age. I felt young and inexperienced. This journey would prove me a warrior as well as a woman and leader.

"What deep thoughts are mulling around in your head, Maecha?" Kelan asked trotting up next to me in the afternoon sun.

I looked at my confident champion and masked my doubts. "I was thinking how nice it would be to beat you and your horse over that hill!" I yelled and broke into a neck-breaking gallop.

Shaking his head, Kelan let me get a head start. Then he whispered in his horse's ear, "Go get her, Octar." The horse took off across the lush green plains. I chanced a look back and saw Kelan gaining on me much faster than I had anticipated. I was not used to my new horse, Finn, and didn't want to push him any harder. I had left my trusted Aeiden at home and hoped that this beast would fill the gap for now. As I reached the summit of the hill, Kelan breezed past and stopped at the top. Octar whinnied and raised its front paws up in the air in triumph. "Good boy," Kelan said patting him.

I took my time catching up. "You and that horse are quicker than the gods, Kelan!" I turned to look for the River Shannon and grabbed Kelan's arm.

He followed my gaze to the river's edge and raised his arm in alarm to the others. Goll mac Morna and Caoilte mac Ronan raced to the top, while the others released their swords in preparation for battle.

"What is it, Kelan?" Goll asked as he reached the top. His question was answered as he stared in horror. As the group of thirty-plus warriors gathered on the hill, they all surveyed the scene below and waited for instruction. Goll took over, "Half go down to see if there are survivors and the other stay up here and let us know if you see the enemy. Caoilte, stay up here and wait for my command."

"I will," Caoilte answered, honored to have Goll's trust. We treaded our way down the hill, closer to the massacre that I hoped was an apparition. The stench was overwhelming and I saw Kelan's jaw clench at the sight of so many dead women and children. We did not know why so many people would be gathered this far from their village, without any provisions or warriors to protect them. Farther along south of the river, Kelan saw armored men and went to look. Fercobh went with him.

"They look like they were dragged here to be killed," I said to no one in particular. I heard a grunt and looked toward Osgar. He was an aged warrior who had seen as many battles as my father. His silver hair was thick and hung down over his forehead. He brushed the hair away and pulled on his long silver beard. The base of his chin and mustache still retained some trace of its dark, black color. He was clad in full leather armor and he carried it well on his large frame. His light blue eyes were scrunched in disgust. No amount of war and death could numb you from the pain of seeing so many people slain.

He put his arm on my shoulder and said, "Aye, I think you are right, daughter of Cormac."

"But who would have done this, Osgar?" I asked wanting to know who could be this ruthless.

"Look at this," he motioned toward a woman sprawled on her back. An elaborate sword protruded from her midsection. Osgar pointed to the detail on the sword's hilt. "These symbols are of Pictish origin. The animals represent their tribe."

I looked closer and could see two wolves with long necks wrapped around each other. The artwork was simple, but clear, and Osgar did not doubt its origin.

"But, what were the Picts doing so far inland and why would they kill all these women and children? And where were the men to protect them?" I asked.

"They were coming to help," Kelan said behind me. His face was drawn tight and I knew his childhood memories haunted him. Kelan saw the sword and nodded his head as if to confirm his suspicions. "It seems that the Picts have ventured further into our land than we had anticipated. From the decay on these bodies, they were killed about the same time that we were attacked. That means that someone planned all these attacks to happen at once. These bloody barbarians might still be in Eire."

"I agree," replied Goll. "Be on alert and stay together. Let's bury our fellow comrades. We have found a shallow passage across the river. We must get over it and have a secure shelter by nightfall."

The men moved about through the motions, but I mourned the children. It took us most of the day to finish. Our bodies were caked with sweat and dirt and my pores reeked of death. I walked my horse through the water and dipped under to clean the stench off me.

We found shelter by a hill, with a cave of stone inlaid within it. It was dry, but not big enough for all of us. Most of the warriors chose to sleep under the stars anyway. Goll and Kelan decided that I would sleep inside the cave with Kelan guarding the entrance, just in case the Picts were nearby.

"Kelan, I can sleep outside. These men need to respect me!" I said not wanting to be treated like a soft girl.

"I understand that you are eager to show your leadership, but you will have more than enough time to do that. Let's make sure that you get into the cave in one piece first," he said.

"Fine," I said, "but I'm not tired and I would like to sit by the fire, if that is fine for an acting queen to do!"

"Be my guest, my queen," Kelan laughed. I brushed past him and joined the men.

Goll passed me a cup of mead and dried meat and everyone settled in closer to the fire. It was a cool, clear night and the moon rose high above us waiting to shine its full light upon Samhain night. Some of the younger men who were huddled near the outskirts of the group were arguing. Kelan recognized the boys as brothers who were aspiring to be great warriors. Goll thought this journey would be a good experience for them.

"What are you two quarrelling about?" Kelan yelled.

The older brother named Aonghus spoke in a vigorous voice. "My little brother, Mairtin, does not believe that the famous Fionn mac Cumhail slayed a serpent from inside its

162

belly." Urged on by the sounds of disbelief amongst the crowd and his brother's cowering stare, he continued. "As a matter of fact, he doesn't believe any of the fantastic stories about the Fianna. I have tried to tell many of them, but alas I do not know as much as I would like."

Osgar Conchobar kneeled over the fire and stirred the kindling, which sent sparks flipping through the air. He stood up and his large frame towered over the warriors. His demeanor and the sparkle in his eyes demanded silence, for he was even better at storytelling than he was a warrior.

"So, you think that my dear friend, Fionn, was a warrior with a fanciful way with words?" He looked at Mairtin and went on. "Fionn Mac Cumhail was no ordinary child. He was born to Cumall, son of Trenmore, and Muirne of the fair neck and given the name of Demne. Bodball the Bendrui and the Gray One of Luachar came and took the babe away from Muirne and went into the forest of Sliab Bladma. This was necessary since Goll mac Morna, in another time and place, had killed Demne's father." Osgar looked at Goll, who nodded his head in acquiescence. "Since Goll had lost one eye in that battle, there were many hostile warriors and sons of Morna lying in wait for the boy.

"As Demne grew, he learned to hunt and to fight. One day, he went out alone until he reached Mag Life. At a certain stronghold there he saw youths playing hurly upon the green of the stronghold. He went to contend in running or in hurling with them. He won. He came again the next day and they put one-fourth of their number against him, and the next day one-third against him. At last they all went against him and he still beat them all.

"They asked his name and he told them, Demne. They told the chief of the stronghold and he said to kill this boy who could beat them so. They did not think they would be able to and the chief asked what he looked like. They said he was a shapely fair (*finn*) youth. The chief recognized the greatness in the boy

163

and said that he should be called Fionn 'the Fair'."

Maecha listened with wide eyes and a heavy heart. She missed Fionn *and* her father. She looked around the fire and saw Goll, the one-eye, staring into the flames. She wondered if he ever felt that he had repaid his debt to Fionn and his father. Maecha no longer doubted Goll's loyalty and understood why her father gave others a second chance. She wondered about the person who had arranged all these battles and kidnapped her father. He would not be given a second chance. She listened as Osgar continued his story, even though the mead had started to make her sleepy.

"Fionn's skill in fighting plus his strength made him a ruthless opponent. He had killed more than one giant in his day."

"Who?" Mairtin interrupted.

Osgar looked at the boy. He took a deep breath and his body seemed to grow even taller over the flames of the fire and he glowed with the magic of a storyteller. "There was a serpent that killed and ate people. The Fianna went to fight it and the serpent ate many of them. Fionn challenged the serpent and it swallowed him. Fionn raised his sword within the belly of the serpent and cut from the inside, releasing the men and killing the serpent. Fionn also slew the monster of Loch Neagh, the serpent of Benn Edair, the blue serpent of the Erne, the phantom and serpent of Glenarm, the serpent of singing Bann and many more. He has slain many a mighty monster and his stories will live on as he does in our hearts," Osgar finished.

"What about Aillen mac Midhna?" Aonghus asked. "Who will fight the monster on Samhain Eve?"

"Ah yes," Osgar said. "Aillen mac Midhna is a demon that causes havoc every Samhain Eve. The story goes that Fionn's father had left Fionn the Crane bag, a bag of treasures he had received from Manannan mac Lir, the Irish Sea God. Among these treasures were the Cap of Silence and a poisonous spear. So bloodthirsty was this spear that the head of it had to be wrapped in seven layers of wet leather and kept in a bucket of water, and it was chained to a wall, so it couldn't escape and kill everyone within reach. The spear's name was Birgha, and it was Aillen's own spear. He had lost it long ago to the sea god and wanted it back.

"On the following Samhain when Aillen came to play his Sidhe music that put everyone to sleep, Fionn put on the Cap of Silence. After everyone had fallen asleep, Aillen started to bellow fire out of his mouth. Fionn attacked him and Aillen ran away. Just as he was about to escape into his Sidhe, Fionn threw the spear and killed him. But different shapes of Aillen come back every year and Fionn has always managed to defeat them. Fionn saved the high king from the demonic attack of that fire-breathing beast. That is how he became leader of the Fianna at such a young age. He proved his strength and prowess and gained more honor that night than a hundred men in battle."

Goll mac Morna spoke. "Osgar, we thank you for keeping Fionn alive in our hearts with your powerful storytelling. We will discuss the problem of Aillen after Maecha and Kelan begin their journey. I will fight this monster myself, if necessary. Now it is late. Let us get some sleep." He turned to Maecha to send her into the cave, but she was asleep against Kelan's arm.

Kelan and Goll both smiled. "It seems that our queen must work on her late night listening skills," Kelan chuckled. Moving Maecha, he scooped her up in his arms and carried her to the cave. When he came out, Goll was there.

"What think you, my friend?" Goll asked.

Kelan knew what his question referred to and he was not about to let any doubts mar his journey. "She is the daughter of the best leaders and warriors I have ever known. She will find her way and when she does, she will shine brighter than her parents. Fear not, Goll, I will protect her with my life and make sure she is ready."

Walk toward the battle. Imbas Skye is released and her eye glows a cold blue. The earth shakes and cracks. Horns protrude from the earth. I run, but trip over the horns and they lift me off the ground. I am thrown. He is there. The man in the helmet. The horns point toward me in anger. The eyes burn with hatred. I shield my face with my arms and Imbas Skye is raised in front of me. A blue light flashes. They are gone.

I woke up in a cold sweat and grasped Imbas Skye. I thought about my dream. The man who had stolen my father's helmet was the man who was responsible for killing all those people by the river, the Fianna warriors, and for kidnapping my father. I touched the closed eye on my sword's hilt, but nothing happened.

We broke fast and continued our journey. We reached the Seaghais River and followed it toward Roscommon. Ferlaigh sent scouts ahead to make sure that the Picts were not waiting for us. Ferlaigh had been on edge since we found the slain victims, because his land was only a day's journey from there. If the Picts had ventured this far into Eire, there was no telling which direction they would continue in.

Upon hearing Ferlaigh's fears, Osgar said, "Afraid for your wife?! Dear man, I would be afraid for any Pict stupid enough to venture into the land of Treasa and her warriors. They patrol and protect your land as good as any Fianna."

Ferlaigh smiled an uneasy smile, but my mind began to spin with ideas. If Queen Treasa and her warriors, who were women, were good enough to serve in the Fianna, how many other female warriors were out there who should be given the chance? I felt a sudden sense of pressure, thinking that their chance lay in my hands. If I failed, then I failed all these warriors. Before the doubt could settle in, I shook it away. I had to survive.

I had to come out of this cave stronger than before. The fate of my father and his kingdom depended on it.

Some time this afternoon we would reach Roscommon and the Cave of the Warrior. I had ridden much of the day lost in my own thoughts about a band of female warriors. Goll's war cry shattered my daydreams. Straightening in my saddle, I rode up to the front. Kelan was there and I chastised myself for not paying attention. A good warrior always knew what was going on around her.

"I've spotted a large band of warriors at the edge of Roscommon's village. I could not identify them, but they are heading our way, prepared for battle," the young scout reported.

Ferlaigh took over. "Were they women or men?"

The young scout laughed. "Women would never band together like that!" He kept laughing until he saw that, neither I nor the elder warriors shared his joke. Ferlaigh looked at Goll, but Goll nodded for him to continue.

"Prepare for battle! We must assume that these warriors are Picts until I establish that they are not," Ferlaigh yelled.

We rode with the three kings in front, Goll, Kelan, and myself behind them, and the rest of the warriors set up behind in a v-shaped formation. To get to Roscommon, we had to venture westward away from the water and had traveled through the forest. We were on the other side of the forest and the land rolled with green fields. Far in the horizon, there was a haze of blackness rising forth from the ground. It looked like an evil spirit escaping from the earth and my heart jumped at the apparition. But, an apparition it was not. The haze formed into a group of seasoned warriors. I had been so enthralled with the vision in front of me that I had failed to see the same thing happen on each side of us. We found ourselves surrounded by about 150 warriors. They did not attack, but they were not Picts. Their leader came forth driving a chariot, which was something that I had only heard about. It was made from wood, the front curved like

167

a woman's waist and the top and sides were trimmed with an ornate black metal that curled into fabulous intertwining knots. The team of horses that pulled it was pure white with eyes as black and dark as the night sky.

A woman drove the chariot. She rode like a queen who demanded respect and punished those who did not give it to her. This had to be the famous Queen Treasa mac Morna of Roscommon. I relaxed knowing we would not be under attack. I felt even better when Ferlaigh rode forward and greeted his wife. I noted that he greeted her as if he were a commoner. Treasa's reputation as a ruthless and dangerous enemy even scared her husband.

Ferlaigh took a moment and told his wife of the king's kidnapping and the slaughter we had come upon. As they spoke, I took note of her warriors. They all wore helmets and full leather or metal armor. Most were on a horse—some with two riders and the rest were on foot. They stood at command and did not move.

Then I looked at Treasa. Everything about her was regal. Her long, black, wavy hair hung down her back and was held off her forehead by a thick gold crown adorned with a green gem in the center. Her skin was fair and her cheekbones rose high on her face, elongating her nose and setting her lips thinly above her pointed chin. She wore ornate gold jewelry everywhere she could, from the gold torc on her neck to her thick earrings, to the rings on her fingers. She was not in armor like her warriors, but had ridden forth as their queen. Her gown was made from heavy wool and was a rich dark green. Her red cloak was held together by a gold brooch, which resembled a bull. It covered her shoulders and flowed down to the ground. Her bare arms bore the gold bands of her sisterhood. She was an amazing sight and I noted how all the men in our group seemed to be affected by her beauty.

Treasa stepped off her chariot and Ferlaigh stepped down from his horse to lead his queen to greet the others. We dismounted our horses and bowed to the queen. She let the men kiss her hands, but her eyes, black as her horse's stayed on me.

"Rise, daughter of Cormac, for it is I who should bow to you."

She bowed with a dramatic flair and then stood up tall once more. "Tell me something, Maecha? May I call you Maecha?" I nodded, but she had continued. "How does a child with limited training get to go on an adventure of such magnitude, without a hint of what you are capable of?"

She turned away from me before I could answer and studied Kelan. Studied was too light of a word. Her eyes dissected every part of his body. Even Kelan looked uncomfortable. "And how do you get such a voluptuous man to go with you!" she exclaimed as she walked around Kelan with her hands trailing wherever they wanted.

It was bad enough that most of the warriors in Kelan's band and the Fianna had doubted me, but now a student of Scathach questioned my right to be admitted into the Cave of the Warrior. If anyone should have been going through this, it should have been Treasa and I'm sure she would have done it better than half the men here. But I still believed with all my heart that I was the person to enter the cave and Kelan was the one to do it with me. I pulled Imbas Skye from her sheath. The pinkish, blue blaze of the setting sun shimmered along her blade and its fiery glow blinded those who watched.

"This sword belonged to my mother, Queen Deirdre, a grand warrior who studied under the tutelage of Scathach. Only those who are blessed by the previous owners of this sword are honored to wield it. I have been given that honor. I have also been given the privilege of leading the Fianna to Alba to save my father. I will serve as acting queen until my father has been returned to Eire. Kelan and I will emerge stronger. I ask that you allow us to venture into your land, so that we may enter the portal stone that leads to the Otherworld," I finished.

"I can see that you have inherited your parent's gift for words, but words will not save you on the battlefield. You have asked my permission and you are wise to do so, because not even my husband's word allows you to go forth." Ferlaigh looked embarrassed. "I am a reasonable woman, so I will let you come into Roscommon...on one condition." Now Ferlaigh looked enraged, but he did not step in, for his wife had the right of sovereignty to do this.

"This is what you must do to earn entrance to the cave. As every Fianna warrior knows, there are three physical challenges that are part of the initiation into this prestigious group. Have you performed them?" I looked at Kelan, because we had not.

"My lady! I am Goll mac Morna, current leader of the Fianna, upon the unfortunate death of Fionn mac Cumhail. Our band agreed to allow Maecha to join the Fianna and lead our group to save her father. It is customary that these challenges are performed after the warriors come out of the cave. As you are welcome at Tara for the Samhain celebrations, you may witness them there," he said.

Once again Treasa dissected Goll like she had done to Kelan. She was fond of standing close to people and she did this to Goll while studying his eye patch. "I remember the stories about you and your family, Goll. I could never figure out how your family could forgive the mac Cumhail's so that you could be a puppet under his leadership."

"Enough!" Ferlaigh interrupted.

Treasa turned on him. "I just wanted to know what could make this man so loyal to King Cormac and his daughter. Why didn't he just usurp everything for his own? For all I know he could be involved in the kidnapping and these attacks!"

"Goll mac Morna has proven his loyalty to the king and the Fianna. He does not have to answer your questions or defend your accusations, woman!" Ferlaigh yelled, nigh upon hysteria.

Kelan looked at me and nodded. I stepped forth. "Queen Treasa!" This time I moved close to her and she stepped back. She liked to be the aggressor, but appreciated those who stood up to her. "I understand your reservations about Goll mac Morna, for I had the same reservations when these tragedies occurred in our land. However, Goll has proven his loyalty to my father and to Fionn many times over through the years and, because of that, I trust him. He has pledged his loyalty to me and is bound to me through the code of justice, trust, and honor. He has vowed to bring down the traitor who has done this and has brought us thus far to you. I stand behind him, as I believe all his men will do.

"I know these challenges well, for it has always been my dream to become a member of the Fianna: stand in a hole up to my waist while nine warriors cast their spears at me; run through the woods with my hair braided while being pursued; leap over a bough as high as my forehead while in full flight and pass under one as low as my knee and draw a thorn from my foot without slackening my pace. These are the challenges that I know of and will complete under your judgment," I finished.

Treasa nodded with a look of mischief in her eyes. Stepping away from me, she walked to Kelan. She was as tall as Kelan and looked him in the eyes. I could see Kelan's jaw clench, but he kept still. She placed her hands on his chest and caressed it. My face went red and I tried to hide it. Nothing seemed to embarrass Treasa. "And you. You can either take on these silly challenges or you can satisfy me and gain entrance through my loins," she had whispered, but all of us heard as if the wind had carried her words to our ears. I knew that it was the right of the sovereign queen to take whatever man she deemed worthy, but I couldn't help but feel bad for Ferlaigh and I did not want Kelan to bed her.

Kelan took her hands and put them to his lips. He kissed each one with the respect due to a queen. He whispered so that

171

only she and I could hear. "As much as my body would enjoy the pleasure of your company, my heart and destiny are held with another and I must acquiesce upon fear of the Goddess. I will take the challenge with my acting queen."

Treasa stepped away with a stately bow and yelled for her warriors to escort us to her land.

Kelan and I rode in silence as we ventured toward their rath. We rode over the hill where I had seen Treasa and her warriors arise in the black apparition. As we crested the hill, my breath caught at the beauty of their estate. Water separated us from the castle. The fields were still green and surrounded the castle for miles around. The bridge to the castle was so wide four horses could walk on it side by side. Three towers stretched across the front, with the middle one rising high above the others. A guard on top yelled to lower the gate.

As we walked through the gates, the noise of the daily market shook me out of my revelry. Wooden houses were lined up against the inner stone walls. All types of wares were being sold. As I passed, the marketers paused from their bickering and negotiating to look up at the newcomers. Many did not know me, since I had never ventured this far from our kingdom and the poorer folk had never come to Tara for festivities. The travel was too dangerous.

However, the nobility did recognize me and bowed as I passed. I tried to appear regal. We passed through another entrance and were in the private area of the castle. Stable boys came and took our horses to feed and rub down. I patted mine before letting her go.

We walked up stone steps into a large assembly area. Treasa turned to us and said, "You must be tired from your journey. You will be shown to your rooms, where you can wash and then meet me here for some food. You will need strength for your challenges. Since you must leave in two days, you will rest today and then tomorrow morning, it will begin."

It was late in the day, and by the time we had washed and eaten, I could barely stand. I retired early, not caring what remarks followed me.

My room was lit by the glowing embers of a warm fire, and I looked forward to sleeping right next to it. As I turned, I caught the outline of a shadow behind the door. I acted as if I had seen nothing, but unsheathed my dagger as I appeared to undress. I saw the shadow elongate as it tiptoed toward me. I let it get closer and closer still. I grabbed my assailant by the cloak and stuck my dagger to his stomach.

"What do you want?" I snarled. A high pitched laugh escaped from my female assailant. Pulling back her hood, Treasa smiled and began to clap.

"Well done, child. I had my doubts about your ability to use those weapons, but I may be wrong," Treasa said.

"I will do fine, Treasa and I will succeed in all of my challenges," I said, not masking my irritation at her invasion.

"I hope you do, Maecha," she continued as the smile disappeared from her face. "Much depends on you being able to overcome your fears and succeed where no woman has ever even tried. Even Scathach has never been given this honor and she is ten times the warrior that you are. You must be destined for greatness. You do realize that if you fail, the Fianna will fall apart trying to get a new leader and your father will rot away in Alba before you ever get the chance to save him," she finished.

She was right, but I didn't appreciate her reminding me. "I know what I am up against and I believe that I have been blessed by the spirits of my sword. I know that I have much to learn, but I also know that I am capable of learning it. I am a good warrior," I said, trying to sound confident.

Treasa's eyes softened. "You are all these things and I

believe that you will do well. If you do, then I promise you that I, and my warriors, will assist you in any way we can. I have grown used to a life of comfort and I don't take it lightly when some flaming Picts come and challenge that. I will stand behind you Maecha, if you pass the tests. And perhaps my warriors will help you with your fighting skills, just to see how well you were trained."

"I would be honored with any training you would provide, my Queen. But I do assure you that Kelan is one of the best swordsman in our land and he is a good teacher," I said.

"Hmm," she said raising her eyebrow. "And what else has your champion taught you? I would love to know! I'm sure I could teach him a thing or two!" she laughed out loud.

My red face told her everything she needed to know.

"Don't worry, my dear. When the time comes, you and your champion will learn more than either of you could ever imagine," she said as she walked to the door. "Goodnight."

My face burned from her last comments. I thought of my mother and all we had missed together. I lay down on my cloak wanting to be close to the fire. The next thing I knew, I was shaken by a firm hand. Opening my sleepy eyes, I saw Kelan. I grabbed his hand to my chest.

"Ah, Maecha?" Kelan said embarrassed.

"Hmm?" I said still enjoying my dreams. He pulled his hand away and I jumped up. "What happened? What are you doing?"

Kelan backed away and stammered, "I, uh, just came up to wake you, since you haven't been down to breakfast and the challenges would be beginning soon."

I jumped up to run out the door, but Kelan stopped me. "Treasa wants you to wear these," he said as he pointed to the bed. Laid out on top of the unused bed was a tanned leather vest laced down the front, a short leather skirt, and laced boots.

I turned to Kelan and noted that he wore about the same

thing, except he had knee-length linen pants. I wished I had the same, but didn't have time to make such a request. I dressed and braided my hair. I ran down to eat and Treasa sat at the head of the table, with a look of contentment on her face. "You and your champion make a fine looking couple, Maecha," she said eyeing me. "I didn't want to hinder your movements, so allowed you to wear the training gear of my warriors. I hope you like it."

"Thank you for your consideration, Treasa," was all I said as I ate my bread with honey and cold porridge. Treasa left me to my food and I followed soon after. As I came into the market area, I saw all the villagers gathered to watch the challenges.

Treasa stepped onto a platform and raised her hands. The crowd was silenced. "There are two contenders who have been offered the chance to join the elite Fianna. These two warriors will face the initiation challenges here before they go to the Cave of the Warrior."

We were led outside the castle and over the bridge to the green fields. The sun shone bright in the sky. Two holes had been dug far enough away from each other so that the warriors could stand around each one to attack the contender.

I hadn't thought about how I would pass these challenges. I hadn't spoken to Kelan or Goll about them. I felt my body would know what to do. I knew that I was destined to go into the Cave of the Warrior and come out renewed.

I smiled at Kelan and stepped into the hole. The top of the hole came up to my ribs and I pressed my feet around in the dirt to gain leverage and balance. I closed my eyes to summon the strength of the Goddess and the souls of Imbas Skye. I didn't have her with me, but I could feel her. I was given a round shield to deflect the spears. I turned so I could not see Kelan. I didn't want any distraction. Goll looked worried, so for once I gave him a secure and confident smile. The furrow in his brow eased. The warriors circled around me and Treasa explained the rules.

"Before each warrior throws his spear, he will yell. The

spear cannot touch any part of your body. You can catch it in your hand, block it with your shield or you can bend out of its path. If it touches you or draws any blood, then you have lost the challenge. Good luck," she said and stepped back.

Treasa raised her hand and let it drop.

"AHHH!"

The first spear flew at me. I saw the tip come toward my face. It seemed to slow down and I leaned to the left and turned my right shoulder back and watched it fly past and land in the dirt behind me.

"AHHH," from my left side. Twisting toward that direction, I lifted my left hand and stopped the spear in mid air. I threw it aside and turned behind me as I heard another scream. I blocked it with my shield. On and on it went until the sweat poured into my eyes and the dirt was caked into my skin.

Only one warrior was left and he held two spears. He lifted them both in the air. Treasa never said anything about two spears at once. Kelan was out of his hole, looking as dirty as I felt. He looked angry. The warrior yelled and the two spears soared at me. I shifted to my right leaning my head back. I raised my left hand deflecting one and blocked the other with my shield swinging it down so that it broke to the ground. A pair of hands lifted me out of the hole.

"Well done, Maecha Ruadh," Kelan said and he kissed the top of my head.

"I say the same to you, Kelan."

Treasa clapped. Kelan let go of me and approached her. "You shame the Fianna by making up your own rules, Treasa. By no means should you have allowed two spears to have been thrown at Maecha."

"Calm down, my big man. She passed, didn't she? I wanted to make it more interesting, that's all," she said with a smile that tempted Kelan to say more.

Kelan turned and looked at Ferlaigh. He shrugged his

shoulders. I hoped that Treasa's games were over and that the challenges would go forth as they customarily did. I would soon find out.

We were ushered to the next challenge. "This next challenge shall lead you into the woods, where you will be pursued by five warriors. Your braided hair must remain so. If you venture out with a twig or a hair out of place, then you have failed. If you don't venture out again...then you have failed."

"My lady," Osgar interrupted. "I am concerned for my queen's safety. I fear that there are Picts in these woods."

"Osgar, I assure you that my scouts are out in these woods, even as we speak. There have been no sign of Picts or any other type of enemy. The path through the woods is marked by strips of cloths on the trees. They only need to follow this path, without being caught by my warriors. Of course, if they go off the path, I cannot guarantee their safety. They are warriors. This should be a simple task," she said.

Osgar looked at us. Kelan nodded and I know that Osgar wanted him to look out for me. On this challenge, we would start out together, but there were two different paths to follow and five warriors for each of us. I didn't know how long we would be able to stay together.

We walked to the opening of the woods. Kelan leaned over to whisper to me. "There is a bee hive around the first bend in the path. We have some time before the warriors begin. Take some honey from the hive and smooth it on your hair. It will be clear, but will hold your hair in place."

I looked at Kelan in shock. "Is that fair?"

Kelan smiled at me. "It's called beating the hands of fate. Every Fianna challenger has known this secret. The hard part is escaping the warriors who chase you."

I started to ask how he knew this secret, but someone yelled from behind us. We found the tree with the bees working in and around it. Kelan held his breath and placed his hand in the hive. He brought out a handful of honey, enough for both of us. After we smoothed it on our hair, we started down the path.

The path was smooth and clear with the cloths marking the way. We heard another yell and knew that the warriors were on their way. "Maecha, stay on the path toward the left. It brings you back to the field and you have less chance of getting lost. Good luck," he said and went on his way.

I ran toward the left. I felt comfortable having Imbas Skye at my side and tried to listen for any sounds of warriors. The path I followed became narrow and I could understand why others before me used the honey. I was grateful for the secret.

I heard shouts behind me and picked up my pace. A warrior yelled and I turned for he was right behind me. He could not have come from the start of the path, but I didn't have any time to think further. I had to react, for he swung his sword at a dizzying speed. Without knowing it, I had unleashed Imbas Skye and blocked his blows. Knocking his sword down into the dirt, I swung my sword up high and clanked him on the head. He went down.

I ran faster with my sword in my hand. There were still four more warriors that I would have to contend with. The path split and I turned toward the left. A huge warrior was in my way, so I ran back toward the right, thinking that I could cut over after I escaped from him. Two warriors jumped out. One was in front of me and one was in back. I saw a long, solid branch and picked it up to defend one side. I tried to remember 'Mikala's' teachings on using a stick for defense and attack. They attacked at the same time and I moved to put both of them in front of me. One warrior had a flail and swung it toward my head. I wondered how far they would go to capture me. I had not considered death in this challenge, but I had seen how Kelan had swung his and this warrior looked just as serious.

As the flail came closer I swung the stick straight at the weapon and the balls swung around it. I yanked hard and as he fell toward me, I hit the warrior on the head. I had no desire to maim these men, so hoped they would go down with one hit. He did and I let go of the stick. Holding Imbas Skye with both hands, I parried hard back and forth with the second warrior. His sword arm was strong and my body vibrated with each hit. He tried to push me off the path.

Someone grabbed me from behind in a bear hug. I swung my head back to hit his face and felt his grip loosen. I elbowed him in the stomach, and turned toward him and butted his ribs with the pommel of my sword. He fell back into the woods and I fought harder with the one still standing. I forced him back with each swing until he was at the edge of the path. I noticed a pond behind him amongst the trees. I hit his arm with the flat edge of my sword. As his arm went down, I jumped up and kicked him with both feet. He fell back into the pond.

One more left and I knew it would be the hardest. My path led toward the right and further into the woods, but I didn't want to take the chance to meet up with the large warrior again. I slowed to a walk, listening to the sounds of the woods. I heard the birds chirping in irritation at all the noise, water flow over rocks, and yelling from somewhere deep in the woods. The sun found its way to me through the tall trees. Its warmth revitalized me and I wanted to be finished.

Something passed in front of the sun and sent a chilly shadow over my body. I looked up and saw it again. Each time it moved lower and its shadow lingered on me chilling my bones. I stood still, wondering what type of animal could swing from the trees in such a fashion. It was large and very agile. I found my feet and tried to continue on my way. The cold shadow dropped in front of me and all warmth left my body. My teeth chattered to look at this monstrosity for that was the only way to describe it. It had the shape of a man, but its back was slumped forward and its arms hung low down to its knees. I couldn't distinguish any other features, because its body was charred black. Its eyelids drooped, but didn't hide the hatred focused on me. As I wondered how it could be right in front of me, I thought about what I should do. A voice inside my head screamed, *"RUN,"* and I followed its orders.

Grunting, the thing took off in pursuit. I ran back the way I had come. Now I hoped I would run into the large warrior, for surely he would help me against this invader. Treasa had said her warriors guarded the woods. How could they not see this atrocity? My lungs hurt when I found the fork in the path. I turned sharp to the right to follow the path out to what I hoped was the field. But the path stopped. There was no exit, only brambles of thorns, vines and whatever else had grown here untamed for years. And yet I saw the white cloths leading me this way and wondered what magic Treasa possessed. She said she would stand behind me, if I passed. Did she not want me to pass? Was she behind the attacks? Her husband was spineless, so I was sure she would be able to reign in whatever fashion she chose.

I turned back and there it was. I grabbed Imbas Skye and sang to the spirits that were sworn to protect me.

"Mothers of the sacred light,
Protect me from this evil of night.
Give me the power to do well
For on this land, it should not dwell."

I felt them lay their hands on me. I heard them whisper how to wield the sword against the evil that lurked in front of me. I saw them swirl around me, and so did the creature. They scared him. I swung Imbas Skye over my head and sliced it from the right shoulder to its left hip. His scream should have awakened the dead.

"Maecha!" I heard from the distance. The sound of my name drummed through the air and it summoned me to be stronger. I was entranced in the warrior's dance of death and the

180

spirits led the way.

My single slice did little to discourage the beast. As I raised my sword to slice him again, his low hung hands grabbed me around my waist and squeezed tight. I screamed as my breath left me. The chanting of my name kept me conscious. I couldn't reach my dagger and had to raise Imbas Skye high to pierce my enemy in what I supposed was its face. The sword sunk into his charred flesh and its silver blade melted his face further. He howled and released me. As I fell, he kicked me in the side. *"Get up! Maecha!"* the voice screamed in my head and once again I listened. This time I took out his leg with two swings and as he went down I stabbed him in the back. I was so angry that this foul creature had touched me I sliced him to bits until I heard someone screaming in my ear to stop.

I turned and saw Kelan. "Are you all right?" he asked pulling me toward him.

"I'm fine, but I haven't finished," I said, tears threatening to overtake me. My battle frenzy was gone and the thought of what could have happened took over my emotions.

Kelan said, "I'm sure that Queen Treasa will understand and will allow you to continue tomorrow."

Queen Treasa. My anger returned. I didn't know what her involvement was, but I wasn't going to let her win.

I straightened my body and winced as I felt the pain in my ribs. "I will finish, Kelan. I don't know what Treasa is trying to do, but I will find out."

He nodded and, as I ran along the path, I saw the opening to the field that was not there a few minutes ago.

I ran onto the field amidst the cheers of the crowd. I searched for Treasa and saw that suspicious, crooked smile on her face. A warrior whispered something in her ear and she motioned to a group of horsed warriors. They left toward the woods.

"Well, Maecha. I am sorry that you met more of a challenge out in my woods. My warriors have gone out to pick up the remains of this thing to see what it is and to make sure that we don't have any more surprises. But the fact remains that you have not finished your challenges. You only defeated four of my warriors and you have yet to leap over a bough and go under it, while taking a thorn from your foot. Do you give up?"

My body wanted to give up, but my spirit was on fire. I replied, "I will do what is needed to convince you that I am a capable and strong warrior. I cannot fail, Queen Treasa, for my father's life depends on my success."

"Well said, my child. And so you shall continue. In the field there is a bough that you must jump over without touching and then just after you must crawl under another. Do not break your stride while running to remove your thorn and be prepared for anything," she said.

I unsheathed Imbas Skye. Her blade was as bright as the first time I saw her. I looked at the bough and nodded. Someone yelled. I ran faster and faster until I could no longer tell which foot was in front. I switched my sword so that her blade was toward the ground. When I came close enough to the bough, I jabbed my sword into ground and catapulted myself up and over the bough. I came down on both feet with my sword still in my hand. The other bough was so low I wasn't sure I could get my body under it. I lay down on the ground and shifted my body like a snake. I could see the finish line and I began to run with renewed vigor.

I felt something stab my heel and remembered the thorn. It burned my foot. Again I stuck Imbas Skye into the ground and as I jumped up into the air, I bent my foot up and removed the thorn. I landed on one foot.

Then I stopped. Right in front of me was the very large warrior who chased me in the woods. I had forgotten about him and all my energy left my body.

"My Queen!" yelled Kelan. "You said that the challenger

had to defeat five warriors in the woods to succeed in the challenge. Maecha did fight five warriors and beat them all. This last one would mean six. She has surpassed all the challenges. You should grant her entrance to the Cave of the Warrior."

Treasa stepped down from her platform and walked to Kelan. "Although I must say Maecha fought well, the challenge was to beat five of my warriors, not some beast."

"My god, woman. What are you trying to do to her? Can't you see that she has done far more than any challenge could possibly dictate?" Kelan said.

Kelan was right. I looked down at my side and saw blood where the beast's claws had tore my skin. I wished I hadn't seen it for now I was light-headed. I felt strong hands, and turned to see Goll and Osgar holding each of my arms, so I wouldn't fall.

Treasa's warriors moved in around Kelan, ready to tear him apart at one word from their leader. Treasa waved them away. "I think that it is touching how much you care for your acting queen, so I will make you another offer. You can fight my warrior and if you win, you both will have earned access to the Cave of the Warrior."

"Kelan, I can fight him!" I yelled, trying to muster up some type of energy to sound confident.

Kelan came over to me and spoke low. "Maecha, you don't realize how hurt you are. Let me fight him and we can leave. I feel less safe here than I did by the river. Something strange and powerful lurks here and I'm not sure if Queen Treasa is on its side or ours. This is why you have a champion."

I looked at Goll and Osgar and they both nodded in agreement. I stepped away from them to address Treasa. "My Queen. My champion and advisors have urged me to accept the offer that you have proposed. I do then agree to let my champion, Kelan Mac Nessa, fight your warrior," I said.

"Then let us finish these challenges," Treasa spoke.

I walked to Kelan and touched his arm. "Thank you,

Kelan. May the Goddess bless you with her strength and grant you victory," I said and leaned on Goll to walk off the field.

Kelan unsheathed his sword and picked up a shield. He still wore the leather armor Treasa had given him, but now put on a helmet, which still exposed his face. His opponent held a two-handed battleaxe with a butt spike on the end. It reminded me of Goll's weapon of choice. All I could do was watch. I was very confident of Kelan's ability as a fighter, but even though Kelan was a large man, this warrior towered over him by at least two heads.

His name was Flidais and from the murmurs of the crowd, he was the best warrior in Roscommon. His height was intimidating, but so was his face and build. His hair was bright orange and wove around his head like angry snakes. His deep brown orbs stared at Kelan without mercy. Perched on top of his eyes were the bushiest eyebrows I had ever seen and were the same color as his hair. His nose was flat and crooked from being broken too many times and his face was set in an unrelenting grimace. He chanted strange words to himself.

He did not bother to wear a helmet nor any armor. He wore a short-sleeved lime colored tunic, covered by a shorter gray one. They were held to his waist by a broad leather belt that was inlaid with silver. His legs were bare except for fur straps that were tied around his calves. His feet were also bare. In his hands he held that battleaxe with ease and his forearms flexed as he turned the axe over and over.

Once again, someone yelled and the fight began.

As I watched, the battle worked in slow motion. Flidais stepped forward and with all his weight swung down against Kelan's shield. Kelan turned and the blow forced his shield against his body. Again Flidais swung down, but in the other direction and his powerful blow spun Kelan around. Kelan's muscles strained against the assault and I could see the anger and desperation in his eyes as he tried to figure out what to do next.

The pounding on his shield forced him to one knee. Kelan protected his face with his shield.

I went to intervene, but Goll grabbed my arm. "Patience. He is fine, Maecha."

I looked at Goll and wondered if we were watching the same fight. I turned back to Kelan and as the latest blow hit and compressed his body further to the ground, Kelan shifted and nailed Flidais' shin with the flat end of his blade. It was enough to make Flidais stop and that was all that Kelan needed. He stood up and gathered his composure.

Angered, Flidais moved with the same back and forth swinging motion, but this time Kelan moved in the opposite direction. Every movement that Flidais made, Kelan would anticipate it and be out of the way. Flidais stopped to catch his breath. He leaned on his axe and watched Kelan. Kelan dropped his shield and grabbed a staff. They circled each other. Kelan was in a very low position, prepared to jump in any direction. Flidais swung with both hands on his axe. As he came down, Kelan leaned back and then forward hitting Flidais across the face with the staff. Kelan stayed in close, so Flidais' axe was useless. He kept jabbing Flidais' body with the staff and caught him in the face with another swing. Flidais was stubborn and refused to go down. Kelan stepped back and swept Flidais' feet out from under him and thrust the spiked edge toward his throat. The crowd was silent.

"Do you submit, Flidais of Roscommon?" Kelan yelled.

Flidais tried to rise, but the staff's sharp edge caused blood to trickle down his throat. I glanced at Treasa and saw that her face was tight.

"Aye, I submit," he said and Kelan stepped away.

I turned to Queen Treasa and spoke, "We have passed all the challenges that you have set for us. Do you now grant us permission to pass through the Cave of the Warrior?"

The silent crowd waited for Treasa's response. "You have

both fought braver than I had expected and you are dedicated to one another and the Fianna. Therefore, I shall grant you permission and welcome you to a feast tonight in your honor."

The crowd broke out in a roaring cheer and many scurried away to prepare for the night's festivities. I wanted to collapse.

"You fought well, Kelan. I thank you for taking this fight for me. I'm not sure that I would have been able to handle it, although I would like to learn your staff fighting," I said.

"I'm not sure if I can remember what I did, Maecha, but I could try," Kelan said wiping the sweat and dirt from his face.

"We can teach you all you need, Maecha! Your man was lucky," Treasa said from behind.

"You think that you can teach her something I don't know, my Queen?" Kelan said, used to Treasa's harmless mockery.

"I most certainly can and I can also teach you a few things after the young one goes to bed," Treasa teased.

My cheeks flamed, but I laughed. Kelan winked at Treasa and replied, "Let's stick to fighting."

"Who said it didn't involve fighting," she retorted and her band of women broke out laughing.

I intervened. "Treasa, I would be honored if you would show me your fighting techniques, especially with my dagger."

"Of course. Why don't the two of you wash and rest. Tonight we will celebrate your victory and have a little fun," Treasa said pushing us along to the castle.

Everyone else wandered off to rest or to find some form of entertainment. I went to my room and it was only when I sat down on my bed that I realized how tired I was. I laid back and was fast asleep.

"Maecha. Maecha. Wake up!" I heard a voice say.

"I don't want to. Go away," I replied.

"Well I guess you will have to miss the festivities and your training with the female warriors," the voice said back to me.

I was sprawled out on my back and I struggled to open my eyelids. I tried to sit up, but my body was one sore lump and I had ignored the cut on my side. Kelan helped me to sit up.

"I need to look at that wound," he stated as he looked at my side. "I think you had more of that beast's blood on you than your own. Get in the bath while it's warm and wake your body up. The festivities will soon begin. I'm going to find something to eat. My body cannot wait any longer for food."

I just nodded.

"I'll send someone in to help you."

A few moments later, two of Treasa's handmaids came in and hauled me onto my feet. They stripped off my tattered clothing and placed me into the water. My body started to relax and I forced myself to wake up. By the time I was finished, I was ravenous. I dressed in a short leather tunic with leggings and boots. I went into the hall to find everyone. I didn't have to search long, because the noise coming from the main hall sounded like a battle. I had strapped Imbas Skye and my dagger on and rushed down to see if we were being attacked. I ran into the room and laughed. Kelan was surrounded by at least five of Treasa's female warriors and they were making him work.

The yelling came from the crowd placing bets, mainly on Kelan's downfall. Even our own men bet against him. Kelan moved to keep the women in front of him and used one as a shield against another. He held his own until a smaller female went behind his legs and knelt down behind him. The others pushed him back and before he knew it, he was sprawled out on the floor and all the warriors had their swords pointed at his throat. Kelan raised his hands and smiled in friendly defeat.

"Well done," I heard Ferlaigh say. I was surprised to see him addressing the crowd, since Treasa had held complete control of his domain since we had arrived. Treasa was not in the room.

I walked over to Kelan. "You did well, Champion. Although I think you planned it that way," I said.

"Sometimes you need to know when to give in, Maecha," he said as he smiled and put his arm around me.

We sat with our group and listened to a bard sing about the day's adventures. We drank imported wine from silver cups and waited for the meal of venison and pork to be served. There was a drum roll and the huge door of the hall opened. The tables were arranged around the room in a large horseshoe shape, so everyone had a view of the center. A lone rider stood in the doorway. I recognized Treasa, even though she wore a green mask and green leather shirt and pants. A sword was strapped on her back and daggers lay at her sides. She sprinted and reined in her horse so that he shimmied high on his hind legs. As the horse came down, Treasa jumped off and landed on her feet. The horse ran back out the door and Treasa stood posed for battle.

Next, ten fully armed warriors with black masks entered. With a magical grace, Treasa withdrew her sword and faced the first warrior. He yelled as he ran toward her with his sword over his head. Treasa deflected his downward blow. She swung her sword around and his sword flew out of his hands. Treasa turned to the next warrior. He was paired with another and they circled around her. Treasa turned with them waiting for their attack. They withdrew short daggers—one in every hand. The first lunged and Treasa caught his dagger with her sword and drew her own dagger and blocked his second strike. She twisted him around so that his partner could not get around. She shoved her attacker away and he tripped backwards. His partner jumped over him and Treasa swung at his feet. He jumped again, but she took out his legs with the flat side of her sword and he joined his friend on the floor. Her sword never stopped. She took each warrior out with a single blow. I was amazed and could tell Kelan

188

was impressed. Treasa ended her battle to the uproar of cheers from the crowd. I looked at Ferlaigh and understood what he saw in this woman. His eyes were full of love and amazement for his queen. She came over to her husband's table and bowed in front of him, showing him the respect that she had been lacking for him since we had arrived.

Everyone sat down to enjoy the feast. The finest portions of boiled pork, beef, and ox were given to us and the king and queen. The rest of the meat plus fish with honey, milk, and cheese were shared amongst the other warriors and guests.

After dinner, Treasa invited our group outside where a huge bonfire burned. The night was cold, but the bonfire's flame warmed us. Drunken couples went to find a place to cuddle and others fought mock battles and tried to fight like Treasa did earlier. Still others kept on entertaining with music and dancing. Kelan, Osgar, Goll, and I settled on a blanket near the fire to watch the activities.

"Where is Caoilte, Goll?" I asked.

Goll motioned toward a tree outside the light of the bonfire. "It seems as though our little man has found a special friend," Goll said.

Caoilte, and what looked like one of Treasa's warriors, had slipped behind a tree. Their giggling disappeared with them.

"Well good for him."

We listened to the music and relaxed. Then Treasa and two of her warriors jumped in front of us still dressed in their gear. "Are you ready for your first lesson, Maecha?" Treasa asked smiling.

I had forgotten about my request and did not have the desire to lift my sword again today. But this was an opportunity I could not miss and I knew I would need all the help I could get. "I am," I said. Kelan laughed. "And what is so funny, Kelan?"

"Oh, nothing. It's just that I started out that way, too. All excited and confident," he said.

189

"Hmph. You just started like that so you could give up and look like a weak man who needed some loving care. Disgusting!" I said and kneeled down to fetch my sword. I whispered to him. "Don't worry. I will learn the proper way and then you can give in to me." Thrown off by my forwardness, Kelan raised his eyebrows and was silent for once.

"She's learning," Treasa said.

We remained in front of the fire. Our long shadows danced over the others who had gathered to watch. I was intent on Treasa's words, so I didn't notice how many people had come to watch the lesson. Kelan sat up and I knew he absorbed everything he saw.

"Now," Treasa said. "Your dagger is long enough to use as a shield and then as a weapon." She motioned for one of her warriors to step forward. "My enemy swings her sword down at me. She wants to cut me from my neck to the other side of my body. That swing is strong and powerful. You must brace yourself to take the blow and then be able to react with your own powerful strike. Keep your legs in a strong balanced stance, and keep your knees bent. That will help you protect yourself and then allow you to move in any direction necessary."

Ciara, one of Treasa's warriors, moved around and swung at Treasa from different angles. Treasa moved with ease blocking the swing with her dagger.

Treasa stopped and Ciara moved back to the edge of the circle that had been formed. "Come forward, Maecha," Treasa said. I held my sword and dagger. "Swing your sword down like you saw Ciara do." I did. "I step in and block your swing with my dagger. The crossguard of the hilt will stop the oncoming sword. Swing your own sword around and hit the enemy in the face with the pommel. If another attacker comes, swing your sword at that attacker and put the first attacker in front of that person. Use her as a shield. Keep your enemies in a line so that you are only fighting one person at a time. Now you try."

First, I practiced getting used to taking my dagger out fast enough to block the swing. Then I tried to attack with the pommel and then fight two attackers at once. Once it felt comfortable, we tried another technique.

"You need to be close to your attacker to make this work. Of course with any dagger move, with the exception of blocking, you have to be closer to the fighter. If someone attacks you with a sword and shield, use your sword to hit the shield so that it deflects back toward the body. If that person's shield is pressed against her, then she can't bring her sword arm around to hit you. Stab your dagger into her eye, her neck, or her side, if she doesn't have armor on. It's quick and you need to be fast in a fight," Treasa explained.

This time I practiced on Ciara and it seemed like an easy technique. Seeing that it was too easy, Kelan got up and stepped in for Ciara. When I tried to hit his shield into his body, he didn't budge. He spoke. "This move is good for someone who is about your same height and weight. It is harder when you have a larger opponent as I did today. You have to take them by surprise and you need to use speed, not power. You don't have the arm strength to match me. What else could you do?"

We moved around and I tried to find a way to beat Kelan and get in close enough to use my dagger. The crowd livened up and offered advice. "Just kill him with the sword." "Run away!" "Ha, Ha, Ha!" They enjoyed themselves, but I was frustrated.

Then I heard that familiar voice in my head. *"Kick him! Kick his shield and then move in!"* I moved around, making Kelan think I was still frustrated. Then I backed up and took two quick steps forward and kicked Kelan's shield right in the middle with what 'Mikala' had called a heel kick. The surprise of the move and the power behind it, forced Kelan's shield to hit his body. I stepped in and hit him again with my sword and managed to touch his side with my dagger.

"Excellent!" Treasa said. "It seems that your student has

picked up some techniques that neither of us has shown her. Interesting."

"Yes, it is," said Kelan.

"Maecha, I think that you have done well and the crowd has appreciated such wonderful entertainment," Treasa said.

I looked around and saw that most of the crowd had shifted from their activities to ours. I was glad I didn't make a fool of myself.

"Queen Treasa and King Ferlaigh," I said, motioning to include him. "I would like to express my deep gratitude for your hospitality and my appreciation for your fighting skills. You and your warriors have an open invitation to my father's rath at any time. Now it is late and we have a big challenge to take on tomorrow, so I will bid you all a good night."

Kelan didn't move, so I nudged him. "That means you too, Kelan. You would do best to get ample sleep and not stay up late this night."

"I'm coming," he said, reminding me of how I would boss him around when we were younger.

Block with dagger, hit with sword. Hit shield, stab with dagger. "You did well tonight, Maecha," *Michaela says stepping from behind a tree.*

"Thank you. I want practice, so that it feels natural." *Michaela watches Maecha and then does the same with a sword and dagger in her hand.*

"I think I have another one," Michaela says. "Would you like me to show you?"

"Yes, I think I am ready."

Michaela explains each step as Maecha watches. "First, an opponent swings the sword down over his head. Step in with your dagger forward and block the oncoming sword with yours. Bring

192

your arm under and back over your opponent's arm and bring the dagger to his throat or stab him. Your sword holds the other sword in place so you don't have to worry about it. He is defenseless and you can take him down quickly. At this angle, you can also do what we call a sweep. With your arm at his neck still, take your front leg and put it tight behind his and kick back while pushing on his neck. He'll go down. Now you try."

They practice all the moves learned tonight. Exhausted, Maecha drifts into a deeper sleep. Michaela watches over her. "Good luck, my friend."

5

The entrance to the portal led into the side of a hill and barely reached my waist. The chamber was formed by two upstanding stones and the roof was a capstone.

All those who traveled with us now gathered around in a protective circle. Goll and the others would ride hard to make it back to Tara for our return and the Samhain festivities. Treasa and her warriors stayed a respectful distance away. I turned and waved to the exquisite queen, not knowing whether to trust her yet. She had helped me, but she had also made my time with her very difficult.

I turned to the group of Fianna warriors who would send us on our way. With their hands clasped on one another's shoulders, the men raised their eyes to the sky and chanted a blessing:

"Blessed are the Fianna
For they protect the poor and weak.
The Cave of the Warrior holds their secrets,
And of them, they must never speak.
The Gods' Blessings go with those
Who now venture on this quest.
And for those who never make it back,
Amongst fellow warriors you shall rest."

194

Kelan and I looked at one another, smiled, and crawled into the portal. A bright light consumed us and our journey began.

Blinded, I felt for Kelan's hand. The light disappeared and darkness overwhelmed me. I couldn't find Kelan and, when I opened my mouth to call him, a rush of wind took my breath away. Becoming accustomed to the dark, I could see images like white clouds forming around me. They moved with ease and, when they came closer, I felt cool air rub along my body. One image stopped in front of me and it formed into the shape of a person. Its face looked like a man and I recognized my father. Overjoyed, I reached out to touch him. But when I did, a searing pain ripped through my hand. The image flew above me and turned into a fiery-red ball of flame. It shot at me and I screamed in pain as its fire singed my skin. It hissed. I turned and saw more images float toward me, but they were no longer the cool breezes of light clouds. They were fiery dragons with blood-red fire seething from their roaring mouths. They had the strength of the gods and they hit me hard from all directions.

I stood up and ran toward what I thought was the back of the cave. "Kelan! Kelan! Help me!" I screamed. They encircled me and I no longer knew which way I should go. They formed into one mold and each time they hit me, it felt harder. The dragons disappeared and the form solidified. A bright red flame exploded in front of it and a warrior walked through the flame toward me. His face was red and scarred from fire. His helmet was made of a human's skull with thighbones hanging from each side. He towered over me and I could see more bones around his waist. Dangling from them were, I assumed, his victims' forearms and hands. I didn't want to add my arms to his collection, so I pulled Imbas Skye from her sheath. She was weak and I knew I had to defeat this demon to get out of here. Upon seeing my sword, he growled and lunged toward me. I stepped back to avoid his grasp and swung my sword toward his head. Our swords met and I heard the screams of the dead calling for me to join them. They wanted my blood and he wanted my soul. We swung and blocked for what seemed an eternity. My arms burned and I could no longer feel my hands. They were numb from the clashing. I had to defeat him soon or else I would fall from fatigue.

I changed my strategy. I began to thrust my sword high and then low to get closer to his body. Beyond him I could see a light toward the ground. I turned to get closer to it and the light began to grow taller. It was the portal, whether to the Otherworld or reality, I didn't know. Nor did I care at that moment. My enemy was getting angrier, but he was also slowing down. Swinging Imbas Skye, I hit his sword arm hard enough to turn him away from me. I pulled out my dagger and thrust it into his side. He screamed and from his wound hands reached out and grabbed my arm. I swung my sword down and only managed to slice his arm, where more hands grabbed at me. They were the souls of his victims and they wanted to pull me into his body. I could hear the dead laughing at my capture. I had thought to kill him like any enemy, but I had been wrong.

I cried for my mother to help me. I screamed a warrior's cry and kicked and sliced at this monster that grew every time I touched it. My left arm and leg were now trapped.

"Macha, Goddess of War, I invoke you!" I screamed above me. Breathing hard I held my sword up in front of my face. I left my fate in the hands of those who had held this sword before me. I felt its warmth. My right hand began to throb as the power of the spirits was awakened. Imbas Skye began to glow. The Celtic knots on her blade began to move. They encircled the blade in a slow dance and as they came to the tip of the sword they turned into snakes. They hissed at their enemy and he hesitated. The rest of the blade was aglow in a white light and it traveled down my hand to the finial.

The stone began to shimmer and I could see a blue light.

I looked into the light and I saw an eye peering around. Satisfied that it had seen its enemy, the blue light became stronger. The souls screamed in fear and they recoiled as the light traveled toward them. My left arm had been freed, so I held the sword tighter and the power of it surged through my body. The demon was afraid, but he was also angry and so raised his sword for one last blow. When he did the blue rays shot out and struck him in his chest. He howled, shocked at the hole in his chest. The power of the impact knocked me toward the cave's wall and blackness.

I woke up to find Kelan rubbing salve on my burns. I tried to stand, but he stopped me. "Just lay still, Maecha. Give your body a chance to heal," he said.

Realizing that I was in another area of the cave and out of danger, I asked, "Did you see the demon, Kelan?"

"I'm not sure what demon you speak of, but I did see you flying out of the cave like a fire ball," he said.

"We're out of the cave?" I asked, excited. "Are we in Tir-nan-Og?"

Looking around, Kelan shook his head and said, "I'm not sure where we are, but I don't feel safe being here much longer." He helped me up. "Look for yourself."

I did and was shocked by the sight. All around us were bare trees and desolate lands. The sky seemed to be enclosed by a black cloud which let in very little light. Hanging from the leafless trees were skeletons of warriors who had failed their passage. Their heads hung askew and worms crawled through their eye sockets and their mouths were forever opened so that the wind echoed their painful screams. We noticed their weapons against their tree graves. Some of the swords were beautiful and would make a wonderful addition to my father's collection. I walked over to one sword that had rubies along its hilt. It glowed just like Imbas Skye and I thought it might have unique powers. I bent to pick it up and was yanked backwards. I fell back to the ground, but jumped up with my weapons ready.

"Kelan! What are you doing?" Silencing me with his finger, he pointed to another tree. There was a skeleton hanging with his sword below him. Holding the sword was another warrior skeleton. I understood and we turned to leave this land of death.

"So what do we do now, Kelan?" I asked not knowing which way to turn.

"This path seems to be the only way to get through this forest. Let's follow it and be prepared for whatever killed these warriors."

Unsheathing Imbas Skye, I was reminded that she saved me from the demon warrior and gave silent thanks to the Goddess Macha and the spirits of the sword. I looked at the eye stone, but she was asleep once more.

As if alive, the forest floor moaned against the weight of our steps. We walked for a long time in silence and I noticed that there were fewer skeletons hanging from the trees. The silence was maddening. "Kelan," I began. "What did you see in the cave?"

Stopping, he waited for me to walk beside him. "I saw many wondrous things. I saw my father sitting amongst druids and he invited me to dine with them. So I did. He told me that he was proud of me and that I was on the right path. I'm not sure what that meant, but it made me feel better about my journey. They told me about the Otherworld and the key to our surviving here. One druid spoke in a riddle. He said:

> "There is one that is two,
> There are three that we must do.
> When we come out anew,
> To each other we will be true."

"Do you know what that means?" I asked.

"Not really, but I think there is hope and we will be successful if we follow the order of the riddle. We will have to take each step as it presents itself to us," he said.

"Were you attacked by anything, anyone?" I asked.

"No. They were all quite friendly and helped me to find the path to this forest," he said walking with ease.

Stopping, I could only stare at him. "I too saw my father, but was burned when I touched him and this disgusting demon tried to tear my insides out and feed me to his dead victims! Why was I attacked with such violence and hatred? Could this be a bad sign for me? Maybe you are the only one who will make it out," I said staring at the ground.

Walking back to me Kelan touched my chin and lifted it, so that I could see his emerald eyes. In them I saw the reflection of a child and felt foolish for thinking that I could conquer the Otherworld and go back to my land as a great warrior. Sensing my fears, Kelan said, "Everyone's experience in the Otherworld is as different as each one of our lives at home is unique. We are tested by our fears and your fears are so strong right now that they are suffocating your strengths. Believe in yourself. Believe that you truly belong here and this land will accept you. I believe in you and I will follow you, but you must learn to lead, Maecha."

I was lost in his words when I felt something tug on my leg. From the look on Kelan's face, I knew he felt the same. Branches entwined themselves around our legs. The trees had begun to move and their branches were the henchmen who had brought so many men down. Springing into action I yelled, "My sword is not cutting the branches, Kelan!"

"Nor mine," he replied looking around for another answer. "Maecha, take your dagger and stab it into the branches."

Not wasting time, I stabbed down on the three branches that had entwined both my legs together. "Oof!" I said as I was pulled off balance. I noticed the branches began to ooze and the more they oozed, the thinner they became.

"When the branches get thin enough, try slicing through them again," he yelled as his right leg was freed.

I did the same and my legs were released just as my sword arm was caught by another branch. Many more were coming and I was afraid that they would overcome me. "Keep stabbing, Maecha," Kelan yelled as he sliced the branches that had me trapped to the ground. "Let's go!"

We ran and the wind began to howl and the skeletons began to swing and clank together in a death dance that was made for us. "Kelan! Look!" I said pointing in front of us. Beyond the trees was another lighted portal and it pulsed with an energy that made the trees shrink away from it.

"That must be the doorway out of here," he yelled. The tree roots were breaking out of the ground blocking our path. I tripped on a root and fell face first into the dirt, only to be pushed up by a bony hand encircling my neck.

The dead had come alive and this one wanted my soul, so it could go back home. The wind seemed to howl, "Kill the woman! No women allowed!" and that only made the hand tighten. I kicked and stabbed my blade into its useless dirt-filled eyes, but it was Kelan's sword slicing its arm in half that saved me.

"Run to the light!" he roared grabbing my hand. Not looking back we jumped through the doorway.

"Woaaaah!" I screamed as I started plummeted down a cascading waterfall surrounded by rocky caverns and lush green trees. Kelan fell faster than I, so I saw the dagger-shaped talons that scooped him up out of the air and the thunderous wings that rhythmically flapped to keep him from falling. I felt a different set of talons take hold of my arms and I looked up to see the beak of the biggest Griffin I had ever seen. Not that I had ever seen one. Our druids often told the story of the origin of these magnificent beasts. They are the offspring of the eagle, the monarch of the skies. Their feathers could cure blindness and a drinking horn from a Griffin's claw would change color in the presence of poison. Normally the claw was red, but with poison, it turned blue.

I didn't feel fear, perhaps because of my relationship with Aeiden. I knew they wouldn't hurt us, and that no matter where we were going, they had at least saved us from the dangerous waters. Looking around I saw a land full of thick green forests. We had passed over the river where the waterfall met the splashing waters and the caverns disappeared behind a mountainous peak. I could see animals in a valley that looked like deer, but they had huge antlers and they rivaled the size of the Griffins. The Griffins slowed down and lowered us into a valley. The trees were so thick it seemed the only way to venture in here was to fly. They placed us on the ground and moved away from us.

I walked up to the Griffin who carried me and he looked at me with his big gray eye. "Thank you for delivering us, my friend. I know I will see you again," I said touching the side of his neck.

The creature fluffed his long brown feathers and bowed his head in acceptance. Screeching, he and the other flew straight up out of the valley and disappeared amongst the trees.

"Well that was interesting," said Kelan looking a little pale from his ride.

"That was glorious, Kelan! Those birds are beautiful! Aeiden would have loved to fly with them," I said as I looked at our new location. "Look, there's a hut just beyond the trees."

We knocked on the door. When no one answered, Kelan pushed down on the wooden handle and called, "Hello! Is anyone here?"

A fire burned in the middle of the room. We walked in and the door closed behind us and disappeared. The wall past the fire changed into a doorway and was illuminated by an orange glow. We followed it and walked along a stone passageway that descended down into the depths of the ground. The air became cooler and water trickled along the moss covered, stone walls.

The passageway curved and spiraled lower until we could only walk one at a time. There was an opening and Kelan pushed his bulky body through. He called for me and as I came through the opening I was met by the infamous faery folk of Tir-nan-Og.

Two of them guarded a doorway. They were half my size, but their spears, which were crossed in front of the doorway, reached above my head. We waited and a small man came out to greet us. "Welcome. I am Tannackta, Keeper of the Passageway, Protector of the Doorway to the Lord of Tir-nan-Og. What is your purpose here?" he asked Kelan.

Kelan glanced at me and then spoke. "My name is Kelan mac Nessa of Tara, and this is Maecha Ruadh mac Art, daughter of King Cormac mac Art and acting queen of Tara. We have come to meet the challenges of the Lord of the Otherworld, so that we may join the brotherhood of the Fianna."

Tannackta looked at me with blue eyes that sparkled like sunlight on water. As he moved, his long golden-white hair shimmered and moved like snakes around his neck. He wore a conical shaped hat that had red stones encircling the rim and I noticed a crystal around his neck that glowed as he spoke. "And how did a creature such as you come to this place?"

I responded, "I came because my deepest desire is to be a member of the Fianna and I must save my father."

"You must know that a female has never come into the Otherworld in this manner," he stated. When I nodded, he continued, "I do not know what my lord's reaction will be to this, but I will warn you that many do not live past this meeting. If you are not deemed worthy, you will die."

"I understand the consequences of my decision and I believe that I am worthy to battle alongside this elite group. I only ask that I be given the chance to prove my worthiness," I said.

"Very well, you both may enter," he said as he clapped his

hands. The two guards moved aside and the doorway to the Lord of the Otherworld, and Tir-nan-Og, was opened.

6

The room was encased in crystal. The water dripped from the cavern ceiling into a dark pool before us. A crystal bridge extended over the water and we walked along the bridge toward the throne. I looked over the edge and could see bubbles under the water. A scaly creature jumped up and just missed my face. I fell back into Kelan who grabbed and steadied me. We heard a laugh from beyond the bridge. "Do not dally amongst my pets, unless you wish to be their next meal," a deep voice spoke.

We crossed the bridge, but still did not see anyone. Crystals hung from the ceiling and glowed along the walls revealing images of the outside world. I saw a shepherd gathering his sheep in a storm, families shopping at a fair, and a village being attacked by invaders. They were only glimpses, but their images stayed with me. In front of us was a crystal wall that pulsed with the white light that we had seen before we fell over the waterfall. It pulsed stronger and began to shift. The whole wall turned and a black crystal chair appeared. The Lord of the Otherworld appeared in the chair as if he flowed through it. We bowed down to the ground.

"Please rise so that I may see the unique creature who has dared to come into my presence," he said.

We stood and he stared at me in silence. His black hair

flowed long past his shoulders and his beard and mustache blended into his hair. His eyes were large and black and stood out from his worn, kind face. He wore black robes, but they shimmered like a clear night sky filled with endless stars. It was hard to focus on him, because his whole being shimmered and moved like there was two of him.

"Maecha Ruadh mac Art," a female voice whispered. I looked around. "I am here, Daughter." I turned forward and the Lord of the Otherworld now appeared to be a Princess of the Otherworld. Her hair was white as snow and covered the front of her gown, which shimmered silver white. Her small face was pale and she smiled shyly, but her eyes sparkled like blue opals. Her chair was clear crystal and the Lord of the Otherworld was no longer there. I caught sight of Kelan's gaping mouth. The Princess laughed. "I enjoy the look on the men's face when they see me."

"You are female?" I began.

"And male," the Lord said and his black image shimmered back into focus. "We are one and the same and we accept all those who come and understand our oneness."

Kelan couldn't find his tongue, so I asked. "Does everyone who has survived the Otherworld know this?" They both nodded. "Then why aren't women invited here? Why were we never told?"

"Don't be angry, my child. All who fight with the Fianna are sworn to silence about the Otherworld's secrets. They could have encouraged women to come, but they have not. They want to keep their elite group male. And that is where they fail. You were meant to lead their way. Only those who accept the knowledge that all are male and female will prevail," she smiled and at last Kelan closed his mouth.

I continued. "So that's why we were both able to come down together."

"Yes, it is. You both hold great promise for your world and for ours. But you will only succeed as one. Your journey together here in the Otherworld is one of growth and bonding. You must learn to trust one another as you would trust yourself. To betray the other is to betray your own self. This is the only way you will succeed."

"But how do we achieve this oneness?" I asked.

"You will have two challenges that you must overcome together. As you do so, you will feel an emotional bond, like no other. I cannot explain what will happen between you. It is different for all who choose to accept the oneness of male and female. If you overcome these challenges, you will each have a challenge that will decide whether or not you go back to your world. You must complete this last challenge alone, or neither one of you will go back," she said.

The Lord of the Otherworld shimmered through the Princess. "Know this. You are bound by our secret. Further, as the two who will become one, you are bound to protect us from the outside world. If by some chance, one who is not worthy enters here to do us harm and we cannot protect ourselves, you must obey and come to us when we call."

Kelan spoke, "How will we know when you need us?"

Two faery folk appeared out of the crystals. They were young and wobbled like toddlers. In their hands, each held a crystal attached to a leather strap. They stood in front of us and Kelan and I knelt down while each faery tied the crystal around our necks. There were three clear crystals that were connected at the top. We stood up and the Princess explained. "These are the Awen crystals. They are sacred and hold the powers of the Crystal Palace where we live. The Awen crystal symbolizes the Three Realms of our worlds. The first ray on the right symbolizes the male force, the left symbolizes the female force, and the center symbolizes the balance between the two. Without this balance, the worlds of the Upper World (sky), Middle World (Land), and the Under World (Sea) cannot exist together. You will achieve this balance as your minds bond. If you live through your challenges, part of their powers will be yours.

When the crystal glows red, one of you will know that the other is in danger. When it glows green, then we are in need of your assistance. When it turns black, one of you has died or lost the crystal and your powers are broken. When you have completed your bond, you will know, because the crystals will shine yellow like the sun's precious rays and your journey will be complete. These crystals are the light of the Otherworld. You will feel its power and you must trust what you feel and take action. Any other powers will reveal themselves as you are deemed worthy."

As one, the Lord and Princess rose. The Lord spoke. "It is time for you to begin your journey. What you accomplish here will affect those in your world and those to come. Your father must rule to keep your land prosperous and strong. Beware of the evil that lurks all around you. Be strong in your faith and believe in one another."

"Be true to one another and know that there will be those who will try to break your bond. This bond will bring you much jealousy and many enemies. Be as one and do not disappoint me, Daughter," the Princess smiled at me like a mother.

"Take this," the Lord said passing a rolled scroll to one of the faery folk, who placed it in my hand. "As we have said, the first two challenges must be done together and you will each have a final challenge that you will overcome alone and that challenge will bring you home. Commit it to memory. Tannackta will bring you to the beginning of your challenge. Good luck, my children."

We bowed and followed Tannackta to a large oak tree that loomed tall through the top of the cavern. "Sit here and read your scroll. When you are comfortable with what it says, place it in the water and walk to the sacred oak tree that ties all the three worlds together. It is your doorway back to your path. Good luck and may we meet again as friends," he said and disappeared into the crystals.

We sat down and I opened the scroll.

I.
FIND THE MAGIC STICK
IN THE WATERS OF THE SEA.
THE ROCK WALLS MAY SURROUND YOU
SO BEWARE THE ENEMY.

II.
FEEL THE STRENGTH OF ONENESS
ITS POWER WILL MAKE YOU WHOLE.
FIGHT THE WARRIORS TOGETHER
AND YOU WILL HAVE ONE SOUL.

III.
KELAN MAC NESSA
THE LONG GREEN SERPENT MAY KILL YOU
ITS TEETH HOLD A VENOMOUS BITE.
TAKE THE TOOTH AND IT WILL SUSTAIN YOU
USE IT WELL AGAINST THE EVIL YOU FIGHT.

THE EYES OF THE GODDESS ARE UPON YOU
SHE TRUSTS YOU WILL KEEP HER DAUGHTER SECURE.
WHEN THE EYES FALL UPON YOU
YOU ARE BOUND TO HER FOREVERMORE.

III
MAECHA RUADH MAC ART
MANY DANGERS WILL AWAIT YOU
FIGHT THE ONE WHO HAS NO NAME.
IF ITS POWER SUCCEEDS TO BIND YOU
HERE YOU WILL REMAIN.

THE CRYSTAL LIGHT WILL CALL YOU
BUT YOU MUST COME ALONE.
TOUCH THE LIGHT WITH NO CANDLE
AND YOU WILL MAKE IT HOME.

After committing the words to memory, we placed the sacred scroll in the water by the crystal bridge. As the water began to bubble, a hand reached up, and pulled it down into its depths. Kelan and I walked to the oak tree and touched its thick bark. The mighty tree began to moan and split in half to reveal the forest. We walked through and when we looked back, the forest had hidden the oak tree and the crystal cavern.

I turned to Kelan before we went any further. "Can I trust you, Kelan?" I asked knowing that the answer would keep us alive and strengthen this bond.

Kelan paused and looked at the ground. He turned and held out his hands. "Put your hands in mine." I did and I felt the inviting warmth of his skin as he held them. He took my hand and placed it over his heart. "As long as you feel my heart beating, you can trust me. When our souls have passed onto the Otherworld, you can trust me. I will die for you, Maecha and, as long as I have breath, I will try my hardest to never let you down."

I felt the strength and sincerity of his words. I placed his hand over my heart and replied, "I will do the same for you no matter what the circumstances or what duties will call. You are a part of my life that can never be separated and I will honor that forever."

"Now that we have each other's trust, let find something to eat. I'm starving!" said Kelan. We laughed and picked luscious berries that the forest provided. Brina had packed some dried meat and bread and the river that ran along the forest gave us fresh sparkling water.

We settled down for the night. A faint glow illuminated the warm night sky and we enjoyed the silence and solitude of this strange forest. Lying down on my cloak, I stared at the crystal that the Lord of the Otherworld had given us.

"This land is so magical and beautiful, isn't it, Kelan?" I whispered.

He moved closer to me and I could feel the warmth of his body reaching over to mine.

Looking into my eyes, Kelan touched my cheek and said, "Yes, it's beautiful."

I smiled, suddenly feeling nervous around my childhood friend. I took his hand and holding it in mine, fell asleep into my world of dreams.

"You have come back," Michaela says to Maecha.

"Yes. I have a need to know more about your fighting skills. I am interested in that stick that you swing around like a sword," Maecha replies watching Michaela. "I must learn all I can to bring my father back to me."

"Ah, so you have lost your father, too," Michaela says.

"Yes, where is yours?"

"He was killed by someone very powerful who could get close to him," Michaela states.

"I am sorry for your loss. My father lives, but a strong enemy has taken him. I must pass through this place, called the Otherworld, so that I can lead my warriors to find him. Your way of fighting can help me I think."

"Maybe that is why I am here." Michaela swings her tonfa stick around in a series of motions forming a kata.

"Come and I will show you how to use this weapon and maybe help you get your father back. It will be more than I could do for mine."

Michaela continues, "When using this weapon, you must be close to your enemies. This will distract them, since sword fighting is usually done at a larger distance. The tonfa, which is made of wood, will not protect you from the blade slicing down, but if you can get close enough to block the arm, like so, you can move in and block up or to the side or down. Then you can thrust the head of the tonfa into your enemy's face, groin, stomach, or any spot that is soft and not protected by armor. In my time, we do not have armor like yours, so the tonfa is a very powerful weapon. You would need to add a spike to pierce another's armor. Do you understand?"

"Yes, I think I do. Can I try it on you?" Maecha asks and they practice until, even while sleeping, Maecha is exhausted.

Kelan woke up to sunlight streaming through the trees. He reached for Maecha, but only felt the ground. He jumped up and scanned the area for her. Amongst the trees he saw her swinging a stick through the air, jabbing it forward and thrusting it down. Kelan had noticed that her fighting skills were different since her fall and he questioned her.

"What are you doing?" he asked.

Surprised, Maecha turned around. Her fiery-red hair flowed around her body and glistened in the morning sun. Her eyes were aglow with excitement and knowledge. Kelan couldn't help but smile.

"Good morning, Kelan. I was practicing some fighting techniques that I thought would improve my chances of surviving this place and getting my father back," she said taking out a dagger to hone the ends.

"What is this weapon that you hold in your hand?" Kelan asked. Maecha held a thick stick with a branch protruding from its side to be used as a handle. The stick was strong and she sharpened each end of it to a deadly point.

"This is called a *ton-fa*," Maecha answered. "Let me show you how it can be used."

Maecha proceeded to fight with her trainer and was excited to teach him something. She used the stick to block his sword's downward swing and noted Kelan's discomfort when the stick hit his arm. Then with the pointed edge she displayed its ability to slice her opponent's face, eyes, neck or to be thrust into the body. Kelan was impressed and desired such a weapon. Upon

211

finding the perfect piece of wood, Maecha sat down and began to prepare its edges for him.

"Maecha, where did you learn about this weapon and how to use it? You seem to have come upon some type of fighting that I know I did not teach you," he asked.

Maecha stopped cutting. She looked at Kelan. "You have known me for my whole life, yes?" Kelan just nodded. "And you have seen the power of my mother's sword and what it has done to me and to us. This whole journey is a transformation of you, of me, of us. I'm changing and so are you. Even before the Lord of the Otherworld spoke of our bond, I could feel you in ways that I've never been able to feel before—you are close to me even when I can't see you. Have you felt that?"

"I…I don't know," Kelan said. "I know that I am very aware of you and I just took that for…attraction," he said looking down.

Maecha moved closer. "Look at me." He did. "It's more than attraction. Do you feel anything else?" Kelan stared deep into Maecha's eyes until he felt lost in her, like a force pulling them together.

"Yes," he whispered. "I feel like a part of you is with me."

"Good," Maecha said. "Then maybe you'll be able to understand what I tell you next. When I fell and hit my head, I met someone and I dreamed of her while I slept. She is a warrior, but she dresses strange and she fights with both her hands and feet. We fought each other, but neither of us could win. She lives in my dreams and teaches me how to fight with this style called *cada'me* and to use this *ton-fa* weapon. She lost her father, too. I know it may be hard for you to understand, but somehow she is a part of me right now. She calls herself 'Mikala'. I think she may help us get my father back and somehow I feel that being here will help her."

Kelan nodded. "'Mikala'. Yes. She has come." Maecha looked at Kelan with suspicion. He continued, "I have seen this

212

woman that you speak of and I have called for her to come. Macha, Goddess of War, had enlightened me with a vision of a warrior much like you, who was needed to complete this bond. I did not know where or when she could help us, but it seems as though she is here and I agree that she will help us with your father," he replied in acceptance.

I sighed with relief upon confiding to someone about this. I was glad it was Kelan. "So it seems we are closer than we even knew."

7

Dream Journal—October 5, 2000, 1:00 AM

Dreamt I am in Ireland. I see a woman who I feel is me. She is dressed in a long blue robe and her face is barely visible under the hood. She walks up a grassy hill. A tall, old man, with long white hair, beard, and mustache chants behind her. A congregation of people follow. I see warriors close by. They scan the area in the early morning light.

The woman steps into a solid circle of stones. The stones only reach about waist high and they are flat on top. There is an opening at the top end of the stones. Two flat stone slabs stand close together in the center.

I walk to the other slab and everyone gathers around the outer circle. Candles are lit and they contrast against the hazy, pink glow of the rising sun. The druid steps forward and raises his hand over my head and says some type of prayer. A female druid called a bendrui steps forward. She is clad in a white gown and her black hair flows to her knees. She is young, but she has power almost equal to the male druid. Another woman steps forward. She removes her hood and I see a woman who does look like me, but her hair is redder. The bendrui removes the robe and the woman is naked. She neither shivers nor appears embarrassed. She sits on the cold stone and waits. The bendrui gives a jug to the woman who drinks from it, then lies down and closes her eyes. The druid sprinkles her body with water and his incantations become louder. The bendrui joins in and they are drunk with the power of the Goddess. As they sing, they sway back and forth.

A light appears around the inside slab of stone and the young woman's body jerks like she is having an epileptic fit. The circle swirls around faster and faster and my mind gets dizzy from all the faces whirling in front of me. Then it stops. The young woman is curled up on her side. The huge warrior with green eyes wraps the robe around her, but does nothing more. All eyes are on the inner stone slab. Another woman has appeared in the same fetal position, but is gasping for air. She is naked and the bendrui steps forward with a black robe to cover the woman. Both women stand, and still shaky, walk over to each other. They are now covered in their robes. They smile at one another and hug. Then they walk out of the circle, holding hands. They are sisters of the past and present. They are the same and everyone bows in wonder.

Shannon closed Michaela's journal. Michaela hadn't commented on this dream and Shannon could understand why. The images were so powerful, it almost seemed like it happened. Shannon hadn't had much luck figuring out how to get her sister back, but she had a feeling that this dream might be a clue.

Shannon remembered Michaela telling her about the dream seminars she attended. If you have an intention for your dream, you must state it when you lay down to sleep. It is helpful to hold a possession of the person you wish to dream of. Shannon held Michaela's journal in her arms. She laid on Michaela's bed and thought of her sister. She breathed deep and was soon asleep.

"Michaela?" Shannon asks as she floats over a green meadow searching for her sister. She sees Michaela dressed as a warrior and steps toward her. "Michaela?" she asks again.

Maecha turns and sees a woman dressed in druidic robes, with her hair piled on top of her head. Maecha bows and Shannon stares in confusion.

"I can see you are here on some important business," Michaela says, stepping out from behind the tree.

"Why am I dressed like this?"

"We all dream as we see ourselves and you have come as our advisor, so speak before your mind takes you away," Michaela says.

"Have you found the man that looks like father?" Shannon asks. The two warriors look at one another. Michaela speaks. "He is Maecha's father, High King Cormac mac Art and he has been taken by an enemy across the sea. We believe that someone close to him might have had something to do with it."

"I fear it could be my brother," Maecha confesses.

Shannon nods in sympathy. "Watch yourselves, both of you, for the enemy lies within your circle as he does in ours. Ricky Cartillo is somehow involved, but he's not responsible for the attacks on you and Uncle Frank is just…useless."

"Stay away from Ricky and protect yourself. Look for someone in the Brotherhood."

"What Brotherhood, Michaela?"

"You know that Ricky is involved, but there is someone else who Dad trusted beyond all doubt. He is the other enemy and he lies within. Keep to those who are loyal, as we will," Michaela says as they fade away from one another.

Shannon woke up. Her heart beat fast and hard against her chest. She understood what her sister meant by her exhausting dream world. She looked at the clock and couldn't believe it was morning. She felt like she had been awake all night. Her dream was disturbing, but she couldn't deny that what Michaela had said could be true.

The phone rang. "Hi, Uncle Frank. I'm glad you called."

"Shannon I think I may have some leads. I'll talk to you tonight. Everything will be fine!" he finished out of breath and hung up before Shannon could tell him anything.

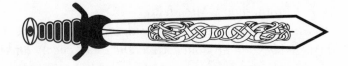

8

Kelan and I spent the morning combining our new weapon with the sword. By lunchtime we were hot and hungry.

"Come," said Kelan. "Let us move on and find some fresh water and this magic stick. It's time for us to meet our challenges."

"What do you think this first challenge means, Kelan?" I repeated it out loud, "Find the magic stick in the waters of the sea. The rock walls may surround you so beware the enemy."

Kelan thought. "Perhaps the magic stick is like the one you made. It could be a weapon. We should search for a stick in the water by large rocks. 'Beware the enemy' could mean that this stick will be well guarded," Kelan finished.

"Well said, Kelan. Let's meet our enemy."

We headed toward the edge of the forest. As the trees thinned, we could smell the freshness of the river. The land roughly sloped downward as we reached the edge. I watched the water gush over the still rocks. The copper brown color of the water mingled with the frothing white bubbles as they flowed around the rocks in agreed harmony. Each gave a little so that both could live together. I longed for the chance to live in harmony with my brother, but instead of giving, he was like a dam that refused to let a trickle of water flow through.

Rocky crags hugged the water's edge and rose up toward the sky. Trees hung along the crags from their last roots, clinging to their right to be there. Plants forged their way through the rocks and grew where nothing had grown before. The water looked inviting and I walked downstream.

There was a pool of water almost surrounded by the tall, gray rocks. I moved along some flatter rocks and stepped in, clothes and all. The water was shallow, so I walked to its center.

"Remember the challenge, Maecha," Kelan warned and smiled despite the danger he knew lurked around them. Kelan was reluctant to follow. He had always been a strong swimmer, but the touch of flowing water on his skin brought back the horrid memories of his family's death.

He remembered that day even ten years later. His sister and mother were at the river behind their hut, washing clothes. Kelan was with his father. Hearing their screams, both father and son rushed to their aid. Five armed warriors had grabbed his mother and sister in the water.

Yelling his battle cry, Kelan drew his sword and attacked. The blood that flowed turned the water red. As Kelan tried to reach the last warrior attacking his mother, she screamed from a knife wound to her stomach. He swam out to try and save her.

As he did, he heard the battle cry of enemies reaching his village. His father yelled for Kelan to save his mother as his father carried Kelan's sister to safety and then ran to defend his land. Kelan fought with the bravery of a warrior, but he was young. He killed the last man, but he and his mother were swept along the river current. Kelan was later found unconscious and barely alive, but his mother had been lost with the flow of the river. His village was destroyed and his father and sister were killed, their heads taken as a sign of their enemies' power. Kelan was saved by the power of the goddess and from that day on lived with King Cormac.

Maecha's voice brought Kelan back. "Let them come,

219

Kelan. I am ready for these challenges. I will claim my prize," I said.

The earth shook. Rocks rose out of the earth like pillars. Kelan swore and jumped into the water.

"Uh!" I yelled as my feet flew up in front of me. I hit the water and struggled to get up before something held me down.

Kelan had reached my side. "Are you all right?" he asked.

"Yes," I said as the water bubbled. In some areas the bubbles became bigger and more rocks pushed their way toward the sky, dislodging themselves from the confines of their murky underground homes. But these rocks were different. As they grew taller, they uncurled, crackled and moved, so that they resembled rock warriors.

"I think we have found the enemy," I said as one warrior turned and moved toward us. They were slow, but stood a sword taller than Kelan. Their arms were their weapons and they pounded down on us like a hammer pounding steel. Instead of blocking, I used my speed to get out of their way. As I stepped aside and behind one rock warrior, I swung Imbas Skye at its legs and shook from the impact. The rock chipped, but otherwise my attack did not affect my enemy.

"Any suggestions?" Kelan yelled, as he was surrounded by his own rock army. It seemed they felt he was the dangerous one and tried to get rid of him first. I looked around me at the rock walls. I noticed an outline of a rock that resembled the rock warriors.

"Kelan, lure them toward the edge of the water by the jagged rocks!" I yelled while positioning myself out of the water to wait for them. As they came closer, they hesitated. Large boulders protruded out of the water that made it treacherous to get to the shore. As a rock warrior came toward the boulder I stood on, I began to chip away at him. First, I swung at his rock hands and they fell away crumbling down to their birthplace. Then I hit their arms and Kelan began to do the same. They reached toward us, but could not step over the boulders. One rock warrior leaned too far over and went tumbling onto the boulders. We chopped at him and Kelan even picked up a very large boulder and dropped it on the warrior's head, breaking everything to pieces. The rock warrior was silent. The others tried to turn back, but their bulkiness hindered them and we destroyed those standing. The one rock warrior that had been fighting me was still in the water and we attacked feeling secure about how to bring him down.

We had managed to break this warrior apart and it was on its knees. As I swung Imbas Skye down, the water began to bubble again.

"Maecha! Behind you!" Kelan yelled. A huge rock hand grabbed me around my waist and I was lifted high above the ground as an enormous rock warrior pulled itself up out of the water and roared its fury at me. I was at his mercy and one twist of his wrist would break me in two.

This rocky beast brought me up to its face and he glowered at me with his huge eye. Not waiting to see if it ate humans, I turned Imbas Skye down and stabbed hard into his orb, blinding him. The monster screamed in horrendous pain and swung me around, without mercy. He swung his arm up to throw me down onto the rocky edges.

"Save me, Mother!" I called as I held Imbas Skye's eye up toward the sightless beast. Her powerful blue rays shot out at the enemy and shattered his head into pebbles. The monster trembled and shook, but could scream no more. He was doomed, but so was I, since he still held me. I turned Imbas Skye's eye to the hand that held me prisoner and she destroyed it as well. I dropped as the last rock warrior fell inches away from me.

"Maecha!" Kelan called. "Where are you?" The breath had been beat out of me, so I could not answer. I held onto my precious sword and, as the eye fed my spirit, I felt stronger.

I kissed my sword to give thanks once more and called,

221

"I'm over here!"

Jumping over the now lifeless rock, Kelan fell into the water to pull me up. Seeing that I was fine, he exclaimed, "What was that?"

Laughing I said, "That is the power of the spirits, may their magic always find its way to my sword."

Kelan held my shoulders. "You and that sword are amazing."

I smiled in return, but again the earth trembled and the water bubbled between us. We looked at one another and jumped up to defend ourselves from whatever creature was going to show up. Instead of a rock protruding from the ground, a silver ball appeared and moved up into the air between us. I reached out and put my hand on top of it. The ball glowed and a long wand protruded out from the bottom. The wand glittered and sparkled like gems. I turned it over and an iridescent light followed in its path. The middle crystal around our necks began to glow a pale yellow and I felt my body get warmer. Kelan felt it, too. I took his hands and the warmth from my body traveled into his and his into mine. I could sense his emotions and my skin tingled. The iridescent glow had surrounded us and we were in our own world and our minds were linked.

"Kelan, can you hear me? Don't be afraid of it. Let it flow through you. You can trust me. I will never hurt you," I said to myself.

Kelan looked up from the ground and I saw tears threatening to fall. I filled my mind with good thoughts and my emotions affected his. This oneness could prove very useful.

As the glow faded, our bodies returned to normal—almost normal. I could still sense Kelan's thoughts and his sensations seem to trigger a reaction in my body. He was becoming a part of me and yet we had never done more than hold each other. I felt that I knew him better than any woman could ever know a lover. I had yet to be with a man, but was comfortable knowing that Kelan would be mine, someday.

Kelan was the first to speak. "How did you speak to me without moving your lips?"

"Oh, so you could hear me?" I asked. "Each challenge will change us somehow and the Sorcerer's Stick has brought us closer. I believe that it is part of the power that will bring us closer to this Oneness," I said amazed. I had heard of how this magic stick had been used to turn people into animals and make rain pour for days and lightning strike a single person. But I never dreamed that it could do what it just did to Kelan and me.

"What are you feeling, Kelan?" I asked wanting to be sure that he was fine with all of this.

He came close and cupped my face in his hands. "I feel you, Maecha. I feel all of you," he said and he kissed my forehead. I shut my eyes to control the overwhelming rush of emotions that flooded my mind and body. It was too much. I touched his hands and pulled them away from my face.

Kelan looked surprised and a little hurt. "Are you all right with this…change, Maecha?"

"Yes, I'm just overwhelmed. Let us leave this place," I said. I remembered the wand and realized that it was suspended in mid-air. "Close," I said and the beautiful wand disappeared. I placed the silver ball in my pouch to explore later. Kelan didn't move. I took a deep breath and held my hand out to him.

He took it and we left the treacherous water. We climbed back up the ledge to the path that nature's rain had made through the forest. As we walked in silence, I admired the trees, old and new, mingling in unity with the grass and bushes. The various plants speckled the forest with shades of purple and magenta. Fallen birch trees made homes for the tiniest creatures and the world went silent as we passed through. The roots acted as steps toward our destiny and as we traveled down another hill, the water's mist cooled our skin.

The sun was overhead and it shimmered through the tall

trees, as it shed its light on the rocks around us. I slowed down to admire my surroundings. The damp forest scents lingered heavily in my nostrils. The harmony of the Otherworld entranced me. Even the rocks and roots were entwined with each other, much like the Celtic knot that maintained our people's heritage. Our harmony should stem from an interlocking world of unity. I envied the forest its peace and unity.

My peace was broken. Kelan walked ahead of me and a rock hit him square in the head. He grabbed his head and cursed. I looked up to see where this rock had come from and saw a hideous beast hanging from a branch.

"Kelan, above you!" I yelled, running to catch up. A huge warrior bounded down behind Kelan. He was the queerest look-ing fellow I had ever seen. He towered over Kelan and had one leg and his foot was the size of a shield. His two arms grabbed Kelan in a torturous bear hug and his third arm reached for Kelan's weapons. His face was as black as night and he had one eye in his forehead that glowed bright orange. He wore a gray tunic, red breeches and a black hooded cloak made of deerskin that could have served as a tent. His broad shoulders were twice as wide as Kelan's and he squeezed with all his strength.

As my crystal burned bright red, I jumped into action. I swung my makeshift *ton-fa* at the giant's knee. He bellowed in pain, but did not loosen his grasp. His third hand released Kelan's weapon and tried to grab me. I pounced in and out and hit him in his knee, ears, and head. I could see that I was more of a nuisance to him, so I had to try something else. I unsheathed Imbas Skye and yelled to the giant. "By the power of the goddess within my sword, release this man or meet your death."

His orange eye turned black and he snorted a toothless laugh. Kelan was no longer struggling and so I plunged the sword into the monster's side. Green blood shot forth and I jumped back from the stench and decay that erupted from his insides. His eye turned all shades of blue, white, red, and then green. He released his hold and Kelan fell to the ground. The monster turned to me. He grunted in pain, but was alive. I spun Imbas Skye over my head and with all the strength my body could muster, I sliced his head clear from his putrid and infested body. His body writhed and shook, and his head rolled over the cliff. I ran to Kelan. He opened his eyes.

"Are you all right, Kelan?" I asked.

He nodded and grabbed my hand to pull him up. As I did, a bright light flashed where the giant's body had fallen to the ground. We both fell back blinded. When our vision readjusted we saw a handsome young man where the giant's decayed flesh had lain.

He stepped forward, kneeled, and bowed his head to me. "My lady," he began. "My name is Lon, son of Liomhtha. I am a master craftsman and teacher of smiths to the king of Lochlann in Bergen. I thank you with all my heart for releasing me from this life of despair. I most humbly beg your warrior's forgiveness for attacking him. My actions were beyond my human control."

I motioned for the young man to stand. "You are most welcome, young warrior. But, how did you come to be such a hideous monster?" I asked.

"I came here years ago, wanting to be a member of the Fianna. I was attacked in this very spot by a gruesome beast with two heads and fangs that dripped with the blood of his enemies. I had to answer a riddle before I could pass. If I did not, then he would rip me apart, like he had done to the other warriors who had dared to pass this way. Alas, I took up his challenge, but could only answer part of the riddle and so he made me a deal. He said that I could take his place here, but would have to take the shape of a monster. When another warrior came that I could kill, I would take his spirit and return to my normal self. It has been years since someone has chosen this path. So when I saw a strong warrior, I knew this was my chance. But what I don't understand is how I lived when you, fair lady, took my head."

"My name is Maecha Ruadh mac Art. I am the daughter of the High King Cormac mac Art. This is Kelan mac Nessa, my champion. We also desire to become members of the Fianna. You live because the Mother Goddess deemed it so," I said.

The boy's shocked face amused me. "Much has changed, since you have been in our world. You have been blessed by the power of the Goddess. You should thank her, not me. You are free to continue in your travels and finish your challenge if you so desire. But you must do it on your own. Our own destiny calls us another way."

"Thank you, my liege. I do so desire to become a brother to the Fianna and I would be honored to serve you as well," he said alive with excitement.

"Good. Then we must bid you goodbye, so that we may continue our journey," I said.

"No!" he exclaimed. Kelan stepped forward. "What I mean is that I wish very much to give you a token of my thanks. I have lived here for some years and I have forged weapons from the magic rocks and trees that are abundant in the Otherworld. A year ago, I made two matching weapons, except one was larger than the other. I never knew what inspired me to do this, but I see the wooden weapon that you used to hit me. Please come so that I may give them to you. I now know for whom they were made."

Kelan and I looked at one another. He shrugged, but I could tell he wanted to see them. He had a love for unique weapons and this did sound interesting.

We walked up a steep hill away from the water. At the top of the ledge was a simple hut, made with sticks, grass, and mud. Next to it was a large hearth with smoke streaming from the fire. Surrounding the hearth were anvils with sledgehammers and swords.

Lon went inside his hut and reappeared with two bundles of cloth. He knelt on the ground and unrolled the smaller one. It was the *ton-fa* that I had seen so often in my dreams, but it was different, blessed by the magic of the Otherworld.

Lon picked it up and passed it to me. "This is Iron Wood made from the mystical oaks of the Otherworld. This wood will not break, it will not rot, and as you use the handle, it will mold to your hand."

I placed my hand around the handle. It was black and glossy and looked like the onyx rock that dwelled in the deepest caves. The handle connected without a seam to the arm of the weapon. It was also made of the same material, but the outer edge and the rounded sides were covered in glowing silver metal. Elaborate Celtic knots wove around the edges and a falcon soaring over a lady was etched in its center.

"Aeiden," I whispered in awe. But that was not all. On the front head of the *ton-fa*, protruded a spike made of the same metal and was so sharp, it would prove fatal with the briefest swipe.

Next Lon opened Kelan's weapon and indeed it was the same majestic piece, but bigger to fit his frame. In the center of the glowing metal were a man and woman riding together on a horse and above them in the clouds were glowing eyes watching over them.

"The Eyes of the Goddess," Kelan stated. We knew who the two riders were and my cheeks felt hot.

"Lon, the gods have blessed you with a skill that few could ever match. I thank you for the precious gifts that you have bestowed on us. Know that when you enter our world again, you and your skills will be welcome at my father's rath."

Lon kneeled again in front of me and spoke, "I thank you, my lady."

Eager to look at his other weapons, Kelan and Lon entered the small hut and stayed in there for what seemed an eternity. I sat down on a bed of leaves and leaned my body against a large oak tree. The day's fighting had tired me out. I closed my eyes to welcome sleep.

"'Mikala'!" Over here," Maecha *screams.* Michaela *runs toward Maecha and stares at the hoard of warriors attacking her. She swings her tonfa right and left hitting the warriors low. Maecha and Michaela fight side by side and the warriors fear them. They retreat and the women remove their helmets. The warriors scream and run away.*

Kelan watches from afar. He knows his love is for Maecha and knows his responsibility is to get Michaela back home. Maecha smiles and yells for Kelan to come.

"Kelan!" Maecha calls in her sleep.

"Maecha," a soft voice sounded in my ear. "Wake up, you are dreaming."

I lifted my heavy eyelids and saw Kelan kneeling next to me, smirking.

"What?" I croaked.

"You were dreaming, my sleepy queen, and it sounds like I was in it," Kelan said laughing and pulling me to my feet.

"What did I say?" I asked.

"You spoke my name," Kelan said. "Is there anything you need to tell me?"

"Yes, you were in my dream, Kelan, but not as you are thinking," I said, laughing at his feigned disappointment. "I dreamt that 'Mikala' and I were fighting side by side and warriors were afraid of us, especially our faces. We look very much alike."

"Hmmm," Kelan thought. "Maybe she is your spirit from another time. Together you might be powerful enough to succeed in our journey. We will let the dream world tell us more."

The sun was lower in the sky. We said our goodbyes to Lon and hurried on. Kelan chattered on about Lon's weapons and I knew he looked forward to seeing him again.

"It's almost dark. We should find a place to rest," said Kelan.

As if by magic, we found a small hut hiding in the trees, which was well supplied with straw beddings, blankets, and food. As we ate the dried meat, cheese, and bread we talked about the next challenge. "I think we have to stay together. We'll have to try to keep our backs away from the enemy and not get surrounded," Kelan said almost to himself. He lay down on his bed of straw and just about talked himself to sleep. I sat there watching him and felt his mind drift toward his dreams. I wondered if I would somehow be able to connect to his dreams and became nervous about what I would find.

I thought about what happened today. This first challenge had changed us and I wasn't sure how far this oneness would go. Would there be a physical union? The image on Kelan's weapon seemed intimate. With my mother dying so young, I never had the chance to learn about pleasing a man and the thought frightened me.

Kelan opened his eyes and saw me still sitting up. He opened his arms and I crawled next to him. His warmth soothed me and I fell asleep.

Dance with Benjamin Walker. Twirls me around and my gown flows about me like an endless carousel. We come together, our bodies touching. We kiss.

"Shannon. Where are you?" whispers Michaela. Shannon turns and Benjamin Walker fades into the darkness.

"Damn," Shannon says.

"Who was that?" Michaela asks.

"What? You could see that?" Shannon asks shocked.

"Yes, I could see that. We are in each other's dreams and you were looking mighty cozy."

"It's Benjamin Walker, Uncle Frank's partner. I feel that I can trust him. I want to see if he will help me. Listen. I don't know how long I can stay in this state, so let me talk. Uncle Frank called about having some leads. He sounded agitated, but excited."

Michaela thinks. Her gi turns into a leather tunic and a pointed tonfa appears in her hand.

"Shannon, I'm so sorry about this. I wish I could figure out how to get back to my body, but right now Maecha needs me and until I help her, I don't think I'm going anywhere. So it's up to you. Find Natalie, Shannon. She is the key to all of this. See if this Benjamin friend of yours is for real. See what Uncle Frank thinks about him," Michaela says as her image fades.

"Take care, Michaela," Shannon yells.

"Kiss Vince for me and trust him," Michaela whispers.

"Who is Vince?" Maecha asks coming up behind Michaela. Michaela walks toward her Celtic friend, her leather tunic hard against her skin. Maecha is dressed in a light, see-through gown.

"He is a special man in my life back home," Michaela replies.

Maecha asks, "How do you know that he is special and... how do you show it?"

"You know this, because you can't live without seeing him all the time and you try everything to be within his touch. Your hearts sing together and you are the most comfortable with him. You show him this by displaying your love and telling him how you feel. Don't be afraid of Kelan," Michaela says and Maecha blushes.

"I adore him, but I don't want us to change. We are such good friends and I don't want to lose that. Plus his emotions are filled with pain and confusion. I cannot take all the emotions I feel from him," she says and an upset Kelan appears behind her.

Michaela yearns for Vince, but knows she must help this girl right now. "Don't fight the feelings. Let them flow through you and keep them in one part of your heart. You have to be strong for this next challenge and you have to learn to keep your emotions under control when you fight. Fight the enemy, not Kelan, and your love will come."

9

I opened my eyes to the sun streaming through the cracks in the small hut. I looked around and saw Kelan sitting against the wall watching me. "Good morning," I muttered pulling myself away from my dreams. After I had said goodbye to 'Mikala', my dream world was filled with Kelan. Just thinking about them made my skin turn hot and I hoped our dreams weren't connected.

"Good morning to you. You look refreshed," Kelan said with a whimsical smile.

"Yes, I slept well, but it looks late. We should leave," I said and walked outside. Kelan followed.

"I found a path along the river," he said. "I think we should follow it."

"Then, let us begin," I said and we set off on the next part of our journey. I ate bread as we walked through the still forest. We did not know when the next challenge would be upon us, so it was necessary to be wary at all times. I smelled the fresh scent of spraying water and saw a break in the trees. As we walked through the opening, the turbulent water flowed out of a cavern in the rocks. Lush trees protruded from the jagged cliffs and the wildlife was abundant and loud. I could hear a distinct calling that was louder and more persistent than all the other sounds. I looked into the sky and saw a huge bird circling above the cavern. I thought of Aeiden and wondered how he fared without me. As the bird flew lower, I realized it was the Griffin who had saved my life and befriended me. The Griffin flew over our heads and headed downstream.

"This way, Kelan," I said and began to walk along the cliffs, the water on my left. Kelan knew better than to question me when it came to birds. He had seen the unique relationship I shared with my falcon. We came to a flat area of the cliff and the Griffin screeched and landed.

Walking up to the Griffin, I patted his beak. "It is good to see you again, my feathered friend. Do you wish us to go with you?"

The Griffin bowed its head and I pulled myself up onto its back. I beckoned for Kelan to do the same and we flew off following the winding path of the river. We entered into a mist and the world turned white. We came out upon a magical place where a palace sparkled with precious stones and metals, and was surrounded by endless fields overflowing with flowers. The Griffin lowered us close to the palace. I said goodbye once again to my Griffin friend and knew that I would see him again. We walked toward the palace, shielding our eyes from its brightness. It appeared to be deserted. Kelan unsheathed his sword, but I stopped him.

"Do you hear that?" I asked. I could hear music. It was slow, melodic, and soothing. My body began to feel heavy and relaxed.

Kelan listened and replied, "Yes, it sounds like the music of the faery folk. Beware its enchanting sound, Maecha."

As he spoke a beautiful woman appeared with her arms raised in joy. "Ah, you have arrived, my children. My name is Gaia and I welcome you," she said as she came and kissed me on each cheek and hugged me close. She smelled of wildflowers and hyacinth and, combined with the music, I felt intoxicated. Then she turned to Kelan and taking his face in her hands, kissed him on the lips and, as he inhaled, I could see that the woman had the same effect on him, but more.

I watched her as she stepped away. Her gown was white and barely covered her naked body. Gold bands wrapped around her upper arms and folds of cloth flowed down to her fingers. Her shining black hair was long and hung past her waist. She wore a band of flowers around her head and her sapphire blue eyes were big like a doe. She entranced Kelan and I felt a twinge of jealousy as this beautiful woman swept him away.

A tall, handsome man strolled out of the palace. His skin was dark and smooth and he laughed and embraced me like a long lost lover. He wore a vest and light pants and his body danced as he turned and walked with me. "I am Aeric and I welcome you to my home, Maecha Ruadh mac Art." Aeric held my hand up to his lips and kissed it as he spoke. His copper eyes lustily held mine. I fell into them and let him lead me to the center court. A band of young girls ran over to us. Soon the palace was alive with laughter and song and beautiful people kissed and hugged one other.

Two girls came up to me and bowed. They took my bag and *ton-fa* and tried to remove Imbas Skye. I stopped them, but Aeric put his arms around my waist and removed my sheath. "We are a people of peace. We do not like to subject our children to the crude weapons of death. They will be safe here. You do not need them anymore," he said and I let him take my sword. Before I could feel its absence, they placed a wreath of flowers and ferns around my head and the scent further intoxicated my mind.

I tried to keep it clear to speak to Aeric. "Where are we?"

Aeric gave me a gold cup filled with mead. We drank as a sign of friendship and peace. "We are the people of Tir-nan-Og and you are on the Isle of the Blessed. We are what you may call the faery folk and we live here happy and free. We stay forever young and all who stay with us may live as we do. We love, laugh, sing and dance. The land provides all that we need and we provide to each other everything else," he said.

"Oh," I wondered what everything else meant. "What is that lovely music?" I asked.

"That is the melody of the apple-branch that blooms crystal flowers. It is soothing, yes?" He smiled as I nodded. "Come, we have a feast tonight and you and your friend are the guests of honor."

The mead hall was enormous and all the faery folk gathered together to feast. There was no order to where they sat. Men, women, and children mingled and dined wherever they wanted. The hall was enclosed by tall marble pillars and overhead a balcony surrounded the pillars. Little children ran around laughing while being chased.

The food and drink were plentiful. The mead flowed from an endless vat and Aeric did not waste time in getting plenty of it for me. Tables overflowed with roasted and boiled pork, beef, ox, and fish covered with honey, butter, milk, cheese, wine, mead and beer. There were no quarrels over the food, just joyous feasting. After the meal, pastries covered with honey were passed around.

Although not as elegant as Gaia, most of the women wore the same sheer gown and precious stones glittered in their hair. They wore crystals on their ears and necklaces that lured the men to them. I touched my chest to make sure my Awen crystals were still there.

Most of the men wore a vest without a shirt, but some were bare-chested and gloated when the women placed their hands over them. Lovers lay all around on lush furs, and I blushed at their physical contact. I searched for Kelan and saw him lying on a rug with Gaia, enjoying the festivities. Jealousy rang through my head and I couldn't relax.

Those who were not enjoying one another on the rugs stood up and began to dance around the hall. The music was loud and boisterous. I danced with Aeric and was lulled into this enchanted place.

Later that night, the children were carried off into another room. People slept wherever their philandering left them. Aeric had fallen asleep on some large, soft pillows in the hall and I slid away from him to find Kelan. I found him wound around Gaia at the other end of the hall. Anger surged through me. I bent over to shake him and felt a hand on my arm. I stood ready to hit the person stopping me. It was Aeric.

He pulled me to him. "Leave him be. What happens on the Isle of the Blessed is the wish of the Goddess. Be with me, Maecha," Aeric whispered in my ear and kissed me. His lips felt soft like rose petals and my body relaxed and molded into his. Aeric led me away.

Let's see how Kelan feels, I thought.

Kelan forced his eyes open and lifted his head. "Maecha?" he called, but Gaia once again lured him back to her intoxicating love.

The feasting went on for days. No one needed to till the fields or work. Each morning the hall was clean and the food abundant. The faery folk would go outside during the day to run and frolic. It was hard to separate the children from the adults, since they all played together. They were carefree and the thought appealed to me. I let my world and Kelan slip further away from me. I enjoyed Aeric's company. He kept me fed and he taught me the ways of love.

After countless days of idleness and lovemaking, I dreamed.

I run through the woods surrounding the Isle of the Blessed. Aeric playfully chases me. He catches me and brings me to the ground. The leaves and grass are soft under our bodies and I welcome him to me.

"NO!" a voice yells around us. Aeric jumps up, afraid of the

voice. I look around me and just beyond some trees I see a body lying on the ground. I run over and 'Mikala' is lying unconscious. I cannot awaken her. The Goddess's voice bellows through the clouds. "She is lost in your inebriated world. You are killing her with your lack of direction and your lust. Remember your promises and your duties. Remember Kelan. He will stay here forever if you don't stop this foolishness."

Waking, I looked around me. I had forgotten about Kelan and why we were here. We had been in this land too long and if we did not leave soon, we would stay forever. I was upset by the sight of 'Mikala' and felt terrible that I had ignored her. I didn't realize that my actions affected her. But my mind was still enchanted by the music. It was late in the evening. Aeric, sensing my mood, pulled me up to dance. My heart leapt with joy and I felt like this was where I belonged. We danced and swung in the circle. Everyone cheered and sang. The mead was once again poured into my mouth. The music slowed and Aeric held me close in a rapturous dance. I could feel every part of his body move with mine and I wanted him to be even closer. He lowered his face and his lips touched mine. My lips tingled with his magic and I felt myself slipping away from my body. "I'm dying," I thought, but it was fine as long as I was with Kelan.

Kelan. I pulled away from this faery magician and looked around. Over the music, I could hear my champion's laughter. That sound pulled me out of my drunken fantasy and I turned to find him. Aeric tried to swing me around as the music picked up its beat again, but I saw him. I saw Kelan, my champion, my would-be lover, entwined with Gaia like an overgrown vine. My mind cleared and I looked around at everyone. Perhaps their joy was real and they were content with their blissful life. But I did not belong here and neither did Kelan. I thought of my father and remembered where my destiny lay.

"Are you ill, my love?" Aeric asked.

I feigned a headache. I didn't know what he would do if he knew I wanted to leave. "My head hurts. May I go lie down?"

"Of course," he said and led me to an elaborate room. The walls glittered like crystals and the bed frame was bedecked with jewels and a canopy of silk. The bed itself was overlaid with plush pillows and it looked very inviting. My bag was there, but I noticed that my weapons were not. Aeric leaned against me and kissed my forehead and said, "Is there anything that I can do to soothe your mind?"

"Perhaps later," I said kissing his cheek. I lay down on the bed, so that he would leave. I thought of Kelan and knew that I had to form a plan or else he would be spending the rest of his life here. I tried to reach him with my mind. *"Kelan. Kelan. We need to leave. You must come to me."*

"Ha, ha! Gaia, Gaia, Gaia, you enchanting woman. I want to stay with you forever," was all I needed to hear. Anger filled me that I couldn't break into his thoughts.

I removed the flower from my head and splashed water on my face. Feeling better, I grabbed my bag and peeked out the doorway. An almost naked man and woman were enjoying each other's company on the stairs, so I couldn't leave that way. I walked out onto the balcony. It was too high to jump. It was a clear night lit bright by the full moon. A huge creature flew overhead. My Griffin. I whistled as I had always done with Aeiden and the Griffin once again came to my aid. I stood at the edge of the balcony and he scooped me up in his talons and flew toward the open fields. I noticed something protruding out of the ground and pulled on my friend to let me down. The Griffin did and waited for me to scratch behind his eye.

"You are a dear friend and yet I don't know your name," I said while rubbing his head. The Griffin stared at me with his great big eyes and cooed. "You are worthy of a king, my friend, and I think I will name you after the king that I love. I shall call you Art." He nodded his head with delight and flew away. The sky was clear and the moon shown like a huge red disk high in the sky. The palace was still close and glistened like a second moon. What had attracted me were standing stones lined up in the middle of the fields.

There were thirteen stones and they all stood tall in a circle. I touched one and tried to feel the spirits of the ones who had built these magnificent stones. Great magic always occurred within the stones and as I stepped into its circle I prayed to the Goddess Macha that I would be accepted.

I peered at the moon and its face was bright, but menacing. The moon's eyes glowed orange and its mouth frowned at my presence. I reached for Imbas Skye, but remembered she was gone. It didn't take long for the evil spirits lingering in the ground to realize that I was vulnerable and for me to realize that I did not belong here. A huge man stepped out from behind the standing stone. His long yellow hair was held down by a wolf mask, which covered his face. His eyes glowed yellow and he laughed at me. He carried a huge axe and a *seax*, a single-edge knife. He snarled and lunged for me. I felt defenseless without my weapons. I managed to dodge him twice, but knew that I would not be able to keep up this pace.

"*Use cada'me!*" I heard a voice yell. 'Mikala'. As the warrior swung at me, I stepped under his swing and kicked him hard in his side. He fell forward and hit his head on a stone. I grabbed his axe and managing to lift it over my head, swung down hard to remove his head from his body. An evil, demented spirit escaped from his lifeless form and disappeared into the night. Other warriors appeared wearing different animal masks: snake, tiger, bear, and eagle. They attempted to encircle me, but I kept my back close to a stone. They raised their voices in a battle cry and attacked. The axe was cumbersome. I swung at bear's arm and he dropped his club. I finished him and his club became my weapon. I blocked and struck with the club to keep their menacing weapons from removing my head. I hit one warrior in the

238

head and his snake mask flew off. He glared at me and his glowing eyes shot flames of fire at me. I fell back to the ground and another masked demon sliced my arm open. I screamed as my blood flowed into the sacred ground and I knew that more demons would rise.

"KELAN!" I screamed and grabbed a sword and dagger. I swung out in a battle frenzy to save my life. They came at me from all angles. A warrior swung his sword at me. I blocked with the dagger and hit him in the face with the blunt end of my sword. I sliced another attacker with my sword and forced the one that I still held in front of an oncoming sword. I shoved the dead warrior away from me and waited for the next enemy. I swung and jabbed, removing limbs, masks, and anything that came in my way. I prayed for Kelan to reach his senses.

I felt something warm on my chest and thought that I had been stabbed. My crystal glowed and I hoped that Kelan still had his around his neck. Fatigue set in and the enemy grew stronger. A monkey warrior jumped at me. His dance distracted me and it took all my concentration to keep track of his movements. He carried two daggers that flew through the air and came too close to me. Dropping my weapons I thought of 'Mikala's' teachings. I I stepped back and hit his hand toward the ground and grabbing it, flipped him over onto his back. I removed his dagger, but he jumped back up and lunged for me. The others stopped to watch what they believed would be the end. He lunged and I tried to get out of the way.

"Ahhhh!" he screamed and fell dead to the earth. A sword protruded from his back. I looked up and saw my champion swaying from intoxication. But the battle frenzy was inside him and, as he threw Imbas Skye and then my *ton-fa* to me, he retrieved his own sword and sought to destroy the rest of the demons. With Imbas Skye in my hands again I screamed for blood and raced after my enemies. Imbas Skye sang in triumph as her sacred eye sought its victims and shot out her fury. The enemies seemed endless.

The challenge had begun and I remembered its words—
'Feel the strength of oneness, its power will make you whole.
Fight the warriors together and you will have one soul.' As I
fought I began to feel a fluidity of movement and I could see that
Kelan was fighting in unison with me. Our bodies flowed
through the steps of cada'me that we both had just learned. We
swung our swords as one and blocked and jabbed with our tonfas. The warriors encircled us and we pulled together back to
back in a fighting stance to protect each other. Our movements
were mirrored, fast and powerful. Our bodies melded together
and we danced with death as one. We were one. I saw what he
saw and we reacted together. As the demons fell to the ground in
pools of blood, their spirits screamed in protest and rose into the
sky. As the last one disappeared, the moon's red glare softened to
a pale white.

When they were all dead, I lowered Imbas Skye. Her blue
eye closed like it had been praying instead of slaying endless victims. We both dropped to the ground back to back.

"Maecha," was all Kelan said as he turned to me. We knelt
and leaned into each other, our foreheads touching. Our crystals
were a brighter yellow than before and the spirits of Imbas Skye
soared around us in triumph.

Placing our hands together, we looked at one other.

"How did you know?" I asked. Kelan pointed to his chest
and I could see a mark where the glowing crystal had burned him
with its urgency.

"It certainly broke whatever spell had been set on me," he
said and he lowered his face. "Maecha. I don't deserve to be your
champion. While you were here fighting for your life, I was
enjoying myself and being…unfaithful." He shook his head in
shame.

This time, I cupped Kelan's face in my hands and lifted it
so he could look at me. "What we have done was the will of the

Goddess. There is no shame. You came for me and that is all that matters. This journey is a test and we are being tested in all areas of our abilities and feelings." Still sensing his disappointment in himself, I continued, "Kelan, you are destined to be my champion…and more. You protected me once again and I will be forever thankful."

"No. It is you who protected me from an uncertain fate," he responded.

"Then we have a great deal to be thankful for," I said and kissed him. Kelan pulled me tightly to him. Where it had felt nice with Aeric, with Kelan it was stimulating. Every part of my body wanted to be connected to his. Our souls had united.

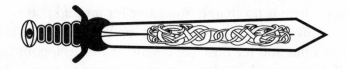

10

I awoke with Kelan's kiss lingering on my lips. I still felt the sensation of his body touching mine. I wanted to feel it again, but he was gone. I had my belongings and weapons, but my champion had disappeared and so had the faery folk. We had won both challenges and now it was time to prove to the Lordly Ones, and myself, that I was a warrior worthy to be initiated into the mighty Fianna. I thought of Kelan and prayed to Macha, Goddess of War, to protect him.

The cool wind swept my hair off my back. I listened to the sounds around me—birds, animals, water, and wind. Then I turned within me. I heard a voice and it wasn't 'Mikala's'. *"Maecha. Think like a warrior. Be the warrior that I know you are and come back to me."*

"I will, Kelan," I said and I stood to begin my final quest. Throughout our journey, the water had been our guide. We had been swept along the currents and nature molded our very beings. We had both changed and now the final transformation would decide who would survive. I was motivated to pass this challenge, so I could be initiated into a group that I had forever admired. But I also wanted to see Kelan and to experience our oneness in the 'real' world.

I was at a cliff that looked down upon the water. I saw a

path that led to a smaller waterfall. I stepped down along the roots so that I faced the water. I smelled the damp earth and the water's mist chilled my skin. The thunderous sound of the water pouring over the rocks blocked out my ability to think and I allowed it to do so for the moment. I stepped further down so that I was next to the flowing water. I sat down. My heart raced and I needed someone's comfort. I closed my eyes and prayed to the Mother Goddess to guide me so that I could help my people and save my father. I waited.

A peace encircled me and spirits hugged my soul, bringing me strength. I could do this. When I opened my eyes, I saw that the falls had parted and a bridge led to a cavern. On the edge of the bridge, I saw my mother. She was dressed as a warrior. She wore a leather tunic and woolen breeches. Around her neck was her gold torque and her crown encircled her wavy red hair that blew with the wind. I stepped onto the Bridge of Swords. The bridge looked simple with its wooden floor and rope handles. But above me were rows of swords covering the bridge like a canopy, their tips touching in challenge to their next opponent.

My mother had walked onto the bridge. She looked happy to see me, but I noted a sadness lingering around her eyes and wondered what could sadden her in this enchanted land. She held her hands upward and out and looked around .her. She warned me to watch myself, to be aware. I heard screeches from below and, although I could not recognize their sounds, I knew that they were eager for someone to fall into their watery grave.

The first part of my challenge echoed in my head—'Many dangers will await you. Fight the one who has no name. If its power succeeds to bind you, here you will remain.'

Hearing steps I turned to see a warrior at the other edge of the bridge. Long hair covered his lowered face and he held his sword by his side. His tunic and breeches were tattered and stained. He was a formidable opponent. I walked toward him.

"What is your name?" I asked, wanting to know who I

was about to kill.

Remaining silent, he lifted his head. As his hair fell away, I could see his face or lack of. His eyes stared at me from bony sockets and his skeleton mouth chattered at me in nonsense.

"Do you have a name?" I asked again not knowing what to make of this creature. He answered with his sword. "Prepare to die, No Name," I said and attacked. He swung his sword down and I stepped in jabbing him in his stomach with my *ton-fa*. Not affecting him, he came back at me and I met his sword with the strength of the spirits that existed in Imbas Skye. The spirits of the women who had owned this sword before me sang out a war song and gave me strength. Our swords clashed high, then low. I did not have a shield, but protected myself with the *ton-fa*. I blocked No Name's sword arm with the *ton-fa* and jabbed his bony face with its sharp point. He felt the pain and I swung my sword to rip through his side. He checked me and we stopped. Our sword arms were locked in a battle of strength. Knowing that mine would not last as long, I kicked him in the groin and sliced his arm. He fell to his knees and I raised my sword to remove his head.

He turned to me and his skinless jaw said, "My name is Each-luath. I am a member of the Fian from the Otherworld. If you will be merciful and let me live, I will be honored to serve as a member of the Fian under your command." He bent his head down revealing a spiny neck to await my decision.

I knew the power of the Otherworld Fian and I knew that Each-luath had once saved our infamous leader Fionn mac Cumhail. He had walked into a flaming cave, where Fionn had been trapped by an enemy. He died saving Fionn and some had said that his skin had been burned down to the bone. I could see that this was true and understood that he tested my ability to fight. He had been allowed to live as one of the protectors of the Bridge of Swords.

I thought of my challenge and believed that I had won

and could be merciful. Besides, the Ring of Mercy glowed. I lowered my sword and spoke, "Rise, Each-luath of the Fian. You have shown that you are a most worthy member by saving your leader and I would be honored to have such a brave warrior help me." Each-luath rose slowly. He stood as he had done when I first saw him—his face hidden by his long hair. His body shook and I saw tears dripping from his sockets. "Look at me *feinnidh*," I said.

He did and I saw the face of a boy who had lost his body so long ago in heroism only to have it given back now. His long hair was now silky blond and his brown eyes stared at me in awe. He bowed in front of me, touching his head to his sword. "Thank you, Maecha Ruadh mac Art, for sparing my life. You have the power of your father and the mercy of your mother. Those qualities together make you a true leader. I must go now, but will always be there when you call the Fian." He turned and disappeared into a mist that had begun to surround the bridge.

The mist became thick. My eyes were clouded by the white flow of thick air that threatened to overtake me. I heard hissing sounds. They were all around me and my mind became as clouded as my eyes. I turned trying to pinpoint the noise.

"Aarghh!" I yelled falling in pain. Something stabbed me in my back and I felt the blood flow down my legs. I did not know how another could have seen me and cursed myself for not being quieter. I stuffed a cloth inside my tunic, where the leather had been pierced. I stood up.

As fast as the mist appeared, it shrank low underneath the bridge and I saw everything. I saw clearer than I would have ever wanted to see and I cursed my eyes for bringing me the knowledge that I had held secret in my heart. With the blood still dripping from his dagger, he watched me. The man's face was covered in a unique helmet. But this wasn't just any helmet. It was the helmet my father had collected off the head of the Scottish king's son. It had the horns and tail of an animal. Only the smallest part of the enemy's eyes could be seen and, while the nose and jaw were covered, the mouth was open so that the mortally wounded would see the terrible grin of their enemy. This was the helmet that disappeared from my father's armory.

As I stared, I recognized the evil grin and spirit of my enemy. "Cairpre," I said. His image became cloudy and I forced myself to keep my eyes open lest this evil spirit of my brother killed me. I knew he had a role in my father's capture, just as I knew he had taken my father's treasured helmet.

I raised my sword to rid the Bridge of Swords of a wretched enemy. I heard my mother's lamentation beyond me. I knew now why her spirit was here. She wanted me to show mercy to this man that I had once called my brother. But the Ring of Mercy was dark and I knew what would have to be done.

"AHHHHhhh!" I screamed and swung my sword with all my strength at this demon. My sword went through his image. As I turned to look for him, I felt something entwining itself around me. When I tried to run the bindings became tighter. They glowed like fire and I could feel them burning into my skin. I tried to swing Imbas Skye, but my arms were soon tight against my body. I was overwhelmed and fell to the floor of the bridge. My sword fell out of my hand and my brother appeared over my head. I wanted nothing more than to wipe his nasty smile off his face, but I could not move.

Cairpre saw my sword and his greedy eyes lit with delight. He picked it up and held it close to his face. The Celtic knots wove around the blade and Cairpre swung the sword screaming with victory. He thought that he had won the sword.

Distracted as he was, I reached into my pouch and grabbed the magic ball that I had found fighting the rock warriors. "Open," I whispered. The ball became the magic stick and I pressed it on my bindings. The light began to fade and the bindings loosened their death grip on me.

Imbas Skye was awake and Cairpre tossed it from one hand to the other. The handle glowed like a sword in a blacksmith's fire.

"Give me the sword, Cairpre. It is not for you. It is only for those worthy to wield it," I warned.

Cairpre spit at me. "You think that you deserve this sword just because our mother held it? Anyone can hold this sword, even a man." He laughed and then the blue eye opened. She saw me, then saw my brother. She grew brighter and I had to shield my eyes. She shot at Cairpre's eyes and singed them. Cairpre screamed and dropped the sword.

My bindings dropped to the ground and I retrieved my sword. Cairpre still managed to get up and lunged for me. I stepped aside and hit him with the side of my sword. I no longer wanted to kill my brother, I just wanted to leave. I lost a great deal of blood from my wound and I needed to get help.

Cairpre grabbed a sword from the bridge and swung at me, even with singed eyes. His blows were tremendous and each strike weakened me. He grabbed another sword and swung both in a dizzying sword dance. I could no longer follow his speed. He swung his right arm in at my head. I blocked it, but his left came down over my head and just missed. I never saw Cairpre drop his sword and grab a dagger, and so I fell to the ground as his dagger found my flesh again.

"'Mikala'! 'Mikala'! Where are you? Please help me. I'm so cold," Maecha calls as she drags herself along the chilled ground. Maecha stops and lays her face down, too weak to move.

"I am here, my friend," Michaela says. She picks up the wounded warrior and lays her down on a bed of soft grass. The images around Maecha change as the world she enters is now Michaela's.

Michaela silently tends Maecha's wound, not knowing if what she does here will benefit her friend in the Otherworld. She had watched in frustration as Maecha fought her brother and wondered how long she would remain in this state. Maecha sleeps and

Michaela sets up a vigil to pray for her friend's recovery. Maecha's life in Ireland and Michaela's life in New York City depend on it.

"Bring her by the fire, my dears," the sidhe said. "Our young queen-to-be has been touched by the poisoned Dagger of Ocmar."

Most would-be members of the Fianna would not be helped in the Otherworld and the lethal wound from the evil spirit would have meant instant death. However, the Otherworld's safety was at stake and it was now necessary for Maecha to be healed in order to finish her journey. The three daughters of Beag, son of Buan had seen the power of Maecha and had watched in fear as she had been wounded. These three women were the guardians of the Well of the Moon. This was the sacred well in Tir-nan-Og and it had the power to grant knowledge and skills to ordinary men and women. Along with the power of knowledge, it could heal one from death when water was drunk from the sacred Cauldron of the Tuatha De Danaan's 'Good God' Eoghan Ollathair. Also known as the Great Father, Ollathair had two special attributes, his club and his cauldron. His club was such that one end killed the living and the other revived the dead and when he dragged it behind him, it left a track as deep as the boundary ditch between two provinces. Known as the Vessel of the Otherworld, the Cauldron brought endless satisfaction to the one drinking from it and had the ability to heal those deemed worthy.

The sidhe, Sean-Gharman, had been prepared in the event that Maecha would be wounded. She had been a long-time friend of Queen Deirdre and had helped her often from the Otherworld.

"Hold her mouth open, so that the water will flow in," the sidhe said to Ailbhe, the eldest daughter. "Elen, Goddess of healing and water—Save this child as she is the link to the goodness of her father. Her victory will bring peace to her lands and will serve as the protector of the Otherworld. Protect her now and she will be forever tied to the Lordly Ones. Blessed be thy name, Oh Holy Mother of Life," Sean-Gharman chanted as the other sisters held their hands up to the starless night and added their prayers.

The water sparkled as it flowed into Maecha's mouth and ran down the sides of her face soaking her hair. She gagged and choked pushing the cup away. "Drink, little one," the sidhe said smoothing her hair. With her eyes still closed, Maecha took the cup and drank until her body was content and her mind brimmed with the knowledge of the Otherworld.

Maecha dreamed of her father leading his men into battle. While running toward the battle his war cry was cut short from a spear tearing through his back. He stopped and looked down bewildered at the direction of the spear. Maecha heard a laugh from behind her father. She turned to face this enemy from within; only to be faced by her brother. His laugh turned to a sneer and he lunged for Maecha.

11

Shannon cancelled her morning appointments. She thought about her sister. She knew Michaela was OK, if you could call being trapped in some time warp OK, but she was scared. Everything was closing in on her. She was worried about Uncle Frank. She had left a few messages for him that morning and Ben had called her to say that he couldn't find him. He wasn't at home and he hadn't shown up for work yet.

Sonya's voice interrupted her thoughts. "Yes, Sonya, what is it?"

"Mr. Cartillo is here to see you again, Ms. Sommers."

What more did she have to say? That man was a thorn in Shannon's side. No maybe a knife and he wasn't going away.

"Show him in please," Shannon said.

Ricky walked in and Shannon noted his disarrayed appearance. For a man as anal he was, one hair out of place would be enough to know that something was wrong. His eyes were black and he looked pale.

"Mr. Cartillo, are you ill?" Shannon asked concerned in spite of herself. She motioned for him to sit down and she sat across from him and waited.

"Ah, Shannon. Where do I begin? I must tell you a couple things that I hope will not tarnish your image of me."

Shannon raised one eyebrow and waited.

"As you know, I came to this country many years ago, because my family could not support me. Now I support my family. With my successful business I have done that and more. My ambitions run deep and I will do everything I can to make sure that my family is well taken care of. I have grown used to a lifestyle that sometimes my business was not able to maintain, so I have taken up a type of business that your father did not approve of. Not that he ever approved of me, but I thought you must know," he said.

"So it's true that you are in the drug business?" Shannon asked.

"Yes, but not what you would call hard-core drugs. These are fun drugs. You must have tried Ecstasy? It is the love drug; the latest craze at these rave parties. The kids enjoy it. It helps them to lose their inhibitions and get the most out of life."

Shannon was livid. She answered, "No, I have not. Nor do I care to try any. It seems that your side job has been the cause of all the misery in my family's life. Do you know how many of those kids come in here, because they have lost control of their lives?!"

Ricky did not appear ashamed. "I am not here to apologize for what I have done. Everyone is responsible for his or her own actions. What people do with what I supply them is their problem. As long as I keep business going, then my family is safe. That is all that matters to me. I still consider you family and your suffering causes me pain." He paused and looked at Shannon. "Plus, I miss Michaela."

"What about my father?" Shannon asked.

"Your father," he said.

Shannon stood up and walked over to Ricky Cartillo. She was no longer afraid of this man. She felt rage toward him and knew that he was the one behind everything.

"Did you kill my father?" she asked.

Ricky Cartillo studied his polished nails…and lied, "No."

Cartillo was good, but she was trained for this. It was the same with her patients when she asked if they were using drugs again. They would look to the left and deny everything. That meant that they were making up some story again so she could tell their parole officers that their treatment was complete. Shannon knew better, and she was smarter. But, she had to take no for now. She needed proof and she needed this Natalie girl.

"Fine. I accept your answer and I don't care about your business or your life anymore. I want to get my sister back and be done with all of you. Can you help me with this?" she finished.

Ricky smiled like a snake snagging the egg that had been guarded so well. "Yes, I can help you, but you must know some things. I believe that Captain Newman may have been responsible for your father's death and your sister's disappearance."

"Captain Newman?" Shannon retorted.

"Do you think that everyone plays by the rules like your father? What about Frank? What is he doing? How long do you think you will last if you do not let this go?" Cartillo kept asking questions, forcing doubt to invade Shannon's mind.

He continued. "I am trying to help you, Shannon. I tried to protect Michaela, but…I failed," he stammered.

Shannon wasn't moved by his show of concern. "Protect us?! I think you caused all this! I don't know exactly what you or Captain Newman did, but you won't get me!" she screamed.

"Shannon, I am sworn by my love for your mother that I did nothing to your sister. Before your mother died, I promised her that I would do everything in my power to protect both of you," he pleaded.

Shannon walked to the window. Her hands shook and she couldn't breathe deep enough to calm herself down. She didn't want Cartillo to think he upset her. She turned and studied Ricky Cartillo. She could see the pain in his face and the anguish over her sister's disappearance, but he was unfazed about her father's death. Even if he wasn't responsible, this man was dangerous. She decided to play along with him.

"What do you want from me?" she asked.

"I need to know what happened to Michaela and get you both away for a while." He looked at Shannon. Her pale skin was flushed and Cartillo took a moment to appreciate her beauty. "I will also need to know if a small girl named Natalie tries to contact you. I think she has certain information that could be bad...for business," he finished.

"You want me to help save your ass?" she asked.

Ricky smiled at her audacity. "In a sense, yes."

"I'll see what I can do," Shannon said.

Ricky stood up. "Wonderful! I look forward to talking with you again. Perhaps you would like to dine at my mansion and I can update you on anything I find."

"You can call me, Mr. Cartillo," Shannon said.

"Fine. Fine. Whatever you wish, my dear. Know that I will search far and wide to bring Michaela back to us," he said as he kissed her hand and left.

Shannon thought about the complex man who left her office. For the first time she envied Michaela being stuck far away in some strange land. At least she was safe.

Shannon went home. It was useless to stay at work. She waited for Uncle Frank's call.

The phone rang. "Uncle Frank? I can't hear you. It's a bad connection...What? Was that gun shots? No, don't hang up!" Shannon yelled.

Frantic, she phoned the precinct for Ben. He raced over.

"Frank called me this morning, saying he had found a lead about Michaela and he would call me. I heard gun shots, Ben."

Ben asked, "What's going on here, Shannon? I told you I wanted to help you find your sister and I meant it. Frank isn't telling me anything and he is distracted. As his partner I need to know what he is involved in. I had a partner before and we were always honest with each other. I don't trust Frank and that scares me."

"What happened to your partner?" Shannon asked.

"He was killed in a car chase. I was apprehending a perp on foot and my partner, Sam, was chasing another guy in a car. Sam crashed and the car exploded. I tried to get him out, but I couldn't save him. I guess Captain Newman thought Frank and I could help one another, but half the time Frank isn't even with me," Ben explained.

Shannon thought about her sister and how she warned her to not trust people outside their close circle. People who her dad thought were friends had turned on him and now she wasn't sure who she could trust. She watched Ben as he spoke. She admired his smooth, square chin, his cropped blond hair and his blue eyes glowing with passion. She trusted Benjamin Walker and she could sense her father's approval.

"Ben." She kept eye contact. "There's a lot going on here. I don't know how much you want to know, but if I tell you then you are a part of it and I don't know how safe that is. I also don't know how safe it is for you to be with me."

Ben slipped Shannon's hand into his. "I'll take my chances." Shannon looked at their clasped hands and felt safe. With that Shannon told him everything—who was involved, what happened, the dreams. When she was done, she felt drained, but better.

However, Ben didn't look too good. "Now, I have to tell you something. You mentioned how your sister thought someone from within the precinct was involved with your father's death. I don't know if this is anything, but Captain Newman took me aside yesterday and asked me to keep a special eye on you as a favor to him. He said that Frank was too close to the situation and wasn't using good judgment and I was to let him know if anything strange happened around you. I thought he was concerned for your safety, but now I'm not so sure."

Shannon thought of Michaela's words—Brotherhood. Ricky told her Captain Newman killed her father. If the captain was involved, was she safe now that she revealed everything to Ben?

Ben noted her fear and eliminated it. "Don't worry, if Newman did this, he'll regret the day he ever thought he could use me. I know of your father's reputation. He was a man of conviction and he didn't give a damn what he was up against. If Captain Newman is responsible for your dad's death and the attacks on your sister, then he'll pay dearly. We just need some proof," Ben exclaimed.

Shannon squeezed Ben's hand. "Thank you, Ben. I didn't know where else to turn."

"I'm going to look for Frank. Everything will be all right," Ben said standing to leave.

"Please let me know as soon as you hear anything and be careful," Shannon pleaded.

"I will."

It was late. The last student had left the studio. Vince brought equipment into the back storage room. He hadn't locked the doors, and was surprised when he heard the front bell jingle. On edge since Michaela's disappearance, Vince peered around the door. Three oversized guys walked around.

"Are you looking for something?" Vince spoke. They stood there with their hands in their coat pockets not answering. "The studio is closed. Leave now."

One man in a long, dark brown overcoat lifted his hand up. "Calm down, mate. We're just looking for someone." He looked at his buddies and since it seemed he was in charge, he kept talking. "We are looking for the lady who runs this place."

Vince sneered. "Why?"

"Our boss wants to talk to her," he said.

"Yeah, and who's your boss, because I would like to talk to him," Vince spat.

"Hey, Mick," an even taller guy said from behind him. "Let's cut the crap. If this loser isn't going to talk, then I'm gonna bust him up." He pushed everyone out of his way and Vince prepared to take all his anger and frustration out on this dummy.

"Chill out, Al. I'm in charge," said Mick.

"Not anymore," said Al. He swung wide and fast toward Vince's head. Vince ducked out of the way. He chopped his opponent's groin, knocking him forward. He dropped to one knee and punched his assailant's ribs, then elbowed him to the ground. Vince kicked the man called Al in the ribs, forcing him over onto his back.

The silent one lunged forward flipping a butterfly knife through the air. Vince backed up, letting the guy strut his stuff. When the knife was thrust toward him, he was ready. He stepped back, blocked and grabbed the arm, breaking it. He swept the thug's front foot out so his legs were spread wide. Vince snap kicked him in the groin and twisting his arm back threw him to the ground. Mick, the leader, yelled and came for Vince. Vince turned toward Mick who also produced a small blade. He tossed it back and forth between his hands. As he tossed it again, Vince jump kicked and knocked the knife into the air.

Twice the size of Vince, Mick grabbed Vince around his arms and pulled him off the ground. Vince smashed his head into Mick's face, breaking his nose. Vince was done with these guys. He side kicked Mick in the chest. Mick took a painful step back. Vince did it again and again, until Mick fell back into the mirror. Vince grabbed him and flipped him onto the ground. Vince twisted Mick's arm until it cracked and Mick screamed.

"Who sent you?!" Vince yelled.

Mick was silent, so Vince slammed his face into the floor. "Aagh!"

Mick passed out. So Vince went over to the last one still conscious. Holding his broken arm, the man spoke, "Please don't hurt me anymore, man. I can explain."

Vince grabbed his throat. "You can explain while you're gasping for air! Who hired you!?" Vince asked.

"I...I don't know. They didn't tell me. They just wanted to know where this woman was," he stammered.

Sheer anger overwhelmed Vince. "Tell me what you do know and maybe I won't break your other arm."

His assailant swallowed hard. "They need to find this woman, so she can tell them what she knows. They are also looking for some young girl with red hair, who may have witnessed a crime. They think that this little girl is with the woman."

Natalie. Vince thought. Was Michaela right all this time? Enraged, Vince pounded the guy's face and knocked him out, too.

He reached for the phone, but once again someone entered the studio.

"What the...?" was all Vince had time to say.

Of all the people Vince wanted to see, Ricky Cartillo was not one of them. Vince lunged for him and threw Cartillo into the wall. "What did you do with Michaela!? If you don't hand her over to me in five minutes, I'll ram my fist through your face!"

Before Cartillo spoke, Boris had his gun planted against Vince's head. Vince retreated, but was ready to attack.

Ricky looked around and then he spoke to Vince. "These, my friend...."

"I AM NOT YOUR FRIEND!" Vince interrupted. Boris hit Vince on the side of the head. Vince went down to one knee. Blood streamed down the side of his head. He tried to stand up again. Boris was ready to hit him down again, but Ricky nodded for him to let Vince stand.

"You will listen to me or else you will get your head blown

257

off. Do you understand?" Ricky asked.

Vince nodded.

"Good. First of all, these are not my men. But I believe I know whose men they are." He had Vince's attention now. Ricky turned to Boris. "Get these men out of here. They do not need to know anything else. Tell them to warn their boss not to come here again." Boris hesitated. "He is fine. He will not attack me anymore. Will you, Vincent?"

"No," Vince said.

Striding around the floor, Ricky took off his black leather gloves and continued, "I have already spoken to Shannon, so it is no secret. I informed her that I believe Captain Newman from her father's precinct is behind this." Ricky laughed at Vince's expression. "I wonder how none of you think he can be involved. And yet you look at me as the typical villain, who has everything to gain by getting rid of Michaela and her father."

Vince spoke, "That's what Michaela thought."

"Michaela. She is a wonderful woman and I enjoyed getting to know her better." Vince started for Ricky again. "Ah, ah, ah. You do not want Boris to shoot you right through the window, do you? I think in time, she could have grown to love me, but until I find her, I will never know. I never tried to hurt her, Vincent. I only wanted to protect her. I need to know where she is."

Vince sneered. "First of all, there is no way that Michaela would ever love you. She loves me and even if I knew, why would I tell you?"

Ricky grinned. "Because, I may be the only one who can keep her and Shannon alive. The walls are closing in now and if you do not act soon, a lot of people are going to die. The good old captain is looking to protect himself and he will kill anyone who tries to sabotage his plans. And I mean anyone."

Vince looked at Cartillo. "Frank."

Cartillo was very serious now. "Yes, Frank probably knows more than he should. But that is all I will say. I will keep

258

an eye on all of you. Just to make sure you are safe, of course. But I implore you to give Michaela to me soon, before it is too late."

"Who's this little girl that everyone is looking for?" Vince asked.

Ricky's eye twitched. "She is my problem and none of your concern. Watch yourself, Vincent." Ricky left the studio, agitated.

Vince called Uncle Frank.

"Yeah, I need Officer Goodale, fast," Vince stated.

"I'll connect you," the receptionist said.

"Officer Goodale's office. This is Officer Walker. Can I help you?" Ben Walker said.

"Ben. This is Vince Cardosa, Michaela's friend. Where is Frank?"

Ben was silent and then said, "I don't know where he is, Vince. I've been out looking for him. He has been missing since last night."

"Ben, listen to me. I think that someone is going to kill Frank. I just had some mean dudes at the studio looking for Michaela. Then this Ricky Cartillo guy comes in and says that Captain Newman is involved and is going to have Frank taken out."

"Newman," Ben said.

"Do you know something I don't know?" Vince asked.

Ben replied, "Newman asked me to keep an eye on Shannon, but I didn't know why. When I asked for any explanation, he tore my head off! Shannon told me everything, Vince. I have to find Frank."

"Meet me at Shannon's apartment!" Vince said and hung up.

Shannon paced her apartment. She hated sitting around waiting for Ben to call, but she didn't know what else to do. The pieces were coming together now. Her father never would have thought his own captain would turn against him. This knowl-

259

edge put all of them in danger. The thought of having Cartillo as the one they could trust upset her even more.

She had tried to get through to Uncle Frank to tell him and wasn't able to. She also tried the studio and couldn't get Vince. No one was here to help her and her nerves were ready to break. "Riiiing, riiing!" Shannon jumped. She peered through the peephole and didn't see anyone. Who was it? The doorbell rang again. Something told her to open the door and do it fast. She did. A raggedy girl with dirty red hair stood there. She held a grimy sash that looked like it had once been pink. Shannon just stared at her.

"I'm Natalie. Can you help me…please?" she asked as tears streamed down her face, making a path along the encrusted dirt.

Shannon woke up as if from a dream. "Oh, my God! You're real. Quick, come in!" Shannon said as she pulled Natalie into the room and locked the door. Shannon looked around and realized that all the curtains were up. She ran and closed everything. Then she turned and looked at Natalie. The poor girl looked as if she had gone through the Holocaust. Her dirty clothes were hanging from her thin frame and her eyes were puffy and red. Even through the dirt, Shannon could see bruises. Shannon couldn't imagine what she had been through.

Shannon walked to her, kneeled down and placed her hands on the little girl's shoulders.

"Where's Michaela?" Natalie asked in a small voice.

Shannon smiled. "First, you need some food and a bath. Then I will explain everything."

Natalie gave her a small smile. Shannon picked her up and brought her into the bathroom.

Shannon and Natalie ate at the table. Natalie had spent the last hour and a half in the bath, telling Shannon everything and now she was drained. She thought about sleeping in a nice warm bed. The doorbell rang. They both tensed and didn't move.

The doorbell rang again.

"Shannon, open the door!"

Shannon ran to the door and let Vince in. "Vince! What happened to you?" Shannon exclaimed.

"It's a long story and we have little time." He stopped and Shannon followed his gaze to the small girl, sitting at the table. Beautiful, shiny red curls encircled her scared face.

"It's OK, Natalie," Shannon said walking over to her. "This is Vince, Michaela's special friend. He is here to help us."

"What's she doing here?" Vince asked.

"She found me," Shannon said. "Now have a seat and let me look at your head." Vince obeyed. "Tell me what happened."

Shannon sat still with Natalie on her lap, when Vince finished. They all felt the weight of what Vince had just said. Vince was now up-to-date on everything, except one part. It was time for Shannon to fill him in.

"Vince, I know where Michaela is."

Something in Shannon's voice told Vince it wasn't going to be a simple explanation. Vince waited.

Shannon retrieved Michaela's dream journal and explained about all the entries on past lives and this Celtic world.

"I've been there," said Natalie. "I've seen Michaela dressed as a warrior, riding on a horse. She saved me."

"So what are you both trying to say?" Vince asked.

Shannon slid forward and took Vince's hand. "Michaela was taken to another place in time. I believe that she was somehow transported to third century Ireland. She disappeared at that deserted mansion. The man who owned it had Celtic origins and there's no trace of her anywhere! Plus the owners of the inn said that this man Finnius disappeared, too. Maybe Michaela is with him!"

"That tells me nothing!" Vince exclaimed. "All I have heard are some dreams, a haunted house, and Michaela's obsession with Celtic literature. Of course she dreamt about it, that's all she ever read. They are only dreams. Everyone has been lying to us, so of course they are lying to us about Michaela. They want us to think that they don't have her, so we'll back off. But I'm not backing off! I can't lose her, Shannon!"

Shannon stood next to him. "I know, Vince. None of us can lose her." She paused for a long time. "I can prove it. There is only one way, but you have to be openminded. You have to be open to the possibility that she is in another time. I've been able to contact her in my dreams. We can see one another and we talk. We can see what is happening around each other. And from what Natalie has told us about her visions proves that I'm not hallucinating. You can see Michaela if you try. Will you try?"

Vince looked at the two of them. His eyes overflowed with tears of frustration and loss. He whispered, "I'll try."

Vince lay down on Michaela's bed next to Max. Max whined and snuggled in the crook of Vince's arm. Vince welcomed him and closed his eyes, like Shannon had told him. "Think of her, Vince. I'm going to go to sleep alongside you. Natalie will wake us up if she hears anything. You have to want to see her. She will come."

Vince nodded with his eyes still closed. Soft Celtic music flowed through the room and Vince let his body succumb to it.

"Shannon," Vince whispers. His body feels cold as he walks through a fog.

"I am here, Vince," Shannon said and she grabs his hand. They walk along a soft bed of grass and the fog lifts. Michaela is sleeping under a tree. She is worn from Maecha's injuries.

"Michaela!" Vince yells. Michaela jumps up, surprised and armed. She searches the land around her and sees Shannon first.

"Shannon. I thought I heard Vince."

"You did," Vince says and comes toward her. They hug and cry.

"How?" Michaela asks.

"I believe it all Michaela and I'm so sorry I ever doubted

you. But you don't look well. Are you ill?" Vince asks.

"I'm all right, Vince. I'm very fatigued and out of sorts, which is only natural considering where I am," Michaela replies, trying to make light of her pale, thin face.

Shannon interrupts, "Michaela we have to talk quick. We are in danger, and I can't stay away long. We have Natalie."

"Thank God! Is she OK?" Michaela asks.

"Yes, for now. But Uncle Frank's life is in danger. We think Captain Newman is involved. Ricky has been looking for you and he has told both of us that Newman was the one who ordered you to be taken out. I still don't trust him though."

Michaela lets everything sink in. "You must hide Natalie. Find Frank and go to someone he can trust completely. There has to be someone! I will find a way to get back to you as soon as I can."

"'Mikala'?" They hear a voice from the trees. Maecha emerges leaning on a tree. She is in her full Celtic gear.

"Holy Christ!" Vince yells.

"Ahhh!" Vince yelled and sat up. Shannon followed. "Who was that?"

Shannon spoke, "Michaela said she loves you. The other woman is named Maecha. I believe she is Michaela's past life. She is a daughter of the High King Cormac mac Art who lived in third century Ireland. According to this book I found in Michaela's room, he lived in Tara and was the High King of Ireland. Apparently, he was well-liked by his people and he was responsible for forming a warrior band called the Fianna. Michaela told me that he has been kidnapped and she is helping Maecha prepare to get her father back. Michaela is needed there and I don't think we'll see her until she is done. She's safer than all of us right now."

"I can't believe this," Vince said and the doorbell rang for a third time that night. "I hope that's Uncle Frank and Ben."

Shannon ran to the door. "Ben?"

"Yeah, it's me," he spoke.

Shannon opened the door and a very somber Ben walked in and hugged her.

"What's wrong, Ben?" she asked, not sure if she wanted to know.

"Shannon, I'm so sorry. I should have been there," Ben said shaking.

"It's OK, Ben. Tell us what happened," Shannon said.

"I...I'm not even sure what happened. I went to the dispatcher to see if Frank reported where he had gone. Then I heard there was an officer hurt. It was Frank. I raced to the scene. He was heading toward Ricky Cartillo's mansion. His car was pulled over on the side of the road. I don't know why he stopped, but he was found shot dead in front of his car and there were tire marks on the side of the road in front of him. They blasted the hell out of him, Shannon!" Ben cried. "I joined the force to fight the bad guys out there," Ben pointed toward the door. "How could they be within the precinct; all around me?"

Shannon cupped his face in her hands. Ben looked like a lost boy with tears rolling down his cheeks. In a short time, she had grown fond of this man. She spoke to him. "It's hard to accept, Ben. People disgrace themselves for the most selfish reasons. Brothers turn against brothers for greed. Newman isn't the only enemy. There are others and they fooled us, just as they fooled my dad."

Shannon held Ben, while Natalie cried in Vince's arms.

Shannon looked around at everyone. "It's the four of us now. We need to get Michaela back and help Natalie. She has some vital information that needs to get into the right hands. Now we just have to make sure who those hands should be and not get killed doing it."

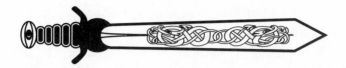

12

Kelan woke up from a night of alluring dreams where Maecha's kiss had turned into more passionate embraces. He looked around the thick forest and it took a moment to realize that he was alone and far away from the Isle of the Blessed. With one kiss, Maecha had broken all the locks that had chained his heart for years and he longed to hold her. Even more, he worried about her. He knew she could take care of herself, and it was time to prove that she could lead. She had to find her way out of Tir-nan-Og alone.

For that matter, so did Kelan. He gathered his weapons and listened to the sounds of the forests. He heard animals rustling through the leaves and the chitter-chatter of birds as they flew along the treetops. He also heard the now familiar sound of the water that flowed down the endless river. Kelan looked across the water to the rocky crag that ran along it. He searched for something that would give him a clue as to where he should head. He closed his eyes and spoke the words of his challenge. "The long green serpent may kill you. Its teeth hold a venomous bite. Take the tooth and it will sustain you. Use it well against the evil you fight."

He opened his eyes and saw an opening in a rock. It appeared to be a cavern. He noticed a green glow around it and decided to see what was inside. The only problem was to get there. Kelan walked along the water's edge looking for a way across. He hadn't seen any bridges, but he saw rocks protruding out of the water. He thought of Maecha and his family. This was his chance to make everything right.

Kelan swallowed hard, took a deep breath, and stepped out onto the first rock. It was dry and he stepped to the next and the next. As he looked down toward the next rock, the water swirled around it. Then images appeared. He saw his dead mother floating face up. Her hollow eyes accused him of leaving her behind. "No, Mother, I tried. I'm so sorry," he moaned, trying to keep control. Guilt and pain tore through his insides.

"Be still, Kelan. You are a warrior and I need you. Come home to me," a voice whispered in his ear and he was calm.

"Thank you, Maecha." He moved forward. He was in the middle of the river when something jumped up and flew across his face. "Ahhh!!" Kelan yelled and regained his balance. Arms held out straight, he looked into the water to see what type of flying fish had almost sent him into the water. All was clear so he stepped again. Splash! Another jumped up and this time Kelan saw it. A rather large fish tried to catch Kelan's arm with its sharp fangs. "What kind of fish has sharp teeth like those?" Kelan yelled out to anything that would listen.

Another fish jumped up at him. They thought a tasty meal was waiting right within their grasp, so they were joining forces to share it. Removing his spiked flail, Kelan fought these monster fish. He slammed his weapon into the first one and it gurgled in pain. As it fell into the water, the other fish tore at its flesh. The taste of blood made them crazy and two or three jumped up at Kelan. He began to run along the rocks swinging his flail and smashing the fish into their watery graves.

Kelan reached the other side of the river. He looked back to see the water bubbling with a fish feast and gave thanks for his safety. Kelan entered the glowing cavern. The interior was dark, but along the ground was a path that was the same color as the outside of the cavern. Kelan followed it. As the opening of the cavern disappeared, Kelan stopped. He heard a hissing sound and it echoed all around him. The cavern smelled foul. From battle he only knew too well the smell of rotting flesh and human feces. Kelan unsheathed his sword and as his eyes adjusted to the darkness, a huge tail whipped out at him and knocked him against the cavern wall. Shaking his head clear, Kelan turned to face the glowing eyes of a huge green serpent. Its tongue flickered in and out in anticipation of a tasty kill. Dead skin and other human body parts hung off its teeth and Kelan held his breath as the snake's hiss poisoned him with its stench.

"Sorry to disappoint you, but I'm too tough to eat," Kelan said. The serpent displayed its teeth dripping with poisonous venom and attacked. Kelan lunged under its belly and jumped over the serpent's back stabbing it. The serpent roared and lurched upward. Its tail whipped around and grabbed Kelan by his leg swinging him up and off the ground.

He swung his sword trying to get close enough to the snake. He pulled out his dagger and waited as the serpent curled its huge head and body around to survey its catch. It hissed with impending victory and opened its jaws wide.

As soon as he was close enough, Kelan jabbed his dagger down into the serpent's tongue and held it there. Its tail uncurled with the pain and as Kelan slipped out he grabbed onto the serpent's mouth. He removed his sword and held it up so that it couldn't close its mouth. The serpent was so huge Kelan could stand up in its jaws. He withdrew his dagger and still holding up his sword, swung his flail high over his head and landed it against the serpent's teeth. One tooth cracked and fell to the ground. With a twist of his sword, Kelan removed it and jumped out of the beast's mouth. He rolled onto the ground, picked up the tooth and stood to run.

"Hisssaahya!" the serpent screamed in fury. The green

monster swung its tail back and forth knocking rocks off the cavern walls. Not able to see the entrance, Kelan was trapped in the serpent's lair and had to avoid getting crushed by the serpent or the rocks. Shoving the oversized tooth in his pouch, he tried to run around the monstrous beast. Once again the serpent's tail hit him in the chest and Kelan fell back against the wall hitting his head. The serpent lurched forward trying to bite the warrior. Kelan jumped out of the way and looked for a way to run. Then he saw the glowing white light. It was the same one that had led him through the first part of his journey and he trusted that it was the way out. He jumped toward the serpent and, with his sword pointed toward it, he jabbed his sword into its scaled skin and flew up over the enormous body. He could hear the monster scream in pain, but didn't look back as he escaped victorious.

Kelan had the tooth that held the healing venom of the mighty Green Serpent. The venom had been used by the druids to make a potion that could restore someone who was almost on the other side of death. He remembered his challenge: 'Use it well against the evil you fight,' but didn't know what other powers it might contain.

The white light had delivered Kelan into a scintillating crystal room. The room was small and shafts of sunlight glistened through it displaying a bright spectrum of color. Kelan shielded his eyes and walked toward a wall. Although the room seemed small, Kelan couldn't reach the other side. He looked behind him and the room appeared to be the same small enclosure and yet he could keep walking. As he did, he noticed eyes along the walls that watched him. The sunlight streamed through their pupils and warmed him.

Kelan knew his next challenge was upon him—'The Eyes of the Goddess are upon you. She trusts you will keep her daughter secure. When the eyes fall upon you, you are bound to her forevermore.'

Kelan felt sleepy. His steps slowed. A strange, soothing

sound echoed around the chambers. It sounded like women chanting, but Kelan did not recognize the words. He tried to pull out his sword, but his body had lost its power and his mind had lost its ability to protect itself and the desire to do so. He closed his eyes and the 'Eyes of the Goddess' were upon him.

"Wake up, Kelan...," a myriad of female voices sang through his head. Kelan had been dreaming of Maecha, but he let go of his vision and struggled to open his eyes. A beautiful woman stood over him. She helped him sit up. He watched her. She seemed to float rather than walk around the room. Her body was enfolded in shining robes that sparkled like the crystal walls he had seen earlier. Her hair was yellow and shined bright like the sun and her eyes sparkled and sang of the bright blue ocean. He could not look at her for too long—her being was too over-whelming.

"You have done well, my son," she began.

"Your son?" Kelan asked. He looked harder at this celestial being, but could not.

"Yes. The goddess appears in whatever shape you desire most. I have watched you from the other side for years and I am so glad I am able to speak with you now, if only for a short time," she replied.

"Mother?" Kelan said. She moved closer to him and once the shimmering lights stopped moving, he recognized the face of his mother who had been slain so many years ago. He picked up her small hands and kissed them. "I am sorry I could not save you from those...men and the raging water!" Kelan exclaimed.

"There is nothing to be sorry for, my son. You were a young warrior and the Goddess favored you that day by saving your life," his mother comforted him.

"She saved me. Why didn't she save you?" Kelan asked.

His mother smiled and touched his face. "The Goddess needs all of us in certain places. She needs me here and she needs you alive and committed to her."

"I have dreamed of seeing you for so long," Kelan hesitated and looked up at her. "Am I dead?"

"No. Have no fear. You have not passed into this world forever. I am a messenger of the eternal goddess and I must help you move on to the last step of your journey. You have done well and have won the challenges that were set before you. Now the last, and perhaps the hardest challenge, is upon you and once you have accomplished this, you will be sent back to your home…and Maecha."

Kelan's heart raced at the mention of Maecha's name. He wanted so much to tell his mother about her, but he had an idea that she knew all there was to know and more. "What must I do, Mother?"

"First, you must know that the tooth of the Green Serpent has very strong powers and you are urged to never let it get into the wrong hands. It has the healing powers of the gods, but it also carries a stroke of death that will destroy a man from the inside out if he uses it for his own personal gain. Use the tooth well and the gods will preserve you," she said.

"Second, you must accept the Goddess and respect the bond that she will instill in you. You and Maecha are close?" she asked, looking at Kelan's face.

Despite his best efforts to hide it, Kelan's cheeks burned red and he mumbled a 'yes.'

"Don't push her away. I know you have had a hard life and that all would have been different had our family lived. Remember, everything has a purpose. Your purpose is Maecha. Be true to her. Bond with her and together you will both bring peace and unity to your land. Don't allow your heart to remain closed forever. Now is the time to open it or else your bond will be tainted. Do you love her, Kelan?" she asked.

"I didn't know it until this journey. I feel what can only be called love for Maecha. As much as she can make me mad, she makes me laugh. I cherish her Mother and I realize that even more being away from her. I want her to be all right and that, I think, is my purpose in life—to protect her as well as love her," Kelan finished realizing the strength and meaning of his words. He only wished that it were Maecha who stood next to him, so he could show her what he meant.

"That is good. Your feelings are pure, so your bond will be strong. As you know, others will test your bond, but to each other you must always be true or else your world and mine will suffer. Now it is time for you to finish your journey. Trust your heart, my son, and your love will always ring true," she whispered as her image faded away into the light of the crystal walls.

The light consumed Kelan and he shut his eyes against its brightness. As the light dimmed Kelan stood in a passageway. He felt a cool breeze along his body and, with only a loincloth covering his manhood, he walked along the white path. A voice whispered, "Kelan, come to me," and all he could do was comply. At the end of the path was a large pot resting on a burning fire. The liquid in the pot bubbled and hissed as the fire heated it to its boiling point. Kelan stopped in front of the pot and waited.

A strong female voice spoke, "Kelan mac Nessa, son of Niall, son of Ronan. Do you accept the Great Queen, the Mother Goddess, giver and taker of life?"

Kelan breathed deep, "I do."

"Do you accept King Cormac mac Art as the sovereign King of Ireland as bestowed upon him by the Goddess of Sovereignty?"

"I do," Kelan said.

"Do you accept his daughter, Maecha Ruadh mac Art as the next heiress to the throne, only upon the death of the true king?"

"I do," Kelan spoke stronger.

Kelan waited through the silence. "And do you accept beyond all life to be the protector of Maecha Ruadh mac Art and the Lordly Ones joined to her from Tir-nan-Og?"

Looking up Kelan saw the Eyes of the Goddess. "I do,

Goddess. With all my heart."

"Then step forward and connect your soul to the one who is bound to you forever," she spoke.

Kelan stepped up to the large pot and bending forward placed his bare arms on it. Sweat flowed from his brow and through the pain his one thought was of Maecha. He stepped back and two young women dressed in the sparkling white robes of the Goddess held Kelan's forearms up.

A woman dressed like his mother approached him and placed her hands on his arms. Her touch was cool and it soothed his burned skin. As she held him, she chanted:

"Power before you
Power below you
Power above you
Power beside you
I am the Power within you
Go in my name."

The Goddess placed her lips upon Kelan's and breathed part of her spirit into his. "Go in peace Kelan mac Nessa. The Eyes of the Goddess will always be upon you."

For the last time on his journey Kelan was consumed by the radiant light.

He knelt on soft grass and surveyed his surrounding. The sight was pleasant. Goll mac Morna and Caoilte mac Ronan stood close to him. They seemed unsure of whether to approach. Beyond them were hundreds of warriors who had gathered to bear witness to this historical event. Some undoubtedly would like to see Maecha fail, but there were others who were anxious for her return. Leann-cha'omh, Cormac's bendrui and healer still looked at the cave's opening with fear that the king's daughter was lost.

Kelan stood up and held out his arms to welcome his

friends and they all gasped and stepped away. Leann walked forward and touched his arms. She shut her eyes and her body shook. She released Kelan and turned to the large crowd and spoke so that all may hear, "The one true Goddess has spoken and the 'Eyes of the Goddess' are upon Kelan mac Nessa, son of Niall, son of Ronan. He has been blessed as a protector and we should be honored to embrace him as a member of our people and a member of your Fianna."

"What about my sister?" a voice yelled out from the crowd. Cairpre's rogue of warriors shoved their way through the crowd leading him to the bendrui. Cairpre's eyes were covered with a bandage. He stepped in front of Leann. "It seems as though the sword of the gods has fallen upon her and shown its displeasure. The gods will only honor men in this journey. It is time to move on. She has failed. She has not emerged, so now listen to me, the true heir of Tara."

Leann spoke, "I see that Mother Goddess has shown her displeasure with you, Cairpre. What happened to your eyes?"

Everyone murmured their curiosity and waited for an answer.

"That's none of your concern! I had an accident, but I will be fine and I will be able to rule! Now is the time for change. Maecha is a foolish woman, who will not return!" he yelled to the crowd that he could not see.

A few in the crowd mumbled their assent, but most yelled against Cairpre. Kelan moved forward to speak, "The Goddess has not destroyed Maecha. In fact, she embraced her. As any *honored* member of the Fianna knows, everyone emerges from the Cave of the Warrior when the Lordly One see fit. Maecha is not finished with her journey."

Cairpre felt the sting of Kelan's words, but he fought back. "And how do you know that she is still alive?"

Kelan, who stood a foot taller than Cairpre, stepped closer so as to look down upon Maecha's brother and spat, "Because

I know."

Cairpre felt Kelan's presence and stepped back, which signaled an entourage of yells from the crowd asking him to wait a little longer for Maecha to emerge. Goll spoke up, "There is no harm in waiting. What seemed like days in Tir-nan-Og are only hours in our world. The Festival of Samhain is tomorrow night. We shall continue our preparations and wait until the morning to make our decision."

Cairpre grabbed the arm of one of his men and stormed away. Goll turned to Kelan and embraced his new brother. "You have done well, Kelan. Let us hope that Maecha emerges soon. It seems as though the enemy within has revealed himself."

Kelan squeezed his friend's shoulder. "She will emerge, Goll. She has to."

13

The Crystal Light will call you
But you must come alone.
Touch the light with no candle
And you will make it home.

I woke up. A burst of stars flashed in the night sky and the moon cast a soft light upon the land. I could see a well and the caverns. The Bridge of Swords was no longer visible, but I was on the other side of the river, so somehow I made it across. I thought about my visions. My brother had betrayed me and our father. I know I had maimed his eyes and could only wait to see if his scars of treachery would be apparent in the real world. I had to pass this test so I could move against him with the strength of the Fianna. Only then could I help my father.

I faintly remembered 'Mikala' helping me, and an old woman forcing me to drink some potion. I didn't know how long I had slept, and I wanted to continue my journey. I walked over to the well to take a drink. As I bent forward I heard an echo of a woman's voice. It crackled against the sides of the well. I listened.

"Go, Maecha. The time has come for you to claim your destiny. Be one with the Goddess. Her powers will protect you

275

and light your way."

I stepped back from the enchanted well. Once again I heard a voice, but it came from the caverns. Gathering my belongings, I moved closer and the voice sang:

"With the power of the Goddess upon you,
Walk through the cavern of light,
The magic of the Goddess will enfold you,
And mark you forever white."

The inside of the cavern was illuminated with a soft white glow, and I was surrounded by its warmth. The path was narrow and I followed it to a vertical wall of rocks. The rocks were marked with interlocking circles that represented everlasting life and unity. The light shone at the top and I began my ascent. I placed my feet in the ridges and climbed up and over the edge. The light wasn't as strong here, but I could see around a corner and it shone like a beacon to me. As I walked toward it, the light surrounded me and I could no longer move. My arms were stuck to my side and I could only turn my head. A glowing light came toward me and transformed into a man with long white hair. His eyebrows grew past his eyes and his moustache and beard covered his mouth. His eyes gleamed silver and huge pearl wings hung from his back. His alabaster breeches twinkled with sunlight and it was hard to look at him without hurting my eyes.

He walked close to me and asked, "What do you seek, Daughter of the Light?"

"I seek the light of the Goddess and the wisdom of the Gods. I seek this for the good of my people and for the love of my father," I replied.

"What you seek will bring you knowledge and with that knowledge comes power, but also responsibility. You have drunk from the Cauldron of the Dagda, so you have the knowledge that you seek. You must find the strength in yourself now. The power

I give you, no other can take away, but you must use it for the good of your kingdom and the good of the Otherworld. Are you prepared for this?" he asked.

"I am," I said. I wasn't sure what these powers were or where the knowledge was inside me. I knew that I could feel thoughts that weren't mine; I could see images that were never known to me before; I felt the spirits of the greatest warriors encircle me and bless me as their leader. I felt ready.

The winged god stepped aside. I walked to him and faced him. He held my arms. Looking up he spoke:

"Let the light fall upon you
My power I give to thee.
Bless her, my true Goddess
The Daughter of Light is she."

Bowing to me, he whispered, "Go."

I walked around the corner and saw the light with no candles. The light was on top of a small hill. There were candles that led up to it and as they flickered, images of the gods and goddesses were illuminated on the walls. I saw the Good God, Dagda, the Goddess Dana, Anu, the Goddess of prosperity; Manannan mac Lir, the Sea God; Macha, the Goddess of War, and many others. I thanked them for allowing me passage through this sacred place and I walked up to the light with no candle. The light flickered in the air and I could not begin to understand the magic and power that lay within its glow. I knelt before it and closing my eyes I breathed deeply. I placed my hands on each side of the flame. I could feel its heat burning stronger. I opened my eyes and closed my hands around the light.

Intense flames shot through my hands and hit my eyes. My body reeled back from the pain and then was catapulted through a sheer ray of light. It was a tunnel and I traveled through it with great speed. Heat radiated through me and my skin was soaked with sweat. I tried to focus on what was around me, but the light was too intense and I had to close my eyes. My body stopped and I was upright, although my feet were not on the ground. Still surrounded by the blinding light, hot rays began to shoot at me. My entire body was consumed by fire.

"Aaaaaaahhhhh!" I screeched as I took all the light in.

It stopped and I was face down on a cold stone floor. A male voice rang out, "The Light of the Goddess is upon you, my child. Go in peace and love."

A light consumed me again and as it disappeared, I found myself kneeling on a bed of grass. Blinded, it took me a moment to gather my surroundings. I looked around without lifting my head. My hair hung around my face, but I could see that there were people around me moving forward with hesitation. I felt Kelan stronger than ever. He stepped close to me.

He bent forward to help me rise, but I put my hand up and he stepped aside. I stood and as I did I lifted my hair back away from my face. Everyone gasped. I knew not what I looked like and could only imagine how the Goddess had changed me. I turned to Kelan and he touched my hair. I took a handful and saw the streak of white that flowed through it. I was touched by the wisdom and power of the Gods and Goddesses and now all who saw me would know of it. I smiled at him and clasped his forearm with my hand and he did the same. I saw the Eyes of the Goddess upon his arms and thanked them for bringing us home.

I turned to the crowd that had gathered. I saw my faithful followers and those that I did not know. I removed Imbas Skye from her sheath and raised her high above my head. She glowed in the glory of my victory, our victory, and people shielded their eyes from her light.

I spoke:
"Strength before me
Truth above me

Honor beside me
Justice below me
Power within me
Art holds all that I am
I rise in his name."

I heard a screech in the sky and raised my arm. My faithful falcon landed and screeched again in welcome and victory. The throngs of people around me bowed. That was not my intention, but they would not listen to my plea to stand. The Goddess whispered to let them honor me, so I acquiesced. As I looked among the crowd of loyal friends, I saw a band of men standing in defiance of me and all that I had worked so hard to accomplish. I saw a man astride a horse, his eyes bandaged. As his horse reared on it hind legs, he raised his sword and pointed it me. I saw my brother, my enemy.

I pulled out the silver ball that had transformed Kelan and me in the Otherworld. "Open," I said. The magic stick revealed itself. Upon seeing it, everyone else, including Cairpre's men retreated away from him. Smiling at my evil brother, I pointed the stick at him. With a force only the gods could muster, Cairpre was thrown off his horse and into the standing stones.

I turned to Kelan, "Capture him and bring him to me."

With a raise of his hand, Kelan's band of warriors ran toward Cairpre. Cairpre's men knew that their leader's boldness would lead to this, so they were on their way to him. They swept him up onto the back of a horse and took off toward the forest. Kelan's men followed them with vigor.

Still displaying the stick with it Otherworldly glow, I exclaimed, "Is there anyone else who would dare to challenge me? My brother is not fit to be a king. He has betrayed our kingdom. He is responsible for my father's disappearance. I took his eyes in the Otherworld. I will take his life to bring back my father."

I walked amongst my father's people, who have loved him and followed his leadership with faith and strength. I loved these people. I grew up with them. I would not let them down, but they had to trust me. I continued. "I have done what you have asked. I have done what no woman has ever done before. I have performed the initiation rites, I have gone into the Cave of the Warrior and I have emerged victorious and now ask to be a respected member of the Fianna."

I walked toward the standing stones and the crowds moved aside. I touched the cool stones that had given me strength before my journey. I turned back to the crowd and yelled, "Whosoever should challenge me—do it now; I have a king to save." I looked around and no one moved; no one disagreed. There was a marked silence, as the crowd no longer knew what to do. Then as Goll mac Morna and Caoilte mac Ronan approached me, the crowd let out a victorious roar, and our Fianna brethren surrounded us.

14

Kelan walked into the mead hall of the rath of Tara. The walls rose to the upper level where a balcony surrounded the circular room. A large table that could hold 50 men stood in the middle of the massive room. Four mighty carved, wooden pillars surrounded the table at each corner making the table appear to be in its own room. Kelan leaned on one such pillar and watched the kings and the leaders of smaller raths settle into their seats to wait. He knew that it would be hard for Maecha to convince them to cross the waters to Alba to save the king, no matter how much they loved him. They were unsure of her abilities. Kelan had been unsure before they had begun their journey.

However, when Maecha entered the hall, her transformation was so amazing, Kelan knew she would do whatever she set out to do and he also knew that he would follow her to the end of the world. She had proven to be a born leader. She strode toward the table with confidence, her head held high; her demeanor proud. The short time in the Otherworld molded her body into a muscled warrior. Her strength and fighting skills rivaled Kelan's and her ability to read people's thoughts was unnerving. Her fiery red hair was tamed by the pearl streak that now ran through it. She exemplified power, but she also respected it and knew the purpose of her goddess-given gifts. His oath to the Goddess had made his bond to Maecha even stronger. Ever since she had come out of the cave, his thoughts were consumed of her. He wanted to touch her and accept the complete bonding of their experiences together. He felt close to her, he could hear her thoughts, which made him want her more.

Afraid that his feelings might show, Kelan concentrated on who had arrived. There was Aonghus of Craoibheach, a leader of the Fianna in Mumu, the southernmost forth of Ireland. Eoghan mac Mail, the king of Ulaid had come, even though King Cormac and he had been feuding for years over the entire reign of Ireland. Mail could never get enough support from the Fianna, so any of his advances toward King Cormac were always eliminated. Kelan noticed that he refused to make any kind of eye contact with the other men and hadn't spoken a word. He listened and took everything in. Kelan made a mental note to keep an eye on him. Osgar Conchobar, Ferlaigh mac Morna, Goll mac Morna, along with other Fianna captains, sat at the other end of the table. Caoilte stood at attention by a pillar behind Goll. The king of Laigin had not yet arrived and it was thought that perhaps he was still dealing with some raids from the Picts. It was on the border of his land where the slaughter had taken place and Kelan did not know how many of his men had been killed.

A trumpet blared and everyone rose to acknowledge the acting queen. As she walked closer, her eyes met Kelan's and stayed there until she came to the head of the table. Kelan smiled at her and everyone else noted the way they looked at one another.

Kelan's longing gaze caught my attention as soon as I entered the room. We had not spoken about our last challenges or the changes that were happening within our bodies and between our minds and souls. I looked forward to our final union, so I was relieved that he felt the same way. But Kelan would have to wait. I studied each king standing around the High King's table. Maintaining my silence, I walked to my father's chair and only then motioned for all to sit.

I could tell by their fidgeting that some were still not comfortable with my position as acting queen.

Still standing, I addressed them with a voice that I hoped was as strong as my father's. "I am Maecha Ruadh mac Art, daughter of King Cormac and Queen Deirdre, acting queen of Tara, and leader of the Fianna." I let the words soften their doubts and then continued.

"My father has been kidnapped by a band of Picts and has been taken by ship to Alba. This scheme was acted out by the Picts, but it was masterminded by my brother, Cairpre mac Art. Many of you were at the Battle of Gahbra and saw a man on horseback watching the slaughter. He wore a helmet with horns and tail that was taken long ago from the son of a Scottish king. My father killed that man and took his helmet. Until last week, that helmet was in my father's armory.

"When I was in the Otherworld, I was attacked by a man who wore this same helmet. His body reeked of the evil that consumed him. This same man somehow gained access to the Otherworld to do me harm, as he had done harm to my father and all of the Fianna warriors who were butchered that day. He wounded me, but I managed to maim him. The Sword of Souls took his eyes. My brother is just as much an enemy as the Picts. As acting queen, I will wage war against these enemies and retrieve my father back to his rightful place—here with all of you. Saving my father is my only intention. I do not plan to usurp the crown for myself or murder my father when I find him. I pledge my loyalty to him and the Goddess who has blessed me with these special gifts and position.

"Let it also be very clear that anyone who defies me shall

suffer by penalty of death! I believe that all of you sit at my father's table in peace and loyalty and that we share the same goal. I also know that there are those who do not agree with me," I said, letting my words sink into their hearts to forge their unity with me.

I heard a whisper of dissent somewhere along the lengthy table, but no one would come forward. I had proven myself worthy enough to be leader of the Fianna in the Otherworld and passed their initiations. I was blessed by the Goddess and the white streak that flowed through my hair proved it. But some men still didn't believe in me. I didn't have the experience behind me that they required. I was not proven in battle. I had never rallied them to continue on when all was thought lost. My father had. Their loyalty was to my father and I was just an instrument to get him back. They had lost sight of who my father was and maybe each was seeing himself in my father's place.

I moved from my chair and strode around them. "Have you forgotten my father?"

They all muttered, "No."

"I see the doubt in your eyes. My words have not moved you. King Cormac is the son of Art and the grandson of Conn of the Hundred Battles, both monarchs of Erinn. He is a great reformer of our military, always supporting the Fianna in every endeavor they have ventured on. He is responsible for forging the Brehon laws that wield us as a united and peaceful kingdom. He is a great patron of literature and art. He introduced the watermill, which is erected on the slope of Tara. Thanks to King Cormac's government, our rivers have abounded with salmon, our fields overflow with wheat, and animals are plentiful and strong. Each one of you enjoys this prosperity and has grown fat by its abundance!

"It is our time to fight back. How many more must die?! We are still mourning the death of our greatest leader, Fionn mac Cumhail. He is no more. The Gray Man's three sons live no more;

the Red Spears are no more; the One-wright's sons are no more. Iodhlann son of Iodhlaoch, Flann the eloquent hero, the three sons of Criomhall, the faultless Green Fian, Daighre the bright lad are no more! Fionn's off-spring, Oisin of admirable warrior-skill was slain.

"Too many have died. I know that each clan prides itself on being self-contained, self-providing, and self-existing in almost every respect. But without the High King, your current life would not be possible. He has brought peace, justice, and prosperity in a land that has seen too much bloodshed. We owe him this loyalty and I cannot do this without each of you," I finished, worn out by my words and the desperate need to begin this journey.

Those I knew would support me, stood up and placed their fists over their hearts—Osgar, Ferlaigh, Goll, Caoilte, and Kelan. The other men remained silent and unmoved. I was angry that these leaders had to think about saving their king, but I knew that any more words were useless.

The silence was shattered by a loud bang at the main door. The intruder did not wait to be welcomed, but swung both doors wide so that three warriors abreast could enter. They entered fast and fully armed.

"Maecha, step back," I heard Kelan say.

But I didn't, because I did not fear these warriors. Aeiden flew to my arm and waited as if he had been expecting them. As they came closer, I noted the emblems on their shields. It was a falcon with a sword in his talons.

Before the leaders around the table decided to attack, I raised my hand. "Stop! These are my welcomed guests." Their leader glided forward.

No longer dressed in her regal garb, Queen Treasa removed her gold helmet. She was dressed in the leather armor similar to what she had given me. She kneeled on the floor at my feet and spoke, "Maecha Ruadh mac Art, you are worthy of the

Gods and Goddesses of the Otherworld. You are a strong leader and warrior. You have passed all challenges set before you and the Goddess has blessed you with success and her powerful gifts. Your father shall be proud of you. I have one hundred warriors who would be honored to follow you to Alba to retrieve your father. I would be honored to follow you and have the blessings of the Otherworld to accompany you."

Still kneeling, Treasa held her hand open and revealed a tiny crystal that I recognized from the Cave of the Warrior. She looked up at me and winked.

Smiling, I spoke so all could hear, "Arise, Queen Treasa, for it is I who should be kneeling before you. It appears that we are both blessed. I am grateful for all of you and would indeed welcome you on this quest."

"Thank you," Treasa said.

I embraced her and whispered, "We have much to talk about." Treasa smiled.

I turned to the kings still sitting around the table. "So, my kings! Queen Treasa of Roscommon will support me next to her husband, King Ferlaigh as well as King Oscar, Goll and my Fianna warriors. Will any of you follow their example?"

One by one the kings pledged their support. I hoped their support was true, because I couldn't afford another betrayal. Eoghan of Ulaid's hand was soaked with sweat when he took mine and I glanced at Kelan and could sense the distrust in his mind toward this man.

Once all pledged their loyalty to me, we spoke about strategy. The second time that night, the main doors were thrown open. My messenger, Ferdia, was thrown into the room, while his assailants ran away. Two of Treasa's warriors pursued the attackers. I ran to Ferdia. He was dead. He had been stabbed many times and his hands had been cut off. I said a prayer to bring his soul home.

I took a deep breath and addressed everyone. "I had sent

Ferdia to my brother, Cairpre, to ask him to surrender and this is how he responds. He will be punished, as will anyone who assists him." I chanced a look at Eoghan and his face was pale in the candlelight. He rubbed his sweaty hands and looked for a way to leave. I nodded to Kelan and he moved behind Eoghan to watch his actions.

"It is late and the Samhain festivities have begun. Enjoy what you can tonight, for tomorrow we prepare for Alba."

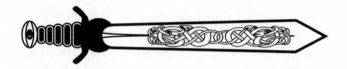

15

It was the night of the New Year, the time between times. The sky was clear and the stars were brilliant. The crisp chill to the air only added to the exuberance of the evening. Large bonfires burned throughout the fields and any animals not needed for breeding had been slaughtered and roasted on the flaming spits. Mead and beer flowed from one cup to another and loud music surrounded the villagers with mirth and excitement.

My arrival with Treasa's band of warriors, along with Kelan and his large band silenced the crowd. It was Treasa who saved the evening by grabbing me and joining in with the raucous dancing around the fire. Kelan laughed and hit Ferlaigh on the back and said, "I don't know how you do it. You are quite the man to keep up with a woman like that!"

"Aye, I am!" Ferlaigh smiled with appreciation, because Kelan gave him credit where he wished he had more.

Treasa and I swung around together until we stopped, laughing and out of breath. We drank some mead.

"To our future battles and camaraderie," I said to Treasa.

Laughing and shaking her head, Treasa added, "To consummating whatever bond you have with that lustful warrior is what you should be toasting to!"

I choked and spit out my mead, "Treasa is that all you

ever think about?"

"If I can help it! A young lass like you should be anxious to get your legs wrapped around a mountain of a man like that. Just look at him!" she exclaimed.

I did and I felt a tickle at the bottom of my stomach, which traveled lower. I looked at Treasa and she must have seen the anxiety in my eyes, for she wrapped her arm around me like a big sister and said, "You and Kelan have a special relationship. You are destined to be together, to make great changes together. I know of the bond that you are both sworn by."

I looked at her and was ready to question her on the crystal that she had presented earlier.

"No, I have not been fortunate enough to have journeyed to the Otherworld, but I did have an otherworldly visitor. The Goddess of the Otherworld came to me and said that a wonderful, but young warrior would approach me for help. It was my sworn duty to serve the Otherworld by helping this warrior. To be truthful, I thought the warrior was going to be a man, so I felt that this obligation could be fun. When I saw you, I saw the strength of the Goddess just waiting to flow out of you. When I saw you next to Kelan, I knew that the two of you were destined for something even greater."

"But what about all that joking and flirting with Kelan?" I asked.

"That was real enough. Bond or no bond, if that man would have given me any reason I would have had him. The Goddess would have approved."

I laughed. "Treasa you are an amazing woman and warrior. I envy your ease with men."

"Let the bond works its magic. Let the magic of Samhain weave its power through you. When our world opens to the Otherworld, let the power of the spirits fill you. You will know what to do. The Goddess will help you. Now go find that man, before he is filled with mead and finds his loving elsewhere!"

"Thank you, my friend. Until tomorrow!" I cried.

I went straight through the joyful crowd to find Kelan. I caught sight of him and began to run toward him. He was close to the fire and as I ran I saw his expression change from joy to fury. I stopped and realized that the earth was shaking. The music had stopped and all eyes had turned to look beyond the bonfires. A flame, brighter and hotter than the largest bonfire, consumed the earth.

Aillen. The demon of the Sidhe had come. I grabbed Imbas Skye and ran toward the open fields, where all the land was ablaze. Treasa grabbed me and shoved something in my hand.

The flames rose and stayed in one place like a wall. I waited. I heard a low hum that seemed to come from the earth itself.

"Put this over your ears," she yelled and she did the same.

I pulled the Cap of Silence over my head and ears. The Cap of Silence was a treasure of Fionn's and I did not know how Treasa came to have two of them. I did not have time to ask. I walked as close as I could to the flames.

I saw his eyes. They were engulfed with the fire that surrounded him. His shadow rose high over us, and it was hard to tell how big he was. I couldn't get too close, so I waited for him to work whatever magic it was that he did. He played his flute and wherever people had been running, they stopped and fell to the ground, fast asleep. Even Kelan and all the warriors had succumbed to his music. Treasa and I waited while this creature played, wrapped up in his own melody. We hid behind some barrels and watched as he walked amongst my friends, looking for someone in particular.

"Fionn mac Cumhail!" he yelled.

He didn't know that his greatest enemy was dead. I stepped out with Imbas Skye raised high in front of my face.

"Fionn is dead, Demon!" I yelled.

Aillen spun around and eyed me with suspicion. He was smaller than I would have imagined, his skin was dark, but smooth. His red eyes burned mine when I looked straight at them, so I tried to avert my gaze, without appearing scared.

"How did my fearless foe die?" he asked as if we were friends catching up on the latest adventures.

"He was killed in battle, protecting the king," I replied.

"Well that was a worthless deed," he sneered. "And where is the king? Does he now send his women to do his bidding?"

"The king's whereabouts are none of your concern, Demon. Your only concern should be to turn your black tail around and head back where you came from," I taunted.

This angered him. He raised his hand and a red ball of fire appeared. He lifted his hand and the ball clung to his palm. He laughed and threw the flame at me. I sliced the burning sphere in half and prepared for the next.

"Not bad for a child," he said and threw two more at me. I managed to slice the one and as I moved toward the other, it singed my hand.

Treasa screamed and jumped behind Aillen and sliced his arm clean off his body. He screamed a thousand cries and I watched his arm burn to ashes on the ground. He turned and threw the same fire balls at Treasa. Instead of using her sword, she jumped and flipped out of harm's way. The balls were lighting the grass on fire and I knew that we would have to kill this animal fast before the fields and the people nearby burned. His sleeping spell would remain as long as he was in this place and so I motioned to Treasa to lead him away from the people.

Treasa ran toward the trees and Aillen followed in anger. I raced after them. As we left, I could hear the warriors rousing from their sleep and I heard our names being called. I couldn't stop, but told Kelan where I was and heard a low murmur of understanding. Aillen had chased Treasa to a raised mound near some trees. I recognized it as an entrance for the Sidhe, but wasn't sure if it was his. She stood in front of it and he shot flames from his remaining hand and also his mouth.

"Aillen!" I screamed to stop his attack. He swung his head around, his mouth agape with flames shooting straight across. I was right in the flame's path and I pulled the silver ball from my pouch. "Open!" I screamed and the ball spread into a large fan that screened me from the flames. Then it changed to the magic stick and I pointed it at Aillen.

"By the power of the one who rules the sky, the earth, and sea, I return you to your place amongst the ashes. May your flames never again enter our realm. May you burn forever in your misery and release us from your grudge now and forever more. Die Demon, for your powers are no more!" I yelled this prayer into the night's sky and I watched as Aillen's eyes widened in fear.

"I will kill you, woman!" was all he had time to say as his own flames burned his body into a pile of ash.

I ran over to Treasa who had many burns on her body and helped her to her feet. "You did fine, Maecha. I think we fight well together," she smiled and winced in pain.

I yelled to the others, "Over here!"

Kelan and Ferlaigh were the first to approach.

They stopped in front of the ashes and they both looked at us in awe. "Is that really him?" Kelan asked.

"Yes, that's him, Kelan. Now help me with Treasa. I fear she's been burned a few times with the flames."

Ferlaigh had grabbed one side of Treasa and Kelan grabbed the other.

"Let me help her, Kelan," Goll said stepping away from the ashes of Aillen. Make sure that Maecha is all right."

"I'm fine, Goll."

"You are more than fine, my liege. You are an incredible woman. Both of you have done what we mere men have been try-ing to do for years," Goll said and all the others agreed.

"The power of the Goddess was once again upon us and I must thank her for her protection," I said. I put my arm around Kelan. "Let us go back and finish our feast. We have much to celebrate!"

The fires of Samhain were built up once again and the bendrui, Leann-cha'omh, entered the center of the stones that glowed against the flames. She raised her hands high to the star-lit sky and spoke:

"Tonight is a night of such sadness and yet joy. The time between times brings the spirits of the past together with our present souls. We fear the loss of our king, taken from us and cast away amongst the seas to the far reaching Alba. We cry in anguish as the treachery of his son is made known to us. And yet the Mother Goddess does not cry for she knows that the power was not in the son, but in the daughter. We have been blessed with the king's daughter. Her strength, courage, and power shall lead us forth and bring her father home.

"We can rejoice that Aillen, the Demon, has finally departed our world and entered into a world most formidable. We thank Maecha and the great warrior, Treasa of Roscommon. For without them, our kingdom would be lost.

"We mourn the death of our Fianna leader, Fionn mac Cumhail. Even now his soul is soaring among us, pleading for us not to mourn him. He is at peace and he shall find his way back to us. So many of his warriors have fallen, but they fought well and died a warrior's death. Maecha Ruadh mac Art took the pledge of the Fianna and she has done all that was required of her to do. We must honor our pledge to her to be the leader of Ireland's Fianna. She is bound to her champion, Kelan, and together they will save their kingdom and restore King Cormac to his rightful place.

"There is much to mourn, but much more to rejoice. Welcome our members of the Fianna," she finished and opened her arms. There were hundreds of Fianna warriors who traveled from all areas of Ireland to help save the king. Kelan and I had been brought to the center of the stones where we knelt on the cold earth. Leann put her hands on our heads and we held one another's hands. The other warriors gathered around the stones in a circle of unity. They chanted,

> "Honor in our hearts,
> Strength in our hands.
> Truth in our tongues."

Goll stepped forward and stood behind us with his hands raised over us.

"This is our pledge to you. We hold the good of the people in our hands. For them we will do no wrong. We hold each other as brothers and will die for one another. We honor you both as our brethren and welcome you." Before the crowd could raise an uproarious cheer, Goll raised his hand high.

"Please stand," he said. He motioned to Kelan who took a step back next to Leann.

"Maecha Ruadh mac Art. You have proven yourself to have the strength of ten men, to have the heart of twenty and to have the loyalty of thousands. I have pledged myself to you as our acting queen. Now I shall pledge myself to you as your most humble and honored brethren and will protect you and sustain you as the rightful leader of our Fianna clan," he said, and then he and all the other Fianna kneeled.

I was so taken by his words that I had lost my own. I felt Leann's hand on my shoulder and took a deep breath.

"My brethren. All my life I have desired to be one of you. I have watched you and tried my best to mimic your beliefs and learn from your outstanding actions. As I have said before, I will never expect to replace our beloved Fionn. But I will continue his leadership in the way that he did best—with honesty, trust, and justice. I welcome all of you as my brothers and am honored to be your leader," I said and bowed my head.

Now everyone yelled. Kelan picked me up on his shoulder and people cheered my name. I was overwhelmed by the support and anxious to put it to use. The music started and the dancing and drinking began all over again. It was a night to remember. Reading my mind, Kelan slid me down off his shoulder against his body.

He whispered to me, "Do you really want to make this a night to remember?"

I smiled and tears of anticipation came to my eyes.

"Yes, I do," I whispered back and we left the celebrations.

Kelan led me to a hidden cove surrounded by a canopy of trees. Once we stepped into it, it was hard to see that it was even here. Blankets were laid out and mead, cheese, and bread were arranged on a tray to the side. The moon was bright enough to glow through the trees and I could see the anticipation on his face. I suddenly felt self-conscious. I thought of Treasa's words and said a silent prayer to the Goddess of the Otherworld to bless our union and to guide me in whatever way was needed.

Kelan kneeled down and looked up at me. "Maecha, come to me," he said. I kneeled down and I felt something warm on my chest. I pulled out my crystal and so did Kelan. They both glowed bright yellow.

"I don't remember what they said this color meant, do you?" I asked trying to break the tension.

"I think it means that it is time for us to be closer." Still kneeling we leaned toward one another. Kelan touched my face and kissed me. He opened his mind to me and I felt all his pain, his loss, his heartaches fall away. I felt a wonderful man who could now love and I, in turn, opened myself to him. As we kissed, our soul's united and swirled around each other, until they were indistinguishable. Our crystals glowed with the brightness of the sun. Our spiritual bond was complete and our physical union was about to begin. I welcomed our union, his love and whatever our life together would offer us. The Eyes of the Goddess shone bright on us this night and we reveled in the power of her love.

16

Shannon settled Natalie into Michaela's bed. Max circled the bed and then crawled up and lay on the pillow next to Natalie. Natalie wrapped her arm around Max's neck and the two were asleep within minutes.

Closing the door, Shannon looked at Vince and Ben. They looked horrible. Vince had a bandage on his head and one eye was swollen. Ben looked defeated, his blue eyes bloodshot. Shannon grabbed everyone a drink and sat across from them. They were all happy for the silence.

Ben spoke up. "What do we know for certain? What hard evidence do we have that could implicate either Ricky Cartillo or Captain Newman? Natalie saw Ricky Cartillo shoot your father, plus she said that he shot this guy named Roger, who isn't even in the police file. Now did they or someone on the force remove his body before all the other investigators came?" Ben looked at the photo that Natalie had guarded. "We can request a subpoena to search the restaurant."

Ben looked around. Vince shrugged, because he had no idea, and Shannon seemed to be off in her own little world.

Ben continued. "I did review Jack Sommers' case and Detective Scott Malowski was in charge of it. Does that name ring a bell?"

Vince snorted and said, "Yeah that's the loser who came to the self-defense seminar we had for new officers a couple weeks back. He was a ball buster and all the rookies were intimidated by him. I almost had to knock some sense into him."

"That's good, Vince," Ben said. "Maybe Malowski is somehow involved. I read in Frank's notes that Michaela was attacked two different times. Any idea who would want to prevent her from asking questions about her dad?"

"I think that freak, Cartillo, is involved. He always seems to be around after something happens to Michaela. Then he shows up at the dojo when those lowlifes were attacking me," Vince offered.

Ben nodded and wrote some notes. "What was Michaela's relationship with Ricky Cartillo?"

"Here we go," Vince said as he rolled his eyes and stood up. Shannon had her eyes closed.

Ben shook her and asked, "Shannon, what was Michaela's relationship with Ricky Cartillo?"

Shannon opened her eyes and stared at Ben. She stammered, "Michaela. We have to get her back. She's...sick."

Vince leaned over to Shannon and took her hand. He could see that she wasn't quite awake yet. "It's OK, Shannon. Tell us what is going on with Michaela."

Shannon turned toward Vince in recognition. She shook her head to help her think. "Michaela is ill. I just saw her. She was on the ground and some women tried to get her to drink something. I yelled at them to leave her alone. She has become very thin, her skin looks yellow. I think she has to get out of this dream world. It's killing her!"

"All right, Shannon. Michaela is strong and she'll be fine. Did you see anything else that could help us?" Vince asked.

"No, but in the distance I could see a bright yellow light. It seemed to be draining all of Michaela's energy," Shannon cried.

"Shannon, is there any way you could get in touch with

this Maecha woman and ask for her advice? Maybe they are more adept at helping in this situation," Vince asked.

"I'll try, Vince. I just need to get some sleep. Are you two OK out here?" Shannon asked. She had brought out some pillows and sleeping bags for them.

"We're fine. Let's get some rest tonight and then we'll figure out what to do tomorrow morning," Ben said. "Goodnight, Shannon."

"Goodnight, Ben and thank you. Goodnight, Vince."

"Sweet dreams, Shannon and tell Michaela I love her," Vince said.

Wind blowing sand in eyes, mouth, can't see or breathe. Hear crying, someone yelling. Fall to the ground to crawl to the voices. Feel a foot, leg, someone's body.

"Help me get her to the cave!" someone yells and we lift a body and walk toward a black opening.

Enter cave and all is quiet. Cough and spit to remove sand from mouth. Wipe eyes to see. Michaela on ground unconscious. Maecha watches Michaela, but holds her own head in pain.

"Your sister is sick. I think she needs to come out of my dream world," Maecha says.

Kneel next to Michaela.

"How long has she been like this?" Shannon asks.

"Since last night," Maecha replies.

"Are you sick, too?" Shannon asks Maecha.

"My head is in pain."

"Is there someone who can help you and Michaela?" Shannon says.

"Yes, druids," Maecha whispers as she falls over next to Michaela.

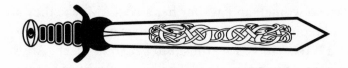

17

I don't know when the pain started. Kelan and I lay together after our final bonding and as the full moon moved across the sky, I fell asleep in his arms. Then I dreamt of 'Mikala' and her sister. I had sensed that Michaela was weak, but with all the excitement of the cave and the assembly, I had ignored her. She was very ill and I couldn't wake her. Then the pain came. Daggers pierced my eyes, I felt agonizing pressure in my head and when I tried to sit up, the sky spun all around me.

I fell back on Kelan and he woke up with a start.

"Maecha," he whispered and leaned over me. "What is wrong?"

I spoke, "'Mikala'. Dying. My head. Need help."

Kelan carried Maecha's limp body back to the campsite. It was still early and most of those who had celebrated lay on the ground still wrapped in their revelry. Treasa saw Kelan and hurried over.

"What happened to her? Is she ill from that demon?" Treasa asked ready to go back and rekill Aillen from last night.

"I don't know what is wrong. She has pain in her head and

she said that 'Mikala' is dying. She needs to come out," Kelan said while still walking fast to Leann's tent.

"Who's 'Mikala'?" was all Treasa could say. She didn't get an answer.

Leann walked out of her tent, followed by the Head Druid Finnius Morgan.

Kelan almost dropped Maecha from the surprise of seeing the druid. Finnius had disappeared years ago and all thought him dead. Now he was here when Kelan needed him most. Kelan thought that perhaps he came back from the dead on Samhain night.

Kelan bowed his head to honor Finnius.

"Nonsense, nonsense, my boy. It is I who should honor you. You have kept this child safe and have bound her to the Otherworld forever. Your union is one of joy and great tidings," Finnius said as he looked at Maecha.

"It has gone on further than I thought. Leann, prepare the stones. It is time to meet 'Mikala'," Finnius said. "Kelan, bring her in the tent and then gather all around the circle of stones."

Kelan laid Maecha on the straw bed and kissed her forehead before he left her. He clasped forearms with Finnius and left to gather everyone.

The pain receded and I opened my eyes.

"Finnius," I whispered. "You came back to us."

Finnius chuckled and pulled on his long white beard. His eyes twinkled at Maecha as he spoke, "How could I miss the celebration of a lifetime? Your father would be proud, my dear child. You have entered a land where no woman dared venture, you have been blessed by the all powerful Goddess, you have defeated that demon, Aillen, once and for all, and you have bonded with a man who is like a son to me. So now, my daughter, you must again be brave and help bring 'Mikala' to us. Her journey is not done and she can do no more where she is. Come. Let us go to the circle of stones."

I knew not what would be expected of me, but I trusted Finnius with my life, as my father had. I followed Finnius along the dew covered fields toward the circle of stones. The sun was a pale pink in the sky and its light illuminated our path. I did not need the sun, for hundreds of candles burned on top of the sacred stones. I followed Finnius into the circle; my long royal blue robe covered my nakedness and hid my face. Leann followed behind chanting to the Goddess of the Otherworld to bless this undertaking.

Two slabs of stone stood in the middle of the circle. I looked past the candles and could see Kelan watching me, his eyes wide with concern. All of my fellow brothers gathered to watch a mystery unfold that could only serve to heighten my acceptance. Treasa stood next to Kelan, her face void of all emotion, stoic as the warrior she was.

I turned back to Leann. I removed my robe and sat on the cold stone, allowing the spirits to flow around me in comfort. I did not feel the cool crisp air. I felt 'Mikala' weak and limp. I looked forward to meeting my sister and hoped that it wasn't too late. I closed my eyes and supported her.

"Drink this, Maecha," Leann said handing me a bowlful of mead with hops to help me sleep.

As I lay back onto the stone, Finnius' chant grew louder. As I felt my body lift and be free, Finnius' words filled my head.

Spirit of the Mother
Rise to meet us.
Spirit of the Mother
Come to greet us.
Spirit of the Mother
Gather around us.

Spirit of the Mother
Set her free.

Leann moved her lips in a silent incantation and sprinkled water over Maecha's body. She and Finnius shared the liquid from a drinking horn. Finnius motioned for Kelan to come into the circle. He did and stood in between the two flat stones. Maecha's head faced the other stone, so Kelan could hold her hand. He drank from the horn and closed his eyes to accept whatever power would overtake his body.

The incantations grew louder as they all swayed back and forth. As the sun rose, its rays warmed Maecha's body, but she began to shake.

Leann stood next to Maecha while Finnius walked to the empty stone slab. They chanted, while her body writhed side to side on the stone. Maecha shook so hard it appeared that a demon had taken over her body. And then she was still. She cried while Kelan still held her hand. Now she was cold. Leann covered Maecha and waited for the strange woman to come forth.

Michaela lay on the cold damp earth, unable to raise her head. Her mouth was dry, her muscles weak. She covered her face with her hands, trying to stop the pounding in her eyes. Then she heard the chanting. It was so far away, but then it became louder. As it neared, the pain in her eyes receded enough so that she could open them.

Once again, there was her dream warrior, beckoning for her to come to him. He held his strong hand out to her. Sunlight shone around his dark head and his green eyes held hers. Michaela knew she had to go with him. She took his hand and a flash of white light consumed her and she knew nothing else.

I felt the warmth of Kelan's hand and I held on tight. I felt a power run through my limbs and escape through my hand. Kelan yelled and his body shook as hard as I'm sure mine had done. He fell to his knees as a bright light consumed us all as it had done in the Otherworld. Kelan still held my hand and I leaned up on my elbow to see that his other hand was hold-ing...'Mikala's'.

The change was hard for 'Mikala'. She gasped for air. Kelan released our hands and stood up. Finnius wrapped 'Mikala' in a black robe and held her to stop the shaking. I looked at Kelan and thanked him with a weak smile. He helped me up so that I could see her.

She was the same as in my dreams, if not a little tired and thin. Her reddish brown hair fell around her robe, but I could not see her face. I walked up to her and Finnius.

"Well done, Maecha. Welcome your sister," Finnius said.

'Mikala' lifted her head and we both smiled. It was as if I was looking at myself in the water. Her features were mine and as we both smiled, we cried and hugged one another.

We turned and looked out at the crowd. They gasped in surprise as they stared at the woman who looked like me.

Finnius' voice rose above the clamor. "'Mikala' and Maecha are sisters of the present and future. 'Mikala' is blessed by Buanann, the 'Lasting One', the 'Mother of Heroes' and she hon-ors us with her presence."

All those around us bowed to the ground in amazement. So much had happened within the last few days. I was over-whelmed myself by the blessings that were bestowed on me. I was fortunate to have 'Mikala' with me. Her skills were powerful and I longed to learn all I could from her.

I heard it as the crowd knelt to the ground. The thunder-ous sound of hooves stampeded toward us.

"Get back," Kelan said.

I pulled 'Mikala' into the middle of the circle of stones. It is against our custom to allow bloodshed with the stones, so I felt safe. But when I saw the line of horses coming toward us, I longed for my sword.

"I need a sword!" I yelled.

"It is here," Treasa said.

I turned and saw her in the circle with her army of warriors protecting us. In addition to my sword, she handed me my tunic and breeches. I placed 'Mikala' in the middle. The scared look on her face told me that her battles were not the same where she came from. I stood up on the stone to face my enemy and I saw him.

The man in the helmet. How he could see after I seared his eyes was not my concern now. How I could remove his head from his body was. That he would dare invade the sacred circle told me what an animal he had become. He rode over people trampling them without mercy. My brother came toward me killing all in his way; his only desire was to get to me. I welcomed him and prayed for victory.

He jumped the stones and I screamed for blood. I felt Kelan call for me, but I could not answer. My eyes and sword were on this enemy of my people. As he and his horse came down within the circle, his sword fell hard upon mine. I blocked and swung his arm out so that his body was open to me. He swung a flail with his other arm and I blocked it with my *ton-fa*. The flail wrapped around my arm and Cairpre pulled me off the stone.

I fell to the ground and rolled out from the horse's hooves before they trampled me. The coward refused to fight from the ground so I fought him where I was. I had lost my *ton-fa*, but still had my sword. I held her high and yelled, "Goddess of the light, destroy this demon, return him to the darkness!"

The eye opened and shot at the demon on horseback. Cairpre jumped off his horse before it could hit him. I had never known the eye to miss and I staggered at the thought. I heard him yell after he was down and I rushed around his horse to see what happened to him. 'Mikala' was standing by him holding my *tonfa*. She had stabbed Cairpre in the leg.

It happened so slow I don't know how I couldn't have stopped it. 'Mikala' stood there after she had stabbed Cairpre. As I yelled for someone to help her, Cairpre thrust his sword into her middle. I felt the pain and I reared my sword over my head and removed his wretched head from his body. He would bother me no more.

"Kelan! Leann! Finnius!" I screamed in pain. I held my hand on her middle to stop the bleeding. When the horsemen had seen their leader go down, they all rode away. Cowards that they were, I didn't have time to chase them down.

"'Mikala', don't go, please stay with us," I sobbed.

"Maecha, my herbs will not heal her," Finnius said.

"Kelan," I said, his thoughts echoing in mine. "The serpent's tooth. Yes, that will heal her."

We placed her on the stone slab that was her birthplace into our land. Kelan pulled the tooth from his pouch. He cracked the top of the tooth open and a soft inside was revealed. Finnius took the bowl of mead that I had drunk from earlier and scooped some of the tooth into the bowl. He mixed it with his fingers and rubbed it on the open wound. Then he placed some of it in her mouth.

We waited. I held 'Mikala's' hand and it became warm and then warmer. Her whole body seemed consumed by heat and I could no longer hold her hand without mine being seared. We watched as the serpent's healing powers worked it magic. Her wound began to close until there wasn't a spot of blood to be seen on her body. She opened her eyes and they glistened yellow like the serpent's eyes. She closed them again and fell into a deep sleep.

"She will sleep now," Finnius said. "Kelan, you have seen the power of the Great Serpent. Guard it well."

I knelt by 'Mikala' and thanked the Goddess once again

306

for bringing her to me and keeping her safe. I could not believe that I had almost lost her. At least Cairpre was dead and she had helped me do it.

"He's not dead," I heard Kelan say.

I turned, "What? I took his head from his body!"

Kelan held the head that was removed from my father's helmet. It was not Cairpre's. My brother had fooled me yet again.

Shannon walks among the forest trees. "Michaela," she calls.
Michaela sleeps on a stone slab, wrapped in a black cloak.
"Wake up, Michaela," Shannon nudges her.
Michaela sits up. Shannon helps her. The hood covers her face. Michaela rubs her eyes.
"Are you all right?" Shannon asks, pulling Michaela hands away from her face.
Shannons gasps. Michaela eyes glow golden yellow.
"I'm coming home. Wait for me at the house," Michaela says smiling.
Michaela starts to disappear.
"Oh and Shannon, bring some clothes."

Michaela woke on a bed of straw, wrapped in heavy blankets. The fireplace was lit and she did not want to leave the warmth of the fire. She turned her head to look around the room. It was a large room, made of stone. The floor was covered with thick rugs. She saw five people huddled around a table, speaking in low tones. She recognized Maecha and the tall warrior from her dreams. She cleared her throat and attempted to sit up.

"Take care, my dear," Finnius said as he moved to steady her. "You have had two very tiring experiences and your body is not ready to be on its own."

"I feel fine," Michaela said in perfect Gaelic. She stopped and looked at Finnius to see if he understood her.

"Ah, so the serpent's tooth does more than heal one's

body. It opens one's mind to all knowledge. Or was it the water from the sacred well that Maecha drank that has provided you with our tongue. Only the Mother knows. But you are truly blessed, my child and we are blessed to have you with us, if only for a short time," Finnius said.

Kelan came over and helped Michaela to her feet. He picked her up and sat her next to Maecha.

"Thank you, Kelan," Michaela murmured, embarrassed now. "I want to thank all of you for what you have done for me. You have saved my life so many times and I have learned so much from you, Maecha."

"As I have from you, Sister. Finnius tells us that you must leave. I wish that you would stay so we could learn more from each other. I have only begun to understand your form of fighting," Maecha said.

"We can still learn much from one another in the dream world. I saw my sister last night. They are in need of me at home. You are a powerful warrior and with your loyal friends, you will succeed. I know how to come back to you should you ever need me. I look forward to it. But I feel my sister pulling me and I must go," Michaela said, feeling anxious to see Shannon and Vince.

"So be it," Maecha said.

Leann left to prepare the portal stone. Treasa hadn't left Maecha's side, even with Kelan by her, but now she walked next to 'Mikala' and guarded her. Treasa felt she had failed Maecha by allowing 'Mikala' to be wounded. She would make sure that the dream warrior would go back to her world safe.

The portal stones stood to the east of Emain Macha. They loomed on a cliff that overlooked the sea. The stones were arranged in a circle with a tall stone in the middle.

Finnius spoke, "You alone must enter the portal. Walk counter-clockwise three times and on the third turn touch the stone." He touched Michaela's arms and kissed her forehead. Take care of my home, 'Mikala'. All that is there is yours. May the

Goddess bless you and keep you close to her heart. Until I see you again."

Next Treasa grasped Michaela's forearm and Michaela did the same. "Protect Maecha for me, Treasa. You are a great warrior and it is my honor to have met you," Michaela said.

"Likewise, dream warrior," Treasa said and stepped back.

Next Michaela walked to Kelan. "Why did you search for me in my dreams?"

Kelan smiled, "I knew that you were the warrior who would give Maecha the strength and knowledge needed to become the leader and warrior she is today. I was drawn to you by the Goddess."

"Thank you for protecting me, Kelan. I wish you happiness and a long life with Maecha," Michaela said.

"No, it is I who must thank you for helping her grow. She has learned much from you," Kelan grasped Michaela's face. "I am sorry about your eyes," he said and he kissed her forehead.

Michaela laughed. "That's all right. I've had too many changes to have golden eyes matter."

Last she came to Maecha. "My sister, I won't know who to talk to in my dreams!" Maecha said, tears dropping on her cheeks.

"Maecha, you will always be able to speak with me. We are connected. You have someone else to keep you company at night. You do not need me anymore. But know this, if ever you do need me, I will be there," Michaela hugged Maecha, blinking back the tears.

"Goodbye, my friends," Michaela called and she walked to the center of the portal stones. She circled the stone once, twice, and on the third turn, she looked back at her Celtic family and touched the stone. A bright light flashed and Michaela Sommers was gone from Ireland.

18

"Hurry, Vince or else we'll miss her. We have to be there when she returns," Shannon chided as they walked through the woods with only flashlights to guide them.

Natalie had insisted on coming and she was the only one who seemed to be finding her way with little effort. They couldn't show up at The Little Lake Inn, go back into the woods, come out with a missing woman, and expect anyone to understand. So they had come in through a back road that they hoped would lead to the house.

It had begun to snow when they had left New York City and the air was brisk. After hiking through the brush and small trees, Vince yelled, "I think I see it!"

They found the house that Michaela had disappeared in. They broke their way in through the front door.

"Which way do we go?" asked Vince.

"I don't know. Michaela said that we would know," Shannon replied.

"This way," Natalie's tiny voice broke in.

They followed Natalie as she walked through a doorway and down the hall. As they turned, Vince and Shannon could see a pale light coming out from under a door. Natalie stood at the door and waited.

"The door handle is warm," she said.

"That must be the one," Shannon said and she opened the door.

The light shone from a small square opening in the wall underneath the bookshelves.

"What do we do now?" Vince asked impatient.

"We wait," Shannon said as she held Michaela's cross hanging from her neck.

They didn't have to wait long. Within minutes, the light grew brighter and they heard a loud buzzing sound.

The sound grew so loud they had to cover their ears. The light intensified and with a loud pop, the room was silent. The light was gone. Michaela lay face down and naked, huddled in a ball. Her long hair lay strewn over the floor.

"Michaela!" Vince exclaimed and ran to her. "Give me a blanket."

He covered Michaela and tried to move her. Michaela gasped as if shaken awake. She sat up. Vince covered her and moved her hair away from her face.

Michaela's eyes were closed. She wasn't quite awake yet.

Vince touched her hair and looked at Shannon. Even in the dim light he could see a long white streak traveled the length of her hair. Vince touched Michaela's face.

"Michaela, you're home. Can you open your eyes?"

Shannon kneeled down next to Michaela. "Michaela, it is all right, now. We are here with you. Come back to us."

Michaela's eyes fluttered and then she opened them.

"Give me the flashlight. What's wrong with her eyes?" Vince asked.

"I thought it was just the dream. Her eyes were golden when I saw her last night, but I didn't know what happened."

"Shannon," Michaela whispered. "I'm home."

Shannon clasped the Celtic cross around Michaela's neck. "Yes you are, little sister," Shannon cried.

<u>Epilogue</u>

I was home. I stared at my reflection, struggling to accept my golden eyes and the streak of stark white that trailed down my auburn hair. It reminded me of a hip Bride of Frankenstein, but that didn't make me feel any better. The trip to Ireland (as weird as that sounded) had changed me more than just physically. I could feel Maecha in the deep recesses of my mind and I knew that if I ventured further, I could find her in my dreams.

But before I could seek her, I needed to find closure in my world. Natalie looked just as I had dreamed she would. In the short time she was with Shannon, her face had grown rounder, but her eyes still held that faraway look. She told Ben Walker about the children, the drugs, the location of the warehouses, and my father's murder. A part of me shattered when she revealed the animal that Ricky Cartillo was.

Ben had gone above Captain Newman's authority to obtain a search warrant for Cartillo's warehouses. I insisted on going with him and what we found was a lucrative business going sour.

It appeared that Captain Newman and Scott Malowski had attempted to arrest Cartillo. Newman was killed from a gun shot to the head and Malowksi clung to life with a similar wound.

We found children in the basement. Most of them were in their early teens. Their clothes were ratty, they lacked for showers, and the ones who were straight enough to stand looked at us with suspicion. It would take a long time to teach these children to love again and to heal. Vince touched my hand and I entwined my fingers in his. His love and support had given me the strength to come and I was glad he would be by my side.

Ricky Cartillo was nowhere to be found. I felt cheated, but satisfied that so many children would get their lives back. I had accomplished what my father had died trying to do. That he would be happy, helped to ease my pain.

I arrived at my apartment to find a letter addressed to 'Mikala' Sommers. My sight blurred as if I was about to have a vision, but I shook it away and opened the letter. It was the deed to the house in the Catskills, with a letter willing all the books and artifacts to me, signed by Finnius Morgan.

My vision wavered again and I welcomed it. I saw my father sitting astride a powerful steed, with his sword raised in salute. Beyond him, Maecha and Kelan sailed on their journey to Alba to save King Cormac. Finnius stood at the helm and waved. I waved back, knowing that it wasn't goodbye. The Mother Goddess stirred the winds to set them forth. I smiled and let the vision fade, for I knew that the Eyes of the Goddess would watch over my friends.

Glossary

Aeiden (*Ay den*): Maecha mac Art's peregrine falcon

Aeric: Male faery from the Isle of the Blessed

Aillen: Demon of the Sidhe

Aire-echta: Personal champion of the king and was responsible for protecting the king and avenging any family insults or murders. Fionn mac Cumhail was King Cormac's personal champion and protector.

Alba: Celtic name for Scotland

Awen Crystals: The Awen crystals symbolize the Three Realms of the Celtic worlds. The crystals are worn as a trio and are attached by a leather band. The first ray on the right symbolizes the male force, the left symbolizes the female force, and the center symbolizes the balance between the two. Without this balance, the Upper World (sky), Middle World (Land), and the Under World (Sea) cannot exist together. Maecha and Kelan are given these crystals as a gift from the Lord and Princess of the Otherworld. When the crystals glow red one will know that the other is in danger; black means that one has died or the crystal has been lost. If this happens all powers are broken. Green means that the Otherworld needs help and the crystals will glow yellow when Maecha's and Kelan's bond is complete.

Bendrui (bun-drooee): woman druid

Briogais: Trousers, breeches

Cada'me: Michaela teaches Maecha karate, which includes kata and tonfa stick. Maecha decides to call it cada'me. Maecha incorporates her sword fighting into this style.

Cave of the Warrior: Entrance to the Otherworld where warriors travel to become candidates for the elite band of Fianna. It is found in the county of Roscommon. The cave is a portal that leads into the side of a hill. Warriors must venture through the portal, which leads to the realm of the Otherworld, and successfully meet their challenges.

Ciara (*kee*-a-ra): Treasa's warrior

Conchobar, Osgar: Leader of the Fianna of Leinster

Corrigan, Aonghus (*ayng-guhs*): Leader of the Fianna in Mumu, the southernmost forth of Ireland

Each-luath: member of the Fianna in the Otherworld

Eire: Celtic name for Ireland

Feinnidh: Member of the Fianna

Fianna: Elite group of warriors led by Fionn mac Cumhail. The warriors were sworn by their leader's authority and often lived outside the realm of normal society. Their purpose was to protect the king of Ireland and all his lands.

Gaia: Female faery from the Isle of the Blessed

Imbas Skye: Maecha's sword, which she named after the Isle of Imbas Skye—the isle where Scathach trains warriors, including Maecha's mother, Queen Deirdre. Only a woman who is deemed worthy by the previous owners of the sword will be allowed to wield it.

Leann-cha'omh (Leann-*cha* om): Cormac's Bendrui and healer

316

Leine: Shirt

Lon, son of Liomhtha: Master craftsman and teacher of smiths to the King of Lochlann in Bergen. Lon is trapped in the Otherworld in a monster's form until Maecha frees him of his curse. He presents Maecha and Kelan with tonfas made from Iron Wood, which comes from the mystical oaks of the Otherworld.

Mac Art, Cairpre (*kair* pre): Son of High King Cormac and High Queen Deirdre. Maecha's younger brother.

Mac Art, Cormac (*kawr*-mak): High King of Ireland from 227-266 A.D., son of Art O'enfher or "Art the Lonely," grandson of Conn Ce'tchathach of the Hundred Battles. He is known as Ireland's first lawmaker and is responsible for setting up the elite band of Fianna.

Mac Art, Maecha Ruadh (mac Art, Ma *ay* ka Ruath): Daughter of High King Cormac and High Queen Deirdre. Heiress to the throne of Tara through matriarchal sovereignty.

Mac Cumhail, Fionn (mac cool, Finn): Historical leader of the Fianna in the 3rd century Ireland.

Macha (*mah* ka): Celtic Goddess of War

Mac Mail, Eoghan (oh *gahn*): king of Ulaid, the northernmost forth of Ireland

Mac Midhna, Aillen (mac *mith* na, *ay* len): Demon from Otherworld, son of Midna, a man from the Sidhe (*Shee*) or Otherworld. Every Samhain he would attack Fionn mac Cumhail, while lulling everyone else to sleep.

Mac Morna, Ferlaigh: King of Roscommon of Connacta

Mac Morna, Goll: Was originally an enemy of the Fianna, but then became its most loyal member. His original name was Aed, which means "Red," but he changed it to Goll, which means "One-eyed" when he lost one eye in a battle.

Mac Morna, Treasa (tree *ay* sa): Queen of Roscommon of Connacta; leader of the female band of warriors in support of Maecha.

Mac Nessa, Kelan (mac Nayssa, *Kay* lan): Maecha's Champion and Fianna warrior. Trainer of Cormac's warriors. Kelan's family died when he was younger and has grown up with Maecha.

Mac Ronan, Caoilte (mac ronan, *kweel* ta): Fianna warrior, Fionn's nephew.

Maol, Conan: Enemy of the Fianna who tried to steal treasures from Isle of Imbas Skye. He was killed by Queen Deirdre.

Morgan, Finnius: Druid from 3rd century Ireland. Time traveled to modern New York. In New York, he was an archeologist specializing in ancient Irish artifacts.

Picts: Were called the painted people because of their blue tattoo designs on their bodies. They were a fierce people who lived in Scotland.

McDermott, Fercobh (fer *kov*): King of Munster

Muirne (*mir* ne): Fionn's mother

Quinn, Aonghus (*ayng*-guhs) and Mairtin: Brothers in Kelan's band of warriors.

Ruadh, Macha Mong (Macha of the Red Tresses): Maecha was named after this warrior who was the first Queen of Ireland and formed Emain Macha (*ev*-in *ma*-cha)

Samhain (sow-en): Was the name for the Celtic New Year celebrated on November 1. All the farm animals were gathered together and those which were not needed for breeding in the following spring were killed for food. Because Samhain did not belong to the old year or the new, it was thought to be a time of magic. Spirits passed into this world to mingle with their loved ones.

Scathach (*skaw*-thach): Woman warrior who trains other warriors on the Isle of Imbas Skye. Her name means 'the woman who strikes fear.'

Sidhe (shee): People of the fairy hills, Otherworld

Tannackta: Faery Folk of Tir-nan-og, Keeper of the Passageway and Protector of the Doorway to Tir-nan-og

Tir-nan-og: Otherworld that is ruled by the androgynous Lord and Princess. They balance the Otherworld and test those who wish to be members of the Fianna.

Uatach the Terrible: Scathach's daughter. Her name means 'specter.'

Note from the Author

This novel was inspired by the strong women in Celtic literature and the wonderful stories of Fionn mac Cumhail. Some of the characters were recorded in history, such as Fionn mac Cumhail, Cormac mac Art, and Goll mac Morna. However, I embellished and altered their stories to allow Maecha her voice and role. Any inaccuracies or imaginative additions are solely my responsibility.

For more information on this time period and the enchanting folklore of a mystical land, please see the bibliography on the next page.

Bibliography

Chadwick, Nora. The Celts. England: Penguin Books, 1971.

Chadwick, Nora and Myles Dillon. The Celtic Realms. Great Britain: The New American Library, 1967.

Clark, Rosalind. The Great Queens: Irish Goddesses from the Morrigan to Cathleen ni' Houlihan. Gerrards Cross: Colin Smythe, 1991.

Condren, Mary. The Serpent and the Goddess: Women, Religion, and Power in Celtic Ireland. New York: HarperCollins Publishers, 1989.

Cross, Tom Peete and Clark Harris Slover. Ancient Irish Tales. New York: Henry Holt and Company, 1936.

d'Arbois de Jubainville, H. The Irish Mythological Cycle and Celtic Mythology. Trans. Richard Irvine Best. New York: Lemma Publishing Corporation, 1970.

Fields, Rick. The Code of the Warrior. New York: Harper Collins Publishers, 1991.

Harbison, Peter. Pre-Christian Ireland: From the First Settlers to the Early Celts. London: Thames and Hudson, 1988.

Herm, Gerhard. The Celts. New York: St. Martin's Press, 1975.

Laing, Lloyd and Jennifer. Celtic Britain and Ireland, AD 200-800: The Myth of the Dark Ages. New York: St. Martin's Press, 1990.

Lonigan, Paul R. The Druids: Priests of the Ancient Celts.

Connecticut: Greenwood Press, 1996.

Mac Cana, Proinsias. <u>Celtic Mythology</u>. New York: Peter Bedrick Books, 1987.

MacNeill, Eoin. <u>Duanaire Finn: The Book of the Lays of Fionn, Part I</u>. London: David Nutt, 1908.

Markale, Jean. <u>Women of the Celts.</u> Vermont: Inner Traditions International, Ltd., 1986.

Martell, Hazel Mary. <u>What Do We Know About The Celts?</u> New York: Peter Bedrick Books, 1993.

Matthews, John and Bob Stewart. <u>Celtic Warrior Chiefs.</u> UK: Firebird Books, 1993.

Murphy, Gerard. <u>Duanaire Finn: The Book of the Lays of Fionn, Part II</u>. London: Simpkin Marshall, LTD., 1933.

Murphy, Gerard. <u>Duanaire Finn: The Book of the Lays of Fionn, Part III</u>. Dublin: Educational Company of Ireland, LTD, 1953.

Newark, Tim. <u>Celtic Warriors, 400BC-1600AD.</u> New York: Blandford Press, 1986.

Rees, Alwyn D. and Brinley Rees. <u>Celtic Heritage: Ancient Tradition in Ireland and Wales</u>. New York: Grove Press, Inc., 1961.

Sharkey, John. <u>Celtic Mysteries, The Ancient Religion.</u> London: Thames and Hudson, 1975.

Sjoestedt, Marie-Louise. <u>God and Heroes of The Celts</u>. Trans. Myles Dillon. London: Methuen & Co. LTD., 1949.